BEST WISHES !

One Hour Martin-izing

Frank Saitta

authorHOUSE®

AuthorHouse™
1663 Liberty Drive, Suite 200
Bloomington, IN 47403
www.authorhouse.com
Phone: 1-800-839-8640

First published by AuthorHouse 10/23/2008

ISBN: 978-1-4343-5788-5 (sc)
ISBN: 978-1-4343-5789-2 (hc)

Library of Congress Control Number: 2008901453

Printed in the United States of America
Bloomington, Indiana

This book is printed on acid-free paper.

Dedication-

To my mother Joyce Saitta
(1939-2007)

Acknowledgements

There are so many people who provided me with encouragement, motivation, expertise, advice and the occasional kick in the pants to go and write. I know I have omitted some of you, please forgive me.

To my amazing wife who read this manuscript many times, made countless pots of coffee, listened to my ramblings and put up with my quirky processes. I couldn't have done this without your love, support and unwavering confidence. You are my hero, thank you for twenty amazing years, you rock!

To the other woman in my life, my daughter, who never doubted that her "old man," would finish this project, you are the best person I know and my love for you knows no bounds. Go Yankees!

To my father Frank for his enthusiasm and opinions- we all got 'em.

Thanks to Laura Alderson, Beth Lieberman and Susan Drake, your advice, tireless editing and encouragement helped immensely.

Finally to my Mom who never got to see this book finished but always told me, "you can do it, Frankie because I love you."

I miss you mom.

1

Why are these blinds open? I'm trying to take a nap. Yes, I know it's four in the afternoon, but my body is telling me to sleep. Should taking a nap be so difficult? Should I have to defend a nap? Yes, I'm talking to myself.

They call me Martin and I own a dry cleaning business in New York City, not one of the Chinese variety, but a simple three-person shop. How I got into this business is baffling to me, I just kind of "happened" into it. Like many things in my life, the illusion of control over things is purely a fairy tale. I can't control anything, my career included.

I had a friend named Bill Meltzy who was a degenerate gambler who has since past and as my mom would always say about someone who was dead, *God rest his soul.* He had inherited the business from his dad and when he lost it to me in a card game; I had no idea that six years later I'd be working it when I had every intention of selling it. But the market for dry cleaning businesses isn't what you'd think, but I am sure you don't think about that.

Most people don't give their dry cleaner a second thought. I mean if we don't crack buttons, ruin garments and the like, we are just here for you and that's it. We are a ticket in your glove compartment or maybe a hanger on your door. By the way, I don't pick up and deliver. Yes, I do still fold shirts and wrap them in brown paper. It costs more, but it is better for these apartment dwellers because closet space is at a minimum in this neighborhood. Most people would trade some kitchen space for another closet in this city.

I digress, but when you are in nap mode it's hard to stay focused. I'm sneaking this nap, if my wife knew I was napping I'd hear about how she is working and I'm not; now don't get me wrong, if it wasn't for my wife I'd be broke and on the street. Cassidy, that's my wife, can squeeze a nickel; she understands the value of a dollar, where yours truly is a hopeless spend-a-holic. I just have trouble saying I can't afford it. It shouldn't be that hard, but I have numerous issues and admitting I don't have enough money for something I want is one of them.

I am sure you noticed that I said for what I want, not need. I like to get what I want. What I need is something else entirely. Cassidy takes care of what I need. This is fine with me because I can't stand the little details; I am a thinker, a creative force, and an idea factory. I just have a little problem with implementation---I have lots of good thoughts and ideas, but no sense for getting them off the ground.

I'm always thinking I'll come up with a life changing idea and somebody will pay me millions and I'll never have to work again.

However, not one has panned out yet. I thought I had a winner with several. For example—when you go to the beach, what is the part you dislike? Right—the sand; my idea is a man-made covering that maintains the sand feeling so you can make the butt groove, but not have a crunchy sandwich. Then once you have eliminated the sand issue, you could rent beach plots daily, instead of folks tip toeing around looking for a vacant space on a crowded beach on hot sand. No one bought it.

Or maybe, "pizza in a cup," especially in New York City; we are always walking and eating so it seemed like a natural, our favorite meal, a slice of pizza and a fork or spoon—again no interest. But that doesn't keep me from thinking.

I run an honest business; all of my customers know that and that's a big part of why they come back.

Back to my image, because after all it's all about image management for me—you see, if you have the address, the car and clothes, it's easy to pass off to others the illusion of prosperity. I think most people judge their insides by your outsides, so I help them feel good.

Cassidy is a commercial real estate broker; she has her own firm and moves a lot of commercial property here in the city and is now branching out to Jersey. My store provides us with WAM (walking around money). Her gig is the one that supports our lifestyle and habits.

I have no problem with that one bit. Some of my friends might not feel the same, but that's their problem, not mine. Cassidy doesn't rub it in my face; she does remind me every so often, but I typically bring that on myself and deserve it. Like I said before, I like to spend money; it makes me feel good. I just need to figure out a way to get more of it.

Speaking of money, it doesn't seem like this nap thing is going to materialize, so I might as well get out of the house. We live in a Brownstone on East 81st between 1st and York. Cassidy found it while working a parking garage deal, eight years ago. The monthly nut is big, but so is the house. Our first year in the house was really tough; since I was just kind of banging around selling Cadillac's for the Potamkins and doing pretty well, but didn't see myself advancing. I had a sales manager who had eyes for Cassidy and I knew it. He would have rather done just about anything other than promote me; it was important for his self-esteem to keep me down or at least, that's the way I saw it. However, the job had perks—a new caddy every three months, a wardrobe allowance, and a sizeable expense account. I had to entertain limousine and car service owners and operators. I was always trying to move multiple cars at once, not quite fleet sales, but three or four at a time. So all things considered, it was a good job. But if you had an

4

off-month, it made it tight around the house, after the house note was paid. But we made it; we didn't set up a budget, we just stayed in—and sucked it up, we had no choice. Those days are behind us and we are a stronger couple because of it, although it didn't feel like it while going through it. But nothing ever does.

I am out the door and headed to the store, it's on 86th and 2nd and has been there for years. I assumed that when I won it, I could just hire someone to run it and I'd collect cash every week. Not so. I must have gone through three managers and each of them ripped me off differently. They were either falsifying the count or not ringing up sales or just stealing clothes. So four years ago, I got involved.

I decide to stop at The Mixer —a bar with no reputation and pretty far from fabulous. Walt tends bar there and we go way back. Walt and I used to get into a lot of trouble together when we were younger and we probably still would, but Walt got sober and his thinking changed. He's quite a character, you don't see too many recovering alcoholic bar-owners, but it doesn't faze him. He put the "plug in the jug" and that was it. In any event, I order an Absolute and tonic or better yet, Walt just puts one in front of me and I thank him. It's about 5 p.m. now and the after work crowd is starting to file in. I have time for a quick one and then it's to the store. We get busy for the next few hours as the folks coming home from work are picking up.

When you deal with the public it's a stressful process. The customers want to impose their will on you, thinking this will get them what they want quicker. There are also the kinds who don't say a thing; they come in, give you their ticket, pay, and then leave. I like them; they don't require any of that clever conversational bullshit that I have to deal with most of the time. Of course, there are the pushy types who think the world should stop and admire their magnificence and see to it that they get what they want, when they want it. Those folks are relentless; they just can't be satisfied. Sometimes I'd like to tell them what they can do with their clothes, but the customer is always right.

It's Thursday and the people are in a hurry and want to get their stuff for the weekend. There is a bonus today and her name is Milagro. She is the sexiest thing I have seen in a long time. She must have been a model or at the very least, a woman who used her looks to make a living. She stands about 5'7" has got a smokin' body and a certain way about her that says: "I am good in bed." She always drops off on Tuesday and picks up on Thursday and I do everything I can to be there so that I can just drink her in. She is right on time today and picks up a couple of suits and blouses. We make the usual small talk—weather—how nice she looks. You know that clever conversation I was bitching about.

When she wheels on her stiletto heel and asks me if we cared for leather, normally, I would have pointed out the sign that says we care for leather, but I don't. I let her know:

"Yes, we do and it takes a couple of days longer than regular dry cleaning."

She smiles and says, "Thanks."

Then out she walks giving me a vision to download to my hard drive for a shower later, if you know what I mean.

The rest of the afternoon is uneventful and a pretty good one at that—we did $3,300 today. I like days like that. Not to mention we took in more clothes to clean than a usual Thursday—must be a big weekend for some of our folks. We even had some new customers today. My assistant Bertha, who has been with me for three years now and is a blessing from heaven, told me about this guy who came in and dropped off two trench coats—nice ones—Burberrys—with the plaid liner. The reason she noticed, was that he had the same phone number as Milagro, my fantasy girl. Bertha has observed me flirting and then looking longingly as she walks out. Basically she "busted" me checking her ass out.

I thought this was a little strange because I never see a wedding ring or any ring on her left hand. Maybe it was her brother, friend, or relative visiting. I didn't think much more about it and we close up for the day.

On my way home I pop over to the Mixer for a drink and to see if Cassidy is there. She stops in looking for me on occasion, especially on a Thursday, because she takes Fridays off. She vowed when she opened her own brokerage firm, that she would have three day weekends every weekend. Business is good enough these days that she can—thank God for that. Any way, I walk in and don't see her, so I grab a table near the door so that I don't miss her if she comes in.

Meanwhile, I get a drink and start watching the news. It's the same shit—market down—a few murders—and—but one item catches my attention. A robbery at the Federal Reserve—no money stolen—just some printing plates. The type of plates the government uses to print money. I can't imagine anyone having the balls to go into the Federal "fucking" Reserve and try to steal anything.

Can you picture the planning? Kind of makes me think of some of the robberies you see in the movies. You know, with Sean Connery or George Clooney leading a gang of thieves into this ultra secure facility and then using high-tech gadgets and schematics of rooms and schedules of security guards—it's almost romantic.

But the next story is about a dog that was supposed to be gassed in a shelter and just walked out of the gas chamber wagging his tail while all around him, were dead dogs and cats! A doggie miracle, needless to say, that dog isn't an orphan anymore.

In walks my wife, wearing a blue Brooks Brothers suit, Jimmy Choo shoes, and her hair pulled back so tight you'd think blinking would be tough. But she certainly looks good. I stand to give her a hug and a peck and get her a glass of Pinot Grigio, her favorite is Santa Margherita. You wouldn't expect that nice of a wine in a place like the Mixer, but Walt keeps some on hand—just for her. She sits and immediately goes into this rap about a client who today, was bullshitting her about this business he was trying to get going and was really pumping her for names of possible investors. This happens all the time. Those in the know come to Cassidy when they need space to expand their business or if they are starting a new one. You see, she only deals in AAA properties; she has the locations for that high profile start-up or that business that is breaking into a big market and needs the right address. So these types come to her and she has a Rolodex of names of the "Who's Who" in NYC, last year alone she did over 15 million in sales. Fortunately for me, we operate the "one pocket" method of finances.

She explains that this venture he is starting up is going to be a cash cow, literally a license to print money, How many times have I heard that, she goes on. Those guys are always the ones looking for a non-recourse loan and want to put down nothing in earnest money—

like their word should be enough. Strangely enough she says he had a car and driver. I know it was his, she remarks, and not a hire because the plates were not the kind you see on most of the limos in NYC—the rental plates.

In any event, she goes on and on about the rest of her day and how tired she is, but she'll have another glass of wine please.

It's about 8:30 p.m. when I start getting hungry, I ask Cass, if she is hungry. She never is after a few drinks, but I tell her to eat because she'll get loaded and there will be nothing to soak up the booze. So we start throwing suggestions back and forth are you hungry for chinks, pizza, pasta or steak. We do the usual dance and end up deciding on pizza. But I don't feel like ordering in; I feel like going out. The one place in this town I got a taste for tonight is Arturo's, down in the village, on McDougal and Houston.

You can always tell a true New Yorker—if they say: "Howston," they are native. If they say Houston like the city in Texas, you are looking at a transplant or a tourist. But that is neither here nor there—back to the restaurant. Arturo's is this little bar/restaurant that has a coal brick oven and makes the best pie in the city—that is—in the "World according to Marty"

So, we hail a cab and head downtown. I taste the pizza already. As usual, the place is packed and we'll have to kill time at the bar before we can get a table. No big rush, so what's a few more drinks.

NYPD detectives frequent Arturo's I'm told. Of course you can't tell who they are, but I certainly can overhear conversations. So we prop ourselves up at the tiny bar and order a couple of drinks—Cass stays with the white wine while I switch to red. I never have trouble switching. You always hear people say stay with what you started with. When it comes to drinking, I have my own set of standards.

The bar is small and cramped so eavesdropping is easy and almost unavoidable. Tonight the bar is filled with a few college kids from NYU who must have been tipped off about the pizza and three men who are engrossed in discussion. I can't help it, but I adjust my listening their way. Cassidy hates when I am looking right at her and nodding as if I'm listening, but then when she presses me for what she said I have to admit I wasn't listening.

The little performance area is being set up. The "performance area" is a piano, a snare drum, and mike stand, so I use the term loosely. That's another feature of Arturo's if you will—a set up perfect for open mike performances—which one appears to be starting soon. Years ago, when I was single and hanging here a lot, it wasn't uncommon to see the likes of Timothy Hutton or Al Jarreau step up and do a set. But times are different and Arturo's is no longer the secret it once was.

Back to my eavesdropping—the three guys are going back and forth and every now and then, one breaks out into laughter. I hone in on some words, trying to put a sentence or two together.

11

Plates, stupid, and money, is all I can make out, I can't put anything together there and listen a little bit more intently. "Balls, mix-up and morons" Still, can't get anything.

"Cass," I said, "let's play 'what's their deal.'"

She tears her attention away from the setting up, and then gives me a nod.

"Me first, okay?"

Ladies first, of course.

Cass looks at a table of three women, and smiles, "These ladies are old college friends who are here on a theater weekend. Watch them Marty. See the way the redhead is mimicking smoking a joint? They must be reliving some old memories."

I buy that. Now it's my turn.

"Look at those four guys in the booth behind us. The two on the outside are salesmen. They're trying to close a deal with the other guys. See how they keep writing something on that pad and showing it to them, I'm pretty good, eh?"

"You're dead on, honey," Cass says. She takes a sip of her drink.

"What about them?" Her head is tilted to indicate the threesome I was eavesdropping on. "I think they are undercover and on a stakeout here because the target of their investigation works in the kitchen dealing dope and using the waiters as runners."

"Whoa! That's a stretch. I don't think so, but they might be cops. I'm replaying my eavesdropping from before and listen in again. This time, I hear "inside job" and "there's going to be hell to pay." Now, it's starting to make a little sense. They are cops. Maybe they were talking about the robbery at the Federal Reserve, the reference to plates, morons, and balls—this clicks with me. I share that with Cass who heard nothing about the Federal Reserve robbery, but then again, she rarely listens or watches the news unless it's something really major that might affect her business. So I explain to her that with a plate used by the Treasury—if someone knew what they were doing—they could literally "print money." She gives me that nod that says: *Martin, come back to planet earth.*

Jimmy gives us a wave and we settle the bar bill and get the table next to the toilet, the bathroom here is unisex, so it's not unusual to see a man walk in and then a lady follow behind to wait in line. It's the only bathroom in the place and it can be a busy one, there is even a working bathtub in there, I don't know why.

But we decide on a pie and a bottle of wine and the evening is a groove. Cass and I joke with the other tables around us and laugh hard with one another. I love my wife, I really do. At about 11.p.m, we head back uptown for home.

It's Friday and I'm up at 6 a.m. Bertha opens up the store on Fridays so that I have a few hours to fart around. First, I go out to

13

move my car over to the other side of the street—if you have ever lived in this city you know all about the alternate side of the "street parking shuffle" that goes on every morning in most neighborhoods in Manhattan. I get my usual spot and grab the paper off the stoop and get inside to drink coffee, smoke cigarettes, and ease into the day. Cass usually rolls out around 8a.m. or so. However, this is my quiet time—which I treasure. I'm a little bit of a coffee freak so today it's Sumatra, kind of mild tasting but it's got the "pop" of a Breakfast blend. I head out onto the patio with the paper. *The Daily News*, not *The Post* which I think is just a little to Enquirer-like for my taste. Anyway, the story I'm looking for is the rip-off at the Reserve. I find it on page three and dig in. Seems that it was three people, two men and a woman, who pulled this caper and they each had a different "costume"—an electrician, foodservice worker, and vending machine refill/repair guy. That's how they got past the first wave of security, which is a receptionist with a sign in sheet. They are then in the promenade, which houses some offices and a bank of elevators. The elevators; however, only go up from the promenade level while all the real security is three floors down. How they got down is still under investigation, but there are some theories, one being employee negligence so I guess the phrase, "good enough for government work" takes on new meaning. Another theory is an "inside job." This seems plausible to me. I am of the opinion that everyone has a price and if approached the right way and assured of no repercussions, they would just about do anything. Well, at least I would—but then again—that's just me and I am not a barometer for society at large. That's for sure.

Once below promenade level, the security and electronic measures taken to protect the money and other things, is thick—ranging from video surveillance, overstaffed checkpoints, armed military personnel, and a series of doors locked with the most sophisticated locks available. Of course, the story is vague because the last thing the FBI wants is a press leak that tells "joe schmoe" how to do this again. That's another thing. Why do some news programs tell you how to commit a crime and get away with it? Or, how to manufacture explosives from products available at D'Agostino's; I don't get that, but then who am I to question?

From what I can gather from the story, the real prize taken was the plates. Apparently, it's the latest version of the twenty-dollar bill, with the new markings and positioning of the counterfeit-proof "tells." So, if the perpetrator has access to the paper, ink, and a means to print, they could conceivably print money. I do know that with today's digital copiers, many people try just copying bills because the quality of the copy is so good that most folks won't be the wiser as the bills go into circulation. So that tells me that the paper and ink must be available somewhere. I guess you just have to know where to look.

This makes me think of how absolutely secure I would be if I could print money—I mean "real money." Not a copy, not counterfeit, but the real McCoy. No work, no hassles from customers, no waking up for something other than what I want to do. Cass could sell the firm and we could loll in the sun on some island in the Caribbean— An island where American dollars command respect and lots of "ass kissing." As usual, I am dreaming just another tool for commandeering the "path of least resistance."

The story goes on to say, that there are no suspects at this time, but the surveillance tapes are being reviewed and the staff is being questioned at length. "Sweet fancy Moses! These guys are gonna get away with this." One can only imagine how THEY feel. I'm excited and I am quite removed from the situation.

Cass comes out looking half asleep, but at 8:15 a.m., most of the people in the city, look this way. She grabs the cigarette from the tray and takes a drag and says "Good lovin' last night Tiger."

After all these years, the sex is still hot. I give her my best "and there's more where that came from look." I then get up to fetch her cup of coffee.

Upon my return she points out the story and says, "Is this what you were talking about?"

"Yep, can you imagine, printing your own money?" I say

"Hey Marty, don't you think Bertha's getting busy at the store. It sure would be nice if you would show up before 10 a.m., for a change."

I get the hint, finish my coffee, grab the paper, and hit the shower. I'm out the door around 9 a.m.

I am at the store before 9:30 and sure enough, Bertha has started the piles for the trip to the plant. I help bag them and mark them: "H," "M" or "L" for starching instructions and "PO" for press only. We ship the dry cleaning to a plant in the Bronx, like most of the stores in town, while we do the laundry here. It works like this—get your stuff in by 8 a.m. and we'll have it ready at 5:30 p.m. the same day. No "one hour martinizing" or pressing on demand. We charge by the pound for laundry and make a nice profit. The day is on and I'm already looking forward to 3 p.m. by then usually, all the laundry is done and folded, packaged, and ready for pick up by their owners. The dry cleaning gets back about 4 p.m. and all we do is sort by ticket and get them racked. Drop offs are fewer today, so I plan on getting out of here at about 4:30 p.m.

I've got a meeting with the bookkeeper at lunch to go over the books for the month and to find out how big a check I can write for myself this week. Then I thought I'd get a manicure before coming back to hand out paychecks and help out at the desk.

I meet my bookkeeper, Sidney, at The Jackson Hole for burgers. Not ordinary burgers—just the best burgers on the planet. Sidney is early as usual—you gotta' like that in your bookkeeper—prompt and accurate. We sit in a booth in the back. Sidney is a pretty uptight Jewish fella, who I don't think, ever did anything spontaneously, but he is a good guy. I order a Baldoni burger and a coke. Sidney orders a patty melt and coffee.

"Sidney, how can you drink coffee with that sandwich?" I ask.

"What's wrong with that?" he says.

"I don't know, it just isn't right," I answer.

In any event, we get down to business; Sidney explains all the money going out and the money coming in. I only have a couple of questions that Sidney answers to my satisfaction. The only reason I even ask is because I know Cassidy will grill me like a whopper later.

The food shows up. These burgers are "knife and fork-ers"— so big you need a knife and fork to eat 'em. The conversation drifts and we end up on the robbery at the Reserve. Sidney of course, can't conceive of a crime, period. Let alone, one that risky and forget about the printing money thing. But he certainly would help take some off your hands for his services.

Sidney shares he had a client one time, who was arrested and did some time for counterfeiting. He said the guy had a good thing going, but he got greedy. Instead of moving around and spending the money in different places, he got sloppy and paid for some appliances for his wife with the fake cash. It didn't take long for word to get out that he had a pile of cash and before he knew it, he was busted in a sting.

Seems that the local gendarme sets up a bogus audio-video shop and in walks Sidney's client who buys a PDA of all things. Cops then check the cash and find that it's fake and dude goes to the joint.

"It's been a few years." The guy is out amongst us now." Sidney says.

Sidney finishes his food. I'm long done and the meeting is over. We set up another one for next month, and then we go. Oh yea, I pick up the tab, because God forbid, Sidney ever buys one of his clients anything. I'll bet he keeps his money somewhere, where he can count it every night.

Just as I had planned, I pop in to see my Vietnamese ladies for a manicure. That's another thing. "Is there some kind of manicurist academy in Vietnam?" Every shop is run and manned by the Vietnamese. Just an observation; they keep the TV on the WB and in the afternoon, you can get your nails or toes done and watch reruns of *Seinfeld* or *Mad About You*. I don't go to a regular girl, just whoever is up and ready. I don't think anyone makes appointments; it's all walk-ins, but everyone for the most part is a regular.

I have this nervous habit of chewing my cuticles and if I go more than two weeks without a manicure, I start ripping them to the point of bleeding. Then I have to wear band-aids which look goofy. So here I am, in a chair with a good angle at the TV, when in walks Milagro. I have never seen her in here and am kind of stunned. I figured her for a spa-type, not a storefront-type, but maybe she couldn't get an appointment, or whatever. I just lost interest in the TV and am focused on her legs. She catches me checking her out and recognizes me.

She points at me and says, "It's the dry cleaner—how are you?"

"I'm terrific and you?" I say.

"A little tired, but okay," she says.

I tell her to just relax and enjoy her manicure. She also informs me that she just dropped off some leather items, but didn't see me. Of course, I instantly start thinking that first, she noticed me gone and second, she was looking for me?

"We'll take good care of them." I say.

I then begin to imagine her in a leather halter with really tight leather pants.

Linda, the manicurist, says: "You wash hands now."

Off to the sink I go to wash the lotion off and then take my seat again for the polish. Milagro is watching TV and paying no attention to the girl working on her nails, which are real, not acrylics.

Realizing I am staring, I move to the polish dryers and look out the front window. As I am paying and getting ready to leave, Milagro asks, "Can you hang around till I'm done."

Without looking at a clock or my watch, I immediately say: "Yes, no problem."

My mind begins to race—what could she want? Is it sex? Is it something she needs to get off her chest? —*ooh* that chest—or is it something about dry cleaning? Heck, she doesn't know my name. I am just the dry cleaner worker, so what else could it be?

My wait isn't long and she is walking out the door with me.

She introduces herself saying: "We've never formally met and I think it's time I know your name, considering that you take care of my clothes."

"Martin," I say.

She replies: "It's nice to meet you Martin, my name is Milagro."

I want to say that I know, but instead I say: "right back atcha."

She laughs at my reply.

I'm thinking, "I'm so *witty*."

"What did you want to ask me, Milagro?" I ask.

21

Here is the moment I have been dreaming about—she'd like for me to come up to her place and have at it on the floor.

"I was curious Martin, how many of those commercial washers and dryers do you have in your store?"

I am sooo deflated that I have to think about those machines. "Four and four," I say.

She looks at me like I have three heads.

"I mean four washers and four dryers. Why?" I clarify. "Are you thinking about opening up a dry cleaning business?" I joke.

She smiles and says, "Oh, no. I am working on a project that might need that kind of equipment and I was curious about the number of machines you had."

She thanks me for the information and says it was nice to see me and she is sure she'll see me again. I say the same and head to the store wondering what the hell that was all about.

At the store, Bertha has all the orders ready for pick up. Our part-time worker of the month is Denise. She has a great smile and a real knack for remembering phone numbers, which comes in handy at the store. The last four digits of your phone number are our reference for sorting on the rack.

I call Denise the part-timer of the month. That is because part-timers usually last about six months, then boogie. The work ethic kids today have is for shit. People just don't seem to want to pursue a career in the dry cleaning industry—go figure.

2

Carlos and Milagro begin walking down Park Avenue about 5 o'clock. Carlos is animated, moving his arms around as he speaks.

"You know storage is going to be a problem?"

"I know, but I think I have a solution, or at least an option," Milagro says.

Carlos looks at her and says: "I hope this is better than your last suggestion."

Carlos Ferrar looks like Armand Asante—chiseled jaw line, thick salt and pepper hair, piercing brown eyes, rugged movie star good looks. He walks with confidence as if the streets are his and the passers by are his subjects; almost regal.

"We need to rent or purchase some killer office space in a swanky building where no one would even suspect or care what was going on. We would just be snooty tenants just like everyone else. Did you ever notice that the people who work in those places don't say hi to the other tenants? They just go about their business and never think twice about the schmuck in the office space next to them." Milagro says.

"You know Babe, it's about time we put the operation into phase two. We could lease about 15,000 square feet for a couple of years and see what happens. I always wanted a corner office with a view," Carlos says.

Milagro looks at Carlos and smiles, "Yes indeed, one for you and one for me. I would love to put my feet up on a teak desk with some lackey bringing me Starbucks. I schlepped my share of coffee for Duane, now it's my turn."

"I don't know about you schlepping any coffee, the only thing I heard is that you went down to get was his johnson."

"Details, my dear. How do you think I got us that security schedule?"

"That is a good point; your talents did pay off in a big way for us. Poor Duane is in a world of trouble now. What goes around, comes around," Carlos says.

"I checked out that firm I read about in *New York Magazine*—the one that is run by that good looking broad. She seems to have the "hot" properties in town these days," Carlos says.

"Good idea. Let me know if you need some help. I am not sure you can be discreet, after all, that's what real money is—discreet."

Thanks Milagro. I'll remember that when I am kicking it in the Caribbean. I got your discreet right here!" Carlos grabs his crotch.

Milagro shakes her head and says, "See what I mean? That shit don't fly uptown, Carlos!"

"Don't you worry Babe; I 'got more class in my little finger than most of those phony WASPS do in their whole damn body." Carlos says.

"That's what I'm afraid of!" she mumbles.

"What's that?" Carlos asks.

"Nothing, Carlos, nothing,"

It's a Friday night and Cassidy and I had planned to stay in and rent a DVD, order in, and chill. We both have had a good, but busy week. Cassidy got a couple of great listings in midtown, while I ran some decent numbers at the store.

Only there was a change in plans—Cassidy booked a late afternoon showing that turned into a meeting with a potential close on some space. She called me at the store about 6 p.m. and said that there was no way she could walk away from this deal and that she'd make it up to me later. I've heard that before.

In any event, I'm not too disappointed, this just gives me a chance to hang out at The Mixer and see what's going on in the neighborhood. Walt has my drink waiting as he sees me walk in and head down the bar. "How ya' doin'?" He says.

"Doin' fine my friend, and you?" I say.

"Got no complaints, Marty, just waitin' for my numbers to hit." Walt says.

"I hear ya', you an' me both."

"Yea, but I ain't married to the James Brown of real estate, so my numbers should hit first." Walt says.

"Screw you ya' bastid, she has to wake up and punch in just like us. It just so happens she has a knack for being in the right place at the right time." I say defending my meal ticket.

"The right place alright; she sells the right places," says my barkeep.

"Walt, you know my dad told me there are three things to look for in a woman."

"What's that Yoda?" Walt replies.

"He said son, you go for a woman with looks, cooks, and a big checkbook."

"All I got was a pain in the ass." Walt says.

"Let's toast to your ex-wife, Walt, how is that ball-breaker doing?" I say sarcastically.

"Marty, I am not going to toast her, nor will I even talk about her. It gives me a headache and reminds me of another bad decision in my life, but by all means—drink to whomever the fuck you want to." he bitterly replies.

27

"Whoa, Walt man, I didn't mean to piss you off. I was just messin' around. Lighten up you fat bastid!"

"Sorry, Marty, I just keep thinking that I was supposed to be someone else, that I was supposed to do something else, something better than a bar owner—ya know?"

"Hey Walt, you got a good life, you make a good living out of this joint, you got a nice roof over your head, and you got your health. Although you should start to consider salads, I'll bet you hear some people who have some real shitty lives at those AA meetings you go to." I say.

"Yeah, your probably right Marty, I just need a meeting. This shitty feeling will pass, they always do," he says.

Walt, sober now for years still has plenty of remorse for his drinking years. It's hard for him to let go of the past when he has lots of reminders in the way of financial amends. He ran his credit cards all to the max, borrowed money to pay those down, stole from his ex-wife, just so he could stay drunk and high. He just never seems to be able to make a dent in his debt; it's always something or someone looking for money from him, if he could only hit the lottery. The bar pays its own bills and that's about it, he draws a salary and that pays his basics, never getting ahead wears on him, wears on him hard.

"Hey Walt, while your mood is passing, can you fix me another Absolute and Tonic, Cass is gonna' be late tonight, so I have some time to kill"

"Oh yes sir. Thanks for gracing us with the extended pleasure of your company. I'll alert the media," he says.

"That's the Walt I love, breakin' balls and sharing the love!" I exclaim.

Just as Walt hands me my drink, I notice that annoying ticker bar on the bottom of the TV screen, flashing the latest headline that reads: *Federal Reserve Heist an inside job, Director of Security in custody.* I can't get that robbery off my mind—actually, walking out of the Federal Reserve with plates that print money. Oh well, someone always has to take the fall. I wonder if they got the plates back. How would you print up the bills? Where would you get the paper, the ink, and the balls?

I shake my head and stare at the screen. The Yankees are losing 3-0 in the 8th. Just when I think those guys in pinstripes got it goin', they drop one to Tampa Bay—the shittiest team in the league. Thank God I don't bet anymore. That would have been one I would have dropped some escarole on. I learned my lesson after missing two payments to Frankie, the WOP down on Mulberry Street. He scared the shit out of me so bad that I had to get a loan on the street to pay him off, so I could save my thumb. Cocksucker was gonna chop off my thumb if

I didn't pay up in 48 hours. I like my thumb, so I got the money and haven't placed a bet since.

After a couple of more pops, I decide to head home to see what Cassidy wants to do for dinner. Walking home always reminds me of how much I love this city. Its 9:30 at night and the streets are still teaming with people looking for fun on a Friday night. There is just this energy that courses through your veins when your feet hit these sidewalks. I love the way this city makes me feel.

I stop at the liquor store and pick up a bottle of Absolute. I feel like drinking some tonight and I think we're out. Cassidy won't mind some V&T's for a change instead of wine. Seeing as I have to be at the store at 8 a.m. tomorrow, vodka doesn't give me the hangover wine does—but that's just me.

Walking in the house, I see it's still dark and Cassidy isn't home yet. I forgot my cell phone today, so she wouldn't have been able to call me if something was wrong. I guess I'll call her, although she hates it when I call if she's in a meeting. Especially if she smells blood—I mean closing a deal. So I make an executive decision and fix myself a drink, slip into shorts and a T-shirt, and fire up the TV. If she's not home by 11 p.m., I'll call.

3

"Well, Ms. Tyroni. I must say that not only will my organization take the space, we'd like to have you handle the financing."

"That's great, Mr. Ferrar. We will make sure that we get you the best deal on both fronts; the price per square foot and the financing."

"I know you will, Ms. Tyroni. Your reputation is impeccable and it's a pleasure to do business with you."

"Call me "Cassidy" and thank you. We work hard to keep our clients happy."

"Well, you can call me Carlos."

"Thanks Carlos, we'll have to do some paperwork at my office on Monday, to seal the deal, but it's just routine."

"Of course, of course. I'll see you Monday at 10 a.m. at your office then."

"Fabulous, Carlos. We're going to see you in that space before you know it."

"We can hardly wait. You'll have to excuse me. My associates need to hear the good news." "Certainly, Carlos. You go right ahead. I'll get this tab."

Carlos gets up and shoots his cuffs, buttons his Prada jacket, and then makes his exit.

An interesting man, thinks Cassidy—attractive and immaculately dressed and pressed, but with shoes in desperate need of a shine. Cassidy also thought it odd that he didn't seem at all taken aback by the prices. I guess he's just eccentric and has some serious cash.

I'm sitting in the den with my hands working the remote like a concert pianist, knowing just when to change channels, so that I never have to look at a commercial. It drives my wife crazy, but I think that might be because she isn't very technically inclined. She has many talents, but working our TV isn't one of them. She just doesn't know how to "graze" channels. Not really a bad thing, unless she has the remote and you are with her. Sometimes I let her "drive" and I must really work on my control issues. I want to grab the thing right out of her hand and start "surfing," but I know that won't score me any points. In the grand scheme of a relationship—critical is knowing when and what to take a stand on. Changing channels and controlling the remote isn't something worth going to the mattresses over.

It's about 10 p.m. and I start watching something on the Discovery Channel. It's a show about early civilization. What I seem to be picking up on is how much time some of these peoples spend on thinking about drainage. I then realize just how important drainage really is. Look around you, wherever you look, someone has thought about drainage—in the streets, in the yards, even on a house. The roof pitch is basically drainage. It hits me square between my eyes; what separates third-world countries from first-rate countries is drainage. Think about it. Every time you see a commercial for a poverty- stricken group of people, they always have puddles around them. The areas always look muddy and half-flooded. They just haven't given enough thought to drainage. Perhaps, if they had, they'd have enough food or at the very least they'd be dry. I take a certain amount of pride knowing my ancestors, the Romans, were some of the first people to pay serious attention to drainage; after all they invented the aqueducts.

I hear my wife turning the key and making her entrance. I can hear her Jimmy Choo's clicking across the hardwood floors—it's a very familiar sound. She checks the caller ID on the handset, as we have no answering machine. It's been years since we did. We realized that we were a slave to the thing. It's just not right that you walk into your house and begin looking for a flashing red light. Besides, my mother always said, "If it's important, they'll call back." Plus, you have some people who know you won't be home and they call, just to leave a message. Now it's on you to call back.

Cass finds me sitting in what she calls a cold, dark room that's illuminated by the blue light from the TV. She immediately turns lights on, which pisses me off. Again, not worth going to the mattresses for.

I ask her where she's been.

She says: "With a client, nailing down a big-ass fee!"

"That's my girl! Who was it today?"

"Some guy who is new in town and wants to make a big impression with his business. You know, it's all about the address and the office."

"Yeah, what does he do?"

"I'm not sure, but I think it's a financial services firm. The guy is Latin, I think—from South America. His name is Ferrar, Carlos Ferrar"

"Doesn't ring a bell with me, but then again, that doesn't mean much."

"Anyway," she says, "he is taking that new listing on Park Avenue—great space, great building—If his business is half as good as these offices will be—he should do well."

"See, honey, what you do is really for the greater good—people helping people!"

"Are you stoned?" she asks me.

"No, just a little high"—as I shake the cubes in my glass. "You gotta problem with that?" "No, but I sure would like to catch up. Why don't you fix me one of what you're drinking." "Groovy, I'll do that while you change and we'll hang here tonight, OK?"

"Sounds like a winner to me. I'll be right down." She says.

I go to the Sub-Zero to pull out a bottle of the chilled vodka, mix the drink and bring it into the den. By the time I get settled again and start grazing on the TV, all I can find is the news, which isn't bad because I haven't seen any today. After the usual murder, crime, and politics, they run another piece on the robbery at the Federal Reserve. This time, they are talking about how much planning, timing, and genius must have gone into pulling this off. It goes on to say they have no leads or anything worth talking about. They did mention that they fired a few people at the Reserve, not for suspicion of involvement, but for negligence. Of course, there is no official comment from the Fed, but they sure do have some egg on their face. The reporter actually showed us what a plate looks like. It's a sheet of metal that is about 4 feet by 4 feet, thin and would fit into a travel golf case when rolled up. Not at all what I thought a plate would look like. I guess the plate fits on to the rollers of the printing press and works that way. But still, man, it is absolutely one of the ballsiest things I ever heard of. Cass comes walking in and I tell her about this and she could care less. As a matter of fact, she asks to change the TV to HGTV so she can look at Extreme Homes.

It's a pretty good episode. Some couple built their dream home 200 feet in the air—a tree house with plumbing and cable. Another guy, an architect, converted a schoolhouse into a seven bedroom house for his family. Of course, the kids are home-schooled.

We drift into a chat about this weeks work highlights and Cass still is wrapped up in her last meeting. She was really curious about what kind of financial service business Mr. Carlos Ferrar was going to be doing in that great space he just picked up.

"What's the big deal, Cass? He has got the "bling bling" and soon you'll have some of it too. Anyway, he is looking to get in next month and begin build out concurrently," she adds.

"That's unusual. It's usually a more drawn out affair—architects, designers, contractors and a host of communications and IT people."

"This is an unusual situation, he assures me. His firm is already established in Amsterdam and in Panama and this move is purely as a convenience for a couple of his biggest clients. Kind of a satellite personal branch, but that was all he said. Not what they do or what exactly they provide for clients. He would be moving 35 people in right away."

The next featured home is built underground, kind of a mole hole for humans, a little dark for my taste, I like some windows. Cass gets up to pee and gets us some more drinks when the phone rings. "I'm not expecting anyone, are you?"

"No, check caller ID."

"It's a Pennsylvania number—Lancaster. You expecting a call from an Amish client?" "Funny Marty, just answer it."

I do and it's an old buddy of mine from the neighborhood, a cat named Space. He is going to be in town next month and wants to get together. We catch up a little, but save some for next month. He is at a funeral in Lancaster, PA and found himself with a minute and decided to call. Space's family has some serious cash. His great grandfather invented of all things, Tupperware, and he is a trust fund baby who can't seem to wean himself off doing absolutely nothing. He is the busiest "doer of nothing" I've ever met. But he is a bighearted good-time loving sincere guy. He just wants everyone around him to have a good time and the two of us have some awesome history together and we stay in touch as best we can.

Somewhere I read that you typically can count the *real friends* you have on one hand. But I think that's because we are lazy and get so wrapped up in what's in front of our faces that we let memories and the people who move away or the ones that we move away from, turn into a Christmas card relationship. It takes work and some commitment to keep relationships and friendships alive and thriving. Someone has to reach out and make an effort; your not living in the same house or seeing them in class or at work anymore. Sometimes over time and it doesn't take long before you start to think that; "Hey, he hasn't called me, so I'm not going to call him...." That is the silliest little thing called pride that gets in the way of most of the honest natural vulnerability that the human condition can muster. We fill in that vulnerability with a host of coping mechanisms, all of them there to hide or mask the way we really feel. We really want to call that friend up and laugh like you used to or hear about what they are doing or tell that same story over again for yet another time. That's the comfort and ease we really need in our lives, but we let pride deny us.

Cassidy says, "Don't forget to tell me when the dates are set so that I can carve out some time to spend with you two and his latest girlfriend."

We finish our cocktails and need more. It's Friday and we love to put a "buzz on" and "dance in the living room" our way of chilling out; we'll end up calling for delivery and stagger upstairs –I love my life.

4

Carlos moves through the metal detectors at Kennedy Airport without a beep or buzz. Now he has to put his belt back on, put on his shoes and not forget his briefcase. The flight to Nashville leaves at 2 p.m. and its 12:30, so he has time to grab a drink and a smoke in the WorldPerks Club. He has been flying a lot for the last two years, organizing this operation and has racked up some serious miles and decided that joining the club would make his time at the airport more productive. Anyway, he likes the free booze and the smoking lounge with lots of phones and computer hook ups.

He finds a spot in the lounge, fires up a Dunhill, and hits the phone. He rings through to Counce, Tennessee, where he has an associate who he'll be visiting this trip. His friend is a guy known as "Sliver," because he is a really big guy (325 lbs.). The genesis for the nickname comes from the way he orders pie—ironically he asks for a sliver—some nicknames stick and this one was long before Carlos came on the scene and he wasn't about to break what seemed like a good thing for the guy.

Sliver answers, "Carlos, when does your flight get in?"

"About 4 p.m. your time. I was hoping to be at the site by 6 p.m. so that we could run through things one more time."

"Sounds good, I'll be here. You remember how to get here from the airport right?"

"Sure do, after all this time you still have to ask?"

"That's my man. You know for a city feller—you are okay."

"From you Sliver, that's a compliment; see you in a few hours and make sure everything is ready when I get there, OK?"

Carlos takes a drag on his Dunhill and hangs up, looking around the club at all the men and women, cradling cell phones and banging away at their laptops, wires coming out of every piece of luggage they carry. It wasn't too long ago that a cell phone, a computer, and these frequent flier clubs were only for the rich, the powerful, but now every joker with a credit card or a job that puts them on the road seems to be a communication and information way station.

The worst, Carlos thinks, is when you get on a plane, there are all these people who seem to have to be on their phone talking about some shit that seems so damn inane, but the way they speak, like they are so damn important—and it's too loud, so all can here the schmuck in 3B say he loves his wife and kids, or the silly sales guy screaming to his assistant—"that's unacceptable!" We used to have these conversations in private, but where has that gone? Why do people think that it's okay to have those talks in earshot of strangers? I don't know, but it annoys the hell out of me. One day I'll be away from all this and never have to deal with these losers and their petty lives again, is all Carlos can think about.

Cassidy is walking around on her heels because her toes are still wet, her phone is ringing in her Prada bag, and she is hustling to grab it. She was expecting the paperwork on that Park Avenue deal with the South American guy to go through today, so on Monday she can turn it over to the building owner and send him her commission bill.

It's her office manager, Stephanie, on the line; "Cass, it's Steph. We have a small problem and I don't know what to do."

"What is it Steph, is it the South American deal?"

"Yes, it is. This guy Carlos, checks out all right but the check he gave you won't clear till Wednesday—foreign bank in Panama City. Those South American banks work on their own system and they'll have to contact their office in Panama City to clear the wire transfer."

"Shit, that sucks girl. Do you want me to call them?"

"Well, if you want this to go through by Tuesday, you'll have to or we can wait—it's your call."

"Let me finish up here and I'll swing by the office and check it out."

"Cool, I'll be here."

Cassidy hangs up, moves back into the spa chair and looks out the window. There was something funny about Carlos, but she couldn't put her finger on it—maybe this was it.

I wish these people wouldn't wait till 2:55 p.m., when they know we close at three on Saturday. It just means we can't get out of here till 4 p.m.

"Bertha, how much more do you have to sort?"

"I think I can be done in 25 minutes if I hustle—why you gotta hot date Martin?"

"No, I just was hoping we could leave at 3:30 p.m. today, so I could be home before Cass."

"Well, it's your store if you want to go, just go, I can handle it."

"Are you sure, I hate to leave you hanging?"

"You aren't leaving me hanging, I don't have to be anywhere and you do."

"Okay then, I'm gonna spilt at 3:15 p.m.—let's get these clothes bagged, quit flapping your gums."

"Martin."

"Yea Bertha?"

"Bite me."

"I love you too."

It's 3:15 p.m. and I'm out—just a little guilt, but I'll get over it—I always do. I want to beat Cass home so I can surprise her with the newest toy I picked up the other day. A sweet bottle opener that makes uncorking wine seem like popping a top on a can. I love gadgets and this one is really cool, so I want to get home and open a couple of bottles, have the wine chilling so Cass can chill after the spa. She'll come home like over-cooked pasta.

We have committed to a small donation to a children's hospital in New Rochelle and part of the donation is this party tonight at one of the board members houses in town. One of those deals I hate. But it's good business for Cass, so I play along. It's a partnership we have and if I have to pretend to be the "trophy husband" sometimes, I don't mind. Cass enjoys rubbing elbows and I kind of like getting dressed up once in awhile. I'll try not to drink too much and use my napkin.

I like to think that I'm a well-connected guy, I have been a New Yorker all my life and with that comes a certain swagger. I have learned that in order to get what you need in this town you gotta' have a guy. A guy for this and a guy for that, regular citizen's use the Yellow Pages, New Yorkers call their guy. When I first started dating Cassidy, I sensed I had to step up my game a notch or two. Meaning that I needed a little schooling in the ways of manners; I knew what the salad fork was and that stuff, but there are some subtleties that I just felt I needed to know. So, I called my guy, Peter who was the maitre'di at one of the finer Italian restaurants in the city and he could help me in this area. So after a few sessions I was good to go. I have learned that knowing what you don't know and then taking the initiative to learn, is what makes you a better-rounded person, of course, if you can put your pride aside and ask for help, that is.

Cass walks through the door at 4, and I'm ready with some chilled wine and some cheese for her.

She smiles and grabs the glass and says; "This is sweet, hon, but I have to run to the office quick to make a call on that deal I cut the other day—a banking issue."

"Bummer, we have to be at the dinner at eight right?" I remind her.

"Yeah, but if we're late it's no biggie."

So yours truly looks at his options and decides that a moment of Zen is required. I have some trouble changing my plans mid-stream; I'm easy going, but when I have my sights set on some wine and some pre-party nookie, not getting it is tough. The wine is fine but nookie is better and I really like having that "knowing" feeling at a party after I have been freshly sexed.

I walk onto the patio and turn on the radio to help chill and hear what's happening in the world. I'm not a news junkie, but before a dinner party, I like to know so I have something to contribute to conversation.

The news has a follow-up on that Reserve heist. The robbers got away with more than previously thought. They got the plates for the new twenty dollar bill—that was known, but what wasn't known was that they grabbed the ink mix formulas. This is a real problem for the Feds. Not only can these guys print twenties if they know what they're doing, but they'll be able to recreate the new patterns and watermarks with that information. This has the Reserve really looking like a bunch of "boobs."

I kind of smile on the inside; these guys have really done the impossible—ripped off government plates and now the new ink formulas. The government can't just turn around, redo the patterns and ink. They are screwed. These robbers are smarter than the average stick 'em up guys.

Milagro is curling her hair; she has to attend a fund raiser tonight in New Rochelle. She is excited because this is a new charity for her. She has been fronting as a professional fund raiser/ party planner as of late.

Latching on to a cause and helping the principals create and execute events to raise the money. She did some of this in Panama. She was one of the driving forces behind the Noreiga Party funding. She was a favorite of El Jeffe, as a matter of fact; she was linked romantically according to the gossip mills in Panama. She was in her twenties and was well-connected then. Her father was a key military leader for the party and she was raised like royalty servants, top schools, and traveled internationally, and was exposed to the best money could buy.

Tonight's event is a simple dinner party for the New Rochelle Children's Ward. It's being held at one of the board members homes. The guest list is small but influential; some leaders of the NY social and business scene will be there.

There were times when she would get really excited for these things, but she has been to so many and her mind is full of other distractions that she doesn't do her usual homework. Things like reviewing the guest list, learning names and likes, making sure that certain folks are kept separated from one another. There are still some feuds going on that below the surface are ingrained and passed down from one generation to the next—the kind of disdain that never really goes away.

But she can't get out of her head the discussion she had the other day with Carlos. He seems to be so cavalier these days; they are so far from the finish line that the mere thought of it is inconceivable. She knows that she has to stay in the moment because he doesn't—once a dreamer, always a dreamer. This time he thinks because there was a little success in the first stage of the plan that the rest will all be downhill. Milagro knows better—she has been around the block before.

Martin and Cassidy show up at the reception about an hour late. The home is beautiful—a six bedroom, stylish condo on Central Park East. Martin is already bored and headed for the bar. Cassidy sizes up the crowd, looking for her girlfriend, Elizabeth. Liz is the one who got her turned on to this foundation; Liz knew that these events would be a target rich environment for Cassidy's business.

She just keeps adding to her roster of clients. She does feel a little guilty for using a charity as a business networking platform, but what the heck, she is donating money after all. She finds Liz near the patio talking to someone Cassidy doesn't recognize, but Liz sure seems engaged, so Cassidy decides to grab a drink then start schmoozing. Martin already has a vodka and tonic in his hand when he spots his wife. Instinctively, he orders her a flute of champagne, her preferred prop for these things. As he walks toward her, he takes a double take because there is Milagro right behind Cassidy. As he hands his wife the drink, Milagro touches his arm so lightly and says;

"Martin, how nice to see you, how long have you been supporting this cause?" Cassidy wheels on her heel to see the sexy Latin talking to her husband.

"About two years, as soon as I found out about it, I couldn't help but want to help."

"Honey, why don't you introduce to me to your friend," Cass requests.

"Oh, what a social retard I am. Milagro, this is my wife, Cassidy. Milagro is a regular at the store, sweetie."

"I'm sure she is. Nice to meet you, Milagro. I didn't catch your last name…."

"It's Perdido."

"I am here to talk with some of the Charity's Board about helping the organization raise some real money—it's what I do."

"How interesting. So you are a party planner?"

"You might say that, but when it comes to this type of fund raising, it's really involved—more than a caterer and an interesting location."

"Well, we wish you luck; Martin, we must say hello to Elizabeth. She is over by the patio. See you, Milagro."

"It was nice seeing you, Martin, and meeting you Cassidy. Enjoy the event."

"Cassidy, that was a little rude. You just kind of abruptly cut her off and pulled me away like a pet."

"Oh well, I'm sorry, Marty. If you want to go back and chat with Conchita, that's okay by me.

It doesn't happen too often, but Cassidy can get a little jealous sometimes if she sees an attractive woman giving me some attention—

you can see her talons come out and she'll turn on that "shark-persona" that has made her successful in the business world.

Some men would get upset, but I am flattered that still to this day, my wife gets jealous. Besides, it also makes me feel good when a good lookin' broad like Milagro, gives me some time.

Elizabeth already has a little buzz on and is working towards a bigger one. Cassidy and I step into her space and wait for a break in her conversation to say hello. She's talking to a guy, who must be at least 10 years younger than her, but Elizabeth is twice divorced and from what Cassidy tells me, has quite an appetite for men—if you know what I mean.

"Cassidy, Martin—so good of you to come." Liz says waving her arm like a character in the Great Gatsby.

"Thanks, Liz. Wouldn't miss it for the world—you always seem to know where it's happening and when—so here we are."

"I want you to meet my new friend, Paul. Paul works for Forsman and Little on Wall Street. We were just talking about all the opportunities for investors in Asia these days."

"Marty, what have you been up to?" Liz asks.

"Nothing Liz, just doing my thing, putting one foot in front of the other and staying out of trouble," I say.

"How boring. I was hoping you had some dirt for me—you are in the business after all." Right about now I want to slap the shit out of this alimony, energy sucking bitch, but I know she's Cassidy's friend and I decide this isn't the time or place, so I just laugh and excuse myself to the bar.

Cassidy gives me a look and I make my way through the crowd. There must be at least 100 people here tonight; perhaps it's the silent auction. Brian Cashman, the General Manager of my beloved Yankees, is tonight's main supplier of items. There are a couple of things I had my eye on, but Cassidy always says we give enough just to be here, so we don't need to buy some shit that I wouldn't even hang on my walls, so I just look longingly.

Three hours of drinking and mingling and I am ready to go. Cassidy seems to be engrossed in a talk with some really old guy wearing a kilt. She spots me and gives me the wink—that's the sign for me to get her out of here. I sidle on over and introduce myself and remind Cassidy of another engagement we must leave for and she apologizes to "Braveheart" and we are gone. As we wait for our car, I can't help but notice Milagro again. She's on her phone talking with some passion, but I can't make out a word as she is talking in Spanish. Even though we were here for some time, I haven't seen her since Cassidy gave her the bums' rush. My loss, but there is always the store—now we'll have something to talk about other than the number of washing machines and dryers—I can hardly wait.

On the way home, Cassidy is just looking out the window. She is so beautiful when she's like this—quiet—thinking, but the silence is broken by her asking me if I'd like to stop off at Elaine's and have a drink and to see if anyone is out tonight. It's still early by New York standards. That's what I love about big cities; you can do anything you want, any time, night or day—they just never close. I love that. I used to rent videos at 2 or 3 a.m. from a 24 hour shop near Gramercy Park, when I lived at the GW. Man, back in the day I used to buy a lot of shit at weird hours. But then again, I functioned at weird hours. I was younger and living 24 hours a day and most of my living was at night. I loved staying up till it got "blue" outside. You know that time just before the dawn's light comes up—it's like the sun's own black light. It's a color that when I see it, I flash back to those times—I dig that.

"Sure, why not? I'm game, and besides, I could eat a little something."

So we're off. We make our way back home to the eastside and park our car. I get a great spot; won't have to move it till Monday— that's a good omen, it brings on a second wind of sorts. As we walk in to Elaine's, we give a quick scan to see who is in the front room and the bar. I spot Dr. Robert; he's a character and always in party mode. I'm not sure what kind of doctor he is, but on occasion, I have seen and heard him say and do doctor stuff, so we call him Dr. Robert—like the song by The Beatles.

We walk up, hug, order some drinks, and engage. The good Doctor has been here for a while. He's got that look about him. You know, the "I've had about six glasses of white wine, but you can't tell look." Anyway, we start telling him about the fundraiser and who we saw and what they served and that crap, when Elaine comes walking over to break the Dr.'s balls—you see, you have to give Elaine a certain amount of respect. Not only does she own this institution for celebs not to be seen, but she also has a lot of influence all over town and she has helped Cass find a few clients—we've always done right by Elaine. After those deals closed, we'd come in and throw a little party, drop some cash, and pay a little homage to the Grand dame of NY night life.

In any event, we start talking about how she thinks those guys who broke into the Fed, did it.

"You know," Elaine says, "I used to date a guy who worked there and he was always telling me that the place ran on such a strict schedule and routine that once someone became absolutely familiar with the comings and goings of the Bank, you could easily find the vulnerabilities and figure out a way to exploit them and make off with the "keys to the kingdom," without ever firing a shot or setting off an alarm. Of course, the only way to become that familiar with that routine was to work high up in security, he'd say, or be on the security review committee which changes about as often as the codes on the vault doors—hardly ever. You have to have some serious clearance to get those gigs. Usually, to some guy who had done good for the company and this was their way of saying thanks, a real cushy job watching computer print-outs of money counts and signing bag tags, bags containing money that is either being put into circulation or being taken out."

"Not only would the job be easy but it could also be the gift that keeps on giving if someone knows what to do with those plates that got lifted."

"But Elaine," the Doc says, "You got more money than you know what to do with. Why would you even think like that?"

"Hell Doc, I don't know anyone who never thought of what it'd be like to print money. I'm just like everyone else, ain't I?"

"No darling, you are not like everyone else, but we still love the shit out of you. Don't we Martin?"

"You bet we do Doc, why just the other day, Cassidy and I were sitting out back and saying how much we love Elaine."

"Oh, shut the fuck up you two. What are you drinking? Doc, I know what you got. Marty? Vodka and tonic? Cass, champagne? Good Jimmy, give these dear friends of mine another round on the Doctor would ya!"

"You guys know I never buy drinks. It's my policy—if I buy one, I got to buy 'em all, it's my hooch anyway and it gets awkward. You guys know how much I loathe feeling awkward"

Before I met Cassidy, I used to hang around with a guy who fancied himself a writer and this guy used to hang around Elaine's all the time trying to meet an agent or perhaps a publisher who could help him get his manuscript published. Well, Elaine being the patron of the written word that she is, let my friend run a tab. Well, he never got that manuscript published and stiffed Elaine. Now one thing Elaine doesn't like is being used so she made it clear to me that unless I paid my friend's tab, I was persona non grata in her joint.

Being the stand up guy that I am, I worked out a trade agreement; I replaced the awning out front and that squared us up. I had a guy who owed me a favor and it got done; that's how things work in "The World According to Marty."

We hang around for a couple of hours, have a few more drinks and a plate of fried zucchini sticks—the French fries of the 21st century says the Doc. I think he said that in the 90's too. But we have a few laughs until we both feel tired enough to call it a night.

While we are strolling home, I ask Cass a question. "Honey, could you imagine if you could print money, like Elaine was talkin' about? How cool would that be. Of course, you'd have to fly under the radar, because the IRS would wonder where the hell this pile of cash came from, but a smart person could figure it out. Hell, if you could get your hands on the plates and figure out how to print it, I'm sure you could figure out how to spend it."

"Marty, have you been thinking like Elaine?"

"Hell yes, ever since I saw the news about that robbery, it's been on my mind. I think it's cool that no one has been charged and that some internal shit is going down. Sure I'd love to print money, or better yet—be really friendly with someone who does—you know?"

"So, I am not the one doing the heavy lifting, just getting the legal tender—pretty cool. Don't you think like that sometimes?"

"Me? Marty, you know me, I believe in working for my millions, not having it handed to me. See, that's you always looking for the path of least resistance"

"Oh Christ, here we go," I think—"another one of those. "when it all comes down to it Marty, why aren't you more like me lectures?"

I tune her out and start thinking about how hot Milagro looked tonight. God! I'd like to have 30 minutes with her, or maybe 5 minutes, six times!

We're home and we throw our coats on the couch in the front room and head up for bed. Well, Cass will be asleep in 10 minutes. I'll stay up and watch the news, have a couple of more pops and head to bed—pretty typical night here.

I crawl into the cold dark room, which is really our state of the art audio/visual room—it boasts of a 60 inch plasma TV, sound system by Klipsch with 10 JBL speakers. I'm a bit of an audiophile, so when we, or should I say, Cassidy, started bringing home some real cash, this was my gift. I watch the TV till 3 a.m., then into the bed and spoon with Cass. Maybe I'll get some in the morning—that thought keeps me going—I'm off to sleep.

Milagro begins her day by taking several calls from Carlos, who is in a very good mood. He kept going on about the trip from Tennessee going smoothly and that the orange juice will have the pulp you like. She knows what that means, but keeps reminding him that when he's discussing orange juice, he should be doing it on the secure phone. Their land line is like a party-line and for the third time, she hangs up.

Carlos is going from room to room in his spacious apartment, just looking out of the windows staring and calculating things in his mind. He is very used to doing the math on this operation in his head, except he hates having to divide these numbers by five; he thinks that four or better—yet two, is a much better number to be dividing by.

5

Sunday morning is beautiful, birds chirping, sun creeping in through the sheers and the smell of coffee in the air. I can hardly wait to empty my bladder, but as usual, I have to start four feet away from the bowl and work my way closer—you know how it is with morning wood. After I brush my teeth and take the meds that keep my high blood pressure and that anti depressant that keeps me from biting the heads off of those I encounter, I am down for that first cup. Grabbing the paper off the stoop and the coffee, I head out back to read in the courtyard, I'll have an hour or two before Cass wakens to enjoy my solitude.

The courtyard is our oasis in the city; we increased the height of the walls to 12 feet so it's very private, Cassidy and I enjoy our privacy, we had it landscaped by Edison Wingate, the urban landscaper to the well-heeled. He looked at the courtyard as a blank canvas and let me tell you, he painted a masterpiece. Ivy climbs three of the four walls; the fourth has a granite wall fountain that gurgles the most serene water sounds. The flooring is made up of imported marble stone tile and a geometric design adorns the center of the space. There are Japanese maples, Italian cypress, jasmine and several varieties of ground cover plantings. I had the audio installers run speaker wiring out here and the sound is provided by Bose outdoor speakers, truly an oasis.

Going through the headlines, I see that the Yankees beat Anaheim and that the US is still screwing things up in the Middle East by trying to make others happy. I notice something tucked inside on page seven. The article reads *Internal Investigation ends with Security Chief of Staff axed.* The article goes on to say that even though the chief isn't connected to the crime at the Federal Reserve, he is responsible for the breakdown in security that day. He takes the fall, is basically the way I interpret this article. The article vaguely describes the possible steps that the perpetrators took to complete the heist. There must have been at least five of them, two more than originally thought, states a Reserve Spokesman. We know this, because it takes two just to get down to the vault secured area where the plates are kept and then another three, at minimum, to get past the two armed guards and deactivate three security systems including digital video, motion detectors, and a temperature sensing system. The third, the heat sensing system, particularly is the most difficult. This system is designed to detect increases or decreases in temperature of less than a degree which would let the system know that another being (animal/human) is in the space. The criminals must have had contact with the system designers or worse yet, within the reserve systems' IT group. The amount of computer hacking required to bring this system down makes launching a worm look like playing Pong. "This is the work of a very sophisticated network of criminals, the spokesman continues. This is an ongoing investigation and we will pursue these plates and people responsible until we can bring them to justice and the plates returned. We feel strongly that the criminals capable of this crime are also capable of a full fledged money printing/ laundering enterprise that has no limits."

Wow, I think….these crazy fucks are really getting away with this. Oh well, they are probably long gone out of this hemisphere by now, setting up operations in the islands off South America or in Belize, Panama or someplace like that. That's what I'd do, but I wouldn't have the balls to even think of such a caper. Heck, I can't even tell a lie without getting caught in it. The crime of the century is what this is. Simply stated—a license to print money, all you want, and all you can imagine. Then you put that lovely money into circulation little by little and build a legitimate fortune through investments, real estate speculation, and some other wealth accumulating methods. Then destroy the plates and you are rich for generations to come. Because money makes money. I can't count how many ideas I've had and said "all it takes is money." Why can't this shit happen to me? Why can't I get lucky and have something fall in my lap? I've been a good guy most of my life—worked hard , put up with more than my fair share of shitty jobs, rude people, helped a few old ladies cross the street…why not me?

I light a smoke, drink my coffee and finish the paper.

6

Agent Garrett Tedia of the FBI is sitting in his cramped office downtown drinking bad "cop coffee" staring at a printout of temperature variances from the Reserve the afternoon of the robbery. The readouts show a constant temperature of 69 degrees. No change all day—not even the usual increases when the guard changes or when an authorized employee enters and exits. That's what makes the FBI and the systems' designers think that the system was definitely corrupted. The person on duty probably wouldn't have noticed, just because nothing seemed out of place. The steady temperature would never have set off any type of alarm or worse yet, the system is literally telling it's keeper that everything is fine, no unexpected visitors. Technology is great, but sometimes we rely too much on the equipment doing the jobs humans need to be doing. The system was programmed on the day of the heist to read 69 degrees, regardless of any temperature change. Sometimes the Reserve IT guys do that when they are working on the system or when there is going to be heavy traffic down on the floors. This keeps the system alarms from going off all the time and in turn, keeps the staff from going through the motions of an intruder. So it's kind of like the system was in lock down. The protocol when this is scheduled is interoffice communications, so those who need to know, do.

But no memo that day—just a call from the lead programmer alerting the security department that this would be happening.

At least those guys on duty—that day— *thought* it was Tom Harvey from IT, alerting them to the "static temp position," which is what it's called when they do that. But Tom Harvey was in DC that day presenting the budgets for the next year. So someone, who knows his voice and knows the inner workings and the routine, placed that call and put the security team on a 'business as usual" mode. But how did they get into the system? That's what is confusing Garrett and his team. This hacker left no breadcrumbs for them to follow. They just simply got in there. A system that was supposed to be impervious to hacking fell prey. Now the process of recreating the events of that afternoon are seriously handicapped.

This has been keeping Garret Tedia awake. This the first high visibility case he's handled since being transferred to Manhattan South and he is not going to screw it up, but he is absolutely baffled right now and feeling the pressure, that his career will stall if he doesn't solve this heist.

7

Milagro agreed to meet Carlos for brunch today and even though they have some serious stuff to get settled, she really doesn't feel like dealing with him today. He can be such a jerk when he is full of himself and this morning on the phone, Carlos was full of himself.

She gets down to the street and starts looking for a cab. Sunday is the day that her co-op let's the doorman take off. All the pampered divorcees and yuppies have to hail their own cabs. Milagro has no trouble, perhaps her mini skirt and heels help the matter. Sometimes the very attractive and sexy take certain activities for granted never realizing their good looks and some sex appeal help in many ways…or maybe they do realize it and leverage it to the hilt. You choose.

The place where Milagro and Carlos are meeting for brunch is the Waldorf Astoria. They meet there just about every Sunday. It's usually crowded with tourists and they make Milagros skin crawl—especially those tourists who maybe spent some time in the city ages ago and still think they know what's going on. This city is a living organism always evolving and always looking to spread out and gobble up more and more people. Too bad these folks didn't get gobbled up. Most people irritate Milagro, unless she needs them for something.

She decided some time ago, not trust anyone or let anyone get too close. She used to be vulnerable, but no more. Once—shame on you; twice—shame on me. So that's why she has an edge, and today the edge is sharp.

She gets to the hosts stand and checks in; Carlos is already seated. That bastard couldn't even wait, she thinks. He has to make me walk in by myself, like some tart that can't wait to see him—she hates that. She follows the host to the table and he's not there, his napkin sits on his chair, but he's gone. Even worse, he can't wait for her to get at the buffet. What an asshole.

The Waldorf is one of mans' finest creations, timeless elegance and sophistication everywhere you turn in this historic hotel and meeting place for the rich and influential. The brunch is certainly all that—a sumptuous buffet, flanked by carving stations, chefs preparing omelets to order, and a sweet table that is to die for.

The waiter comes by and she orders a Bloody Mary. That should help her tolerate Carlos. Just about the same time her drink arrives, so does Carlos. He's got a plate heaped with fruit, breads, and smoked salmon.

"You know Carlos, you can make two trips. You don't have to get it all at once"

"I know my darling, but it looked so good I thought I'd save myself a trip, you know—efficient."

"Oh yea that's right, you are in such demand you need to measure your activities."

"Do I sense a tad bit of agitation darling?"

"You're damn right I'm agitated, I hate this place. I hate these brunches and we should be talking business in private, not in a goddamn hotel ballroom."

"Ah, but you see, I think in broad daylight, in public is best. It gives the appearance of impropriety if we sneak around."

"Like anyone is looking; you are way too pompous for me."

"Let's cut the small talk, Milagro, and get to the real reason you're here. I suspect you are wondering when you'll be seeing the fruits of your labor, right?"

"Well, now that you mention it, I was wondering if you had a timeline."

"Indeed I do, darling. I want you to know that we are all in better shape than we imagined. Those feds are walking around looking at nothing, it's quite comedic, I equate it to a monkey trying to fuck a football."

"Well, I'm glad you feel so good. I still want my end and I want it soon."

"You know I was just thinking this morning about your end— if you know what I mean." "Not in this lifetime Carlos, I may work to help charities but you aren't one of them."

Carlos has always had a voracious appetite for women. With his good looks and charm, he has never had any trouble in this area, except keeping his hunger satisfied and as of late, he has been thinking about the real estate broker, Cassidy Tyroni, and what a nice roll she might be.

8

"Sweetie, I'm going down to the corner store—I need some smokes. You need anything?"

"Grab me a pack would ya'. I think I've got a few, but its Sunday."

"Will do, Babe. Do you need anything else?"

"Nope, just some cigarettes—thanks," She yells back.

Off to the store I go, the corner store is a staple of city living, they usually carry a little bit of everything from milk to porn. As usual, it's Lee, the Korean owner's kid, working behind the counter. There is so much stuff sold at the counter. Lee appears to be framed in lottery tickets, lighters, breath mints, and cigars (blunts). Today, the kids open these blunts and fill 'em with weed and smoke them. I don't get it, but they do and Lee knows what sells.

I grab a donut and the smokes, Lee nods and says; "Good morning," and I pay. Back on the street, I survey the activity. Nothing unusual, just a Sunday morning coming down. I can't help but think of the Johnny Cash song. The lyric that goes, *somewhere, somehow I lost something along the way.* I guess it makes me think back to a simpler time, when the living was easy and I never worried about a soft place to fall.

Carlos decides that he's not too full to go back up for seconds. He grabs some more eggs benny, fresh melon, and returns. He sees Milagro down another Bloody Mary and realizes that he needs one too. It won't be long before he has someone bringing him drinks and ordering food from his own kitchen, once the last part of this caper is in place— he keeps going over in his mind just how simple the whole thing is and reminds himself that now is the fun part. The heavy lifting, so to speak, is done. He has to stay cool and organize his thoughts, stay focused and not get sloppy.

Something about Milagro lately has him concerned; she seems so distant, so pre-occupied—not her usual cool, cat-like demeanor. Cats just never seem to be interested in what you want them to be interested in when you want them to. But it could be 100 things making her act this way. But Carlos doesn't know what, her part in this plan is coming to a crescendo; she needs to make sure things go seamlessly.

The way Carlos sees it, he has reserved the office space, Milagro now needs to do PR for him and promote the business, and things go from there. It's a no brainer. She has all the right connections now and she needs to do the foot work. She's been raising money for charities; now it's time to raise money for him.

Carlos remembers when he first started grooming her for this assignment. She was placed in the security design firm for the Federal Reserve to be a coffee jockey for some poor unsuspecting schmuck that wrote the code for the security system that measures temperature. This schmuck named Duane, had a thing for Milagro and as time moved forward Carlos made it worth her while to respond to Duane. Her part in getting the access codes for the Reserve was beautifully executed.

Now the plan was to fund a financial services firm. Carlos will use Park Avenue office space for the company that will employ investment bankers, traders, brokers and those types. With the economy headed *south*, there are more of these guys out of work than you'd think. Most of them tried their hand at day-trading and quickly lost houses and families. They are desperate so the idea of trading for others will wet their appetites for the rush that comes when you see money double in two hours.

The concept is simple, Carlos thinks, we find these former hot-shot finance guys a little down on their luck and tell them they are trading for someone else. Then, Carlos will provide the "shill client" and then after the broker gets his cut, Carlos will pay the shill and he'll be left with a handsome profit. It's brilliant is all Carlos can think to himself as he looks back at Milagro, smiling.

All the money is in the escrow account Cassidy's firm set up for Carlos's deal. Cassidy kind of gloats to her staff who were freaked out the other day when the banks in Panama seemed to be balking, but Cass is an optimist—a real "glass half-full gal." She is also a lady who can get things done when others can't.

Cassidy decides that she should create a nice setting for the lease signing with Carlos for his new headquarter location. She begins to go back and forth with her assistant on restaurants in town that would be suitable. She decides first, that it should be a steak place; men always get a surge of testosterone when they look at a true carnivore's delight—big ass steaks. How about Smith and Wollensky—that's tradition in NY?

"Naw," says Cass, "They have locations around the country now, and they've become a chain, not exclusive and special anymore.

"I've got it," says Cass. "I'll take him to Brooklyn—to Peter Lugers. That's the place. Sweetie, call and get us a table for tomorrow night 8 p.m. After all, he is going to bring some serious currency into this office. Better yet, Cassidy thinks, Lugar's only takes cash. She bets Carlos is the type who likes to throw cash around.

I'm sitting at The Mixer looking at the Yankee game with Walt. Walt, really doesn't like baseball, but since he got sober, it's amazing the shit he puts up with. He even went out and paid for the YES network, it shows only the Yankees and Rangers games 24/7. For a guy like me, that's bliss. The Yankees are leading; they're playing the Colorado

Rockies—some of that interleague stuff—I'm not a big fan of that, but it's not my league to play with

But as I sit at this bar feeling good about myself, I can't help but think that things are not so good for Walt these days. The bank wants to talk to him about the loan he took to buy the bar. He's been consistently late and they don't want to own his bar, so they want to talk to him about third party management, which eats Walt out from the inside; working for someone in his own bar, now that idea could lead to a drink. I know Walt needs money in the worst way. Cassidy and I offered to loan him money before, but Walt won't have it—he's proud.

Today was a good day for yours truly, I think. The store did well. Bertha is happy and Cass is working late, so for me, no buttons to push—it's all downhill. I'll sit here and have a few drinks, go home, open a bottle of wine, put some *Dead* in the stereo, then turn down the sound on the TV, smoke a joint, and watch the end of the Yankee game; nothing like being stoned listening to Jerry and watching Jeter.

Cass, strolls into the den and looks at me and says; "Are you stoned?"

"Why, what's wrong?"

"Nothing, did you save any for me?"

"Hell, yes baby, here you go."

I hand her the half joint I didn't finish and she lights up, sits down, and gets nice and quiet. She digs the *Dead* too.

After a while, she goes up stairs to get into her sweats so we can chill, better yet, so we can cuddle some. God, I love this woman. I wish I could do more for her. All that I want is for her to be happy, to want for nothing, to ask for nothing, to smile, to be happy, and laugh. I want everyone to laugh...I am so codependent.

Cassidy tells me about the meeting with Carlos tomorrow. She'll be schmoozing her way into some serious steaks.

"Marty, does your friend Eno still work the bar there?"

"Yes, he does and I bet you want me to call him up so you can get the treatment, right?"

"Well of course I do honey, she purrs, what's the point of having a husband who's gotta a guy if he isn't going to share his guys."

For the uninitiated, having a guy is a New York thing. Over the course of a lifetime, you accumulate guys, friends who you can count on to elevate your status or enhance any experience. It's also a rule that if you have a guy then you have to share your guy with your wife, also a guy is for life, unless of course if your guy dies, then you gotta get another guy.

"Well, I guess I can give him a call, I say, but you owe me."

It's about quarter after 11 p.m. and the game ends, so I switch over to the news to see what is going on in the world. The story on the screen is about the Federal Reserve heist. Apparently, one of the guys who worked on the security system—the temperature checking technology—the reporter explains, was found dead in his car down by Battery Park last night. There is a suspicion that he might have been on the take because he was under investigation and now, well, dead men don't talk. Those are the reporters' words, kind of corny, but right on. Of course, the cops have no suspects and are following up on all and any leads.

"Man, check this shit out Cass. This Reserve thing just keeps getting more movie-like every time something comes out. I would love to be in ka-hoots with these thieves. They did it right. No loose ends, no traces—just clean unadulterated robbery."

"Marty, you amaze me. You always root for the anti-hero, never one to root for the good guy—the right side."

"Sweetie, Einstein said it—if you change the way you look at things, the things you look at change."

"Oh, snaps for you Marty, aren't you profound."

"Hell honey, I'm just high. Besides, all wisdom is plagiarism; the only thing original is stupidity."

"Yes, Marty you are an original," Cass says smiling.

Across town on the Westside, Milagro and Carlos are sitting in Teachers, sucking down some mussels and wine. Carlos is in a festive mood; Milagro is pretty happy too. Heck, the whole world is their oyster and tomorrow they'll be setting up the accounts for the business—Conserve-Reserve—that's the name they've decided on. They'll be going after conservative brokers to invest and use Reserve money to seed the phony clients. Pretty ballsy, but only they know.

9

Peter Lugar's is a place that is a throw back to restaurants in the 40's and 50's. No fancy furniture or contrived atmosphere, a bar in front and tables in the back. The menu is simple. Appetizers are a big steak tomato with an onion on top, seasoned with A1, the rest of the meal is real simple—steak for two, three, and so on. The hook is that the meat is so tasty and so fresh, it's like they are butchering in the back room. The service isn't rude, but it isn't that nose-up-in-the-air shit.

Carlos is late, Cassidy swears she told him to be here at 8 p.m. and it's almost 8:30 and he's still not here. Cassidy hates to wait, hates to feel like she is a table of one. So she orders another cocktail from Marty's friend and reviews the lease papers to make sure everything is in order. She is prepared for Carlos to hit on her too. It never fails these wheeler dealer types figure that every broad is romanced by their money, guile, and charming ways. But Cassidy is different; business is business, plus she is still very much in love with Marty. She wants the papers signed, give him the keys to his space, recommend some office designers, enjoy her meal, and then go home. Marty will certainly be up waiting for her; he doesn't like to go to sleep and doesn't like waking up. Besides he knows she's out with a man, but he has his buddy Eno looking out for him.

Finally Carlos walks in; he spots her at the bar immediately and joins her.

"I'm so sorry Cassidy for keeping you waiting; a beautiful woman like you shouldn't be left alone, my sincerest apologies."

"Not a problem, Carlos. I was just enjoying a drink and reviewing the lease and the other paperwork—mere formalities."

"Must we talk business? I was hoping to enjoy your company without being sold anything or thinking about work."

"Sorry Carlos, I have to get these in to the office tomorrow, but I promise it'll be painless."

"If you insist, show me the papers."

"Why don't we get our table and I can take you though this," Cassidy says.

"Okay, Carlos says as he throws a one hundred dollar bill on the bar, let's go."

"It's all standard stuff, the riders you asked for are here, Cassidy says, the owner has agreed to everything you've asked. He is very happy to have the space occupied by your firm."

"Well my associates and I feel lucky to have found the location and we couldn't have done it without you, so let me first propose a toast to you—the most efficient, beautiful and expensive broker in this town."

"Thank you Carlos, that's sweet of you, but when you love what you do like I do, it's an avocation not a vocation. Now let's do this deal so we can eat; I'm starving."

Cassidy procures the stack she has reviewed several times and takes Carlos through each one pointing out the changes he requested and the concessions that the owner has made. Pretty routine stuff, with one exception—the owners want to approve the interior designer and then of course, the designers' plans. Carlos has no problem with that, heck, he can hardly match his clothes. He gladly welcomes the designer rider.

Now that the deal is cemented, Cassidy and Carlos order dinner and some wine. Carlos orders the wine, she wanted red and Carlos chose a bottle. He chose an expensive Stags Leap from California, and he made a show of it.

The waiter brings the appetizers and wine and Carlos begins his rap. Cassidy prepared for this and very deftly avoids his verbal advances without crushing his ego. She's smart. She plans on making some more money with him, so why alienate him completely. She'll flirt a little; she just won't fuck him—plain and simple.

"So Carlos, what's the mystery business you are going to put in that magnificent space you just bought?"

"It's unique. We call it, Conserve-Reserve. It's going to be the only full-service brokerage firm of its kind. Not only will we handle our client's money, but we will create some mutual funds for others to sell for us—very unique. We made it work in Panama and the Netherlands too, but the market down there went bust, after Noriegas's fall all that fine Panamanian money went elsewhere. Things became too unstable for our clients and they got scared and moved their money to Switzerland. But now, that money and confidence is back in a big way. The banks in Panama have become friendly and very solvent again—after the canal was turned over that is, along with some other things and now there is a boom going on down there and there is a lot of currency floating around waiting to be put to work. That my dear is where we come in."

"But Carlos, your space is on Park Avenue. Why not downtown, with all the other brokerages?"

"Well as you know, most of the bigger International Banks are located in midtown and we just want to be a little closer to our clients. Cassidy, the cab fare for a suitcase full of cash is cheaper too." Carlos throws his head back waiting for her reaction. She's a cool customer, this one, he thinks. She didn't even flinch when I made the cash joke. He likes her; perhaps there is another way to use her.

Cassidy thinks to herself, "what an asshole. How much of a bimbo does he take me for? Cash in a suitcase in a cab.....*ugh*."

The rest of the dinner goes pretty smooth; Cassidy spends the bulk of the meal dodging Carlos' double entendres and weak advances. But in the end, she got the business and she senses there is more to this guy than meets the eye, so she plays along. Carlos tells her about how he got started in business and with each story he tells she becomes mildly interested in the man, not just his business. Carlos offers her a ride home but Cassidy declines, she has her own means and of course she has Marty, she doesn't need him to be aggravated; he can be a little protective or territorial.

Cassidy walks into a quiet house, Marty is sacked out, so Cassidy quietly slips into bed and tries to sleep, but for some reason she can't—could it be Carlos on the brain? She tosses in the king size bed until finally sleep comes.

Agent Tedia has been looking over the phone records from the Federal Reserve for the day of the heist, focusing on the ones in and out of the IT Department. Looking for phone numbers and times can be so mind numbing, that you lose track of time passing. Garrett looks at his watch and can't believe it's 4 p.m. already. He got here at 10 a.m. and started with these printouts and now the day is almost gone and nothing to show. He is really beginning to get frustrated with the Treasury guys. He's been waiting for the video from the security cameras at the Reserve from the day of the robbery for too long.

Garrett starts to think that maybe they have something that they don't want him to see; you know, "we'll handle this one in-house." He would be put in a really awkward spot if he starts to feel some push back from these Treasury guys. He hopes he is only imaging that scenario, because if it comes to that, he's fucked. His boss is riding his ass and he'd hate to have to ask for help on this one. He needs to hit this one out of the park, so he's feeling the pressure.

Since the Raynoud Case, Garrett has been assigned to lower profile work. There was a time when all the big, high profile cases came across his desk.

The Raynoud Case was a kidnapping. Walter Raynoud was a delegate from the UK; his nine year old boy was taken from school while his class was on a field trip. Not really that complicated a case, except that the kidnappers somehow tapped into the network that runs the Hilfiger Electronic Billboard in Times Square and had it showing a streaming video of the Raynoud kid chained up naked and blindfolded in a dark basement. The contrast in the basement and the kid was disturbing. He was so pale, it looked like he was backlit and chained and crying without the sound. Times Square became silent that afternoon.

This haunting image stayed on the screen for about seven hours when Garrett and his team got intelligence that pointed to the location of the kid, so instead of working with the kidnappers and getting them what they asked for, Garrett thought "fuck 'em. I'll surprise them and grab the kid." Well, he had the right location, but as soon as the kidnappers, some college kids who wanted to be famous and use their skills to create the ultimate computer game, heard the intruders, they shot the kid in a panic. Garrett's team killed three of the five guys and the other two are doing 50 years each, in Elmira. However, the whole scene played out on the big screen.

The Delegate, because he lost his only son in such a hideous way, turned it into an international incident and really smeared the law enforcement agencies. All cops suffered. They were the butt of jokes, cartoons, skits on *Saturday Night Live*, and *David Letterman*—It was horrible. Garrett was held responsible and never really recovered.

He went into a tailspin, had trouble focusing; he kept playing the scene of the kid dying over and over again. He saw specialists; he tried treatment—all to no avail. Then his wife left him, taking away his children and his connection to the world—his role as husband and father.

Because of the lack of bench strength in his precinct and him being the cop who handles cases dealing with technology, Garrett was handed the Federal Reserve case. He was really in the spotlight again, except this time, he was on a short leash and being micro-managed. But despite the lack of confidence the agency had in him, he knew he could break this and start his career back up. But right now, he was at a dead end. Whoever was behind this caper had some friends in the right places. They didn't even leave a crumb behind.

Even though we're talking about the Federal Reserve, if someone could get that security force field turned off for three minutes, after immobilizing the guards, they could walk right in and grab what they wanted and get out right through the front doors. That is what looks like happened. A humongous breach in the security system that is absolutely untraceable. The system can only be shut down by three keys being turned simultaneously. It's mind boggling to think that somebody first of all, would think about trying to coordinate that for their own benefit, then even more head spinning, to see that they got it done.

Cassidy didn't feel like cooking dinner tonight, so we went back and forth and decided on Italian. We figured that since it was Tuesday, Bruno's wouldn't be too busy. The place only has about 15 tables, so if you don't get there at the right time, you feel like you're waiting for a sitting to end.

There are few things in life worse than waiting for a table in restaurants, especially a small one. You feel so "on the outside looking in." Usually the bar looks into the dining room and every diner seems to be eating so fucking slow and looking at you every other bite. They order dessert, coffee, after dinner drinks, and they linger. You just keep getting hungrier, more aggravated at them, and develop a huge resentment towards them. Before you know it, you hate their faces. You want to take the plate in front of them and shove in their stinking fat face. Instead, you just sit there looking longingly at the dishes coming out of the kitchen and hoping someone will get up, since you've made every move you know and you are the next party to be seated.

"Making moves," is another New York thing, you make "moves" all the time, a good example of a "move" is name dropping. You tell whoever it is, that you need something from all the people you might know that he might know, your "guy," and hopefully he'll recognize that you need special treatment—you're not just another "schnook" as Henry Hill put it at the end of *Goodfellas*.

Well, we were right tonight. Bruno's wasn't too busy and we got seated right away. Tony, the maitre d, is a customer at the dry cleaning store and greets us like we own the place—no "move" required. He makes enough of a fuss that the other diners and bar patrons look to see who it is. You never know, in New York who is what. It's nice to feel like you are a "face;" someone that others wish they were, for that fleeting moment. Women want to sleep with you; men want your power and magnetism. It's an intoxicating feeling—one worth lying for. When I was much younger, I used to say I was Dr. Tyroni when making dinner reservations. They'd call my name, "Dr. Tyroni—party of two!" Oh yeah, that's me. You got better service and a better table, or so I thought.

Tony sits us in the middle of the dining room, a great table, if you know restaurants you don't want a table up front—it's drafty. You don't want in the back near the kitchen, you can hear the staff arguing in god knows what language, and it's warmer back there. I like the middle, the stage of dining—look at us, watch us, see what we eat, wish you'd ordered what we did, wish you got treated like we are—that's dinner in this city, at least in the "World according to Marty."

I'm starving tonight and feel like a big meal. Cassidy orders us some wine, a nice Chianti, the old world Italian kind, with the rope encased bottle—it looks good on the table and tastes good too. I tell Tony to bring us some fried mozzarella and some clams casino. Cassidy likes the cheese, but can't eat more than two and really doesn't care for the clams, so I'm getting a bunch of food by default.

Seated to our left is a party of four. Cassidy catches me looking at them and says; "Well, whatcha got?"

"They are two couples from Columbus, OH, I say, he's got an Ohio State watch and has that Midwestern round plain face. They all seem so taken with the staff because they speak Italian and the menu is in Italian."

"The other couple is from here, Long Island. The two guys went to school together and are catching up on old times. His wife, much younger, is number two and his friend's wife was close to number one, so that's why the ladies don't seem to be into one another too much."

"Nope," says Cass, "They're here for a conference. The men are doctors; they did their internships together and then went their own way. The guy with the navy blazer is from Connecticut. He met his friend, wearing the bad sweater vest, for dinner." She looks back at the group. "The women are both second wives. See the rock on his (navy blues') wife's finger? Too big for someone that age, unless it's a second marriage. The other wife has a small tattoo on her ankle—definitely too hot for sweater vest guy, she's in it for the money. Hey, check out her bag—it's a $600 Prada. She's even got the tan that starts above her ankle. That's from golf at the club. Naw, she doesn't work. She's sleeping with the club pro, but hubby is too busy doctoring, so he is never at the club. Probably the whole membership knows except him."

"Wow, nice work honey; especially the affair with the club pro." It's about now that our appetizers arrive and we order our main courses. I opt for a veal chop, while Cassidy has a plate of gnocchi. We dive into our appetizers and as I suspected, Cass eats two sticks of cheese and leaves the clams all to me.

"So, how was your day? Any new listings, shoppers, or did you fire anyone?" I ask.

"As a matter of fact, you remember that Park Avenue deal a while back? The guy who had that printing money business plan, a brokerage of sorts?"

"Yep."

"His business is called Conserve-Reserve; it's actually a pretty clever business plan. Anyway, he invited the office over for a lunch to show us the work he did with the space, and it was awesome. He had Todd Oldham design it and it is the hippest looking brokerage I've been in for a while. The buzz on the street is that he has secured some old money clients and has a line out the door too. Maybe he really has the magic formula. Anyway, I set up a meeting to discuss our finances with one of his strategists."

"Strategist?" I say pulling the meat out of a clam.

"Yep, that's what they call themselves; kind of cool, huh? Even though I don't care what a man puts on his business card; I care about how much money he can make for us. We meet with them on Thursday at 10 a.m., can you be there?"

"As a matter of fact, I can't. I promised Bertha that day off, so she could get a mammogram."

"Bertha's going to the doctor?" Cass says sipping her Chianti. "She's tough as nails. Is everything alright? Maybe I should call her; it's been a while, besides she can let me know if you are flirting with any of your lady customers, who needs a private investigator, I have Bertha."

"Well, go ahead, but she told me its routine, so don't make a big thing of it. You are a bit of an alarmist," I say sopping my bread in the clam sauce.

"Damn, I told him you'd be there."

"Who's he?"

"Carlos, the principal owner. He wants to meet the man behind the woman."

Now for some guys that would be a problem—the behind the woman thing—but I know Cassidy feels like I do, we walk side by side. No one follows the other or hangs behind. We are a partnership, but I'll play along.

"Well, you go meet with them. You know what our philosophy is, just don't commit to anything till we talk."

"Okay," says Cass, "I'll take the first meeting and if I think it's worth it, you'll come to sit number two; deal?"

"You got it babe—deal."

Our salads come next and then the main dishes. It is so good tonight that I even walk back into the kitchen to let Estelle know that this was one of the best meals I've had. She loves that shit. She's a shy 300 lb Albanian woman who never had a man and just loves the attention. I walk back into the dining room feeling pretty good about myself.

It's about 10:30 p.m. and Cass is getting a little drunk, so I better strike while the iron is hot, if you know what I mean. We pay, hug, make a great exit and grab a cab back to the house.

Back home, I decide to just get right in the bed with Cass instead of my usual night cap and late night TV viewing. I'm sure I'll get lucky, then Cass will roll over and I'll head downstairs for my own version of "Martin after Dark"—the end to a pretty good day.

I'm right and I get over on my wife and then she starts sawing logs, I head down and have a little after hour's party till about 2 a.m. Nothing fancy, a couple of vodka rocks, a remote control, and a joint—it's all good.

"Martin after Dark" was another idea of mine that never got off the ground. It was my idea for a late night talk show. You see I can't believe I'm the only married guy who gets in bed with his wife when he isn't ready to sleep just to appease the wife or maybe get "some stink on his Johnson."

So, I had this idea for a TV show that started with me waving my hands in front of my wife's face to make sure she was soundly sleeping, then I would put on my Dunhill smoking jacket and head downstairs. As I headed down the stairs you would see a helicopter landing on the lawn, limos pulling up, a doorman letting people in past velvet ropes and such. Next you'd see me in the living room sitting on the couch, hosting a talk show, my guests would sit in a wing back chair and we'd watch some late night TV together comment on infomercials or the news. There would be a one man band taking us in and out of the commercials. I'd do a cooking segment and a daily rant called "Marty's World."

I sent in a treatment to MTV, figuring the big networks already had their late night programming set up. After submitting the treatment, I made some follow up calls, tried to make a move, use my guy, but no luck, they just felt it didn't fit their demographic. I left it at that.

I'm up at about 8 a.m. Cass has been up for a little while and has the coffee going. *The Today Show* is on and I'm almost ready to shower and get ready for work, but I want to look at the paper. Bertha is opening and I told her I would be in around 9 a.m. or so. As usual, Cassidy doesn't bring in the paper. She is not a "paper person." She is a non-news person for the most part, so she never gets the paper off the stoop.

I step out into our courtyard oasis and fire up the first cigarette of the day, drink my first cup of coffee, and open the paper—just the way I like to get the day going. I say a little morning prayer, asking for some direction today and the strength to carry out those directions. Better safe than sorry. A little God consciousness never hurts, right?

The headlines today scream about another corrupt politician and his greed. Always makes for good copy—another man's greed gone badly. We're all a little greedy, but some of us are just over the top and get ourselves caught being greedy. When confronted with it, it seems incredulous; same story time and time again; just different names and faces

But on page six, I see a headline that catches my eye: "Entrepreneur donates 5 million." It's a story about the founder of Conserve-Reserve, Carlos Ferrar. The story shares his niece's challenge of living with the devastating disease, cystic fibrosis. It goes on to say that he's a Panamanian immigrant who came to this country 25 years ago with no money, but ambition and dreams…. blah, blah, blah.

Cassidy needs to see this I think, so I get up and bring the paper into her dressing room. Yes, she has a dressing room; the closet was so big, that we chopped it in half and made a dressing room equipped with full length mirrors, positioned so you can see your ass without stretching your neck.

She scans the story and says, "Oh yeah, that reminds me, don't forget this Saturday. We have to go to the Bifada Ball. I took a table for the firm and it's a command performance, so get your tux out."

"Sure, but if you were concerned about this client of yours staying power, I'd say he has some."

"Yep, that's why we are meeting with them," she says returning her attention to her dressing routine.

"Okay then, I'm going back outside to finish the paper; just thought you'd like to read about your newest client."

"Thanks sweetie, I'll be down in a minute," she answers.

I am back outside when it dawns on me, Cassidy knew about the ball last night, but didn't tell me even when we were discussing the meeting at Carlos's firm. She has been spending a lot of time on his account, talking about him; I think I need to meet this guy formally, who wants to meet the man behind the woman.

Down at the shop, it's business as usual; a pretty good "take" this morning, I'd say, it'll be a $2,500 day. Most folks get their weekend dirties to us by now and the stuff for the weekend hasn't come in yet, so telling Bertha to take the morning off was no big deal.

Lunch rolls around and I feel hungry, so I turn to Cheech another part-timer, who is Berthas nephew.

I tell him; "I'll be back in an hour. Would ya' watch the store?"

"No problem boss, Cheech watch store real good."

Isn't that comforting? I've left him before and he is really a good kid, so I make sure he has my cell number and out I go.

I feel like some deli food today, so I take a walk over to Abelboum's for a knish and a hotdog. As I'm crossing Lexington, I see Milagro coming out of Bloomie's, carrying two Big Brown Bags. She sees me and waves me over. I'm frozen for a second, but acknowledge

91

and head her way. In my sick mind, I have the vision of Dudley Moore running towards Bo Derek on the beach in Mexico. Like I said—a sick mind.

I get to her and she hands me a big brown bag and says; "Be a dear and help while I grab a cab."

"Chivalry ain't dead," I say and; "Better yet, *lady M*, I'll get your chariot." She smiles a smile that I've seen her smile in a few daydreams of mine and nothing needs to be said.

"Marty, you can be my knight today."

I am so flirting with her and so loving it, that I can hardly stand myself.

"I'll take that job," I say while looking over my shoulder and standing in front of Bloomies, in the middle of Lexington Avenue trying to hail her a cab.

If there is one thing I have a knack for, it's getting a good parking spot and hailing cabs. I seem to arrive at places at just the right time for someone with a good spot to pull out, as if they knew I was coming. But there have been times when I've been known to circle a lot, going up and down the same rows over and over again looking for "rock star parking."

There is a knack for hailing a cab—you have to just get into the middle of the street and make yourself big, raise your arm and look like you are looking into the driver's eyes as he approaches. The myth is that a strong whistle can help, but they can't hear you a block away, but they CAN see you.

After a minute, a cab pulls up and I open the door as any good doorman or driver would do.

I look in and say; "See ya' round, at the store maybe."

"Thanks, Marty, you certainly will see me again, I promise."

I pull my head out of the cab, smack the cab on the rear quarter panel, as if it were a horse and away she goes. I smile on the inside to myself—what a fortuitous moment that just was.

Cass strides into her office and instantly notices the huge spray of flowers on the reception desk.

She announces: "Who got laid last night?"

"Cassidy, they're for you," the receptionist Janice says.

"Well, I did give Marty a trip around the world last night, but it wasn't *flower-worthy*. Let me see the card. Oh shit, they're from Carlos."

"The guy in the paper this morning?" asks Janice.

"One and the same" says Cass. "You know the guy we sold the Park Avenue space to a month or so ago?"

"Yes, I do. He was smokin'hot, very Andy Garcia."

"Nice Janice, don't forget I told you never let your ink well get dipped in by a clients' pen."

"I know Cass, I know." Janice says walking behind the desk.

"Any messages, Janice?"

"Just a few, but nothing urgent"

"Cool, I'll be in my office with the door closed, but knock if you need me or just buzz. I had a few glasses of wine last night, so I'm about 85% right now."

"Gotcha' boss."

"Thanks Janice."

Cassidy grabs a coffee from the break room exchanges a few good mornings and gets behind her desk and looks out the window. What has she been thinking these last couple of weeks? After the dinner at Lugar's with Carlos, he insisted on lunch two days later and she should have said no, but didn't. Now he's sending flowers and she thinks she likes it.

Cassidy knows that Marty has eyes all over this town and if she is seen more than once with the same guy other than her husband, he hears about it. It's a macho bullshit brotherhood thing. These guinea bastards stick together. It's been a while since Marty did his "jealous" thing. Because he grew up poor, he always feels inadequate around people with money and even more so, when the money is a man showing his wife attention. Instead of being flattered, he gets threatened and acts like a boy.

Cassidy decides she'd better call Carlos and cool him off. Shit, flowers, what was he thinking about? These broads in the office start thinking, and then talking, and the next thing you know, they have me moving to Panama with the guy.

"Carlos Ferrar please," asks Cass.

"Who may I say is calling?" The voice on the other end asks

"Cassidy Tyroni, thank you."

"I'll see if he's in," she says.

"I'll hold, thank you." Cass says.

"Cassidy, how are you?"

"Cut the shit Carlos. What's with the flowers? I thought we said…"

"But Cassidy, didn't you read the card? It says congratulations."

"I don't care what the card said; it could have said Happy fucking Hanukah. These girls in here don't think about the card, just the flowers and to them, it means only one thing." "Well, what can I do to diffuse your situation, Ms. Tyroni?"

"First, don't send anything here other than checks. Secondly, I'll call the shots from here on out." She says and hangs up, looking out the window again wondering what she is doing.

Marty is just finishing moving a load of shirts when he hears the bell ring out front, so he hollers; "Be right out!" He steps out front and there's Milagro, looking great as always and talking on the cell phone. Strike one. She's a "walking talker." I see them all over Manhattan and it just pisses me off. All these people who think they need to be so connected, like what they have to say can't wait till they get to a proper calling place. They talk too loud so you can't help but hear their conversation and it's rude.

I watch and wait as she ends her call.

"Lady M, I don't have anything for you to pick-up."

"I know Martin," she says and closes her phone.

"I came to see you, are you surprised?"

"Why I was just thinking that you haven't visited me to shoot the breeze in a while."

"Martin, you are an amusing man. I do enjoy your outlook."

Amusing, that's a new one I think. No one has ever referred to me as that, but then again, this ain't anyone.

"Glad you stopped in. What's on your mind?" I ask.

"Well, I wanted to thank you for helping me out earlier today."

"You are welcome, my pleasure."

"So I was thinking about a drink, Marty. Can I buy you a drink to say thanks?"

"Well, I'm alone here. I mean, Cheech is here but…" Stumbling all over myself, she is looking at me like I have two heads.

"Cheech, she quieries, what's a Cheech?"

"Oh, he is my store manager's nephew, but he can't close the shop, he's just part-time."

"I didn't mean right now Marty, but soon. What do you think?"

"Heck yeah. You can call me anything you want, but don't call me late for cocktails," I say. Milagro smiles and says, "how about Friday afternoon, say, 4 o'clock?"

"Sounds good to me, I can make that work."

"Good, she says, where's good for you?"

"I don't care, I'm gonna' be in this neighborhood, but I can cab anywhere."

"Don't you need to check with your wife?" She says coyly.

"Now why would I have to do that?"

"Well, most married guys I know don't make a move without their wife's okay."

"Not me, I'm the king of my castle."

Milagro smiles and says, "Okay then, do you know where Jean Lafitte is?"

"Sure do. Fifty-eighth and Sixth, I have a friend who does their desserts, Darrel, is his name."

"Good, I'll see you there?"

"Yes, you will definitely see me there."

Milagro turns to leave and glances at me over her shoulder and slides out of the shop. I turn around and there is Cheech with a stupid smile on his face.

"What the fuck are you looking at Ahab?"

"Nothing boss, nothing at all." Smirking again, he then has the balls to say: "you gonna' hit that Mr. Marty?"

"I'm married you punk, now get back there and start tagging those shirts, before I hurt your aunt's feelings and kick your ass."

"Don't be mad, Mr. Marty, I mean no disrespect. Honest, I didn't. Cheech loves his job. I be quiet."

"Good. Go to work!"

That's all I need; that stupid kid talking all over the shop. Someone will open their mouth in front of Cass and she'll go batshit jealous and it'll be a month before I get a decent conversation out of her, much less sex.

10

Agent Garrett Tedia's next series of investigative actions come as a result of a bunch of things out of his control. First, he still hasn't seen the surveillance tape yet, but the treasury agent, Rogers, assures him he'll have it Friday. The programmer at the security system company is dead and it's not from natural causes. The homicide guys can't help him either. He is assuming the perps feel comfortable enough to start thinking of using those plates and printing money. Just saying that seems nutty, thinks Garrett, but it is what it is.

Garrett decides his next step should be to check out every source the Treasury uses to get the paper used to print legal tender. Maybe he'll be able to find out something there.

Garrett calls his Treasury contact to find out who the government buys the money paper from. He learns there are only four sources in this country for the right paper.

The first one, he checks out is in Western New York in the small town of Hornell. A pretty normal looking town, but the town has a funny smell to it. The paper plant reeks every time a fresh load of paper pulp is processed. Garrett thinks that there are some things in life you just shouldn't have to get used to, and this smell is one of them.

The factory is run "jelly tight." The records for every shipment are triple signed for and finger print scans are recorded for every truck driver. If you were gonna' steal paper from here, you'd have to get through as much security as the gang who ripped off the Reserve. Garrett can't see one single hiccup in the paperwork; every piece of pulp, paper, and tree is accounted for. It's amazing the way a set-up run right, really looks and feels. Everyone knows what everyone else is doing and when. Synchronicity at its best—these people take pride in their operation—they know the deal.

The next plant is much the same. This one is located in Tallahassee; it is squeaky clean with no visible breaches, no paperwork missing and all files accounted for and stored properly. Each shipment is recorded in triplicate and even the office supply procurement department documents everything that way—down to every paper clip. It also has the smell Garrett experienced in the other paper town.

Next stop is some small town that sprung up after the TVA built a dam there. A place called Counce, TN. A little resort town that is about two hours east of Memphis. A really pretty place, but it too, has that distinct smell of paper pulp, but it's not as bad as the plant in NY or Florida. It only wafts through once or twice a day, so it doesn't permeate everything. The lake that came about due to the dam that was built on the Tennessee River, is a big recreational lake called Pickwick—that also doubles as a shipping channel for the barges running from the Great Lakes down to the Gulf of Mexico through a series of locks. The town is one of those classic rural towns with one of everything and everybody still waves at you driving by, whether they know you or not. You wave back out of respect; you don't want anyone thinking you're conceited or haughty. The town is just too small to have that follow you around.

Garrett is having the same experience here as he had at the other plants. Everything is accounted for, the truck traffic is monitored, and records are in place for every driver. Every time the gate for the plant opens, someone is checking it and recording the information. This plant has a very sophisticated video set-up. All entrances of course, are covered, but this plant sets on the banks of the river so barges loaded with the timber used for the paper manufacturing drop their loads at the rear loading docks. A wireless system is set up that projects images from across the river and the dock master can see what's going on—on the other side of the barge or any vessel that comes dockside.

This makes Garrett's investigation take longer than at the other two plants, because not only does he have files and records to pour through, he has hours of tape to review. So he takes a room at the State Park Inn and settles in for at a couple of days.

He also has a copy of the tape he finally got from the Treasury folks; they were ashamed that this could happen, so they really needed to scour the tapes before an outside agency did. Garrett hasn't had a chance to talk with them yet, but they are on his short list.

The tape doesn't show anything they didn't know; three perps dressed as an electrician, a foodservice worker, and a vending machine refill/repair guy. The chick is the foodservice worker. You see them all show their ID badges, sign in, and move out of frame; that's the last you see of them. Frame by frame you see nothing unusual, then BAM; a black screen for three minutes and then back to a scene with no apparent sign of a robbery. Heck, the receptionist is still drinking the same soda she was drinking before. The soda bottle level was checked making sure the tape wasn't doctored and it checked out. Without those three minutes, the video shows nothing, except a bunch of security guards who were knocked out. The criminals hit them with stun guns, but because the system was shut down, the rise in temperature that the gun would have caused, didn't set off the alarms. The guards were the last line of defense watching the new plates that had arrived from Virginia earlier that day. So the crooks knew what was coming in and obviously knew that the shipment would be vulnerable for a very short window. They only took two plates. Two plates are small enough to stash in a big handbag, backpack, or even under a jacket—pretty fucking smart. The bad guys weren't the usual greedy bastards that get sloppy.

This gang was calculating, not biting off more than they could chew, but still, where do you find pants big enough to hold balls that big to even contemplate ripping off a Federal Reserve?

Garrett settles into the task at hand, reviewing dock front footage—it's been a long day. It started off with his Captain grilling him like a whopper; his boss not liking what Garrett was saying, but knowing that the guy was doing the best he could. The Captain was under a microscope too and the Mayor had even called him to see how the investigation was going. Reminding him that lots of eyes were looking at this one, wouldn't it be nice to get some redemption after the UK delegate's kid fiasco. Garrett's Captain was feeling the heat and even though Garrett was a thousand miles away, he had to feel it too. The Captain calmed down and told him to make sure he doesn't miss a fucking thing. Garrett wasn't having a huge self-esteem day and to make matters worse, his ex-wife called him and reminded him that the child support was past due and that he was still a piece of selfish shit.

Garrett married his college sweetheart, Marie Lagano; she was a Mediterranean beauty with a flair for the dramatic. They had two kids together—a boy now twelve and a little girl, nine. Their marriage was a rollercoaster from the get-go. Marie thought she knew what being a cop's wife would be like, but she underestimated that and her neediness as well. Now Garrett wasn't a day at the beach either. He was a little chauvinistic; he behaved as the hunter and gatherer while Marie tended to the little ones. Which at first worked, but as time passed so did the appreciation for each others' roles, and then, the kidnapping case went sideways and Garrett withdrew from the world. Marie had to have an officer of the court serve him with the papers, because he wouldn't leave his apartment and had sealed his mailbox so no mail could be delivered. The cop had to wait outside Garrett's door in silence for almost 13 hours till Garrett opened the door to take out garbage. He didn't contest a thing; he also didn't fight for any more visitations or the amount of alimony and child support Marie asked for—it wasn't even sporting. Garrett just didn't care.

With that kind of morning, a day of looking at dock front video seemed ok, but the committee in Garrett's head kept taking him away from focusing on the tapes. He kept thinking to himself –didn't I see this tape before? That's a common problem when reviewing surveillance videos. Usually nothing unusual is happening, so you begin to wander and that's when you can make a mistake. But he knew he couldn't be watching the same tapes, because the labeling and tape storage was impeccable.

It was about 7 p.m. when he saw it—a barge pulls up and the usual shit was going on. The boat hands unload and the dock master and the captain exchanges paperwork and then does some backslapping and then focuses on the work. Except this time, he notices on the side of the boat away from the dock, a log underneath slips and a pile of logs fall into the water. You can see all the workers on the boat and on the dock look and move towards the falling logs. It's then, when one of the workers reaches down to grab the lever to bring up the holding claw when his hand slips off the lever and he falls backwards grabbing for the lever, but his hooded sweatshirt catches on the railing and spins him off his feet into the workings of the holding claw. Then you see it, his severed arm shoots up into the air and the other workers scurry to grab it and shut down the loader. Garrett had heard about this accident, but that was when he first got here and has since forgotten it. He needs to write this down, so he can go back and review the background action during accident.

Garrett rewinds the tape so that he can see what went on away from the accident; he starts the tape and looks in amazement. As soon as the guy slips, all the attention goes from the falling logs to the worker. The logs just float downstream, where protocol calls for complete retrieval of the logs as the trees are from the government's own birch farms where these "money trees" are grown.

Garrett watches and notices a bass boat zip by the dock, but it's a fleeting image as it speeds out of frame downstream. Now Garrett has seen numerous bass boats by these docks, some of the best fishing on the river is done right here, below the dam. But the hours for fishing are strictly enforced, 5 a.m. to 10 a.m., after that, no unregistered boat traffic of any kind. So this boat doesn't belong here and how would a boater know that this log barge would spill and that a worker would have a near fatal accident that would clear the way for them to zip in, steer the "money trees" into their own cove and haul 'em away? At least that's the conspiracy theory Garrett has formulated.

The next day, Garrett takes the video to the plant manager and shows him the scene.

"Well, I never noticed that before. We were focused on getting my son-in-law out of the apparatus, and then haul all the logs out of the water, per regulation," Charles Worren, the plant manager says.

"Really, Charles, are you sure every log was accounted for?"

"Yes I am Agent, is there a problem; are you saying something else here?"

"No, just doing my job."

"Good, because we take pride in our work down here. I don't know about how you Yankees do things, but here we are serious."

"It's my job to question everything, Mr. Worren, everything."

"Like I said before, every log that fell into the river was retrieved and accounted for, sir."

Garrett knew this was a lie as he had seen a shitload of logs slide by the docks heading downstream before the worker fell, and there was no way that they were corralled before going 100 yards—which is how much more plant property lay past the docks, the paperwork confirming the retrieval was falsified and the manager was in on it, Garrett thought.

This might be his first solid lead, or is it? Maybe the manager just went along with the falsification, because he would be reprimanded for letting "money trees" escape. But how do you explain the bass boat? Garrett has to get this tape back to New York where he can have the video analyzed with some better equipment than he can get here. Plus, if those who are behind this know he has the tape and has found something; the tape takes on a new value.

"I appreciate your commitment to your work, Mr. Worren, and I thank you for your time. I know you're a busy man."

Garrett acts as if the manager's explanation is good enough for him and grabs the tape out of the machine and heads out of the suite of offices, when Worren stops him.

"Mr. Tedia, the tape, please. It is plant property after all, and the warrant said nothing about tapes or files leaving the plant for good."

Now Garrett knows the manager is right, but if he lets this tape go, so does his lead. "Sure," Garrett says and as he hands the tape over.

"Mr. Worren, may I use your phone?"

Worren agrees and leads Garrett into his office. The whole time, Garrett hasn't let his eyes leave that tape in the hands of the manager. Garrett dials and asks the operator for Judge Moore's office.

"Good afternoon, Judge, I hate to bother you, but I need a slight addition made to the blanket warrant you gave me for the paper plants."

Still eyeballing the tape Garrett says, "I need you to add evidence removal if do deemed by the investigating agent."

"Agent Tedia, the judge says, I've got a copy of that warrant right here and it does give you the right to remove evidence. It's on page three, second paragraph."

"Page three? I only have two pages."

"Well stay right there and I'll fax this to you."

"Great Judge, I appreciate your help, the fax number here is 731-689-5677, address it to Charles Worren."

The ring of the fax machine breaks the silence and the two men look at one another, except Charles Worren's eyes show the resignation of a man who has been caught in a lie and has nothing left to save.

"Mr. Worren, the tape please." Garret asks with his hand extended.

Worren's body language sags and he hands the tape over, "I was just looking out for my plant Agent Tedia, I'm sure you understand."

"I'm sure I do." Garrett says as he takes the tape.

Oh, Mr. Worren, please don't make any plans to go on a vacation in the next three weeks," Garrett says, as he takes one of Charles Worren's business cards from a holder on his desk.

11

Carlos tells the driver to take him to Brooklyn, Red Hook to be specific. Red Hook used to be the warehouse district for overflow and storage facilities that contained the contents of thousands of containers from ports all over the world.

Today, Red Hook still has plenty of warehouses, but they're like most neighborhoods in the NYC area that haven't been over run. It is what's called an "up and coming" area, meaning that developers have targeted the yuppie segment to buy lofts, condos, co-ops, and the like here. Downtown Brooklyn and the Promenade have had a tremendous revitalization. Those neighborhoods became popular after shows like Cosby and Law and Order showcased the neighborhoods.

Red Hook is a neighborhood with a tough reputation—crooked longshoremen rules with dingy bars that cater to the swarthy seamen and the hookers who service them. The drug trade is also brisk here; the port is pretty wide-open and has been for some time. If you know the right people, you can get containers of cocaine, hashish, pot, and opium through without an inspector coming near the box. The long arm of mob influence is still alive and well on the docks. When Las

Vegas went corporate, they had to find some place to launder money and drugs, and Red Hook was just that place.

Red Hook housed a few well-placed paid-off politicians, a police force adroit at turning the other way, and some good old-fashioned muscle to make any do-gooders run the other way for fear for the lives of their families. It's so old-school, you could write a thesis on corruption in the Twenty-first century here. All that said, the value of property here has skyrocketed and Carlos is a benefactor, so he needs to visit some of his holdings.

Crossing the Brooklyn Bridge always evokes certain memories for people and Carlos included. He remembers coming to this country for the first time and coming to New York, via Miami. He remembers the lyric *if you can make it here you can make it anywhere*. So Carlos took that to heart and made his way here. Looking at the lower East Side of Manhattan from the Brooklyn side of the East river was one of the first looks at this city he ever had. Now crossing the bridge today with money in the banks and more on the way, he really feels like he's made it here. The song doesn't say how to make it, it just says make it.

Carlos' first real job was in Brooklyn; he was working for some wise guy wannabe who thought he could make a name for himself hijacking shipments into Red Hook. He thought he knew how all the dots were connected and that holding contraband for ransom was a way to make big bucks. Carlos was supposed to meet some guys from Gino "Icepick" Revoli's gang down by warehouse #8. He was supposed to show them the goods, some AK-47's that had fallen off a Beijing freighter and now belonged to Carlos's boss. There were 2,000 weapons in the container and the amount Carlos was supposed to be collecting was $300 thousand, which was a great deal, but the serial numbers needed to be removed and they needed to be converted from semi-automatic to fully automatic. Then they would be worth a lot more.

Carlos was on time as agreed at 2 a.m., but the buyers weren't there yet, so Carlos figured he'd check out the shipment and perhaps take a couple of rifles for himself. What Carlos didn't expect was that not only were there weapons in that container, but also there were 200 kilos of uncut Heroin straight from China. Of course, Carlos's boss knew it was there and so did the buyers, but keeping Carlos out of the loop made for good business. Never let a middle man know everything, this keeps them honest.

Carlos opened the container and to his surprise, saw the heroin and now was really pissed off, because his boss put him in a position he didn't like. It was time to show his boss that Carlos was not a man to be made to look silly. Don't piss on my leg and tell me its raining, he would later say.

The buyers arrived, just as Carlos was exiting the warehouse. They sniffed each others' asses just like dogs, making sure that everyone was who they were supposed to be and not cops. After all the intros and secret handshakes were done Carlos, asked for the money bag. The buyers, two guinea brats from Bay Ridge looking to make some extra money to fuel their own disco biscuit habit, never saw it coming. Carlos shot each of them twice in the back of the head and dumped their bodies into the river after rifling through their wallets and lifting their cash and ID's. Now Carlos had 300 large and a container filled with hot Chinese weapons and 200 kilos of China White. Not a bad calling card to present to the boss of the Bolivian Cartel that was running a distant second to their Columbian neighbors in the city.

Carlos had to lay low for long time after that deal till the peace was made between the two cartels, but with cash, some H, and a hot hand, Carlos of all places, found a hiding place in Tennessee. While in Tennessee, he made a friendship with a real estate broker called "Sliver," a good ole' boy who took a liking to the Panamanian immigrant with the new Cadillac and some serious spending money.

Sliver introduced Carlos to the world of banking; Sliver owned a regional bank that dealt primarily in real estate loans, mortgages, and the occasional land development project. Very conservative stuff, but then again, we're talking about the Bank of Hardin County, TN, not Chase Manhattan.

Carlos was a quick learn and Sliver saw the way Carlos soaked up the business and finally asked Carlos if he would be interested in going into business with him. Carlos never saw himself as anyone's partner, but Sliver saw something in him.

Carlos with his improving English and head for figures, was now part of the American system. He had a social security number, and for a while, was a real citizen. But Carlos wanted more. He didn't see a future in rural Tennessee, but learned that the sleepy town had a secret industry; producing paper for legal tender to be printed by the United States Treasury.

12

"Marty you've got to just let it go, man."

"I know Walt, but it drives me mad when I see someone getting away with something, I'd like to be getting away with, it's like fuckin' nails on a chalkboard."

"Damn, Marty shut the fuck up; you just ain't the lucky type."

"I know, but a boy can dream Walt, a boy can dream."

"You know Marty, if you'd channel your shit right, you could have it all."

"Walt I hear ya', but I want it now, I don't want to do the heavy lifting. I'd like a nice score—one that could set me up for life, just one."

"Well, you got one—your wife man; your lucky to be with Cassidy."

"Oh, can it Walt? Don't lay any of those dime store, twelve-step profundities on me. Nobody loves their wife more than me and it's all good there. But you know, seeing some immigrant win $123 million in the Powerball is what pisses me off."

If anyone could use that money, it was Walt—up to his eyeballs in back alimony; the bank breathing down his neck for their money and the liquor commission threatening his license if he doesn't get current with his liquor distributors. He was so deep in debt, that his dream of owning and running a treatment center in the Rockies seemed so hopeless he could cry. Walt was trapped, and couldn't see his way out.

"Marty go to *your* store and insult some customers, I need the stool."

"Thanks Walt, you certainly have a great bedside manner."

Walking in to the shop, I can see that Bertha has it all under control.

"Marty," she asks, "Can you close tonight?

"Sure, no sweat, I'm happy to, what's up?"

"Great, I've got tickets to see *The Lion King* tonight and I need to get ready and pick up my nephew, Ralphie."

"Well then, finish what you're doing and get outta' here. I can handle it."

"Thanks boss, I'll bag these loads up for tomorrow and it's all yours."

The rest of afternoon cruises by, as soon as Bertha left the store, it got nice and steady, no more than two at the counter at a time, just steady.

It's about 6 p.m., and in walks Milagro; I can smell her from the back.

"Good afternoon Martin, how are you today?"

"I'm great—better than I deserve to be."

"You are so funny Martin; you must keep your wife laughing all the time."

"Well, I wouldn't say all the time, but." Just smile at her Marty you don't have to fill the air with words, just smile…I think.

"In any case, I need to ask you something Martin, can you keep a secret."

"That's a prerequisite for this line of business. You bet I can."

"Good, you remember me asking your washers and dryers?"

"Yes, I do.

"Well, that's the secret, I need your dryers. I need to dry some cash," she says looking into my eyes.

"Cash, like money?" is all I can say swallowing hard.

"Yes, it's for a party."

"Okay now I'm really interested, I say, what kind of party are you talking about?"

"It's a birthday party for our boss; business has been going so well that we want to give him the ultimate birthday cake."

I'm looking at her and my head is tilting like a puppy that is being asked to do something and doesn't understand.

"We plan on stuffing the cake with $50 thousand—a thousand for every year of his life."

"Really?" is all I can muster up.

"It's a big PR stunt you see; it's his money and after the cake is opened and the money is revealed—well more like appears, he in an emotional state, will donate the money to the Adopt–a–Kid Foundation."

"Wow, that'll certainly get him Liz Smith."

"That's the plan," she says.

"Why the dryers?" I ask.

"Well, the dryers will fluff up the money so we can stuff it in the cake; new money is so stiff and hard to crinkle."

"Got it. When do you want to launder your money?" I say with a grin.

"Sunday night—I was thinking instead of drinks at Jean Lafitte."

"Sure, I say, Sunday is fine, 6 o'clock okay?"

"Six is fine Martin; I look forward to seeing you then. Oh Martin, what do you like to drink? I'll bring some refreshments. Do you like vodka?"

"I do; that'll be great."

As I watch Milagro walk out of the shop, I begin to think I can hear myself explaining this to my wife; "honey, I'm going to be at the store Sunday night after dark with a really steamy, Latin broad who is bringing vodka, while we dry her money."

That ought to go over like a lead balloon. I'm going to have to wait for a REALLY good mood, before I lay that one on her. Can you imagine?

13

"Cass, are you ok?"

"I'm fine Melissa, just pre-occupied, too many spinning plates, you know."

Melissa has been with Cass since she struck out on her own, a good soldier, this one.

"Well, if I can do anything to help you just let me know, okay?"

"Sure thing babe, you bet I will. Thanks for asking."

Cassidy is feeling a little sick to her stomach, she's never stepped out on Martin and she has never even thought about it, but for some reason, her judgment went out the window and accepted another Carlos invitation to The Peninsula for lunch. Now, the problem is that Martin has been kind of funny himself, and he might be onto her... or is she just being paranoid?

This wasn't the first time a client has tried to get more than office space from Cass and she has never had a problem letting them down gently, but when Carlos asked her if she'd like to learn about "real money" over lunch, she said, "yes," without hesitation. Maybe that sent the wrong signal to Carlos, but whatever signal he got, Cassidy was hooked. Now she really was conflicted; she couldn't tell Martin. Her business with Carlos was too fragile to fuck with…literally. It happened so fast, she didn't think—just didn't think.

Sliver has been really enjoying his stay in New York; he has been living at the Gramercy Park Hotel and has found himself feeling at home. With a successful play in motion and no end in sight, he has been living like royalty—room service, limos, beautiful girls, great food, culture, and even some friends. He hasn't thought of Tennessee in months—well except for the money he sends back, and when someone makes fun of his accent.

The play is running smoothly, each step unfolding as planned, with luck being on their side each time. But Sliver knows that luck comes from hard work and opportunity and it's only the wise and the experienced that recognize the opportunities that can change lives. Sliver is one of them, a master of the universe.

Life is funny. Sliver thinks, after all he taught Carlos about banking, moving money and making money and now it's Carlos calling the shots. The only twinge of obligation or accountability in his life is to Carlos and its absolutely bearable most of the time, but there are moments when he'd like to see Carlos out of the driver's seat and Sliver at the wheel. He'd make the changes that are needed; he'd stay out of the public eye and keep the operation below the radar instead of trying to jam it. If Carlos could only have an accident; if only an old enemy got revenge…these were Slivers' last thoughts.

Sliver is pulling away from the curb sitting in the back seat of a cab when the door flies open and he turns to see a masked man and the barrel of a gun, he hears the pop then it goes black.

Carlos is sitting in his study when the phone rings.

"Yep, that's great, good job, I'll talk to you later." Carlos says and hangs up.

Reaching into his humidor, he pulls out a Sancho Panza Cuban cigar and cuts the end and rolls the smooth cut end around in his mouth, tasting the tobacco and spreading the taste on his lips with his tongue satisfied with himself. He knows that he now is the only one left who knows the operation from "soup to nuts." Sliver had to go; he was getting sloppy. Some of the finished product had been unacceptable of late, and all roads lead to Sliver. It's not like this is a publicly held company that had to worry about wrongful termination. No one is going to sue Carlos, especially not Sliver; it's hard to file a complaint from the morgue.

"Hey Janice, it's Marty, is Cassidy around?"

"Hang on Marty, I'll check."

It takes a few seconds but finally the phone is ringing through.

"Hey Babe, what's up," Cassidy asks.

"Not much, just wanted to hear your voice, I guess."

"Oh honey, you melt me," she says, "what do you want to do tonight?"

"You know sweetie, I kind of feel like staying home tonight, it's been a while since we stayed in, how 'bout it?"

"I'm cool with that," she says.

"Maybe some take-out, cocktails and maybe a little dancing in the living room—we have been awfully busy lately."

"Great, will you be home by six?"

"Yes, definitely I've only got a few things left here and I'll meet you at home. I'll also pick up some supper on the way?"

"No, don't Cass, let's eat later. You know I hate eating before 9 p.m., okay?"

"Sure honey. No biggie; I'll just come straight home."

"Great – love you," I say.

"Love you bigger," she says and we hang up.

Cassidy forgets, when Marty was a kid his dad was a truck driver and he never got home before eight and his father insisted on dinner together—another one of those goombah things, but in any event, Marty grew up with dinner always after nine, so he has a weird hang-up about early supper.

Marty is such a good guy, that's what everybody says about him. He's a good guy. So he likes a late supper, is that so bad? Is that a reason to contemplate cheating with Carlos? No, of course not. I've got to get that shit out of my head. I'm not going to get myself in trouble. I've got a great life. Why would I want to screw it up, over money? Marty might understand. Who the hell am I kidding, if I've heard him say he doesn't like to share his toys once, I've heard it a million times— even for millions. We watched that movie with Demi Moore, Robert Redford, and Woody from Cheers. Marty said no fuckin' way would I let my wife do that. I don't care if we were living in a refrigerator box. I'm kidding myself, could I live with the guilt? When and how could I ever tell him? Probably never; I'd have to take it to the grave.

"Steve, it's Marty. How are you?"

Steve is my hangar guy, he provides us with our hangars.

"Good Marty, what's up? What are you doing calling this late in the day?"

"Screw you, I work too. It just looks better on me than you."

"Good to hear from you, Marty, what can I do for you?"

Steve and I have some history. When I took the store over, Steve saw that I was at the mercy of my employees who were robbing me blind. It was when I was behind on payments, that he began explaining how the business worked and over time, I got control of the shop back and it started to make some money.

"You know those bags you guys use to collect the hangars Steve, those ones that don't rip and don't get the contents wet, what are they made out of?"

"Tyvek, Marty, why?"

"Well, I need to get my hands on about 10 of them. Can you help me out?"

"Sure thing; when do you need them?"

"Can you get them here tomorrow afternoon?"

"Yeah sure, I'll send a guy by; I'll tell him to leave them with Bertha."

"Great Steve; what do I owe ya'?"

"On the house for a long-time customer and friend Marty, enjoy."

"Thanks Steve, you rock."

Feeling pretty good, I decide to hit The Mixer on the way home.

"So are you over your little lottery lunacy?"

"Yes, Walt, I am. I have seen the errors of my ways and now my good man, pour me a long vodka and tonic."

"Oh, really? Well then, in that case, the first drink is on the house."

"Thanks buddy, how are you?"

"Not bad Marty, no one asks the barkeep. I usually am dispensing the small talk and asking the questions. I'm doing OK, my ex-wife isn't breaking my balls today and my daughter isn't swinging on a pole in some club, so all things considered, I'm good, what have you got going on this weekend that's so good?"

"Well tonight, I have a stay at home date with the lovely Mrs. T and I might even get lucky. Tomorrow, I'll put a few hours in at the store, then I'll get my tux on for some big charity event and rock this town."

"Well my friend, good for you," Walt says as he wipes down a counter.

"That hit the spot," I say downing the drink Walt placed in front of me.

"Walt, you've heard the phrase—be careful what you wish for, it might come true—right?"

"Oh yes, we say that to most newcomers in AA, it usually does, if you work for it."

I hate it when he lays some of that AA shit down and I'm drinking, I think.

"Anyway, I have been thinking about that and have been wondering if what you wish for isn't the right thing, but it's still your wish, can you get your wish and forgiveness too?"

"Marty, you can't save your ass and your face at the same time, if that's what you're asking."

"I thought so, but thought I'd ask."

"What are you into Marty, I'm not sure I like the way this is sounding?"

"Don't worry big fella; it's all good; I was just thinking out loud, that's all."

"I know you Marty, it's more than that."

"I swear, Walt, it's nothing I can't handle. Aren't you the one who says what doesn't kill you, will make you stronger? Well, I'm doing some strength training, don't worry."

"If you say so, suit yourself, but don't come back in here playing the victim in a week or two."

"Does anybody REALLY like you better sober?"

"Fuck you, Marty!"

"I love ya' Walt, now let me have one more before I head home."

On the way home, I'll stop and grab some supplies for tonight. I'm thinking since I'll be drinking vodka on Sunday, that tonight we'll have some wine. First stop is Mikhals, the store is owned by a family from Slovenia, really nice people who really know their wines. The bell rings as I walk through the door, not an electronic one but one of those

127

string of bells that you can hear from the back where they usually are hanging out playing euchre.

I require no assistance, unless they've moved the Santa Margherita, which of course they haven't, and I grab three bottles that should get us through the night. Mikhal is at the register and outstretches his paw and we shake hands and then kiss each other on the cheeks. I so dig the European greetings, it's much more intimate and meaningful then some of the customary greetings we have here in the New World.

"Marty, how have you been?"

"Fine Mikhal, fine and you?"

"Good we good, business is good, how are things at cleaning store?"

"Steady as she goes no complaints."

"Good Marty, good, is that all these bottles?"

"Yep, that's it."

"Marty did you see today's Post?"

"No I haven't why?"

"They ran a picture of a fat man with no face; his face was blown off in a cab."

"A cabbie shot him?"

"No, someone reach in and shoot him, no one see though."

"Oh that sucks, the picture was bad, huh?"

"Yes, very bad," said the man behind the counter shaking his head in disgust.

"That picture shouldn't be in the newspaper, his family will be upset."

"Well, Mikhal that sounds like the least of their problems, but I know what you mean."

"Too much shooting here Marty, too much guns; in Slovenia before revolution, we never shoot each other, we yell, we fight, but don't shoot."

"We live in violent times—greed, envy, and anger. Mikhal, that's the problem, nobody wants what they have, and everyone wants what they don't have."

"You smart man, Mr. Marty, you be careful out there, say hello to Mrs. Marty."

"Thanks Mikhal, same to you."

So now I have to stop by the corner store and grab a Post, just like a car accident, I have to look at the picture, another form of rubbernecking. So I walk in to the Korean store and grab some smokes and a Post. I walk out of the store and open the paper to see the picture but also the headline, *"Murder in Cab link to Reserve Job."*

Walking through my door, I hear some Jack Johnson playing somewhere, probably in our room. Cassidy loves music, playing all the time she says it's like the soundtrack to her life, one should always have music playing, so says my wife. We both appreciate music and we have become audiophiles in the last few years. We recently installed a state of the art audio system that plays throughout the house, a B&O system that cost us an arm and a leg, but is one of the material things that remind me that we are doing OK.

I put some wine in the subzero to chill and then I sit with the paper and read. The story goes on to say that the man in the cab was under investigation for his part in the Reserve heist. Not much more in the way of details, but he was from Tennessee and was living in the Gramercy Park Hotel. Pretty nice digs if you ask me, he must have had some cash to afford that kind of "temporary housing," I say to myself.

What kind of part this guy played in the heist, I wonder. It sounds like the cops might have at least some kind of lead on the robbers, but there hasn't been much press about it. The story also surmises that this is the second murder related to the plate theft. The security executive and now this guy, but connecting the dots is really giving the FBI a run for their money. I'm rooting for the FBI; I guess just like anything, I hate it when someone else is getting away with something I would have liked to have done. Weird, I know, but that's just one of my twisted thoughts. Right now, it seems like I am rooting for the losing team.

14

Carlos is in his office at Conserve-Reserve; his brainchild that is filling the expensive office space quite nicely. He opened the doors with 10 million in assets. Now the firm is handling over 750 million—that's a lot of OPM-other people's money, of course. His scheme is working without a hitch, the brokers are happy, each one of them turning at least one account per week.

Considering Carlos is setting them up with a calling list of guaranteed "hungry whales," they should be doing well. These cats eat what they kill and they're getting fat. Of course, Carlos is backing those whales with the money he is making. Well, making money is technically what he's doing.

Conserve-Reserve is the best laundering systems he has seen work and he has seen or been told about them all. Carlos learned a lot from Sliver while he was in Tennessee.

Shame about Sliver; Carlos genuinely liked the man, but he had to go.

Carlos wasn't surprised to read in the paper that Sliver was under investigation. Sliver told Carlos that some "flatfoot" from the

FBI was asking him about his boat and where he was when the money trees disappeared, but Sliver had an airtight alibi and the paperwork to show that he didn't even own that boat at the time of the incident. The boat was sold and the new owner hadn't put the new registration numbers on her yet. So Carlos felt good about him walking away, but the way the operation was working and the amount of unacceptable product was the issue. Business is business and he wasn't going to let personalities and relationships get in his way. He had hit the mother lode and was going to ride this one out.

Marty pours a couple of glasses of wine and walks into the bedroom to see his wife staring into her closet—her big-ass closet.

"Honey, what's wrong?"

"I have not a thing to wear to the Ball tomorrow night."

"How can that be," I say. "You've got a closet full of clothes."

"Marty, I'm fat right now and all my thin clothes are too tight and I don't have any fat-clothes that are good for the ball."

"I am so not going, you can go by yourself."

"I can't go by myself; these are your clients."

"I don't give a shit, Marty, I'm not going, I look and feel like shit and that's that."

I could plunge a knife into her chest when she gets like this, there is nothing I can say or do to change this mood of hers. I just retreat, leaving her wine behind, I head down to the media room to watch some news and maybe look at a movie from the DVD library. Fuck her, I'm not going to let her mood ruin my night. I've done that before, but after all these years, I figured out that sometimes the best action is no action.

Cassidy grabs her wine and sets herself down on the chaise next to her writing desk and puts her head in her hands and begins thinking of Carlos, the money, the life, and never having to go to another client lunch again or walk onto another construction site. It all sounds good, but doesn't feel good. It feels better than it did earlier today, but still not good. How could she tell Marty? "Oh hi honey, I don't have to work anymore, I'm selling the firm and you can close or sell the store, that's right. How and where did I get the money? Oh that's no big deal, I just fucked one of my clients and he cut me in on the biggest cash cow investments." Yeah, that'll go over well, Marty's head will spin like Linda Blair's, ala Exorcist. Then he'll….oh hell, I can't tell him, at least not like that. I could tell him I closed some really big office buildings, entire buildings it would have to be. I'd have to really get creative. Maybe I shouldn't worry so much and just do it and let the chips fall where they may. Marty says it all the time—just go with the flow Cass, don't try to figure it all out ahead of time, stay in the moment. Ok, Marty, I am going with the flow…going with the flow.

I am channel surfing when Cassidy walks in.

"I'm sorry babe; you know how I get before one of these things."

"Yes I do, that's why I'm down here."

"I hate when we fight; it tires me out—it takes so much energy to get mad and then to stay mad. Of course, I'll go with you to the Ball. I'll find something to wear and I'll be delightful."

"That would be a good idea, since your firm is hosting our table."

"I know, I know, I wasn't really going to let you go alone. Besides, you'll get to meet our new investment guy, Carlos."

"Yes, that's right; the latest client you have decided has some lifetime marketing value." "Well, his firm is successful, he might need more space and besides, he might be able to make us some money."

"Is that what it's all about Cass, making money?" "What the fuck is that supposed to mean!" She raises her voice now.

All my serenity and calm went right out the door. Did you ever say something and as you were saying it, wish you could suck it right back in? Well, this was one of those times.

"Marty someone needs to be mindful of that; you just seem to careen around like a helium balloon with a slow leak." She adds with some venom.

"Marty, don't forget that I never had money growing up, and my parents split up when I was a kid and I never got to know my dad."

She remembers her mom was a secretary for a bank president, who used to include Cassidy and her mom in some family events. So Cassidy saw what it was like to have money and she swore that she'd live like the well—heeled and in order to do that she had to work. When Cassidy turned 13, she got her working papers and started working for the building superintendent where they lived. She did odd jobs, cleaned out empty apartments, organized the files; basically she did a little bit of everything. She was a good worker, never missed a day and was never late. One day the owner of the building, an odd little man named Mr. Schiano, saw her working like a dog mopping up after a pipe burst. He asked the supervisor about her and the next thing Cassidy knew, she was working in the leasing office in the afternoons and on weekends. She was making $275 a week and that was some big money for a 15 year old. But unlike her friends, who blew every penny they had at Kings Plaza on clothes, shoes, and stuff, Cassidy banked her money. Well, she gave it to her mom who had opened an account for her at the bank she worked for.

After Cassidy graduated from high school, Mr. Schiano offered her a full-time job as a leasing agent making $400 a week and 50% off the rent her mom paid. You might have told Cassidy she was Donald Trump, because she hit the ground running. By the time she was 20, she had helped Mr. Schiano sell two buildings for a hefty profit and then helped him fill his most ambitious venture, a 25 story office building on the West Side. Cassidy was making more money than she had dreamed of. She bought an apartment in Manhattan, a one bedroom near Carnegie Hall, and was out on the town three or four nights a week partying with the beautiful people. Well, the only difference was at the end of the night she was taking a cab home while the other partygoers were in their limos going to after hour clubs. They were the idle rich, no job required. Cassidy had to work and it wasn't long before the partying slowed down and the work became her party. Cassidy filled the 25 story building and had filled two more for the firm of Schiano and Schiano. Mr. Schiano brought his son in and he was made a partner, while Cassidy did the selling. In the beginning, the money was so good Cassidy didn't care, but when she started to notice that Charlie Schiano Jr. wasn't working nearly as hard, but seemed to be making the same amount of money, she asked to be made partner. Mr. Schiano offered her more money, but not the partnership she wanted.

She had made enough money and had enough connections to open up her own two-man office and began moving office space. She had made so many contacts while leasing space for the Schianos, that building owners were happy to give her their listings. Heck, one of the old building owners, a 76 year old, John Brompton, asked for her hand. He said, "I can't afford to pay her, so I'll marry her—it's cheaper." Well, Cassidy declined and sold three buildings for old man Brompton. He was right; her commission check was almost three million, but she was cheaper than Leona Helmsley she told him.

It was about then that Cassidy met Marty at one of her client's parties; a good-looking Italian, oozing with charm and street smarts. It was exciting for her. Marty knew another side of this town that she didn't know existed. He was her prince and the city was his principality. The two dated for a couple of years. Cassidy never moved in with Marty; she gave him a drawer in her place. She liked the independence, but when Marty popped the question holding a three karat yellow diamond in a platinum setting, she said, "yes." The successful real estate broker was going to marry a neighborhood kid with connections and a million dollar smile. All her girlfriends told her she was crazy, but Cassidy saw something in Marty no one else did.

Now I was going to be subjected to the "I wish you were more-like-me" barrage of disparaging remarks about my future, work habits, and family. Cassidy never fought fair; she'd go for the jugular every time. I have a little more control; realizing that this would pass, but man, I sure was getting tired of this shit. It seemed that these episodes were becoming more frequent. If this was the beginning of menopause, I was really concerned what full-blown change looked like. These are the times when I ask myself, "What the fuck was I thinking about, when I asked this broad to marry me?"

Cassidy was going off on me, but I had channeled her out. Hell, I'd had heard this shit before. I could see her talking, but it was kind of like when Charlie Browns's teacher would talk all nasal, you know, "Whapp, whapps, whapp, whap, whap."

God, I've got to spend the rest of my life with this woman, was what I was thinking, when I noticed that a graphic of the Reserve heist was on the news. The reporter, Sue Simmons, went on to say that the FBI now states that they have some solid leads and that the perpetrators will be brought to justice.

Over at The Mixer, Walt was listening to Lee, the drunken Korean shopkeeper talk about containers full of cash on a truck heading for Red Hook tonight. Walt had never seen Lee in here before, so he was checking him out pretty closely.

"Where does this cash come from? A money farm I suppose."

"Look, I don't know where the money come from; I know that it come every other Friday, and that it."

"You know fella', I wouldn't come in here talking shit about money trucks and money farms, this place is for working folk," Walt says.

"Me work too, work hard. I see truck last month, while I was picking up inventory for store in Red Hook," The Korean answers.

"Why tell me, what am I going to do about the deal?" asks Walt.

"I think money fake," the Korean slurs.

"What makes you say that?" Asks the bar owner.

"I found a twenty dollah bill near the building where the trucks go in, here look."

Walt examines the bill, it's a fake alright. It looks like it wasn't completed, only one side is done. It's not one of those trick bills you can buy, but by the feel and weight of the paper, whoever was printing this was serious and meant to be able to put this into circulation when finished.

"Say buddy, can I keep this?" asks Walt.

"You buy me two drinks, you keep."

"Done" says Walt, "Now drink up, I'm closing."

15

Carlos is sitting in his favorite armchair in his study while Milagro fixes them both a drink. Looking over at Carlos, she pours the 12 year old scotch into the tumblers.

"Carlos, now that Sliver is gone, who did you have in mind to take over the operation?"

"Well my dear, that is an excellent question, one which I've given a lot of thought to. I was thinking that my nephew Jamie, could handle it. I've always liked the kid and he has been great so far."

Milagro nods her head and says," he is trustworthy and blood is thicker than water."

"I was thinking the same thing."

"Here's your drink Carlos, I've got to run. I have some last minute things I need to do."

"So you approve? You think Jamie is the right guy?"

"Yes, well considering there is only three of us left who know where the bodies are. If you know what I mean, then yes, Jamie is the right guy."

"What have you got going on tonight, Milagro?"

"Just some errands for the ball tomorrow night."

"But tomorrow night's event isn't yours, is it?"

"No, but I have some friends who need help with the valet parking, uniforms, and I have to make sure that they will be ready for the event, so I need to call the dry cleaner and make sure he understands."

"You're going to call a dry cleaner on Friday night?"

"Yes, he is a friend and knows how important this is. You know his wife; she's the shark who sold you the office space."

"Oh yeah, she mentioned they owned a dry cleaning operation and that her husband ran it. What's he like? She is certainly an interesting woman."

"What does *interesting* mean? You want to know her in the biblical sense?"

"My dear Milagro, you think my only use for attractive smart women is between the sheets. Look at us, we have a business relationship."

"Not at first, Carlos, you only wanted one thing from me."

"Not true my dear; once I laid eyes on you, I knew we had a future."

"That was only after you realized that I wasn't going to let you get inside my pants. Then you figured out if I could get you inside at the security firm, I might be useful."

"Once again, you overestimate me, Milagro. That was not my sole purpose for you. I also knew that once things were moving, we, that's right we, would need your contacts to help us look legitimate, so you see, you are functional as well as ornamental."

"That's what I love about you, Carlos; I always know where I stand with you."

"So now that you've poured me a drink, why did you stop by?"

"Well, I need some money Carlos, my account is running a little low."

"Oh sure, come sweet talk Carlos, tell him what he wants to hear and get some money. Wish I had someone like me in my life."

"Look Carlos, I did my part and you know it I have made you look like a goddamn citizen to the outside, so don't give me that shit. I need $100 thousand put into my account. Here is an invoice for my services for your records and for the IRS. When can I expect the money to drop?"

"Darling Milagro, today is Friday, and on Monday, you'll be $100 thousand richer."

"Thank you, Carlos; don't forget to be ready by 8:00 p.m. tomorrow. There are lots of people you need to meet and be seen with to help further our plans."

"Yes, dear, I'll be ready. Be a love and top off my drink would you before you leave."

"Get it your self, *love.*"

"Milagro, what do you know about Cassidy's husband?"

"Be careful Carlos, looks can be deceiving. He has lots of friends and I think he could kick your ass."

With that, Milagro puts her glass down and walks out. Carlos sits back and thinks to himself, *if she only knew…if she only knew.*

Agent Tedia is putting more 3x5 cards on his "board of truth," the board of truth is a method for putting together facts, info, and questions that have relevance to a case. The board is a tool he picked up from his mentor, Woody Carmone. Woody used the board with much success; he cracked many a case and put lots of really bad guys away.

Woody always used to say, "Deal with the facts, what you know to be true, conjecture and theory are fine, but truth is a stepping stone to justice." So, by placing all the case related info on a board, eventually if you get enough evidence, you will see a pattern. Hopefully, before more harm is done. "This is true more than not," thought Garrett; "if I could only get a break."

He thought that finding the bass boat at the paper plant in Tennessee was a "case buster," but after tracking down the boat to the fat guy, he had a link. But the fat man had an airtight alibi, as did the boat's new owner, so it was a dead end, literally. Still the trees were gone and with that amount of "money trees," the crooks could print money for a long time. Now the fat man was dead—murdered execution style in New York City—that is a connection, but to what?

Garrett did all the legwork on the man that was called "Sliver." While in the city, Sliver, whose real name was Kenny Lore, left no paper trail. He paid the hotel weekly in cash; the credit card he put down was a Visa from a bank in some back-ass town in Tennessee called Ramer and was squeaky clean.

He learned that Sliver was a successful business man who lived his whole life in Pickwick. He went to school there, starred on the football team, dated the Prom queen, and when he graduated, he stayed in Pickwick. He was a hustler with a charming smile and a laid-back way about him that oozed confidence and patience. Sliver started selling boats and after a couple of years, Sliver had sold more boats than any other salesman. He had sold some big ass boats to some rich folks, many who took a liking to the young man with the smile and velvet voice. One wealthy real estate developer from Nashville liked Sliver so much, that he opened up an office in Pickwick and let Sliver run it. Sliver didn't know anything about real estate, but he did know the lake, 50,000 acres of pristine waterfront land owned by the TVA. Sliver sold a lot of boats to TVA executives and directors; hell, he knew half of the fucking organization chart. Whenever the Authority needed some money, which was about every five years or so, they would sell some of the land to a local developer, because they wanted the area to maintain its integrity. They could only sell the land at a fraction of the cost, because of some profit percentage clause included when the Authority was established by Roosevelt. He didn't want the authority to turn into a real estate conglomerate. The potential was there and Roosevelt knew it. With the power of eminent domain, the Authority could own and sell land like someone printing money. Need more, just take it, sell it, and do it again, so by preventing profit, the Authority's money making potential was limited. It was better to hold the land, than sell it, because they'd always be selling it way below market value. Yes, they could still sell, but they couldn't abuse it. That was built in to the original draft of the charter of origination.

Sliver would wine and dine and hunt with these good ole' boys and every so often, they'd tap ole' Sliver on the shoulder and eek out a parcel of land, usually 1,500-1,800 acres— never too much, but just enough. Sliver would buy it at usually 50% of market value so let's say an acre of waterfront land with lake rights goes to Sliver for $75 thousand. He could sell that to another developer for $100 thousand in a second. Waterfront land will always sell. You see, there is something primal about the water, something that stirs a mans' soul. Even more so than a beautiful woman; a man will hold his gaze on a body of water longer than the body of a woman. That's a fact and every real estate man or woman will tell you the same; "God isn't making any more waterfront land, so get what you can for as cheap as you can, cause you'll be able to sell it for more—guaranteed!"

The developer, who bought it for $100 thousand, will sell it again for $150 thousand and by the time it gets to the street, the acre of waterfront land with rights goes for $225 thousand. So Sliver was near the top of that food chain and from there, the sky was the limit. He opened banks, did some speculating, built some hotels, and was a very big fish in a small pond.

Why all of a sudden, does Sliver liquidate almost every thing and move to New York City? Perhaps Agent Tedia missed something down there in that sleepy town. If Woody was here he'd say; "Only one way to find out. Go back down there and poke around."

Everyone in Pickwick was pretty closed-mouth about Kenny, aka, Sliver. He may have been that town's Mr. Potter from *It's a Wonderful Life*, minus the enemies. He went to church, lived alone, and threw hellacious Memorial Day parties. His employees adored him; restaurants for miles around loved him, that's why he weighed 350 pounds. The man loved food. He really loved life, according to the interviews Garrett conducted. The man was genuinely likeable and eager to please. At least that was all he could find, there had to be more to this guy; there just had to be.

"Ann, this is Garrett Tedia, I need to book a flight to Memphis, can you help me?"

"Of course Garrett, when do you need to go?"

"Tomorrow, I think there is an afternoon flight out of Newark."

"Yes, there is a 1:50 on Northwest and it's available. Should I book it?"

"Perfect, yes please, and I'll need a rental car too."

"Done, Garrett. I will email a confirmation to you shortly, do you need a hotel?"

"Yes, I almost forgot—there is a Hampton Inn there, can you get me in?"

"I'll check, if there is a problem I will let you know, but you'll be good to go."

"Thanks Ann," Garrett says hanging up.

Perhaps it'll be the familiarity with the place that might jog his mind and he'll be able to connect some dots or better yet uncover some more clues.

Traveling is different today—9/11 changed everything. Garrett misses seeing the reunions that would occur at the airplane gates, the people waiting in a self-imposed line-up leaning forward bending from the waist so they can see their loved one come walking down the jetway. Then the shouts, tears, and hugs, those scenes could change your mood in a hurry; it's hard to stay miserable after seeing the emotion-charged people. There once was a time when Garrett had his family waiting for him when he'd return. His wife would stand behind his kids and let them come running to him and hug him around his kneecaps. She would then walk over after the kids and softly kiss his lips. How he missed those reunions—they were a reminder of his connection to something bigger than himself, a family unit. When he returns home now, there is nothing, except the vacant stares and forced smiles of the passengers waiting to board the plane he just got off.

Walking into the store, I see Bertha just staring out the window. She seems deep in thought.

"Hey, did you have a good time at the show?"

Bertha looks at me as if it's the first time she's seen me, then you can see the recognition as she replies, "yes, we did. It's amazing what they do with production today on Broadway."

"I know, we saw Phantom. I swear that boat was cruising on water, it's really cool."

"My nephew was singing along with the actors; it was priceless." says Bertha

"Just like the credit card commercial—priceless." I say with a smile.

"That's what I was just thinking about when you walked in Marty. How nice having money would be. I could give my nieces and nephews memories and experiences I never had."

"I know Bertha, they say money can't buy you happiness, but I think it certainly smoothes out the bumps on the ride, that's for sure."

"You got that right, Marty, you got that right."

"So, what's going on in here today? Has it been a busy morning?"

"No, not really. We did get a call from your favorite customer asking if those valet uniforms were ready. I told her they had been ready since yesterday, like she'd requested."

"Why don't you like her, Bertha?"

"It's not that I don't like her; it's that I like your wife so much."

"What's that supposed to mean?"

"I guess I see the way you look at her and Cheech told me that she was here and you made some plans with her. He didn't say what, but I just got a bad feeling, Marty."

"I appreciate your concern Bertha, but there isn't anyone or anything that could get between my wife and me."

149

"That's good to hear, because I've known you two for a long time and I'd hate to see anything stupid happen." And with that, Bertha grabs two bags of shirts and heads into the back to sort.

I grab my tuxedo down from the rack in back and examine it before putting it in plastic. It's an Armani, classic cut with the notched lapels. The tuxedo was a gift from Cassidy. She took me to Bijan, on Fifth Avenue, to buy it. What a great day that was; talk about major sucking-up, the store associates were all over me pouring champagne, dressing and undressing me, telling me how fabulous I looked and that I should be a model. Money makes people lie, doesn't it? But it is a stunning tuxedo.

Tonight, I'll wear the black vest with the black bowtie and use the black and gold cufflinks and studs. I'll be dealing with a pretty uptown crowd tonight, at the Bifada Ball. The benefit is held every year and the charity rotates between Aids Awareness and Cancer research. This year it's cancer with the money going to St. Jude Children's Hospital in Memphis. The hospital was founded by Danny Thomas and is now funded by the efforts of his daughter, Marlo. I've always felt a connection to Marlo Thomas, since mom took me when I was 15, to talk to the same plastic surgeon that did her nose job; I thought that was cool when I was younger.

When I was 15, my face didn't fit my nose. My nose had grown, but my face hadn't grown into the nose, so I was teased constantly by the other kids about this nose. But after hearing how they do the procedure, I backed out, which was fine with mom because she didn't know how they'd pay for it anyway. Eventually my face grew into the nose and I considered myself good looking. Never was I called cute, but I did ok with the girls. I was never really super-confident about my looks, but I knew I wasn't repulsive and I could make the girls laugh and I had heard lots of girls say they want a man with a good sense of humor and I had that for sure.

Tonight's affair is at the Four Seasons, so that means big bucks will be raised and with Marlo Thomas's entertainment connections there, there will be plenty of "star power" tonight. So I want to look smart, just in case one of those Hollywood types thinks I have a look that he or she needs for their next project. I'd like to think that's the way people get discovered today. Forget the hard work of theatre, training, and all that it's about—a look, plain and simple.

I dive into some Saturday morning store paperwork, pay some bills, approve hours, and before I look up, its 2 o'clock and my stomach is doing a little talking.

"Hey Bertha, I'm going out for lunch, you want me to bring anything back?"

"No, thanks, I had a big breakfast, but you can continue to kiss my ass, so I don't say anything to Cassidy about your attraction to that Latin Lolita."

"Nice, Bertha, very nice." Then I flip her off and walk into the sunlight of the day.

On my way to lunch, I stop into Jim's for Gents; I need some new socks for tonight. I'm looking for hose more than socks and I know Jimmy has 'em. As I make my way past Jimmy's sales guys to the back to where the socks and accessories are, I see a guy who looks familiar but can't place him. The guy looks squarely at me, but there is no recognition in his face and he looks away. I know I've seen this guy but .....Then it hits me; he's the Latin guy that Cass sold that space to and who donated the money to that charity and got his mug in the paper. Satisfied with my recall, I pay for the socks.

When I overhear the guy say, "I don't care how much it costs, can you get one today?" The sales guy runs into the back, and returns smiling, whatever the guy needs they can get, at least that's the way it looks to me.

"$14.68 for the socks, man," says the cashier. His voice brings me back in and I give the guy a twenty, get my change, and leave the store, wondering what it was the guy needed so bad.

Marty remembers that he's got those Tyvek bags coming today, so he'd better give Bertha a call to let her know. After calling Bertha, he heads across the street and into The Mixer. Marty has got a hankering for a club sandwich and Walt's cook makes a good one, plus it's after 12:00 p.m., so a cocktail is in order too.

The Mixer is pretty much empty, just a couple of guys at the bar looking at the game on the TV with a pitcher of beer in front of them. So I grab a stool at the end of the bar, light a smoke, and get the attention of the man behind the bar. I ask for Walt. Keith, Walt's brother-in-law and partner in the bar says, "Walt had to go to Brooklyn today Marty, so he won't be in till late."

"OK then, Keith, can you get me one of those club sandwiches and some fries and a ..." Before I can finish, Keith puts an Absolute and Tonic in front of me. "That's what I like about you Keith; you are a man who knows actions speak louder than words."

Back at the store, Bertha puts the box of Tyvek bags in Marty's office when she looks down on his calendar and sees "meet with M" in the day box for tomorrow. Shaking her head, Bertha walks back up front and notices Marty's tuxedo hanging on the hook out front that customers use. Again, shaking her head, the stocky woman with long gray hair like Judy Collins, puts her bosses' tuxedo in the back. It's then, when the bell rings and she sees a good looking Hispanic guy standing at the counter. "Hello, can I help you?" asks Bertha.

"Well, I'm not sure, but can you tell me who owns this store?" answers the man.

"That's not really information for public consumption, who needs to know?" Bertha asks while sizing up the man.

"Just an honest inquiry. I've been thinking of opening up a dry cleaning store and had some questions that I thought I could get answered here." Carlos replies. "My name is Carlos Ferrar and I don't mean to be a bother."

Bertha recognizes Carlos from his picture in the paper and she knows he is the one who used Milagros phone number on a drop-off. She remembers from the article that went with his photo that he was a very successful, powerful entrepreneur. Maybe there was an opportunity here for Bertha; maybe he was looking to recruit her for his new store. Bertha's mind was like a fantasy sports car. She could go from zero to ruling an empire of dry cleaning stores in less than five seconds.

"Well, I can maybe help you, seeing as I really run the place for the owner." Bertha says warming up to Carlos.

"Good then, what's your name?" Carlos says with a sly smile.

"Bertha, its Bertha. Carlos, was it?" Bertha says with a sly smile of her own.

"Very nice to make your acquaintance, Bertha," Carlos coolly says.

Very nice indeed, Bertha thinks.

It's 3:30 p.m., and Marty needs to swing back by the store and grab his tux and make sure the bags for Milagro came and check on Bertha. She's closing and on Saturdays Marty likes to make sure that there isn't too much cash in the register, since the store will be closed till Monday.

Marty gets his tab from Keith, slaps a twenty on the bar, and leaves telling Keith to tell Walt he was looking for him. "Will do, Marty," Keith says. Marty just points his finger at Keith, grabs his bag with the socks and leaves the bar.

Walking towards the store, I notice from across the street of all people, I see Carlos walking out of it. Funny, I think.

So I ask Bertha about the guy who's just walked out.

"He was just asking some questions about running a dry cleaner," Bertha says.

"Really, I wonder what a guy who runs a big financial services firm would be doing with a dry cleaning store?" I ask Bertha.

"I thought the same thing, but he said he was thinking about opening a store in Brooklyn—Red Hook to be specific." Bertha added.

Now I'm really confused, but I don't let Bertha know that.

"Hmmm," I say, "maybe I got the wrong impression of him."

"Probably, Marty, this guy seemed for real; he just had some questions about the equipment, dryers, and shit like that." Bertha replied, lying through her teeth.

"Of course you told him that this wasn't the get-rich-quick business, right?" Marty asked. "Oh yes, I asked him if he was a glutton for punishment."

"Good girl, Bertha, good girl. I don't care if he's opening in Brooklyn, its competition all the same." I say.

I then walk over to grab my tux and stop by my office. I see the bags for Milagro and move to check the register. Looking in, I see about $400 and see no reason to make a deposit, so I say, "Goodnight" and head home to get ready for the evening.

Bertha turns from the door and begins rationalizing why she didn't tell Marty the truth. She didn't think he needed to know what she was planning, at least not yet, and Carlos is a piece of her plan.

Admiring the rooms in her home, Cassidy stands in a spot where she can see her family room, living room, and kitchen and takes the journey of her life in her head, where and what she came from to all this. Marty calls the slow spin she is doing, the "decorating dance." She smiles, realizing how much she really loves that silly man. Looking at the wall clock, she sees it's almost 4 o'clock and she still hasn't picked out a dress.

After getting pissed at Marty last night, she had a few more glasses of wine and went to bed early without any supper, so she's feeling thinner today. She makes her way into the closet, figuring that Marty will wear his Armani tux, so she should wear something classic like a

LBD (little black dress) or a maybe the Gucci pants suit that looks like a tux for a woman. Marty hates that outfit though, and she feels bad about being such a bitch last night that she wants to look good for him; he always does such a good job of being her "trophy husband" at her business things that she should try tonight and be his "trophy wife."

She starts trying dresses on and after about three dresses, she begins thinking that maybe something with a little skin showing would be the thing. Sure enough, she tries on the black Versace with the slit up to her mid thigh and plunging neckline that shows a good two inches of cleavage and it's backless to boot. She can't zip it up herself, but gets it on and does the spin in the mirror checking out her ass and liking what she sees and feels this is the dress for tonight. Plus, Marty loves her in this. The last time she wore this was to one of his cousin's weddings and he paraded her to all of his family—look at my "American" wife, but saying it like "med-ee-gon" wife. She knew what that meant; she wasn't Italian and no matter how much fucking lasagna she made, she never would be. Marty always said he'd never marry an Italian woman. He says it would be like marrying his mom and besides, Italian women always end up looking like their mothers, which usually was some fat broad with too much facial hair in a duster or housecoat with tissues bulging out of the pockets, yelling at her husband!

No one at tonight's affair will have seen her in this dress either, which is important, especially during the social season. You would rather be nude than be caught wearing the same dress twice to an event in the same season. That's just not done, another one of those things Cassidy had to learn the hard way. Growing up without money meant wearing the same stuff over and over, not really caring what other people thought, you just wore it till it wore out or you outgrew it. But shortly after opening up her own firm and going to these things to find clients or at a client's request, she wore a dress twice, once to the Rock and Roll Hall of Fame Induction Dinner and then to some fundraiser for "Jerry's Kids" and some bitch had the nerve to say, "she thought Cassidy looked better in it the first time she wore it....last month, wasn't it?" Cassidy didn't know what to do, she felt like such a second-class citizen at that moment, that she vowed never again would she do that and she hasn't since.

Cassidy takes off the dress and steams it with the steamer Marty bought for her. At the time, she thought it a cheap gift, since he had the store and certainly got a deal on it. But years after, she always says what a great gift it was, because it's saved her ass plenty of times. She can't count how many times she's pulled something out wrinkled as shit and then used the steamer and in minutes good as if it just came out of the plastic.

In walks her husband with his tux over his shoulder and a big smile when he sees her putting the steamer handle down.

"You love that thing now, but remember when I bought it?" he says.

"I was just thinking about that; we are so in tune." Cassidy says.

"What about last night, I think we were a little "out of tune" wouldn't you?" Marty says with his back to Cassidy.

"I know Marty, I was a bitch, just a little pre-occupied at work and then not feeling good about my weight, so I lashed out at you. I'm sorry, can you forgive me?" Cass says making big eyes and pouty lips.

"I don't know. How can you make it up to me? He says with a roguish smile.

"Come over here and I'll show you big boy," placing her finger in her mouth and looking at him through the tops of her eyes. Marty does as told and as Cassidy places her hand on his crotch and slowly rubs against him, as she slides down to her knees, then taking him in her mouth, Marty looks at himself getting blown in the mirrors. This is going to be a great night he thinks, as his eyes roll back into his head with pleasure.

16

Landing in Memphis, Agent Tedia begins to smell the BBQ coming from the Corky's bar in terminal B. He is still confused when it comes to BBQ. Growing up in Queens, BBQ meant throwing hot dogs and burgers on a grill. He learned in the South that this is called grilling out, rather than BBQ. He also learned that there is wet BBQ, dry BBQ, rubbed BBQ, pork versus beef, and Texas versus the southern BBQ. It all gets confusing, but it indeed is a subculture down here and the natives take it very seriously.

Everywhere he looks, he sees people walking and eating. He thought that was a city thing, but apparently it's a universal pastime. He just thinks that people are in too much of a hurry. His mother, before she passed away towards the end, was so obsessed with being ready and on time that she would set the table for Thanksgiving on November 1st. Of course, she would dust the dishes, but he always shook his head thinking what the rush was? She had plenty of time on her hands. Senior citizens also seem to wake up earlier and earlier. Garrett used to say of his mother that one day she would "lap" us. She was up at 4 a.m. and in bed by 7 p.m. He missed his mom; sometimes she would call him just to tell him she loved him.

She was afraid that one day she'd be dead and the last thing someone would remember was that she didn't call. So she became obsessed with the phone and sending those cards that make you cry, no matter what the sentiment. His ex-wife just couldn't understand the closeness of his family. She came from a different background, one where saying I love you was a chore, "it was understood" she would say. But Garrett couldn't get her to see things his way and one day he woke up and she was gone—no note—just gone. He did hear from her lawyer when he was served with the divorce papers.

His wife took his kids and Garrett just stood by putting up no fight, resigned to the fact that he was a failure, a failure at marriage, a failure at work, a failure at fatherhood, and he just couldn't find a reason to get out of bed. So he stayed in bed for six months, kind of like Brian Wilson of the Beach Boys did. He took a medical leave of absence with pay and just shuffled around his apartment clearing a path through the debris of cups, pizza boxes, fast food wrappers and beer cans.

He stopped answering the phone, stopped talking, and began what he now calls, a silent retreat. It was then, that he started reading about Eastern religion and philosophy and he found out that he was here on earth to serve—that he was most useful as a servant to mankind. He slowly started to assimilate living. He bathed every day, shaved his five month beard, which was way more salt than pepper. He began answering the phone, watching the news, and before he knew it, he was walking into the field office, ready to work.

However, the agency wasn't sure what to do with Garrett. With the botched kidnapping case still on peoples mind and his "little breakdown," it was hard for the Area Director to put him back on the street. Instead, they assigned him to the electronic crimes division, giving him a desk job in a high profile department thinking this would keep him out of trouble, or at least that was the plan.

Garrett resented what he thought was a lame assignment, but with the help of a meditation teacher he found on-line, he was able to accept the assignment and realize that he could turn this into an opportunity. He dove into his work with new vigor; he created his own job description. He started working on identity theft, then moved from that to institutional hacking and that is where he learned about counterfeiting.

Counterfeiting is something you don't hear about very much anymore, but it is going on in record numbers. Today's photo copiers are so precise and so consistent that some counterfeit rings are successful for a period of time, just using high resolution copiers and parchment dyed "money green." But the treasury department has gotten more sophisticated as well, introducing new watermarks, hidden identifiers, and other means of confirming the validity of the money in circulation.

But the most widely used bill, the twenty, hadn't been changed in years and this year the treasury came out with the "new twenty." The bill was a different color, had a completely different look, and had many new "tells." So when the plates got lifted from the treasury, it sent ripples of panic into the money making branch of our government. They had gone to too much trouble to have to re-engineer the bill, so getting these plates back was a priority. However, the FBI and treasury department wanted to keep this situation under the radar, so that the new administration wouldn't be exposed for the breach in security and perhaps even have an effect on consumer spending. It was that delicate.

So when the case hit Garrett's desk, he looked at it as an opportunity to show the agency that he was back, that he was capable of finding these guys and putting them away. His track record in electronic crimes was good; he put away a bunch of identity theft rings, small-time counterfeiters, and prevented a serious virus from hitting the web. His confidence was as high as it had been in years and he was in good shape, ready for the rigors that a case like this would take to solve. This job also was one where he would get to work on his own, at his own pace, with very little supervision. He liked that part; with his new found spirituality, he began to work with mindfulness—which is key—as what might be seen by another as tedious and dull work. He needed this case; he needed some real validation which was all he realized he wanted out of work was validation—that and piece of mind, a state he describes as one long satisfying deep breath.

Right now Garrett was pretty far from deep breathing and Memphis didn't feel like home, nor did he feel like he blended here. Getting more information out of the residents of Pickwick Dam was going to be tough, but there had to be more, if he could just get a break.

Grabbing his luggage off the carousel, Garrett realizes he should have carried on; waiting for the luggage seemed endless. He'll have to remember that if he ever comes into this airport again.

Memphis International may be the busiest airport overnight, but that is because of nearby FedEx—no luggage handling required.

It's a Monday and the shuttle to the rental car lot is packed. The next time he hears how lucky he is to have a job that affords him travel, he will remind them of the glamour of business travel, crowds, delays, insensitive workers, and getting lost.

Garrett gets his car, a Taurus, and pulls out his map and heads east to Pickwick Dam. It's about two hours due east from the airport and he plans to use the ride to formulate the questions he needs answers to. Why was Sliver in New York City? Who did he confide in and what was he up to? Who would want him killed; this was the sixty-four thousand dollar question?

Garrett had gotten a search warrant for Sliver's storage shed. Sliver had sold his house, most of the contents and what was left he stored in a boat storage facility he used to own. The manager of the facility said that no one had been in the shed since Sliver left; no one cared as long as Sliver paid his bill, as a matter of fact, Sliver had paid a year in advance. He was definitely planning to be away for longer, but then again, no one plans their own murder.

Garrett prepared for the drive slides a CD of *Tibetan Incantations*, into the player and chants along for awhile Ohm Mani Padme Ohm, the sound of the universe. His meditation instructor taught Garrett that right action will always be rewarded, but knowing what was right, that was the hard part.

Garrett could pretty much figure out what the wrong thing to do is, but knowing the right thing, was his downfall. He had a mind that was quick to rationalize and denial was powerful, so he needed to learn how to quiet his mind, so the right thing would come to him.

He'd been driving about an hour and he needed to stretch. With a two hour flight, then right into the car, he was a little stiff and needed to bend his body. Part of his spiritual growth was achieved doing Yoga, so when he didn't get to stretch, he felt restricted, knotted up, blocked. He pulls into a BP Gas station in a town called, Middleton, where they have of all things, a drive thru window. Imagine that one can drive thru and get smokes, beer, and bad sandwiches. How busy can these people be that they need a drive thru window at the gas station?

Garrett climbs out of his vehicle and stretches so hard his eyes water, but that is the desired result, pain to pleasure. Yoga has been around for thousands of years and Garrett has a reverence for things old, so he was drawn to the discipline. He only needed a nudge and he was hooked. Lately he'd been enjoying "Hot Yoga." This was where the class is conducted in a sauna, a really big sauna. This really loosens up the muscles and makes some of the more difficult poses easier, but after an hour or so, the room really stinks of body odor.

Garrett surveys this intersection of rural living. There is a four-way stop that seems to be the focal point of the town. Each corner has a different business; two gas stations, a restaurant, and a video store. Garrett checks all the corners; his observation skills are sharp and he notices an old man sitting on the bench outside the restaurant smoking a pipe. The man looks like he has been on that bench forever. Garrett wishes his life could be that simple, but he knows someday he'll retire and end up hopefully, like that. To be able to enjoy a day by just being still, with no buttons to push and no worries—now that's worth working towards, thinks Garrett.

Once inside the gas station, he realizes that the gas station is also convenience store that sells a little bit of everything from fishing tackle to condoms; the station is like a mini Wal-Mart; it even has a little area to eat, smoke, and shoot the breeze. This is what seems to be going on right now; a circle of leather-faced men wearing overalls, John Deere caps, smoking, and drinking coffee. I'll bet these guys know everybody's business and have opinions on everything. Garrett decides to grab a cup of coffee after using the bathroom and see what he can overhear.

The topic of the day seems to be high school football and the disappointing season the team is having. The old guys reminisce about the days past and how much better the game was then. One old guy even got up to show the others what a real three-point stance looked like, but he needed a little help getting up; this made all the rest howl with laughter. Garrett can't help but join in the laughing, but the old guys don't seem too interested in him they look over, but turn back to their circle.

Garrett knows that if he could get a group of guys like this to talk in Pickwick, he might be able to dig something up on Sliver, but fat chance of that. In these parts, they don't take to strangers too readily. Garrett had heard of Southern Hospitality, but soon realized that it appeared genuine on the outside, but it was really just being cordial—especially if you are a Yankee—they even will call you a *goddamn Yankee,* if you move down here.

After getting the cold shoulder from the old men, he gets back into his car and heads east to Pickwick. He's had enough chanting and tries to find a local station on the radio, so he can get caught up on the happenings around here. He pulls in a station from nearby Corinth, a metropolis compared to the towns he's been driving through. The talk on the radio revolves around the weather, with most of the folks around here being family farmers, weather is critical to the well-being of the local economy.

In all his years, Garrett has never met a happy farmer; it's either too dry, too wet, not enough sunshine, or the bugs are bad. He used to think farmers were ultra conservative, never taking risks, but he now knows that these farming folk are gamblers; they take all their money to buy seeds and put it in the ground and hope for the best.

The radio hosts seem to think that this year will be a good harvest; the weather has been cooperating and the fields look good. They too, discuss high school football like the fellas in the gas station except, apparently, Corinth High has a team that has a shot at the state title. So the radio guys are encouraging the listeners to put up signs of support on their houses and businesses for the team encouraging them on to victory. Like Garrison Keillor and *Prairie Home Companion*, all they need to do is break into a little "theatre of the mind," and it would be complete. Corinth, where the women are beautiful, the men are all handsome and the children are above average.

The show then turns into a trading post or a country version of eBay, with people calling in trying to sell their stuff or find a suitable trade. Actually pretty entertaining and Garrett settles in for the last hour of the ride.

Once he arrives in Pickwick, he checks into his hotel; this time he's staying at the Hampton Inn; they boast of free high speed internet access and it'll help him turn in reports and surf for information quicker. Besides, it's the nicest hotel in town and he deserves the comfort. He only plans on being here for a few days and the $59 rate is well below his per diem; heck, he might even make a few sheckles. The room is nice; some hotel art on the walls, a TV, a clean bathroom, and a work area where he quickly sets up his laptop, plugs in his cell phone, and then unpacks.

One of the things his wife said that drove her crazy was the way he hurried to unpack in hotels, as if he were moving in. So as he's putting his underwear and socks in separate drawers and hangs his pants and shirts in separate parts of the closet—like you'd see in a retail store—he smiles and thinks of some of the vacations they took and how he used to unpack for everyone, making sure that space was used efficiently. God, why did he do the things he did? He never knew his behavior might drive people away. But then again, who does? He misses his family now, but then he took them for granted. It's a funny thing the human condition, we tend to treat strangers with more courtesy then we extend to the ones we love the most, Garrett thinks, sometimes we get the tests first and the lessons later.

Garrett checks his emails and responds to the ones he needs to and deletes all those that are spam. He hates to be away from his email more than 24 hours; he feels out of touch when he is. This is the curse of technology; it's a double-edged sword. It makes you more efficient, but it can turn into an addiction. That's why you hear executives who use the handheld device, Blackberries, call them "Crackberries," because they can't put them down—not even at the dinner table. Even today's kids are being brainwashed with things like Instant Messaging (IM), texting, and My Space. Previous generations used the phone, but today's kid has a computer in their room and unless mom and dad is computer savvy, it's hard to find out who their kids are talking to and what they're saying. Garrett's parents would listen in to his calls; they told him after he'd grown up and had a kid of his own, he'd understand. They recommended he get good at picking up the receiver—very slowly and quietly.

Garrett places a phone call to his office instead of emailing. He needed to hear that New York accent—giving them his phone and fax numbers in case they need to get to him. He then calls Sportsman's Storage to arrange a time to examine Sliver's space and have a manager there to give the warrant to. He talks with a guy named Jeremy, who tells him that he's the manager, but he was leaving for the day and he'd be happy to let him in tomorrow morning if that was OK? Garrett says, "sure;" this frees up the afternoon for setting up and studying his "mobile board of truth" and making sure he has dotted the I's and crossed the T's so far.

He sets up his portable DVD player so that he can review the disc from the paper mill and perhaps find a clue about the driver of the bass boat. He has looked at this footage so many times that he's probably lost perspective, but this is the work, so he digs in.

Next morning, Garrett does some Yoga and gets some breakfast in the lobby and heads to the storage facility. He's dressed in blue jeans, a flannel shirt, and a ball cap; he attempts to dress like the locals. Maybe his attire when he was here last time was just too harsh for these folks; maybe a change in look will open them up.

Jeremy is there as he promised, and reviews the warrant as if he knew what he was looking at and asks Garrett, "What you lookin' for fella?"

Garrett answers, "I don't really know."

"Well, good luck to you; let's get you in there." Jeremy says waving a key set that must have 30 keys on it.

"Great, you lead." Garrett says walking behind the manager.

They get to shed number 47 and Jeremy proclaims, "Here she is; let's see how long it takes me to figure which key opens this here lock."

"You don't know?" asks Garrett.

"I know it's one of these, so we'll get it, you in a hurry?" asks Jeremy.

"Well kind of, but you take your time; I don't want to add any pressure." Garret suggests

"Pressure?" says Jeremy, "My friend you are in Pickwick; there is no pressure here except water pressure thanks to the TVA."

"Great," thinks Garrett. This is going to be a longer day than expected. And with that, the key trial and error project starts. After about half an hour, Jeremy stops and asks Garrett, "You like a cup of coffee?"

"Sure," says Garrett, "I would."

"Great, let's go then," Jeremy says walking towards the office.

Garrett can't help but notice that Jeremy has scooped up the pile of keys he has tried with no success and puts them in his pocket while he leaves the untried ones by the shed door. "Garrett, that's your name right?" asks Jeremy.

"Yes" answers Garrett, "It is."

"Garrett, why do you care who killed Sliver?" Jeremy asks.

"It's my job, Jeremy; Sliver was murdered and that's not cool."

"I know," says Jeremy, "but he didn't have no family, no real friends, so why the work?" "Well Jeremy, we don't see it like that; his life was ended by the hand of another and we need to punish who ever did it." Garrett says taking the coffee from Jeremy.

"Besides Jeremy, he was an important man around here; lots of friends and lots of folk depended on Sliver." Garrett says looking into Jeremy's eyes.

"Well, I reckon you could call some of his acquaintances, friends, but he never really hung out with anyone after that Spanish fella moved away." Jeremy says.

"But that were years ago, and most folk don't remember the way those two were."

Really, who was that?" asked Garrett, hearing this for the first time.

"I don't know, he just was always with Sliver; didn't say much, but had some shifty eyes. Sliver was the only one who liked him." Jeremy adds.

"Then one day he was gone—just like that—kind of the same way Sliver left—just up and gone."

Garrett looks into his coffee and at the storage shed outside. Maybe something will turn up; something has to turn up.

17

Sometimes, I just feel bigger than my body gives me credit for—I think, a really good way to feel before one of these charity things. They usually are a drain and make you wish you could get those five hours of your life back. But tonight, I've got my mojo workin'; freshly blown and showered, as I preen into the mirror. Cassidy is hosting the table, so I will have to be "on." Damn that woman is good; I think she serviced me, so I'd be in a good mood for her table tonight, and it worked.

Cassidy is downstairs and on the phone to Carlos. "You had better god-damned behave tonight, this is important to me."

"Define behave," says Carlos.

"You know what I mean, so just do it."

"Okay," Carlos sighs, "I'll behave."

"Good. Now we'll act like we barely know each other, purely professional."

"Got it," says Carlos.

"I'm hanging up," declares Cassidy, and she does.

Carlos is taken by this woman—he has had women all over the world and now a woman who is married has his attention. Maybe that's why she is already spoken for, but Carlos knows everyone has a price. He wants to bring Cassidy into his inner circle; she can help him complete his plan. He also knows that if he can really trust her-as much as he is capable of trusting anyone, she stands to make a lot of money for herself. Money seems to be her motivator; maybe if he shows his hand, she'll show him her ass.

Cassidy moves to the Sub-Zero, pulling out a bottle of Dom Perignon; unwraps, six twists, and "pop" goes the cork. Cassidy fills her flute and drinks. This is going to be an interesting night. She almost cringes, but another couple of glasses of champagne, and this too shall pass. Just as the thought settles in, she looks and sees Martin coming down the stairs.

"Well, does it still look good baby?" Marty asks.

"As good as it gets darlin'," Cassidy says playfully. Doing her best runway spin, "You like what you see?"

"Me like," says Marty, "me like very much; what do you say we go back upstairs and rewind?"

"You're sweet honey; have some bubbly, baby."

"Sure," says Marty. "So, who is at our table tonight?"

"Well, there'll be Liz and her latest, a client and his wife, and that guy Carlos Ferrar, my South American financier client. You remember?"

"Oh yeah, I remember. He's been busy lately; this should be an interesting night," Martin says turning his flute up and licking his lips tasting every bit of his champagne.

"You are right Marty—interesting." Cassidy thinks turning up her glass and draining its contents.

Milagro, while working the keyboard on her laptop, looks at the clock and realizes she needs to quit and start getting ready for tonight's gala. Since she's been working as an event planner, she enjoys these things much more. She has an appreciation for all that goes into putting one of these events together. She almost gets nervous for whoever is responsible; looking at all the little things—candles, music, lighting, and even the valet parking rhythm. She knows how many moving parts are involved and to see them work like a well-oiled machine is a treat. Tonight's event is one of those gargantuan affairs—an intimate gathering of 1,200—an invite list that looks like a Who's Who in Hollywood and the New York power-broker scene. The location tonight is The Four Seasons, quite possibly the best ballroom in town with a celebrity catering chef who creates menus rather than be told what the menu will be. The cause—St. Jude's Children home in Memphis—maybe the most over exposed charity, thanks to the late Danny Thomas. This will be the event of the year—too bad I have to go with Carlos. I'd rather go by myself, than pretend to be on his arm, but sometimes you have to do a thing that you don't like—that's just the way it is.

Milagro knows that it's better to keep Carlos in **your** sights, because if you don't, you might end up like Sliver. She **doesn't** have to be a rocket scientist to see what Carlos is doing. So far, **two** of his partners have ended up dead and she is the only one left—she'd better be on her toes. But how long can she go on this way; fronting as an event planner, doing Carlos' bidding, and keeping Carlos' public image impeccable.

Keeping Carlos squeaky clean is tough; he just doesn't give off that nice, compassionate guy vibe. You just see a man who likes making money and doesn't really seem to enjoy life. Pretty hard to endear him to the media, let alone the public. But Milagro can't complain about the compensation, its more money than she dreamed of; literally millions a month go through her, and she just takes what she needs to keep up the image. So justifying her actions is pretty easy, money being important to her too. Growing up as she did, she never asked how much something cost; she just made it known she wanted it and it was hers. She was totally sheltered and taken care of. But when her dad went away, so did the life; she never knew what happened, but she sure did feel the effect. It wasn't till she was seventeen that she understood who her dad was—an official in a government that dealt in drugs, exporting, producing, and controlling the market. She didn't believe it, but when she confronted her mother, she told Milagro everything. That her father took bribes and used his influence over Noriega to create a policy for dealing with the South American cartels that still exists today in some South American countries like Brazil and Columbia. It was based on greed; not for the good of anyone, but for those who could abuse their power without any repercussions.

So Milagro worked, studied, survived, and built her own life story. After all, it was Milagro who played the part of assistant in the security firm and stole the script to disarm the system at the Fed. She felt safe right now, but for how long?

Milagro first met Carlos years ago in South America; he was a rising star in one of the cartels and she was just finishing her work in college. They spent an evening just talking about their dreams and their past, both of them wanting more than they had and both of them with a plan. That was it—one night talking until morning, no romance—nada. After that night, they went their separate ways never thinking they'd see one another again. Their worlds had no reason to intersect. But life is a journey with many paths to take and choices to make. Three years ago they reconnected at a fundraiser and before she knew it, she was caught in his web.

Carlos was supposed to pick her up at 7:00 p.m., so she has two hours to get ready. She has her dress out, shoes, and bag, along with her jewelry all laid out. She hates to be uncertain about an outfit; her confidence in part, is fueled by her outward appearance—that's the way she was raised; if you look gorgeous on the outside, people assume your insides are the same. She is wearing a black Dolce and Gabana with a slit up to the mid-thigh and tight, so that her perfect size six body is framed like a painting—striking. She's also adorned her feet with a pair of Manolo Blaniks, with a three-inch stiletto heel that draws the eye to a well sculpted calf; her Prada bag, crusted with black pearls adds an understated elegance, while her David Yurman earrings and necklace don't take away from her classic jaw-line and full lips. Her four-carat sapphire cocktail ring isn't gaudy, just magnificent enough you'd call it "gawky," you can't help but gawk.

She is one well-manicured, buffed to a fine sheen magnificent specimen of the species—a beauty like this intimidates and inspires. Milagro knows she looks hot tonight; she has her hair done in that "freshly fucked" style that is all the rage in town. Her deep brown eyes look herself over and she winks at herself. Genetics are a great thing—thank god the gene pool she swam in had looks; life is easier if you're attractive—much easier.

Tonight will be interesting, thinks Milagro. We're the guests of Cassidy Tyroni, the real estate broker Carlos used to get the Park Avenue space. He's spent a bunch of time with her of late, considering the deal is done and her commission is in the bank, which makes her wonder what he could be up to with her. She also knows that tomorrow she has a meeting with Cassidy's husband, Martin, at his store, with drinks…. I hope he doesn't say anything, but she could tell by the way he looks at her that he isn't telling his wife they have a meeting at the store on a Sunday. Men usually keep Milagro away from their wives, thinking that they might have a shot at her. So Milagro just wonders what conversation will come up at the table tonight; interesting indeed.

Carlos walks from room to room while he is talking to Cassidy on the phone, listening to her telling him to behave; he knows she'll be stand-offish tonight, but that's to be expected—her husband will be there. Carlos now feeling like a little master of the universe, hangs up and goes into his bedroom to dress. The bedroom—a mahogany affair, looks like the inside of a men's club—deep green leather inserts in the paneling, brass fittings, black and white photos adorning the walls, the brown shag carpet looks like a mohair sweater. This room oozes testosterone; it's a Brooks Brothers store on steroids.

The apartment, a twelve-room, four bedroom corner unit on the 30th floor, looks at the East River and downtown. Carlos had Todd Oldham do his condo too; he liked the way he did the Conserve-Reserve offices, so why not have him do his own home. Carlos couldn't be happier, although you'd never know it; to say Carlos isn't emotive is an understatement. Never let them know what you're thinking; everyone has a tell—Sliver taught him well.

Out of his cedar-lined closet, he looks into the tuxedo vault—which one will he wear tonight? Knowing that there will be tons of paparazzi and celebs, he chooses a classic Armani with a shawl collar, brocade vest, a tie, Johnston and Murphy patent leather slip ons, and the look is complete. "Damn, I'm good looking," thinks Carlos, "how can that Cassidy keep her hands off me? I'm money and everything she needs; she wouldn't have to work if she came with me. Her husband… hell, I'll pay him off too—she is the prize."

The front door of the Four Seasons is roped off tonight; guests of the hotel will enter through the side entrance. Tonight the front is reserved for the Bifada Ball. Limousine after limousine rolls up and deposits beautiful people; the entrance is lined with lookers-on, fans, and paparazzi. Tonight a photographer can make some money; with all the movie stars, TV stars, business leaders; the Bifada Ball is like shooting fish in a barrel. Yell the right thing to get your subject's attention, and snap away. You can roll off fifty exposures, one of which could end up in your super market check out line. The photographers have a kind of "honor among thieves" code when it comes to jockeying for position at one of these. Of course, the first-come, first-serve method works, but there can be two to three different events going on in this town and it's not possible to be in three places at once so, they rotate. Giving the "hole-shot" up after they've snapped five to ten celebs, depending on the event, sometimes that number is smaller.

Tonight, the event warrants a two- to three-subject rotation for the free lancers; of course, the big mags—*People*, *In-Style*, etc… have assigned spots and those pricks don't play. They forget that they once free-lanced and had to hustle. Tonight is a special night, so everyone who is anyone is there—a papparazzi's wet dream.

Martin and Cassidy finish the bottle of champagne and pull two more out of the Sub-Zero for the limo. "Are you sure you told them it had to be a black caddy?"

"Yes, Martin I did. We've been together long enough and in enough limos for me to know you won't ride in anything but."

"Damn straight! You won't catch me dead in a white prom special limo."

Cassidy rolls her eyes and lights a smoke to calm her down before this night gets underway; she should smoke a little weed, but she is hosting—maybe later. She'll remind Marty to bring the dugout; a handy little item that let's you light up just about anywhere you can smoke a cigarette. Although Marty brings it to most of these things, it never hurts to remind him. "Hey babe, you bringin' dug?"

"Got it right here," he says, "patting his breast pocket. Don't leave home without it." He remarks.

"Cool," Cass says and drags on her smoke.

Marty looks at his wife basking in her beauty, he really hit the jackpot when he married Cass. All these years and she still gets him "warm for her form." Tonight is no exception; she is magnificent in her dress, her hair and all the accessories. Man, he thinks she is hot, really hot and she's all mine—it's a very comforting and satisfying feeling and Marty lets it wash all over him.

18

Walt parks his car and heads for the address the Korean kid gave him the other night; the address for the place he said that trucks filled with money, deliver to. Walt has a crazy feeling that there might be a score here for him, he needs a big score, he's behind on the bills, his ex is breaking his balls and his partner is seriously considering walking away from the bar and taking a loss. He doesn't know what else to do, sometimes you can take a thief and sober him up and he's a new man, but most of the time all you get is a sober thief. He has dreams too—a treatment center in the mountains and a life of helping others with addictions, he quickly justifies his being here—bad money for good.

It's been a while since Walt has walked around in this neighborhood. When he was still "out there," he used to end up here every so often. There used to be a warehouse down here that was an after-hours joint. You paid fifty bucks to get in, and it was an open bar-beer and wine, that is, if you wanted something harder, it was there to. You just had to poke around—whatever your pleasure—coke, X, weed, H—it was a madhouse—only open on Saturday nights. Walt shakes his head thinking about it. Back in the day, Walt was a doorman at the Marriott Marquis; he used to clear anywhere from two hundred to three fifty a shift in cash. After work, it was "Katie bar the doors." He was off like a rocket. Change into some clubbin' duds and a wad of cash, a little blow to start out, and then a steady diet of booze. Somehow he'd find his way home not remembering the night before-he was a blackout drunk. Finally he got scared; he started feeling jittery in the mornings—he had to quiet his nerves with a couple of shots. This wasn't so bad; he felt okay about it. Actually, he felt very okay about it. He'd seen his dad do it, and thought it was just what the life did to ya'.

But it wasn't long before he shook violently if he didn't have any booze in him. Then he got fired for no shows and for being drunk on the job. He drank constantly, around-the-clock, and then it got so bad he didn't leave his apartment or get out of bed. He only got up to answer the door for the neighbor kid who he paid to get him his booze. He lived to drink and he thought he had to drink to live. Pretty soon, the booze didn't work anymore—he was fucked. He was too afraid and a coward to kill himself, so he had reached the bottom—no where to go.

Then it happened; he thought he heard the door, but when he went to answer it, no one was there. He looked up and down the hall—nothing. When he walked back in on the TV, it was one of those late night PSA's for AA and he called the number. The next thing he remembers, he was in a hospital and there were two men who had concerned looks on their faces. They explained that they came to his apartment and he was passed out in his own shit and piss. They hauled him here to save his ass. Here was the 14th floor at St. Vincent's, the nut ward, where they dried you out for a few days and then sent you on your way into the waiting arms of Alcoholics Anonymous.

He's been sober for a lot of twenty-four hours, which is the way he was taught; that one day at a time is all he's got, so stay sober for that day and don't worry about tomorrow. You're not guaranteed another day and that made sense to him.

It was his dream to own a bar—a neighborhood bar—a place to relax and unwind. Nothing fancy, but a good ole' fashioned corner bar. Somewhere you could watch the Yankees and Giants play. He was walking from his friend Marty's dry cleaning store and he saw The Mixer. He'd passed it before and maybe even drank in there; hell, he drank everywhere so he was sure he did. Someone was locking the door and it was 5:00 p.m.—why would you close a bar then? So, he asked. He was told that the owner's wife died and then the owner shot himself. The bar was for sale by the bank. Walt took that as a sign and called the bank and his brother-in-law the next day and in forty-five days, The Mixer was his. He never re-married; the bar was his wife. He was there just about all the time. His sponsor constantly reminded him that he was making a mistake; it's like giving a pyro a blow torch dealership.

Walt knew he was meant to own this bar and that was it. He would be able to keep his eye on everything. Since he wasn't drinking, he could run an honest business and after all, that was all he wanted—a place to take an honest deep breath, no more lies, no more buying things he didn't need to impress people he didn't care about. He liked himself again and this bar was his stake. It's been his for years now and he never looked back.

Walt kind of recognized the address the kid gave him and he remembered he said every other Friday the money came; Walt had nothing else to do. Why not go see trucks full of money in Red Hook on a Friday night. The only light was that of the streetlamps—kind of eerie, because the streets down here were still the old cobblestone and the curbs of granite, so you couldn't see the street signs until you were on top of them. When he found the address he was looking for, it was 10:30 and the area was quiet; you could hear some horns and traffic roaring by on the BQE in the distance and that was it. Walt walked around the building, or at least the front half; it was a big warehouse probably seventy-five thousand feet or so, big enough to hold two to three trucks—that's for sure. He noticed the drive in entrance was barricaded pretty heavy duty with a pair of 15-foot high doors barring the entry.

He walked back to his car and pulled it so that he could stake out the doorway from afar. He had some night vision glasses he bought on QVC one night. Drinking wasn't the only thing Walt had a compulsion for; he was addicted to shopping late at night on the TV. Sometimes the UPS guy would come twice a day with stuff Walt bought. He talked in his meetings about it and he would stop for a while, sometimes three months, but it made him feel good, so he'd buy. Sometimes for other people, but usually for himself; the night vision glasses were definitely for him.

He turned the car off and sank in the seat. This was fun, even if he didn't know what to expect—just curious he guessed. After an hour and 45 minutes, he heard the rumblings of an approaching truck and as the sound got closer; he realized it was heading his way. Once the truck arrived in front of the building he was watching, he saw two men get out, work the security system and then drive in. Another hour later the truck drove out and away into the early morning.

Walt was now in analysis paralysis; his mind was going one hundred miles an hour. He felt like a car in park and someone was stepping on the gas. He wanted to do something; break in, and call someone—something! But he was stuck, he had no business being there; he didn't know what he was looking for, but some drunken Korean kid said that every other Friday night trucks delivered money to this building and Walt figured the money to be counterfeit. How could he prove that what he was thinking was wrong or better yet right?

19

In the limo I am playing with all the dials and buttons; I always feel like a kid playing with new toys in a limo no matter how many I ride in. Cassidy was used to this routine; she knew the drill. First, I'd play with the lighting, then the AC or heat, and finally the sound system. By the time we arrived at the Four Seasons, I was finally familiar with all the gadgets in the car, but we had to get out.

Getting in and out of limousines is a learned skill; you either do the left leg out first if you're a woman with great legs or you do the hunch down forward walk out. Cassidy had the legs and she knew how to exit a limo. Yours truly hunched down and banged my head getting out; Cassidy stood there shaking her head while I got the driver's name and phone number and gave him some instructions for later.

Dramatically, Cassidy reached her hand out for me and then we glided down the red carpet, into the hotel. I just love that shit; feeling like a rock star walking in like that. In my mind I am, just undiscovered, that's all. We got our table assignment; Cassidy had reserved a table in the Gold Circle so that it would be a table with a view—a view of everyone else that is, a perfect people watching perch.

The pre-function space was converted into a three ring circus, Cirque d' Sole that is. There were contortionists, clowns, jugglers, gymnasts, and of course, a ringmaster who kept announcing something in French. There was so much going on that I felt over-stimulated; I didn't know what to do; watch the acts, get drinks, follow Cassidy, or look for a place to smoke. I had gotten high before leaving the house and this was a trippy scene to say the least, almost Fellini-esque.

Cassidy made up my mind for me. After looking at me stand there with mouth open, she grabbed me and we started toward the bar. She knew she'd need some drinks to get through this night and she didn't want to lose the buzz she started at home. On the way to the bar, she spotted her girlfriend, Liz and some guy with red hair.

"Who is that with Liz?" she asked me.

"Hell, I can't keep track of her men; she changes men like I change socks, so why would you expect me to recognize her dates?"

"Well, I thought she said she was going to bring the guy from her office, but I don't remember him being a redhead."

"Let it go Cass, we'll find out soon enough; then you can grill him like a whopper and find out his life story," I say heading to the bar.

After a short wait, I order a couple of glasses of champagne after seeing them pouring Cristal, I'll mix Dom with that no problem!

Handing the flute to Cassidy I say, "Here babe, no woman in this room can hold a candle to you. I drink to you."

"You are too sweet, Martin. I love you, I really do," says Cassidy and then thinks, "I really do."

Carlos sends the driver to the door to get Milagro while he pours himself a glass of straight Absolute. He'll need this tonight he thinks; with that piece of ass Cassidy at the table, he'll want to play his cards right. He doesn't want Milagro or Cassidy's husband to see him flirt; he's supposed to be a cool customer, a power broker, a man to watch, he can't be seen letting his guard down because of a pair of legs and great tits. Stay cool tonight, be a little aloof, and let the night come to you. While that thought is clearing, the door opens and in comes the lovely left leg of one Milagro Perdido. He gave up trying to get in her pants years ago; she is too smart and too valuable to the operation for him to play that game.

Settling in, Milagro looks at Carlos and says, "good evening, you look nice."

"Thank you my darling, you look fetching."

"Thank you Carlos, a woman needs to hear that now and then." Milagro says while checking her lipstick in the mirror.

"Would you like a drink while we ride?" he asks.

"Yes, do you have any champagne in here?"

"Of course I do", he says leaning into the built-in cooler and pulls out a bottle of Cristal. "Perfect," she says adjusting her dress. "I am looking forward to this Carlos, please be on your best behavior. I see you have a vodka on the rocks. Please don't drink too much; tonight is important to me," she says. "With your birthday party invitations going out soon, we want to make a good impression so we can get some of these old moneyed bores to attend. They can make or break an event and we need them."

"Thanks for the orders, General," he says, drinking from his glass, "just like your father—always giving orders."

"You leave my father out of it. He was a good man who got in with the wrong people and before he could get out, he got thrown under the bus, so don't bring it up."

"I touched a nerve," smirks Carlos, "I'll remember in the future to leave dear old dad out of things, Ok."

"Thank you, Carlos; I don't need that shit and you know it, so don't push my buttons, you hear me?"

"Loud and clear a toast to us, Milagro, a toast to us." Carlos says gulping some more of his drink and looking out the tinted window.

Their limo gets into the unloading line and creeps till it's their turn. The driver stops and opens the door for Carlos who gets out first turning to the crowd who seem to recognize him but aren't sure. He leans in and says, "I thought you'd have photographers here?"

"I do, now help me out and you'll see." She says sticking her hand out for Carlos to help.

She elegantly exits the long black car and turns to the crowd and sure enough the bulbs start going off. "It's the Conserve-Reserve guy," they hear the photographers shout, "shoot." Shoot they do. The clicking and flashing is almost overwhelming, but the handsome Latin couple strides down the carpet flashing toothy grins and giving the peace sign to the fans and photographers alike.

Once inside, Milagro looks to Carlos and says, "Never doubt the long arm of my influence; I make things happen. Don't you forget that?"

Carlos just looks at her and smiles, "Yes my dear, once again you are functional as well as ornamental. You are a professional in every sense of the word. Now let's go have some fun."

As they are guests of the Tyroni Firm, they go to the reception desk to find their table. Again, Milagro takes the lead; getting the table number, signing in, and then looking for the ballroom entrance. Of course they are bombarded by clowns and all manner of circus types, paid to "distract-ertain," Milagro calls it. It keeps guests eyes busy so they don't feel like they are just standing around waiting to get drinks, food, or whatever is the main attraction. She is impressed, Cirque d'Sole doesn't come cheap. This is a first class affair and she could learn a lot here. But her mission tonight is to get Carlos circulating with the right people. He needs to get on invitation lists and maybe even find some investment opportunities. After all, CR can only move so much money; they'll need more places to park the money and the people who come to events like this one, don't invest with strangers. Carlos will have to build a few well-targeted relationships.

Milagro hates having to play second fiddle in this operation, but then again, there used to be five who played fiddle and she is still here. Carlos is a snake and she is in business with him, so she must be on her toes. As long as she is directing him, he can't take her out. Some day she won't have to live with this fear; someday, she will be away from this. She'll go back home to Panama, change her name and live like her father wanted, like a princess—a very rich princess.

Carlos notices a waiter with a tray of drinks. He slips a one hundred dollar bill in the waiter's pocket and says, "If you see me without a drink at anytime tonight, make sure you are getting one for me. Understand?"

"Yes sir, and what would that drink be?" the waiter says knowingly.

"Vodka rocks, my friend, Vodka rocks," Carlos replies.

"Very good," the young man says as he heads to the service bar. As he's leaving, Carlos grabs a glass of champagne off his tray before he leaves and hands it to Milagro. "Here you are, enjoy yourself tonight," he whispers.

"I'm on the job Carlos and you are too. Stay sharp. Here comes someone I want you to meet; his name is Thurman Orsman. His family owns cruise ships—perfect for us—off shore registries, foreign partners and lots of old money."

"Okay Milagro, let's go." He says and moves towards the old man in the Admirals tuxedo.

Milagro makes introductions and the clever conversation begins. Carlos can be charming she thinks, if he wants to, but only if he wants to.

20

Cassidy and Marty weave their way through the crowd to catch up with Liz and her date.

"There you are darling," Cassidy says, "You look divine Elizabeth, divine."

"Thank you. You look fabulous—is that new?" Liz remarks.

"God no, this is my old standby, but thank you. I feel good in it; and who is your friend?" "Cassidy and Marty Tyroni meet John McDeer."

"The pleasure is all mine." The red head says while reaching to kiss Cassidy's hand.

"Oh a perfect gentleman, I like him Liz, I like him." Cassidy says.

"Marty say hello to John."

"Hi, I'm Martin Tyroni, Cassidy's husband, happy to meet you."

The red head reaches out and gives Marty a limp fish handshake; this is going to be some night is all I can think scanning the room for a waiter; I need another drink.

Turning towards the bar, I can see to my left—a juggler working a bowling ball, butcher knife, and chain saw. Transfixed on the man in the yellow satin shirt, I turn back to Liz's date and say, "Why would someone even think they wanted to do that?"

"Probably grew up around it." The redhead says.

"Huh" is all I can muster wondering what that means.

"I represented a guy who worked for the Felds; remember them?" John asks.

"They used to own the Ringling Brothers show, right?" I answer, and then add-on yeah, I do remember. I sold one of his sons a car back in the 80's."

"Well anyway, my client was suing them for breach of contract. I'm an entertainment lawyer and it was pretty cut and dry."

Using my best "I'm really fascinated look" I just nod my head.

"My guy got hurt, of all things, getting shot out of a cannon," the lawyer goes on to add.

"Really," I answer, I've gone this far why not finish the story.

"You see, they don't really get shot out. The cannons have a kind of spring loaded catapult that propels them out, giving the audience the illusion of a human cannonball. The explosion and smoke distracts the crowd and bam—there it is."

"Cool. I always wondered what the deal was, so did your client win?"

"Well, we settled and he got his medical expenses and some walk-away money. You don't fuck with the Felds; they're ruthless."

"What I was getting at, is he was in a long line of cannonballers, and so maybe that juggler is too."

I size up John, the entertainment lawyer, and thinks maybe I was too quick to judge. Liz usually picks old men with money, or young studs for a good workout after the night ends.

"So John, how long have you been practicing law here in New York?" I ask.

"Not too long. The firm moved me here from our LA office three years ago."

"Well, how do you like it?"

"I do. I'm originally from Ohio, but I think I was a nomad in another life because wherever I hang my hat, I feel like I'm home, so New York is home now and that's OK. I guess I'm supposed to be here."

"Interesting way to look at it," I answer, "I've lived here all my life and I sometimes forget there is life west of the Hudson River."

"Marty you and Cassidy really should get away, Liz tells me, you and your wife have your own businesses, so you should travel more. There are so many worlds out there. I came from this small town and I have seen so much; if I hadn't left there, I'm sure I'd have gone mad."

"Well John, we talk about vacationing more, but the furthest we get is the Jersey Shore. Cassidy doesn't like to fly, so that kind of limits us."

"Marty, do yourselves a favor then, go on a cruise that can be relaxing, romantic, and fun."

"I hate to think of being trapped on a boat for days, it sounds confining." I respond.

"Not the case anymore, it's the 21st Century, Marty. The cruise ships today are floating full service resorts—anything you want or can imagine, can be had on a cruise. I like the Costa Line myself, smaller ships, super service, great food, top notch entertainment, and great ports of call. I'll give you my travel agents number, she's terrific."

"Thanks, John, I'll keep that in mind," I say swirling the champagne in my flute.

"So John, how did you meet Liz?" I probe.

"Well, my office is on 54th and 6th and every day at around 10:00 a.m., I step out for a little fresh air and cappuccino. There is a Starbucks on 57th and 5th near Trump Tower and I kept seeing this good looking woman there. A month ago, I was behind her in line and she was fumbling in her purse for change when she dropped her bag. I bent down to help her and we "banged heads" like you see in the movies and we laughed and got her stuff picked up and shared a step and a cup of coffee at St. Patrick's—pretty random, huh." He said with a big smile looking over at Liz and Cassidy talking.

"Pretty neat," was all I could say.

"Yep, we've been dating since. She was really nervous about all of us meeting. She says Cassidy is her best friend and it was important she approve."

"That's nice, want to fetch some drinks for the ladies?" I ask.

"Sure, I've got some clients here who I should say hello to." John said.

All I could think of, I kept to myself. I've got some clients here too, but they don't know their dry cleaner is here.

Cassidy and Liz are doing their best "in a deep discussion" not looking around for celebs and dignitaries; the girls just can't let it appear that they could be remotely star struck—that wouldn't be cool at all. While chatting it up, they spy Regis, The Donald, and Giuliani, but they hold no magic for these two. They see them all the time; they are on the lookout for Hollywood stars.

It doesn't take long and over Cassidy's shoulder, Liz spots Samuel L. Jackson looking sharp in a Prada tuxedo with a black Kangool cap turned around. He looks smaller in real life. Cassidy catches Liz's sign and sneaks a peek. While looking around, she notices Carlos on the other end of the bar talking with that Latin woman and some guy who looks like Captain Stubing from the Love Boat. She quickly looks

away; she's not ready for him yet. She out of habit—looks to where
Marty and Liz's lawyer friend are and see that they've left—to the bar
I'm sure, she thinks. Hopefully, they remember us. But as she turns
back to Liz, she sees her husband and Liz's boyfriend shaking hands
with what looks like Christian Slater. She looks again and sure enough,
that's what it is. Hmmmm, she thinks; I wonder what that's all about?
She really looks hard at Marty, because he has been known to say some
odd things to celebrities—like the time he asked Jack Nicholson to say,
"I'd like an egg salad sandwich," the way he did to that waitress in *Five
Easy Pieces*. Nicholson looked at Marty and said, "what the fuck do I
look like? A circus monkey? Go rent the movie!" Marty took offense
and almost took a swing at Jack, but his buddy Walt, broke it up and
hauled Martin off. Another time they were in Elaine's and he saw
Oliver Stone. This was right after he released, *Natural Born Killers* and
Marty was relentless telling him he needs to turn it into a Broadway
musical. Now can you see Mickey and Mallory break out into song?
That's how Oliver felt too and Marty had to stay out of Elaine's for
awhile. That Elaine has got a memory like an elephant and told us that
her place was off limits to Marty until she felt like he'd made amends.
Poor Marty, he so badly wants to be on "the inside." He did her dry
cleaning for free for months before he was allowed back. So Cassidy
had good reason to worry about Marty and celebrities, but hopefully
with John there, he'd behave.

Cassidy pointed out the group to Liz who immediately said, "Let's get over there and meet him; he's probably one of John's clients." So the two striking long-legged women made their way across the room. On the way, Cassidy feels someone grab her arm ever so gently, looking around it's Carlos's.

"My dear, who is your friend and where are you going unescorted?" says Carlos.

"Well hello Carlos, this is my good friend Elizabeth Basker."

"Pleased to meet you Elizabeth, Carlos Ferrar is my name; Ms. Tyroni forgot to tell you." "Pleased to make your acquaintance, "says Liz.

"The pleasure is all mine," he says.

"Carlos is a client Liz, he runs Conserve-Reserve. I sold him his space—one of the finest locations in the city."

"She said that about every space she showed me." Carlos says jokingly.

"Well, I only deal in the finest Carlos. That's why you came to me isn't it?" Cassidy fires back.

"How's business Carlos?"

"Very good, Cassidy, very good," he says confidently.

Just as he says that, a waiter walks up and hands him a fresh drink. The ladies just look when Carlos asks if they'd care for a fresh one.

"No, thank you, my husband is on his way back with one." Cassidy says and looks over to see Martin still talking with John and Christian. "Thank god," she thinks, "this isn't the way she wants them to meet."

"Carlos, will you please excuse us? We were on our way to the powder room. We'll see you at the table; you know which one we're at don't you?"

"Yes, we do and thank you again for the invite. This is a terrific event." Carlos says winking at Cassidy.

"What was with the wink, Cass?" Liz asks as they make their way to Marty and John and "We weren't going to the restroom. Why'd you tell him that?"

"Not now Liz, later I promise." Cassidy says as they get next to their men out of sight from Carlos.

Liz squeezes John lightly around his middle and he turns and says, "Darling, I want you to meet someone—Christian Slater, this is my date, Elizabeth Basker."

"Nice to meet you Elizabeth, be good to John. He's important to me." He says flashing the smile that has made him an icon.

"Oh, don't worry about that, Mr. Slater, he's in good hands." She says kissing John on his cheek and wiping off the lipstick like lovers do.

"Call me Christian, Mr. Slater is my dad's name."

"Okay, Christian—it is then." Liz says.

"Christian this is Cassidy, Martin's wife." John continues.

"Nice seeing you; I love that name Cassidy—is it a family name?" Christian asks.

"Actually, I'm named after my mother's uncle, so I guess yes, it's a family name."

"That's cool," he says, "I guess you've heard that song the Grateful Dead sings called, *Cassidy*—about that guy who Jack Kerouac wrote about?"

"You bet I have, Martin here, is a deadhead and plays it all the time."

"Really," Christian says. "Marty, me too. I've seen lots of shows."

Now I am really having a surreal moment; here I am at a black tie affair talking the "Dead" with Christian Slater.

"Isn't that right?" Cassidy says, looking to me.

"Oh yeah, I dig me some "Dead." We saw them last summer at Jones Beach, even without Jerry, the vibe and the scene is still pretty cool."

"It sure is," Slater says. "I caught them at Red Rocks that same tour and hung out with Bob Weir. We met at some teachings by the Dalai Lama in San Jose a couple of years ago, and hit it off, so he told me if I ever wanted to see a show as his guest, just call him—so I did."

Now I am getting dizzy—Christian Slater, The Grateful Dead and the Dalai Lama—this is fucking awesome!

Before I can say anything, John says, "Ladies we were on our way to get you some cocktails; I'll bet you're thirsty?"

"Now that you mention it, we are," says Liz.

"Christian, we are on a mission; it was good seeing you and maybe we'll chat later, OK?" "You bet, John, Marty, ladies, it was nice meeting you," he says extending Marty his hand.

"That was cool, John. Do you handle lots of movie stars?" Cassidy asks.

"Some. It depends on who you consider a star—to me they're clients. We have a saying—treat the celebs like regular clients, and the regular clients like celebs—both groups like it that way." John remarks.

I nod knowingly. Yep, that's the same thing we say in the dry cleaning business—thinking to myself.

"What'll it be ladies," John says reaching the bar.

"I'll have champagne honey," says Liz.

"Me too," says Cass.

"Well, that's easy, Marty?" asks John.

"Make it three, I say, looking around and hoping to see more celebs so that John can introduce me.

"My good man," says John, "four glasses of your finest champagne."

The bartender barely acknowledging him, wheels and returns with his order. John hands him a ten dollar bill and dispenses the drinks to the group.

With my back to the bar, my field of vision allows me a panoramic view of the event and it's almost breathtaking. A thousand people or so all dressed to kill, looking and being fabulous.

Taking a deep breath I realize how lucky I am; I guess I should feel more gratitude for all I have, but I don't. I guess I am a little affected by stuff. I need to have good stuff; I want my stuff to be better than your stuff, and I can identify with stuff—it validates things. I occasionally have moments like right now, where I think I have all I need—more than my fair share. This comforts me for a time, until I see someone with better stuff. Then I start thinking about my lack of stuff; I get jealous almost, and it's that jealousy that fuels my ideas from time to time. I know that is dangerous and can put me in a place where I shouldn't go, my mind is like a bad neighborhood, you shouldn't go in there alone. If I put my life on a balance sheet, my Profit and Loss statement would certainly have a high profit margin. If I could only hold onto that thinking—"but this too, shall pass," is a saying my grandfather said when things were good and when they were bad—never holding that thought when things were good. I am hard-wired for good times; bad-times and difficulties were things I push aside. Tonight, all is right with me; I am on top of the world, and I can have fun.

Liz turns to Cassidy asking, "Have you seen any of your other guests tonight?"

"You know Liz, I was thinking that myself; I should be looking out for them, shouldn't I?"

"Well, if you want to work, I guess," says Liz, "they're clients aren't they?"

"Yeah, Carlos Ferrar and Calvin Knowles," Cassidy replies.

"You've seen Carlos, he is the financier who I turned onto that amazing Park Avenue space and Calvin, owns two office buildings in Downtown Brooklyn."

"Cassidy, isn't Carlos the guy who has been in the news lately, donating money and that sort of stuff? He's got a PR machine behind him, it feels like."

"Yep, Liz, that's the one and his business, is booming. I can see another couple of pieces of business with him—that's why he's here."

"Calvin is a longtime client and friend. He was one of the first developers to give me exclusives on his building—when I first opened shop for myself. So, he holds a special place in my Rolodex, and he's turned out to be a steady customer."

"It's Carlos, who I need to work tonight some; I want to make sure I'm his agent of choice. After all, he's got to do something with all that money, right?"

"That's my girl. I love to watch your mind work, Cass" says Liz, "and it's always working."

At that moment it happens, Carlos and Milagro walk up. Carlos moves in on Cassidy with a kiss to both cheeks and then reaches over to shake hands with Marty.

"You must be Cassidy's husband. I'm Carlos Ferrar and a big fan of your wife too. She put me in a space that has been very instrumental in our success at Conserve-Reserve—you're a lucky man."

"Thank you, Carlos; it's nice to meet you. The name's Martin. Call me Marty though. I've heard Cassidy mention your name before. It is good to see you," I say eyeballing this guy hard...

"I think you all know Milagro Perdido," Carlos says looking into Milagro's eyes, and then turning to the group.

"Yes, we met once at a fund raiser in Westchester; nice to see you again," Cassidy smiles.

"Carlos, Milagro, this is Liz Basker and John. John, I'm sorry, I forgot your last name."

"It's McDeer; Carlos, Milagro, nice meeting you." John says.

"Great," Carlos says, "now that we all know one another, I'd like to propose a toast to our hostess tonight—to Cassidy, the loveliest broker in town."

"Oh, Carlos, Cassidy says bashfully—thank you."

As the six raised glasses, I can't help but feel a weird vibe here, but I try not to think a whole lot of it, and instead drink to my wife.

"We'll be joined tonight at the table with another couple, Calvin and Jean Knowles. Calvin is a longtime client and friend; I think you all will like them." Cassidy says.

"Well, this is a lovely affair and I want to thank you for inviting us," says Carlos, "any table where you are, is one lucky table, Ms. Tyroni."

Now I am definitely feeling something strange from this guy and I don't dig all the attention he's paying to my wife, but saying and doing anything about it is pretty far from my mind. I can deal with it; I've seen Cassidy's clients gush over her before, but something about Ricky Ricardo here is unsettling. I'm gonna' keep my eye on this one; I might even say something to Cass when the time is right. But then again, I could just be paranoid because I'm a little high...

21

Agent Tedia and Jeremy finally have gotten the door on Sliver's storage shed open and Garrett now has the task of sifting and sorting through the remnants of a man's life. Garrett knows that you can tell a lot about anyone by going through their stuff; what they liked, what they wore, what they listened to—and who else was a part of their life. Garrett was hopeful, but not optimistic about finding anything that might tell him first: why Sliver up and left for NYC and was there anything that could link him back to that bass boat he saw in the video at the paper plant—or who would want to kill him—execution style?

The first thing Garrett notices is all the books this guy had—books on all random topics, from presidential biographies to a bird-watching guide. There must be over 500 books in here he thinks—this job is going to take longer than he thought. After having that thought, he looks back and sees Jeremy picking through some boxes.

"Hey Jeremy, my warrant is for only me; I'm the only one who can be going through Sliver's things, so I'd really appreciate it if you could leave me alone with his belongings."

"Okay, you don't have to get ornery or nothin'" Jeremy says backing away.

"I wasn't gonna' take nothin', I just was going through some photos lookin' for anyone I know."

"Well, that's fine, but I'll have to ask you to leave now. I'll let you know when I'm through here and before you leave, can you give me the key to the lock please?"

"Yes sir, here it is." Jeremy says handing Garrett the key.

"I'll also need you to put those pictures back, okay?"

"Sure thing," says Jeremy placing the photos back where he found them.

"Thanks," says Garrett and watches Jeremy walk away.

Once Jeremy is far enough away, Garrett moves right to the box he was looking at with the photos. Mostly he sees that they are pictures of Sliver with fish— mostly big catfish and sauger. It looks like Sliver liked fishing. He probably had a lot of time on his hands, with all the successful businesses he had going; he probably didn't have to put in many hours. After looking at what feels like hundreds of pictures of a really fat man, with really fat fish, he comes across one with Sliver and a Latin-looking fellow in front of a house boat. Garrett puts that one in his pocket, since it's the only photo he's found with Sliver and another human and continues to dig; looking for more photos that might help him.

After two hours of sifting and looking through another man's stuff, all that Garrett has to show for his search is the photo of Sliver with the Latin guy, who he assumes is the fella that Jeremy spoke of. So he thinks its good time to break for lunch, but first he wants to show Jeremy the picture to confirm his suspicions.

Jeremy is sitting in the office, feet up, watching Maury help a couple find out if their baby belongs to the guy who has been acting like the father.

Jeremy spotting Garrett, takes his feet down saying, "done?"

"For now," he says, "is this the guy you were telling me about this morning?"

"Yep, that's him," Jeremy says with certainty, "those two were together all the time, but like I said, one day he was gone."

"Thanks Jeremy, you've been a big help. I'm gonna go make some calls, grab some lunch, and then I'll be back, okay?"

"Sure, it's a free country," Jeremy says looking insulted that Garrett didn't ask him to help. "Great, maybe I'll see you later then," Garrett says walking out the door. Jeremy turns back to the TV and puts his feet back up on the counter.

Garrett gets into his car and drives down the gravel road till he comes to Highway 57 and takes that back into town. Noticing the lake to his right, he sees plenty of fishermen out there. He thinks maybe some of the guys in the two or three bait shops in town might be able to tell him more about Sliver. But first he needs to get this photo scanned to see if the guys back home can find any more info on Sliver's friend.

Back at the Hampton Inn, Garrett clears some emails, mostly info on some other cases his team is working on and some internal bullshit. He scans the photo and shoots it off to his crime lab for a run through the database to see if he can find out more. The lab confirms receiving the photo and it'll take a few hours before they can get to it. Garrett replies saying, "that'll be fine; call him on his cell if needed."

Garrett heads into town. He's going to The Broken Spoke for one of their famous burgers. He read about in *The Front Porch*, the weekly newspaper that serves the town. He is hungry all of a sudden and a cheeseburger sounds good to him. Plus, the restaurant is the headquarters for the annual Catfish Derby they hold here. They might be able to tell him something about the fat fisherman who landed all those catfish in the pictures.

Pulling into the parking lot, his Taurus is the only sedan in the lot. All the other vehicles are pick-up trucks and SUV's. It's lunchtime and the guys from the plant have taken the place over. As Garrett walks in, everyone turns checking him out. It's a small town. Everyone knows everyone, so a stranger in town is an event. Garrett finds a seat at the bar and grabs a menu that's resting between a sugar dispenser and ketchup bottle. Scanning the menu for the burger section, he finds what he's looking for. He puts the menu back in its resting place and looks for a server. It's but a few minutes, and a woman with jet black hair, piled on her head like a country singer from the seventies, chewing gum, and holding a coffee pot in one hand and a pitcher of iced tea in the other looks at him and says, "Coffee stranger?"

"Please," he says turning the cup in front of him over and places it in the saucer. Like synchronicity, she pours just as his cup is upright, "sugar, cream?" She asks.

"Nope, black is fine, thank you." Garrett responds looking to make eye contact.

"Know whatcha' want?" She asks.

"Yes, I'd like the Spoke burger with American cheese, lettuce, tomatoes, and onions. And can I have some mayo on the side?" He asks.

"How do you want that cooked, hon?" She asks.

"Well done, please." He says.

"That'll work; French fries or coleslaw?"

"Fries please," he says.

"Got it," she says and walks away.

Garrett seeing the name on her nametag—Vivian—perfect he thinks; this woman looks like a Vivian.

Garrett has been observing people for years and has realized that some people look like a certain name and his waitress is a definite, Vivian, or her name could have been Madge or Florence. He wouldn't have been surprised. She had the look—kind of like the saucy waitress in that show, *Alice*, with Linda Lavin years ago. He continues observing the other patrons, starting with the guys on either side of him. The men all seem to have on a flannel shirt, blue jeans, and a baseball cap. Some of them wear caps that look like they are real old, sweat stained and shiny from the years of wear and hard work. They all seem to smoke. Their fingers have nicotine stains and their fingernails have that dirt that never comes out. These are working men with occupations like factory workers, farmers, laborers—men who don't talk about much, but fishin', farmin', football and huntin' and their trucks. Garrett clearly sticks out. He feels the eyes upon him as he gets up to use the bathroom. He checks out the cashier—a woman in her seventies at least. Her face is weathered, sun worn, and she has a cigarette dangling out of her mouth while she rings up someone. "Jesus," he thinks, the restaurant inspectors back home would shut a place like this down in a heartbeat. He sees at least a dozen violations on his way to the can. Everywhere he looks, he sees fishing memorabilia, paraphernalia on the walls, and a few mounted catfish around too. Inside the bathroom, which is a one-person affair, he notices the stains on the bowl from tobacco juice. He is sure that he saw some men chewing in the restaurant too. This place is the real deal. I'll bet the burgers are excellent. Places like this, only do well when the food is good, the prices low, and the service is tolerable. No fancy fine dining for these folks; just good old comfort cooking is what attracts these guys.

Back at the bar, he watches a dozen or so guys finish up and head out. It's beginning to thin out, as the lunch hour draws to a close and the factory guys have to punch back in. This is what Garrett was waiting for. By the time his burger arrives, the restaurant is almost empty—just him and two tables with three people at each. He takes out the picture of Sliver and looks around looking for some pictures on the wall that might show Sliver with one of those big-ass catfish he saw him posing with in the storage shed. Scanning the bar area, he doesn't see any.

Looking down at his burger, he can't get over how big the thing is. The menu said a half-pound, but it looks even bigger. Vivian comes by and asks him, "is everything okay here?"

Garrett looks down and asks, "Can I get some mayo?"

"Oh crap, I'm sorry hon, I forgot. Anything else?"

"No. Maybe some more coffee when you get a chance," he says draining the cup he had. "You bet hon," Vivian says walking back into the kitchen. She comes right back with a squeeze bottle of mayo and the coffee pot.

"This pot's fresh; just brewed it myself," she says pouring it.

Garrett then says, "Are you from around here, Vivian?"

"Sure am; been here all my life, hon." She says sitting on a stool across the bar from him. "Well, that's great. Maybe you can help me then." He says squeezing the mayo on his burger then cutting it in half, so he can manage the monster sandwich.

"How can I help ya'," Vivian says. This might be the most exciting thing that'll happen to her all day, so she's anxious to hear. Garrett bites into the burger and juice, ketchup, and mayo ooze out onto his hands and he reaches down to wipe his mouth when Vivian leans in and wipes it for him. This takes Agent Tedia back some. He puts the sandwich down and thanks her.

"So, how can I help you—cut your meat maybe?" she asks smiling.

Apparently, Garrett thinks, Vivian has a casual moral attitude as well.

Garrett takes the picture out of his shirt pocket and asks, "Do you know the guys in this picture, Vivian?" As he hands her the picture, a guy in a tee-shirt with no sleeves, walks out from the kitchen. He comes up behind Vivian and before she can answer, he sticks his hand out and says, "Howdy feller. You ain't from 'round here are ya'?"

"No, I'm not." Garrett replies.

"Name's Jay, this is my place, how's the burger?"

"Outstanding," is all Garrett says.

"Best burger near a dam site, get it?" asks Jay.

"I do," says Garrett leaning in to another juicy bite.

"We've also got the best sweet tea in Hardin County too," Jay says and smiles.

"I'm sure you do; I'm just not a tea drinker." Garrett says.

"Too bad, this is some fine tea," Jay says pouring himself a glass. Before Jay can speak, Vivian says, "Yeah, I know these guys—it's Sliver and Jose." She says handing the picture to Jay.

"Yep, that's them alright. Shame about Sliver; no one knew where he went. He just up and left, just like Jose did." Jay said handing Garrett back his picture.

"Who's asking anyway?" Vivian says.

"My name is Garrett Tedia and I'm an FBI agent and I'm here looking into Sliver's murder and thought I could find out more about him down here where he was from."

"Well, we wish we could help more, but besides Jose and his mom, God rest her soul, Sliver kept to himself," said Jay.

"And when Jose left, he didn't come around much. Just spent time on the water fishing and counting his money," Vivian added.

"Well, that's the most I've learned about Sliver all day. Do you guys know when Jose left town?" asked Garrett.

"He left about five years before Sliver did; never said nuthin' to nobody. He talked with an accent and helped Sliver at the bank. Then one day we noticed he was gone." Vivian said. "Huh," said

Garrett diving into the other half of his burger. "How did these guys get together? They seem like an odd couple, don't you think?" asked Garrett.

"Well, one day Jose just kind of showed up," said Jay. "Came into town driving a Cadillac and spending money all over; I guess he met Sliver when he was in his bank." Jay said.

"It wasn't too long before Sliver and he started hanging out all the time. Jose lived in a house that Sliver owned near the water and that was that," added Vivian. The two of them spent a lot of time on Sliver's boat," Jay said.

"Did they have a fight or something; any reason for Jose to just up and leave—that you know of?" asked Garrett.

"Naw, who could tell, they kept to themselves. Some of us thought they might be queer. Jose was always dressed up—you know, a "fancy man," said Jay unapprovingly.

"So, they weren't just fishing buddies?" Garrett continued to probe.

"Nope, never saw Jose bring in any fish. He just kind of hung around. We all thought it was weird. Like I said, we thought they might be queer—it was that weird." Jay said.

"Nobody talked to Jose?" Garrett continued.

"Nope, 'round here people don't ask many questions." Vivian answered.

All Garrett could think of was what a great place to hide; no one cares or sticks their noses into other peoples' business; perfect place to lay low.

"Well, that's all I got," says Garrett "thanks for your help. If you can think of anything else, I'm staying at the Hampton Inn. Please call me," and he hands Vivian his card.

"Sure thing," says Vivian, "what about if I can't think of anything, can I call you?"

"Damn," Garrett thinks, "this broad is hitting on him. He's gotta' come 800 miles to have some redneck waitress hit on him—figures.

"If you like, Vivian—if you like," is all he can think to say.

"Maybe I will hon, just be ready."

"They don't call her va-va-Vivian for nuthin' 'round here fella." Jay says with a real dirty smile that creeps Garrett out.

All Garrett can do is smile and ask for his check, pay, and leave.

Well, that was interesting, Garrett thinks, walking out into the sunshine and into his car. He'd better write his lunch finds down on some of his 3x5 cards for his "board of truth."

Once back at his hotel, he stops by the desk and the clerk steps out and says, "Mr. Tedia, I have a fax for you."

That was quick, is what Garrett thinks. He sent in the photo just an hour or so ago; the lab is getting better these days. The clerk hands him the envelope with the fax and Garrett hands him a couple of bucks. "Thank you, sir," the kid says and heads back into the office.

On the elevator, Garrett opens the envelope and reads the fax, *"Call us right now."* It says with the lab's number underlined underneath the bold writing. "Hmmm," he thinks and as he walks into his room, he sees his message light on the phone flashing and notices a new email on his laptop.

Garrett opens his email message and reads: *the guy in the picture with the dead guy is Carlos Ferrar, and he's here in New York City. Call us right away!* Who is Carlos Ferrar? Why is he in NYC and why is his name not Jose? Garrett can't dial the number to the lab fast enough.

22

Carlos and Sliver had the whole thing laid out; once the plates were secured, they knew what they had to do. The first thing they needed would be a pair of quality high speed printers.

Sliver knew that banks were closing all the time and they held auctions for the equipment they no longer would need. These auctions weren't for the general public, only bank owners and manufacturers or dealers of this type of equipment– due to the sensitive nature of equipment like check sorters, security equipment, and high speed printers that big banks used to print money orders, cashiers checks, and wire drafts.

Sliver knew that these printers could be retro-fitted to accommodate the money plates they sought. He also had the clearance necessary to get into one of these auctions and when the First Bank and Trust of Jackson, Tennessee, was liquidating, he saw on the manifest the equipment they needed. Two Holmsberg printers that were purchased by the bank back in 1986 and had been upgraded last year with the necessary technology that would work perfectly, because they still used the drums that the plates would need to be affixed to.

Once the printers were theirs, they needed to get their hands on the paper that was being used for currency today. This was no easy task. Sliver had lived around that paper plant for years and knew just how tight security was. But Sliver also knew that every man has a price, and he'd just have to find out who was "for sale" in the plant.

Carlos would be in charge of securing the plates; he had called Sliver a while back, letting him know that he had someone on the inside at the security firm that designed the Reserve's system. This person programmed the system that the Federal Reserve was using and he'd have the necessary information to disarm the alarms and surveillance equipment. Then he said, "It's a piece of cake from there."

Sliver had no reason to doubt Carlos; he had been impeccable with his word and delivered on every promise that he had ever made to Sliver. He also knew that Carlos was a genius when it came to acquiring information. Carlos knew information was power and that without any inside information, most big jobs never would have worked. Sliver didn't care or want to know how Carlos got his information; just that it was accurate and reliable.

Getting in and stealing enough of the "money trees" was Sliver's job. He had figured that they would need somewhere in the neighborhood of 100 or so trees to get the "party started." Once they had the core pulp from them, they could create synthetic pulp with just a small amount of the real thing; enough pulp to make the precious paper; enough paper to print money for at least two years.

Then there was the ink—that special green and blue ink that our government uses on all paper currency. Once Carlos shared the formula they had stolen Sliver had a line on some in Fort Worth, Texas. He attended a banking seminar years ago, and one of the workshops was on counterfeiting and how to tell the fakes from the real deal. Sliver made friends with the presenter, who is now retired from the Treasury and in Slivers back pocket.

Two years was all the time they needed to print their fortunes. Once printed, getting the money into circulation would be Carlos's job. Once in circulation, the money would make more money—it's true. All it takes is money to make money.

The IRS might have a problem with millions of dollars worth of unreported, untraceable income—just a little problem. So they had talked about the laundering operation for a solid year. It had to be squeaky clean, so clean that you could flaunt the money. After all, who wanted to have wealth without the ability to spend it? So they plotted and planned, creating a fool-proof operation—thus, the birth of the greatest crime happened on the back porch of Jose's, aka, Carlos's cabin in the woods. The two masters of the universe had devised the perfect crime and then the perfect cover-up to enjoy the fruits of their labors. But they had a lot of work in front of them—planning was one thing—

flawless execution was another. They also needed more manpower, but who could they bring in? There were still a lot of questions that needed answering, but they were focused and in time, they'd pull the trigger.

Carlos had to get back to New York. The wheels needed to start turning and there was only so much he could do from Pickwick. Sliver would handle his end, but Carlos's work was in New York and just as quickly as he blew into town, Carlos got in his Cadillac and headed north.

23

Milagro was acting aloof towards me and I liked it that way. I'd be lying if I said I wasn't nervous that she'd be too familiar with me and Cassidy might get some funny ideas. Even though she wouldn't admit it, Cassidy got jealous when another woman gave too much attention to her man.

She didn't like this Milagro for some reason; there was just something about her that she couldn't put her finger on, but give her some time, and she'd find some reason to dislike her.

It was almost time for them to find their table when the three men decided to get one more round from the bar. "Would the ladies like anything too?" They asked.

All three of them said another glass of champagne would be fine. Milagro and Liz had started talking about shoes. Cassidy had a shoe "jones," so the three of them talked about where they shopped, what they wore, and what the other women in attendance were wearing. It didn't take long before they began critiquing the rest of the women, ala, Joan and Melissa Rivers. Milagro fit right in. Liz seemed to like Milagro; they both worked in the same field. Liz was an event planner too, kind of, except she only had one client, MMG Worldwide—a huge conglomerate that held events ranging from Board meetings to product launches and even golf outings. So they knew some of the same people; caterers, multi-media equipment rental folks, and of course, all of the A-List New Yorkers. Theirs was a small world, so it's a wonder they hadn't met before. In any event, Cassidy was happy with the group she'd put together for this evening.

Cassidy did see The Knowles a little while ago, and they stopped and met everyone, but had to run to catch up with some friends of theirs they hadn't seen in quite a while, but would meet them at the table. Cassidy was feeling a little more relaxed while Carlos seemed to be more interested in bonding with her husband and John, than showering her with compliments which was just fine. Sometimes less is more. This was shaping up to be a nice evening, but there was a way to go and the bulk of it lay ahead. Cassidy needed to stay sharp, so this would be her last champagne for a while as she was starting to feel the buzz a little and it was way too early to be loaded. So, it would be water she'd drink after she finished the champagne her husband was off fetching.

"Cassidy, how long have you and Martin been married?" asked Milagro.

"A hundred years." Cass answered. "Marty and I have been together for almost twenty years. What about you and Carlos?" asks Cassidy.

"We're not a couple; we are business partners." Milagro replies.

"Oh really, I just assumed…." Cass stumbles.

"That's okay, it happens all the time. Although we've been working together for so long that it can feel like a marriage, if you know what I mean," says the striking Latin woman.

"What about a boyfriend?" asks Liz?

"Nope, no one in the picture," Milagro says. "I just don't seem to meet the right guys and when I do, they're already married, gay, or spoken for. You two ladies don't know how lucky you are." She says.

"Don't you feel lucky Liz? I sure do!" Cassidy says facetiously.

"Oh yeah, just like a lottery winner," Liz answers.

"Well, we're not making fun of you, Milagro; it's just amazing that a woman with your looks and talent is single." Cassidy says.

"I might have someone for you to meet." Liz adds.

"Oh, thank you Liz." says Milagro "But I have no time for dating these days; I'm just so busy with work that most of my free time, well, isn't free." Milagro smiles at them both, almost seeking approval.

"I know what you mean," adds Cassidy, "a woman has to work twice as hard to get ahead these days—I hear ya'."

"Oh well," says Liz, "all work and no play make Liz a dull girl."

"Liz," says Cass, "you are an anomaly. I've never met anyone who has the gig you do and gets away with as much, or should I say, as little as you do."

"Hey, I resent that remark—here's to me." Liz says, raising her glass.

Like clockwork as the three women turn up their champagne flutes, the men return with fresh drinks.

"Well, I don't know about the rest of you, but the crowd is heading in and I'm getting hungry, so let's find our table and see what else they've got in store for us tonight." Liz says and grabs John by the hand.

"Good idea, Liz." Milagro says "We'll follow you.

And with that, they walk through the ballroom doors into a huge ballroom with 50-foot ceilings that have been transformed into a factory—complete with conveyer belts and big vats that have steam rising from them. The servers are dressed in work jumpsuits and hard hats; the room resembles a steel mill. The tables are rectangular and have four seats to a side, instead of rounds.

I quickly surmise that this is the cafeteria for a steel mill. Pretty clever; I only hope I don't have to get in line to get my food—I hate buffets. But this is Cassidy's night, so you won't hear me complaining. I know that she has no control over the food or the décor, so I will just sit back and make the most of it. Besides, I get to sit across from his Latin dream-woman. So as far as I'm concerned, it's all good!

The crowd is a slow arriving one. So, there is some time to kill, as the people all find their tables. The process is taking longer, as the guests are awestruck by the transformation this ballroom has undergone.

"Isn't this amazing." remarks Liz. "I don't know if I have ever seen such an extensive and elaborate set-up for a function of this size. You really do feel like you are in a factory, except your co-workers are wearing formal attire."

"I think it's cool." I add. "But I can't figure out what that is over there." I say, pointing to the front of the room.

"It looks like a water tower," says Milagro. "But why would you have that here?"

"I don't know." answers Carlos "Maybe it's filled with something."

"I'm sure we'll find out soon enough." John shoots back.

Just then, Mr. and Mrs. Calvin Knowles arrive and everyone re-introduces themselves and they find their seats at the far end next to Liz and John.

"Wow, this is something else." Calvin says. "It looks like an old mill I used to work at when I was a teenager, well, except for the carpeting, the smell, and the noise."

"Well, that's what they were going for, so I'm sure the organizers would love to hear that." Milagro says.

"I am always amazed at the money spent to raise money." Calvin adds.

"Well, if it wasn't fabulous, the fabulous people with the fabulous money would have no desire to come out and support any cause." Cassidy reminds the table.

"Hence the emphasis placed on originality and spectacle," Liz adds.

"I suppose," Calvin shrugs, "I suppose."

As for me I am just looking around, spotting celebrities and dignitaries and taking it all in, when all of a sudden, I feel a little rub on my calf under the table. Now I know Cassidy is next to me and it's not her, so without flinching, I look across the table and Milagro is looking at me with a slight pout. It's about now that a marching band goes off in my head playing, *"seventy-six trombones"* and I make serious eye contact when I feel the rub again. Now I know for sure it's Milagro. I just act cool, like beautiful women do this all the time to me.

But what I don't see is Carlos raising his glass to make a toast. Instead, I act aloof, until Cassidy nudges me and says, "Honey, are you with us?"

Startled from my moment of Zen, I quickly grab and raise my glass while the man across from Cassidy, makes yet another toast to my wife.

Just like clockwork, a server dressed in work duds, brings over the appetizers.

All of a sudden, I have lost my appetite; as I now know that my meeting tomorrow at the store with Milagro has taken on a different feel than before—the type of feel that says this could cost me a lot more than I'm willing to lose.

Just then I decide I need some fresh air and excuse myself, but before I can get away from the table, I notice Milagro asking the other ladies if they need to go to the ladies room. All three decline, so she asks me if she can walk out with me. I turn my head and give Cassidy a quick look, but she is involved in conversation with Carlos and the lawyer, so with out a choice I say, "Sure, I think it's this way."

As we walk out, Milagro locks her arm into mine and says, "Your wife is certainly attractive and successful. You must be very proud."

"I am," I say, as if I made her.

"But I get the feeling she neglects you and let's her business run the house."

"Sometimes," I say. "Things do get busy, but you have to roll with the punches."

"You are a special man Martin. Your wife is very lucky."

By now, they are outside the ballroom and in the pre-function room. "Marty would you be a dear and get me a glass of champagne?"

"Sure. When you come out, I'll be here with your drink. Okay?"

"Why don't you meet me in the lobby and I can have a quick cigarette, OK? Will you join me, Martin?"

"Well, if you insist. I'll be in the lobby." I say with some hesitation, but you can bet I will be in that lobby waiting.

I quickly finish my business, but spend just a little extra time in front of the bathroom mirror. I spritz myself with some Paul Sebastian cologne, pop a mint, give the bathroom attendant a buck, and a wink, and I'm off to the bar for the champagne. I feel a little nervous and anxious. I have dreamed of time with Milagro and now here it is. It's almost surreal, but I remind myself to remain cool and collected. After all, it's just a smoke, right?

Milagro slinks into the lobby where I am waiting with a flute in hand.

"Thank you, Marty. You are so kind."

"Well, it's my pleasure," I say and light her smoke at the same time. "God," I think. This is the sexiest cigarette smoker I have seen.

I just melt, as she drags on the long thin smoke, leaving a lipstick ring on the white filter.

Milagro surveys the lobby, as if she is scanning for a terrorist, but quickly turns her attention back to Marty. "You know, Marty, I have been watching you for some time now."

"You have?" Is all I can stammer.

"Yes, and I think I need to tell you that I am the trouble you've been waiting for."

Now I am absolutely speechless; all I can eek out is, "You are? Didn't know I was looking for trouble."

"Martin," Milagro continues, "I see in you as a man with tremendous potential."

"Phew, Milagro," Martin stammers, "I have been plagued by that word, *potential,* for all of my life. And to hear it come from you, buckles my knees. *Potential,* has been defined to me many times. It means, *you aren't worth a shit to me right now*—at least that was what I heard."

"Well Marty, that's not how I define it." Milagro says. "I see in you, a man with an appetite that hasn't been satisfied."

"Well, Milagro, I don't know about that. I have a full life; a good wife, money in the bank, a nice roof over my head, and a little business that gets me out of the house. Not to mention, a fair stable of friends and acquaintances."

"But Martin, your eyes tell a different story. I want to change your life."

"Why me?" I ask nervously.

"Because you have been put in the right place and I believe in destiny and I think that our lives have intertwined for a reason," Milagro answers and takes a long drag on her cigarette

"Wow that is mind-blowing. Tell me how are you going to change my life? Because if you mean that you'll take me away from my wife and life; I don't want that kind of a change." "Well, it does involve your wife. It does involve taking you away, but it will take you to a place where you have never been." the Latin beauty remarks flicking the cigarette ash.

"But Martin, more will be revealed to you tomorrow, when we meet in your shop. I'm going to leave it at that."

"You can't do that. I need to know now!" I say, getting excited.

"Sorry Martin, my game and my rules. Now, let's get back to the table before Carlos starts looking for me."

"Why would he look for you, Milagro? I thought you were just colleagues."

"Martin, more tomorrow, let's go." And Milagro leads me back to the ballroom.

Stunned and silent I follow; but I can't help but watch that ass slide under the skin-tight gown. Perhaps a change and a little strange will do me good, but Cassidy can't ever get wind of it, that's for sure.

Back at the table, Carlos is holding court. Everything he is talking about and every gesture he makes is all focused on Cassidy. He is almost like a schoolboy looking for her approval at the end of every sentence and punch-line.

Cassidy is eating it up; she is used to attention, but this is fabulous. She feels all eyes are on her and she couldn't feel more beautiful, wanted, and exciting.

Carlos is just finishing this story about a friend of his as Milagro and I take our seats. Seems this guy, a big loveable bear of a man named Chessie, short for Chester, had a dog—a dachshund, an adorable wiener dog. Chessie was going through a divorce and he had been asked to change his address by his soon to be ex. He rented a place in Queens and took the dog with him. Well, it seems Chessie had been having some issues with the plumbing and had asked the building super to fix it. Now the super didn't know about Chessie's dog and when he came in, he saw the food and water bowl and connected the dots. He then saw the dog. Startled, he backed away, forgetting to shut the door and out went Honeymoon—that was the dog's name.

At that time Chessie had been down to the candystore picking up a pack of smokes and some beer when he turned his corner to see a crowd of people around something. Well, you guessed it. Honeymoon had been hit by a car and lay dead on the street. Chessie overcome with grief, pushes the crowd aside, scoops up the pooch and walks the two blocks to his apartment. Confused and distraught, he puts the dog in the building's dumpster in the alleyway, and then goes up to his apartment. Upon walking in, Chessie sees the food and water bowl and starts weeping. After a while, he takes the two bowls down to the dumpster and leaves them outside the receptacle. People leave stuff out all the time. One man's garbage is another man's treasure....and that's that.

Two days have passed and Chessie finally sees his super and is pissed because he figures he must have let the dog out, but he can't be sure. In any event, he confronts the super who claims total ignorance and is insulted by the accusation. Chessie walks away from the irate Puerto Rican and goes up to his apartment.

An hour later, there is a knock on Chessie's door. It's a guy and a girl flashing badges. They want to talk to Chessie about his dog; it seems another tenant was taking out his trash and opened the dumpster to see the dead dog. The tenant is a tree-hugger, PETA-card-holding animal freak. He immediately called the police to report the abused, dead dog, and wants to see the perpetrator suffer as did the dog.

Well, it doesn't take much digging for the cops to identify Chessie as the owner of the dead dog and now they must do their job.

After confirming that the dog is Chessie's, they ask him what happened to the dog. He tells them about the dog getting out and finding him in the gutter and then putting him in the dumpster and later his food and water bowls too. The cops aren't buying today. You see, Chessies crazy neighbor had them do an autopsy on this dog and the autopsy determined that he was killed by a blunt instrument. They all assumed Chessie must have wielded it and beat the animal to death—a felony. With that, Chessie was cuffed, read his rights, and hauled to the station.

Sticking to his story, because it's the truth, Chessie denies the allegations and wants his day in court. He gets his court date and brings his lawyer who is costing him $350.00 an hour and stands before the court as charged. The prosecuting attorney is a rookie Assistant D.A. and a dog lover! Chessie is fucked. His attorney gets a continuance and tries to plea bargain, but the dog-loving D.A. won't hear of it and wants to make an example of Chessie.

You see, Chessie is 6' 2" and 280 pounds. He looks big, tough, and certainly looks the part of a dog beater, but if you knew him you know he wouldn't harm a hair on that dog's head—he loved it so. It was his connection to a happier time before the shit hit the fan in his marriage. Chessie's lawyer tells him that he is going to try for another continuance and maybe the D.A. might get re-assigned—happens all the time with the case load these guys carry.

Chessie agrees, knowing now this whole thing is costing him about two grand and there is a chance of jail time—he just can't believe what's happening to him—he feels cursed.

The lawyer gets the continuance, but the D.A. stays. In the next 30 days, Chessie has to stand trial. Chessie can't believe this. He is so innocent, but can't get anyone to believe him. No one from the scene where Honeymoon was hit is he able to find, and the super won't budge, because he knows it's his fault, and he ain't going down.

Chessie is tried, convicted, and booked. Son of a bitch—got 30 days and a $10 thousand fine! Have you ever heard of something so innocent, turning so bad for someone?

Everyone at the table is shaking their heads—Chatting and figuring ways that Chessie could have avoided it.

Carlos sits back, sips his champagne and watches Cassidy's reaction. She appears overcome with disbelief and just slumps back in her chair and says, "There's nothing but murderers, rapists, and thieves out there and our P.D. spends time and resources hounding ...pardon the pun, some poor grief-stricken man, ruining his life and reputation. Where is Chessie now, Carlos?"

"Well, that's the sad part. Seems he got so depressed, that after he got out of jail, he couldn't find work, because he now had a record. He decided to eat a 9mm, next to the same dumpster he put Honeymoon in." Carlos answered dramatically.

"Oh my god," Liz from across the table says, "Those bastards."

"Yep," nods Carlos. "That's why I hate the cops—nothing but misdirected ball-busters."

"You'll have to excuse me," Carlos says as he is rising from his chair. "I must use the restroom. Does anyone know where it is?"

"I do," says Cassidy. "I can show you. I need to visit too. Ladies, anyone care to join me?" The other two ladies shake their heads no and go back to their meal.

"Well, let us go then," Carlos says, pulling out Cassidy's chair. "Show me the way."

"Such a gentleman, Carlos," Cassidy adds. The two of them walk away from the table heading out of the ballroom.

Cassidy doesn't even grace me with a look.

As Cassidy leads Carlos to the bathrooms, he says he'll wait for her and they can walk back together. Once inside the bathroom, Carlos grabs a stall and takes out the piece of paper folded like origami and spills some of the white powder onto the back of the commode and takes a twenty out of his wallet. Admiring his work, he rolls the bill and snorts the powder he's cut into two neat lines.

He waits outside the ladies room for Cassidy. He sees the statuesque beauty walk out and moves towards her. He then takes her by the arm and they walk away.

241

"I must see you alone this week. I have a business proposition that I think you'll find very attractive." He says.

Cassidy answers, "If it's the building in Red Hook we discussed, I am already working on it."

"Well, it has something to do with the Red Hook spot, but it's not what you think—that I guarantee."

"Carlos, you are a mystery. You explode on the scene and into my life. Now you have even more to reveal. I am not sure it's a good thing for us to be alone. My husband is a jealous man; it may not appear so, but trust me, if Marty finds out we have been meeting alone, even if nothing is happening, he'll go ballistic. I don't want that and trust me, neither do you."

"Who says he'll find out?" Carlos says, with a certain knowing look.

"Well, you'll have to tell me more about this proposition," Cass says. "Why don't we step outside and I can have a smoke and you can talk, okay?"

"If you insist on spoiling my surprise, then so be it." Carlos replies. "Let's go."

Once outside, Cassidy opens her sleek Prada bag and extracts a cigarette. Carlos deftly strikes a match and lights her smoke, looking directly into her eyes. Cassidy gently touches his hand as she draws the first smoke into her lungs.

"So, talk to me Carlos." Cassidy says. "What's so attractive, that we need to meet alone?"

"Well, let me put it like this, I have another business venture that I need your help with; a business that can provide you with more money than you've dreamed of and I know you dream big!"

"Tell me more." Cassidy says. "I'm listening."

"I need someone whom I can trust and I think I can trust you." Carlos adds. "I will have to ask you to sign some paperwork that binds you to me, if you agree to help."

"I don't know, Carlos. This sounds vaguely dangerous, but for some reason, I'm interested. How can I help?"

"Good," Carlos says. "I need you to help me spend my cash. I need tax shelters, real estate, and some legitimate good investments, but you must never ask where the money comes from or ask to meet my partners. Can you do that?"

"I can be discreet when I need to be, Carlos. I am a professional and if my clients want anonymity as some do, I oblige."

"Marvelous!" Carlos says. "Then you'd have no problem signing paperwork that says that then."

"No, Carlos. I wouldn't have a problem with that. I'll sign whatever it is you need me to within reason, so you can rest assured, I will be a good girl." Cassidy says and drags on her cigarette.

"Well, I am sure you are a very good girl, but perhaps I'll get to learn about that too." Carlos says, looking her over and holding his gaze on her chest and perfect legs.

"A very good girl, I'm sure."

"Call my office Monday, Carlos. We'll take a meeting, then I'll review and then perhaps sign your papers and then we'll start spending your money, okay?"

"Let's not get the cart in front of the horse, my dear. We'll take a first meeting, I'll bring paperwork and then, I'll show you my operation and you can then decide if you want to play with me—if you know what I mean—how's that?"

"That works for me, Carlos. I just want to make money and make money for my partners, so what you're saying is *okay* with me." Cassidy says, putting out her smoke.

"Come on, we'd better get back before they start wondering if we fell in."

Back at the table, Carlos gives Milagro a quick wink and goes back to showering Cassidy and her guests with attention and charm.

24

Agent Garrett Tedia is back in his office in New York; has created a timeline with the help of his wall of truth. All roads now leading to one Carlos Ferrar, aka, Jose; however, he can't connect the dots completely. He needs to talk with Mr. Ferrar and ask him why his old friend Sliver is dead.

Sliver had banking connections, possibly enough information to actually print money—if he had stolen plates—but why is Carlos here?

Why is he, Carlos, and not Jose?

Garrett dials Conserve-Reserve, identifying himself and gets transferred to a voicemail. He zeroes out, but still another voicemail. Looks like he is going to have to pay an unannounced visit to Mr. Ferrar, but first, he reviews the document he requested last week. It's the list of employees at the Security Firm that handled the system at the Federal Reserve. It's amazing, that in the last three years, they have had little turnover—an administrative assistant, a few tech-support people, and that's it. Well, the task of interviewing them shouldn't be as bad as he thought. He'll have his support agents conduct the first round and if anything comes up strange, he'll get involved, but he's just doing due diligence. This case he's handling by the book.

The offices on Park Avenue for Conserve-Reserve are impressive to say the least; beautiful artwork adorns the walls, expensive rugs on the floor, and Remington statues all over. Someone really likes cowboys, Garrett thinks, making his way to the receptionist. Garrett asks the stunning redhead behind the desk, if he can see Mr. Ferrar.

"Do you have an appointment?" She asks.

"No, but this is my card." He says flashing the FBI badge in her face. "This should get me a meeting."

"I'll get his assistant; she can help you."

Garrett takes a seat in the soft Natuzzi leather chair. He knows its Natuzzi, because his wife would drive him crazy about the furniture they owned—always making him be careful not to rip or scratch it with his gun holster or spilling stuff on it. God forbid, he could actually enjoy his house and its contents, but good riddance—he's moved on. Well, at least today he has, there are other days when he'll replay the entire marriage over in his head trying to figure out what he could have done to save it.

He notices that the office is busy with lots of couriers coming and going, lots of clients, and lots of constant phone rings. This place is hopping and it's only Monday. No wonder Mr. Ferrar can be so philanthropic; he's got himself a cash cow here—at least to the untrained eye—that's what it appears to be.

Finally, after a good 30 minute wait and two cups of coffee, Carlos appears and introduces himself. Garrett recognizes him immediately from the photo with Sliver in Pickwick.

"How can I help you, Agent Tedia is it?"

"Well, I'd like to ask you a few questions in private, if that's okay?"

"Sure, let's go to my office," Carlos says. "Can I get you anything—water, coffee, or soda?" "No thank you. Your staff has already seen to my hydration." Tedia says with a smile.

"Very well then," Carlos says, "this way to my office."

Garrett has seen plenty of offices in his day, but this office is unrivaled. First of all, it's enormous. It has a conference table that seats at least 18, a sitting area with a couch, two arm chairs, a big screen wall-mounted plasma TV with the Bloomberg network running, a wet-bar and a teak desk with a black leather chair inscribed with a CF—very much like Tony Montana's in *Scarface*—Garrett thinks to himself.

Carlos steers him to the couch while he takes his place in one of the armchairs.

"So, Agent Tedia, we are in private, I assure you. How can I help you?"

"Does the name Kenny Lore ring a bell, Mr. Ferrar?" Garrett asks, waiting for a facial move as well as a verbal response.

"No, I don't think so." Carlos answers.

"What about Sliver, Mr. Ferrar? Does that name mean anything to you?"

"Well, while I was on an extended vacation several years ago, I met a guy named Sliver—a strange nickname I thought for a big guy."

"So, you do know Sliver?"

"Well, "know" is hardly what I'd say, but, 'yes.' We were acquaintances." Carlos says, shifting in his chair.

"So you remember Mr. Lore?"

"If Mr. Lore and Sliver are one in the same, then I do."

"Well, they are one in the same and Sliver was murdered a few weeks ago. Did you know that?" Garrett leans in asking.

"Of course not, why would I?" Carlos says.

"We are checking all angles, Mr. Ferrar. Sliver didn't have many friends in Pickwick, but when we found a photo of you two together, we thought we should contact you." Garrett says. "We found the photo while we were in Pickwick. The people we talked to called you, Jose. Now, why would they do that? Believe me Mr. Ferrar, everyone called you Jose."

"Look at me Agent Tedia, I am Hispanic-looking and Pickwick isn't what I'd call diverse, so of course, they referred to me as Jose. I never had the time nor was it important to me, to correct them, as I was only there for a short time."

"Is two years a short time, Mr. Ferrar?" Garrett now sensing Carlos's discomfort decides to try to corner him.

"Did you know Sliver was in New York City, Carlos?"

"No, I did not and I think this conversation is over, Agent Tedia. I have a very important meeting in five minutes and I must be leaving. If you'd like to talk more, why don't you schedule some time with my assistant." Carlos says buzzing for her.

"If you like, Mr. Ferrar, but I'd prefer if we could continue right now." Garrett says in an official tone.

"I think I made myself clear, Agent. I am late for a meeting." Carlos says, getting up and opening the door to his assistant—a bulldog of a woman, who quickly gathers Garrett's coat and is ready to escort him out.

"Mr. Ferrar, I won't need to schedule an appointment. I believe I'll be back with a warrant and we can continue this downtown in MY office." Garrett says grabbing his coat and walking past the assistant and out of the office.

"Get Oscar on the phone, Lindsey. It sounds like I'll need to talk to my lawyer. Now, be a dear and ring him up. Thanks." Carlos says walking away to pour himself a drink from the bar.

That went just as he suspected it would, Garrett thought. He knew that Carlos would initially deny any connection to Sliver, but he was too smart to lie when there was evidence of their relationship. For the first time, Garrett thinks he might actually have a solid lead or at the very least, a source for answering a few of the questions he has. He also knows that the next meeting with Carlos will be much different. Carlos will have a lawyer and Garrett will have to be very clever—very clever indeed.

25

Johnny Cash is playing in the den, when Cassidy finally comes down from the bedroom. I've already read most of the *Sunday Times* and am on my third cup of coffee and lighting my second cigarette. "Well, good morning sunshine. How did you sleep?"

"Must you be so damn perky?" Cassidy says in a husky voice.

"Why honey, are you a little hung over today?" I say sarcastically.

"I guess I didn't realize how much I was drinking, until we got in the limo coming home. It hit me like a ton of bricks. The last thing I remember is dropping Liz off and then you helping me out of my dress." Cassidy says stealing a smoke from Marty.

"Did I do anything stupid or do anything that I have to apologize for?"

"No, you were fine. I think everyone had a good buzz on, especially Carlos. He was a wired-man and he didn't shut up—one story after another." I add.

"I learned last night he can be pretty random at times; it was hard to follow him sometimes, but no, Cassidy, you have no apologies to make, except to me."

"Why you, Marty" asks Cass, grabbing the real estate section of the paper.

"Well first, you disappeared twice with Carlos and then you left me with Liz—and you know how I feel about that." I say, turning up Johnny Cash singing *Sunday Morning Coming Down.*

"Oh honey, I'm sorry. Carlos wanted to talk business and I promise I won't leave you with Liz again. Forgive me?" Cassidy asks now cozying next to me on the sofa.

"Why don't you come back to bed and we can spoon some more. Whaddaya say, babe?"

"Naw, I'm up now and don't feel like it, another time soon—I promise we'll have a "bed-in" like we used to." this I say while reading the Arts and Leisure section of the Times at the same time.

"Okay, be that way, but it's your loss big boy—your loss." She says kissing my neck.

"Are you hungry, Cass? I can fix some eggs."

"Thanks hon, but my stomach isn't receiving right now—if you know what I mean."

"I do. How about the hair of the dog? You want a Mimosa, bloody mary, or can I interest you in a screwdriver?"

"God no, I am getting nausea just at the thought." She replies.

"Well, I have to go to the store this afternoon. I have some paperwork. I promised Bertha that I'd have it done for her before she opens on Monday. So, I'll be there for a couple of hours. Okay?" I ask, casually hoping that Cassidy will think nothing of it.

"Sure sweetie, that's fine. I can relax, and then cook us some supper. How does that sound?" "Great Cass, I'd love some ravioli in a crème sauce and some sausage. Can you oblige?" I ask.

"If that's what you want, that's what I'll make. Let me check the kitchen and see if I need you to get anything at the market before you leave, because I am not leaving this house today. Hell, I might not even get dressed."

"Cool by me. You deserve a day of nothing. Enjoy!" I say with feeling. This means I'll have no worries about my meeting with Milagro today—no worries, except for what she plans on telling me.

Cassidy walks into the kitchen and checks the freezer, then the pantry. "Marty," she yells, "we need ravioli and a jar of Bertolli. I'm not making the gravy from scratch, okay?"

"No sweat, babe, I'll run out in a little while before I leave and get you set up." I say. "Thanks, and get me some smokes too. I think I smoked all mine last night."

"Okay, give me a few minutes and then I'll run to D'Agostino's." I say while folding the paper. I figure if I jump when she asks, she'll have no reason to question this afternoons meeting. I can't help but be a little paranoid, but the anticipation of Milagro's promise is powerful.

Shutting off the expensive stereo system, I walk to the hall cedar closet and grab my favorite leather jacket, and out the door I go.

Cassidy hearing the door shut, runs to the kitchen window to see Marty walking down the block. She heads up to the bedroom and dumps the contents of her bag onto the bed. Fishing around, she finds what she is looking for—Carlos's cell-phone number. Digging her cell phone out of her briefcase, she dials the number.

"Hello Cassidy, I've been expecting your call." Carlos says with an evil smile in his voice.

"When can I see you Carlos?" Cassidy asks almost desperate.

"How about this afternoon?" Carlos replies.

"Well, I was kind of planning on staying in, Cass says, but if you're ready to talk business, I suppose I can meet you at my office at 4:00 p.m. or so."

"Oh, I'm ready to talk business Cassidy, I'm ready," again with that sly smile in his voice.

"Okay then, my office at 4:00 p.m. today, Carlos." Cassidy says.

"See you then." Carlos says, hanging up.

Always leave them wanting more, Carlos thinks to himself. This is going to be too easy; he smiles as he tightens the silk belt on his Dunhill robe.

26

Milagro is stepping out of the shower, her brown skin glistening in the soft light of her bathroom. She is truly a magnificent specimen of the species, lithe, trim, and proportioned perfectly. Her long brown hair is shining as she begins brushing it out; she is pleased with herself this day. Last night went as planned and today will go equally as smooth. Marty confirmed the meeting an hour ago and he sounded spirited. She just has to get ready and make one stop before meeting him at the shop. He moved the meeting up from 6:00 to 4:30 p.m., but that was fine with her. She could have been ready even earlier; she is fastidious and nimble and always prepared for a change. She already has the booze and mixer on ice for the meeting. She has the fifty-thousand in a briefcase and has reserved a car to pick her up and take her to the dry cleaning shop—as it's not wise to walk down the streets of Manhattan with fifty-thousand dollars in cash. Preparation is the key to success in any operation and Milagro is the queen of planning—that's why she is so good at her day-job.

Milagro goes to her closet. She needs to wear something that will distract Marty; something low cut and tight on the ass, with a serious leg show. She pulls out the Armani dress that she bought last week, knowing that she'd need it for today. First she slides on a powder-blue thong and matching push-up bra. On second thought—no bra. Give him a peek—he is an Italian after all, and they love boobs. Dropping the dress over her head, it slides down fitting her curves perfect as if painted on. The top is revealing enough that any man will be hard-pressed to keep from staring.

She thinks to herself that this is going to be too easy and smiles while admiring herself in the mirror.

Marty decides to stop in The Mixer on his way back from D'Agastino's. Walt opens up after 1:00 p.m. on Sundays. He gets a good crowd during football season and the regulars appreciate him being open.

Walking in, Marty notices four people at the bar and a few tables occupied. Walt is tending bar and his niece is waiting the tables. The kitchen is open and the cook today is only doing burgers and cold sandwiches, so even with a crowd, it's manageable. Besides, it's Sunday. People aren't looking for a bar and grill to deliver too much, at least those who frequent The Mixer.

Walt sees Marty and waves him over to the bar. Pouring Marty an Absolute and Tonic, and says, "Well good afternoon, Mr. Tyroni. What a pleasant surprise and to what do I owe the pleasure?"

"Nothing special, Walt, just a trip to the market for Cass and I. Figured I'd just stop in for a quickie. I've got a meeting at the shop later, so what the hell."

"A meeting on Sunday, what's up with that?" asks Walt.

"Well, I'm doing a favor for a customer and she made me an offer I couldn't refuse." Marty says.

"A *she*, Marty?" Walt asks with a big smile.

"Yes Walt, a *she*, but get your mind out of the gutter, this is business."

"Whatever you say, my name is Walt and I'm gonna halt."

"Cute Walt, cute, but it's really just a quick meeting to discuss a project she is working on and she needs my dryers." Marty says, taking a sip on his drink.

"Needs your dryers, is that what they're calling it today, huh?" Walt says with his back to Marty.

"Let it go Walt; it is what it is."

"What have you been up to, Walt—anything new?" Marty asks looking to change the subject.

"Funny you should ask. You got a minute? I need to talk to you about something, Marty." "Sure, Walt, for you, I got all the time in the world. What's up?"

"Not here. Let's go into the back, okay?" Walt leads Marty back by lifting the end of the bar, so Marty can slip under and go into the back office.

"Okay, spill it Walt, what gives?" asks Marty.

"Well, a few weeks ago, Lee, the Korean shopkeepers' kid, came in here drunk and talking about some trucks that are full of cash making drops at some warehouse in Red Hook. So, I gave him a drink on the house and got the address out of him."

"Wow Walt, do you actually think that some drunken shopkeepers' son could actually know about that?"

"I thought the same thing, but I got a vibe off him and followed up on it. Marty, I sat there on stakeout and the truck came in, just like he said." Walt now was getting excited.

"So did you check the truck for cash?" Marty asked.

"Of course not, but I'm going back this week to see if it happens again like he said it would." "What if it does, Walt? What are you going to do, hijack the truck?"

"Don't be silly, Marty, hijack is a strong word, but perhaps something could happen to that truck and I could put myself in a position to help the driver and myself out."

"What are you thinking, Walt? I see that look in your eyes."

"Nothing really, Marty, until I know that this truck runs on a regular schedule, I can't think anything." Walt says.

"When is the next delivery supposed to be?" Marty asks.

"According to the kid, they come every other Friday, so this Friday should be the day." "What time do these trucks come, if I may ask?" says Marty.

"Well, the last one came in about 2:00 a.m.—nice and quiet down in Red Hook." Walt says with a real sly smile.

"Well, I guess we have nothing more to talk about Walt, until you confirm the delivery this week, right?" Marty says scratching his head.

"Right Marty, but don't tell anyone about this, not even Cass, okay?" Walt asks.

"Sure Walt, you're my bud it's strictly between us." Marty says extending his right hand for a shake. The two men shake hands and head back out to the bar.

I drain my drink so that I can put Walt's crazy story out of my head and before Walt can pour me another, I'm out the door and on my way home.

With D'Agostino bags in hand filled with groceries and cigarettes for Cass, I'm a little nervous. I haven't been alone with a woman in a long time other than Cass and I'm getting such weird signals from this Latin beauty, especially after the little chat last night and the mysterious undertones for today's meeting, I can't help but have what I can only describe as butterflies; before I can think anymore, I'm home.

27

Carlos picks up the phone with the secure line and dials his nephew, Jamie. With Sliver out of the picture, Jamie has been running the operation from the printing, to the warehouse delivery. The operation couldn't be simpler, the Holmsberg printers they had purchased, turned out to be exactly what they needed. Give Sliver credit for that, and the paper he produced, was beyond reproach. Once they retrofitted the printers for the stolen plates, it was a mere matter of getting the ink mixture right and then manually feed the paper and then they were printing money.

"Jamie, its Carlos, are we set for this Friday's delivery?"

"Yes, Carlos. We should have another 25 million loaded and ready for delivery by Thursday, if the printers hold up." Jamie adds.

"What does that mean? Is there a problem?" Carlos asks with concern in his voice.

"Well not really. Number two was making some error prints. The paper wasn't staying lined up and we had to throw away some paper."

"Throw away? You mean incinerate don't you, Jamie?"

"Yes, Uncle Carlos, we burned it." Jamie answers quickly.

"Good. It's the little mistakes and slip-ups that will put us in jail; you do know that young man, don't you?" Carlos says now sounding almost mentor-like.

"Yes, I do. You told me over and over again, to be careful and I am." Jamie responds.

"Well, you'd better; I'm not going away, because of your mistake."

"I promise, Carlos. All is well. The truck will be there Friday night."

"It better," Carlos says and hangs up.

Carlos now feeling just a little uneasy about the exchange decides to call Milagro and check on her.

"Hey," asks Carlos, "are you still on, with the dry cleaner today?"

"Yes, I am. His name is Marty." Milagro fires back.

"I know I was with him last night too." Carlos says.

"Yes, things are all set; he is eager. He moved the meeting up to 4:30 p.m., so I'd say, we are right on track." Milagro answers.

"What about you, Carlos, are you all set?" Milagro asks.

"You bet, honey. This chick is playing right into my hand, so I would say; we'll be on our way as planned."

"Good, because if this doesn't work, we're fucked you know." Milagro says with authority.

"Don't forget whose running this show lady, it's me and I do the ordering, okay?" Carlos fires back.

"Well let's not fight," says Milagro, "we have a lot to do before we are home free."

"You're right, but I just got off the phone with Jamie and he still makes me nervous." Carlos says with an unusual vulnerable tone.

"I told you taking Sliver out wasn't prudent, but you had to do what you wanted." Milagro says in disgust.

"Don't second guess, Milagro, it's unbecoming and unproductive. It's done and we have to play the hand we have. It'll be fine. I just need to stay on top of him." Carlos says, as he picks out a jacket for this afternoon's meeting with Cassidy.

"Okay then, Carlos, stay on top of him and I'll stay on top of things on my end. Sometimes a little nervousness is good, you know." She says seeking approval.

"I hear ya'." With that, he hangs up and focuses on his closet. Maybe I shouldn't wear a jacket he thinks; it's Sunday and maybe, less is more.

28

Garrett Tedia is feeling pretty good; he thinks he saw something in Carlos that might indicate he knows more than he is letting on. It's a hunch, but in the detective business, a hunch is worth plenty.

After leaving Carlos's office, Garrett headed back downtown to his office in the Battery and began gathering the information he'd need to get a warrant to search both Conserve-Reserve and Carlos's apartment. Even though he has the photo and testimony from the folks in Pickwick, he really doesn't have much else, other than Carlos's admitted connection with Sliver, which is completely unrelated to the Reserve heist. His boss is going to really "grill him like a whopper," so he needs to be able to connect the dots for him. Show him the videotape with Sliver's boat at the paper plant, connect that boat to the stolen "money trees" that were never accounted for or retrieved, and then link Carlos to Sliver, via, the photo. He needs to do this before his boss will even let him get near a judge in order to obtain the warrant. If he only had something that was more definite; if he only could find a document or a phone record that would show that Sliver and Carlos communicated, while they were both in New York. If he had the warrant, he could subpoena phone records—business and residential. But he doesn't have the needed evidence, just his hunch, and a judge doesn't give a rat's ass about a detective's hunches.

Garrett's history doesn't give him even the benefit of coming in with incomplete evidence; he'll need to have something really concrete linking the two men. He goes through his notes, reviews his wall of truth, reviews his case file, and knows he doesn't have enough. All he's got is a photo of two guys at a lake and nothing more than some stories from some lake folk that connect the two. Just because Carlos didn't want to cooperate, it isn't a crime. He was well within his rights. He's smart and powerful—heck—he might even have some of the judges as friends or clients. He appears that well connected. Garrett stares out his window, hoping that something will come to him. He notices through the dirty window of his cramped office, a Waste Management truck making a pickup of a dumpster. The truck is making all kinds of noise when the dumpster is dropped back in its place. It's then that Garrett gets an idea. Garbage once out on the curb, is public and can be looked through. It's pretty rude, but not illegal. You hear about the press going through celebrities' garbage all the time, trying to find something juicy that might sell some tabloids. He can also put a tail on Carlos, and follow him for a few days and see who he associates with and what his habits are. Garrett can only think of one guy for the job—someone who always flies under the radar, when he has to—Snuffy.

Snuffy and Garrett have some history; Snuffy used to be a hacker and a crackhead when Garrett first met him. He used Snuffy as a snitch. He was a good informant, reliable and easy to find. Wherever the rock was, you'd find Snuffy. Snuffy ran into some bad luck; he was smoking some rock when his propane gun exploded, burning his face pretty bad. After a couple of months in the burn unit, Snuffy hit the streets, sober and saved. Garrett had turned some recovered addicts onto Snuffy, while he was hospitalized and now Snuffy was clean—full of the spirit and ready to start a new life. Garrett helped him get his P.I. license and because Snuffy was an informant, he had a clean record. Thanks to Garrett, he was able to get his carry permit. Snuffy was in business; a private detective who knew the streets and could navigate his way through any computer operating system.

Garrett had used Snuffy before, when he couldn't use agency resources. Snuffy was forever in Garrett's debt for helping him change his life, so when Garrett asked to meet Snuffy, there was no hesitation. He simply said, when and where.

29

Back home, as I walk into the kitchen with the grocery bags, I begin putting things away. First, I put the ravioli in the fridge, while leaving the jar of cream sauce out near the stove. I then put the French bread loaf on the counter, but before I finish unloading, I tear a hunk of the bread off and shove it into my mouth, just as I look up to see a freshly showered and dressed Cassidy come into the kitchen.

"Hey, don't eat all the bread before dinner." She says while smiling at her hopelessly Italian husband.

"I can't help myself; it's fresh and was calling my name. You want a piece?" I ask while chewing.

"No thanks, hon, my stomach still isn't right from last night," Cassidy says with a frown. "See what happens when you drink too much? I warned you, but no—you had to be a big shot in front of your clients and by the way, don't think I didn't notice the flirting with you and Ricky Ricardo."

Cassidy genuinely surprised says, "His name is Carlos and he can be a bigger client than Martha Stewart was during her heyday. Do you remember the commissions I made getting her operation expansion done? Carlos has that potential. So don't confuse work with flirting, young man. Besides, why would I want hamburger, when I've got steak right here?" She asks, kissing Marty just behind his ear.

"Flattery will get you everywhere, Mrs. Tyroni. Can I show you my sketches upstairs?" Giving her a wink, knowing she'll decline an offer for daylight sex; it just has never been her thing. Cassidy can be traditional when it comes to sex—dark room and at night—that's her M.O.

"Actually sweetie, I'm going to run down to the office and pick up some paperwork. I've decided to work from home tomorrow and if I get a few of the files, I can really knock out some busy work."

"Really," Marty says, "I thought you were housebound today, what happened?"

"I don't know, just some sudden burst of motivation, but I need to hurry so I can get back and cook supper at a reasonable hour, okay?" she says hurriedly.

"Okay, I'll see you when you get back." I say kissing her cheek as she readies to leave.

Five minutes later, I hear the door close and I'm alone. It's 3:30 p.m. and I have some time to kill, before leaving for the Milagro meeting. Still feeling a little uptight, I decide to pour a drink. The drink I had at The Mixer tasted good, so another will taste even better. I fill a tumbler with ice and pull the Absolute out of the Sub-Zero and

One Hour Martin-izing

pour two fingers worth of the clear syrupy liquid and head into the family room for a half hour or so of TV.

Plopping into my favorite chair—a black leather Herman Miller, I turn on the Yankee game and begin fantasizing about what this afternoon might turn out to be. Perhaps there is a chance Milagro was just a little drunk last night when she talked about changing my life, but it still has me wrapped around the axle some. I can only imagine what she meant. It won't be long before I know precisely what she was talking about.

Did you ever notice time sure does move slowly when you want it to go by quickly, and then moves too quickly, when you want to savor the time. It's kind of like wearing a hat all day. While you wear the hat, it doesn't feel like there is anything on your head, but take the hat off, and it still feels like it's hugging your melon—go figure. I can't. That kind of distractional thinking takes my mind off of the clock. Looking at the TV screen, I can see my beloved Yankees coasting with a 10-2 lead over the Orioles, so right now in my world, things are as they should be. I take a good pull on my drink and daydream about Milagro.

Cassidy grabs a cab and heads to her office; she is anxious and nervous like a schoolgirl. She is attracted to this man and she can tell he wants her. Is he worth it, she asks herself? How much money can she make off him? Is it worth risking her marriage? Marty will never

269

find out, and he adores money. Is it a means to an end? She has never felt so dirty.

The cab ride seems to go on forever. "When the hell is this cab driver going to go around this bus," she thinks.

"Hey Mac, I'd like to get to where I'm going today. Can you step on it a little?" She barks.

"Lady, I'm not gonna' risk a ticket for you; we're almost there." He remarks.

Slumping back into her seat, her point made, she looks out the window at the Sunday shoppers on Madison Avenue.

I finish my drink, shut off the TV, and head towards the door. On the way, I hit the bathroom, check my look in the mirror, as I shake the piss off my dick—and I'm off.

Walking down the street, I slide on my Maui Jims and scan the neighborhood like a king looking down from my castle on my subjects. This is my world and these people are just passing through. Turning the corner, I pass a woman walking a great dane. She is long legged, blonde, and striking. I look across the street and see a brunette bending over to grab a *New York Times* from the box, showing me a fine bottom. Straight ahead, a redhead in a mini skirt and black leather boots approaches.

Goddamn! Is it me, or is this city just full of hot chicks—or perhaps it's like when you buy a new car? Before you bought the car, you didn't notice how many other of the same make were out there, but now that you have one, it seems like everyone has one.

I guess I'm just anxious, I have never really contemplated stepping out on Cass and right now, I feel guilty and pretty dirty.

30

Garrett is sitting in a booth, wondering how he is going to spin this job to Snuffy. He needs to make sure he doesn't let Snuffy know the whole deal, but he needs to know enough so he understands how important Carlos is, and how much Garrett needs some intelligence on him.

He's almost afraid to share the possible connection between Carlos, Sliver, and the stolen plates from the Federal Reserve. Even Snuffy might scoff at him and right now, he's working a hunch and it's hard to get others to feel the same. But he feels in his bones, that there is more than meets the eye when it comes to Carlos Ferrar—much more.

Garrett can't afford to be seen with Snuffy right now, because his boss told him specifically—no outside help on this one. So, he asked the ex-informant, crackhead, hacker-extraordinaire, and now, bible-thumper, to meet him at Jeremy's Ale House—a beer garden by the Seaport that is frequented by college students and tourists. Surely, no one there will know Garrett or Snuffy.

He's ordered a pitcher of beer and two glasses. He knows Snuffy doesn't drink, but he doesn't want to draw attention to them at all, so a pitcher is what everyone orders here, because they're students with no money. Garrett tries to blend in. Snuffy comes through the doors and squinting from the sun into dark change, he sees Garrett and heads right to him.

"Hey buddy, how are you?" Snuff asks.

"Just great, my friend, just great," Garret answers.

"Well you look good," Snuffy says, "I mean that in the best possible way, of course." "Thanks. You don't look too bad either; your face has healed nicely, after three years those burns have really faded." Garrett remarks.

"Well, without your help, I would have never been able to get the treatments I received, so it's all because of the grace of God and you." Snuffy says, showing a mouth-full of gold teeth.

"Well, that's nice of you to say so, let's get down to business. I can't hang around. Have a beer." Garrett says pouring and pushing the glass across the table.

"You know I don't drink, Garrett." Snuffy says.

"Yes, I know, but we won't be here long and it's the house special, so just pretend to drink it and listen." Garrett says.

"Okay. Don't get hostile pilgrim—I'm listening." Snuffy says, while eyeballing the agent.

"Good, here's the job." Garrett hands a photo of Carlos to Snuffy.

"See this guy? He lives here." He pushes an address over to Snuffy. "I need you to follow him close for a week. I want to know where he goes, who he's with, how long he stays anywhere, and I want you to go through his garbage too."

"What!" Snuffy says. "Man, I don't do that shit. I have some scruples, you know."

"Since when?" Garrett barks back. "Please help me out and do this. I need you to find me some phone bills and the garbage is where you can start—everyday, too."

"This one's gonna cost you, Tedia." Snuffy says sitting back in the booth.　　　　——————

"You owe me this, Snuffy. I hate bring it up, but I really went out on a limb for you.

"Well, when you remind me like that, I guess you got a point. Okay? I'll tail this guy."

This time, I'll take photos and download them everyday and e-mail you, so you don't have to call me every fifteen fucking minutes, like you did the last time I tailed someone for you." Snuffy says, pouring the beer back into the pitcher with some disdain.

Garrett reaches his hand out and Snuffy looks at it, and then reluctantly shakes with the agent.

"So, we have a deal, right?" Garrett says.

"Deal—I'm your man." Snuffy says.

"You'll hear from me Tuesday. Got it? Don't call me. I'll call you—you got that officer?"

"I hear ya', now, get out of here before someone sees us." Garrett says.

Snuffy rises up and leans down to whisper into Garrett's ear—"Be thankful my brother, that we don't get what we deserve, or you'd be one fucked up cop."

Before Garrett can register and respond, Snuffy's back is to him and out the door.

Garrett hopes Snuffy will find something that'll help Garrett get closer to Carlos.

31

Arriving at my dry cleaning store, gliding on air, I unlock the cage, pushing it to one side, then unlocking the front door locks. I walk in, disarm the security system, and turn on the light. There is just something about being here when it's quiet and closed—like it is right now. The machines are off, the smell is different, and it's cool. No matter what, when the washers and dryers are on, the humidity and temperatures get high and it's uncomfortable. Especially in the back —while up front, I have fans and crank the air conditioning, so the customers don't feel the heat.

I go to the back and turn on the lights in front of the two dryers. Then I make my way to the office, where I turn on the main power switch that controls the washers and dryers.

Milagro did say she needed the dryers—albeit for money.

I check the clock and notice it's twenty-five past four. She'll be here soon. Next, I walk in the bathroom and pee again and check my hair. "God, I get better looking every day. I can't wait till tomorrow," I say to myself, while laughing and just as I am zipping up, I hear the door and her voice.

"Martin, are you here? It's me, Milagro."

"Back here. I'm coming." I say walking out.

"The door looked open, so I walked in." Milagro says. "I think we should lock it. I have a lot of money in here."

Marty looks down and notices her suitcases; two pieces of Hartman luggage.

"Of course," I say, "Give me a minute."

So, I step out, pull the cage closed, and shut the door by turning the two locks.

I turn back to her saying, "We're locked in now," not even thinking about what that really implies.

"Where are the dryers? May I see them?" The Latin beauty says. It's just then, that I really check her out. She's wearing a killer outfit—nice and tight. I can clearly see she's wearing a thong and the cut is low in front, showing a good two inches of cleavage, and man do I love boobs. Her hair is down and her legs are spectacular. I pause for what seems like five minutes, drinking her in and lead her back.

"Here they are," I say. "These babies will hold everything you have in those suitcases, that I assure you."

"Well, I don't think we want to put this in the dryer." She says, pulling out a brown paper bag from the zippered front pouch.

"What's that?" I ask and then realize before she can answer, that it's a bottle of vodka and a plastic bag with ice.

"I promised you a drink—I'm a woman of my word." She says, setting the bottle on the folding table.

"Great! I'll get us some glasses and we can get started—drying the money, that is." I say, as I walk into the break room or the oversized closet that I converted into a break room. There is a refrigerator, a bridge table, three chairs, and an old 13-inch TV mounted on the wall. Opening the cabinets that Walt installed next to the fridge, I pull out two glasses, not matching, but they're clean at least I think—holding them up to the light checking for spots.

"Here we go. It's not Rydel, but these will have to do; I promise they're clean." I say as I put them on the table.

"Oh, Martin, they're fine. No reason to feel formal around me; we're friends right?" Milagro says, as she rips the plastic bag holding the ice and drops some cubes in both glasses. She then pours some vodka into them and puts the bottle down. Milagro hands me a glass and then takes one for her.

"Let's make a toast, Martin. She says while raising her glass. "To you and me. May we live long, love hard, and prosper."

"I'll drink to that," I say taking a long swallow.

"I knew you would," Milagro says. "Now, let's get down to the business at hand."

"Let's do it," I say; "then wait to see if she gets my double entendre."

"Well, I'm sure you didn't forget our chat last night outside the hotel when I said I was going to change your life— you do remember?"

"Of course, I do. Who could forget that?" I say looking at my feet avoiding eye contact.

"First, let's get this money into your machines and we can discuss the meaning of my statement."

"I've got you some Tyvek bags, Milagro. After we fluff this money up, it might not fit in your luggage."

"My, my, my, you are prepared, Marty. May I call you, Marty?" the siren asks.

"I wish you would. All of my friends do." I say, shyly.

"Marty, would you please open the suitcase for me?"

I wheel the suitcase and lay it down in front of the dryers and unzip it all around. I lift the top and find myself staring at five vacuum sealed clear plastic bags, containing what looks like bricks, but I know that's not what it is, because I could tell by the weight.

"Go ahead, Marty, take the bags out." Milagro says.

So I pull out one of the bags and pierce the bag; reach in and pulls out packs of twenty dollar bills—crisp, fresh, and beautiful. The only time I can remember seeing this much cash was in Atlantic City. Cass and I were there on a weekend getaway and some guy cashed in his chips and was handed the cash. Sixty thousand on a silver platter to boot, a nice touch; it was beautiful. Security escorted him to the elevator and that was the last I saw of the lucky gambler.

But these stacks of twenties in front of me, were brand new—I could tell. I have seen what the new twenty looks like. I occasionally get them when I go to the bank to make change or make a deposit.

"There's ten-thousand in each bag. Remember, I said I would bring fifty-thousand?" She smiles and taking a sip of her drink, she gives him a sexy look.

"Yes, you did and here it is. A woman of her word I like that." Marty says, throwing a smile her way.

"Here goes." Marty says, as he breaks the paper seal holding the bills together and separates them while putting them in the dryer. He also puts in a 1 lb. dumbbell wrapped in a towel.

"I use this when someone wants their jeans relaxed. I learned this trick from the guy I got the place from. This should help age the money and fluff it up too."

"Very clever, Marty, I would have never thought of that." Milagro says.

"Well, it's just one of the many things you didn't know about me, Milagro. I'm clever and resourceful."

"Yes, Marty, I can see you are," She says sitting down and crossing those gorgeous legs.

I can almost feel the blood rush between my legs; any performance anxiety I might have had, because I hadn't been with anyone but Cassidy for years— was gone!

I program the dryer for 15 minutes, then hit the power button and the thumping begins. It's almost rhythmic and semi annoying.

"Why don't we go into the back office? We can get some relief from the noise and you can tell me what you had in mind last night when we talked," I say while turning back to Milagro.

"Good idea, again," She says, this time rising from her seat and giving me my first gaze at the ass that could stop a train.

In the office, I offer Milagro the desk chair, but she declines saying, "that's your chair and you look good in it."

She settles into the armchair Bertha put there after she found it on the curb. Again, I am mesmerized watching her cross her legs.

I come back to focus when she says, "Marty, how would you like access to more money than you ever imagined? What do you think?"

"It would be great, and what do you mean by access?" I ask.

"Just that, Martin, Access, whenever you wanted or needed some cash, it would be there." She says licking her lips and pouring some more vodka into both of their glasses.

"Well, that sounds great, but what do I have to do, kill someone?" I laugh.

"No, nothing that dangerous, but it would have some risk." She says.

"Okay, I'm interested. Tell me more." I say, sipping my drink.

"You see Martin, Carlos and I have a business together, that is ready to expand again, and I need to take on a partner."

"Why me?" I ask, "and why now? I'm confused here."

"Of course, you are. I thought we could go over some of the details now and the rest later—at my place."

"Okay, let's start with this business. What kind of business?" I probe.

"You don't need to know about the business, you'll need to help me with the proceeds—the cash."

"You need me to dryer it?"

"No Marty, this job today is a one-time thing. What I need from you is to help me store and transport the proceeds. I trust you. You have a solid life; you don't need to steal from me—at least that's what I think. Am I right, Marty? I can trust you, can't I?" Milagro asks as she's reaching down for her purse and fishes out a cigarette, giving me a good look at her tits.

"Yes, Milagro, I can be trusted, but again, I hardly know you and yet, you want to trust me with your cash, why?"

"Martin, I told you last night, I've been watching you. I watch the way you run this store. I have seen you with your wife more than you know; people trust you."

"Wow, Milagro. I am flattered and blown away, at the same time. What can I say?"

"Say you'll work with me, Marty." Just then she reaches her hand out and places it on my knee. So, do you want to work with me?"

Looking down at her hand and then back at Milagro; I can see she is looking right at my crotch, then into my eyes.

"Yes, I think I want to work with you, I do" I reply growing more confident with each word.

"Good, very good," She says and just then, the buzzer on the dryer goes off, startling us both. We realize what it is and laugh.

"Let's see how our experiment turned out." I say and stand up to walk to the dryers. Milagro gets up at the same time, and blocks my path. She reaches down, grabbing my crotch and says, "I like to experiment, do you?" Before I'm able to say anything, she is shoving her tongue down my throat and reaching around to squeeze my ass.

32

Finally, the cab pulls up in front of Cassidy's building. The cabbie drops the flag and says, "That'll be $13.75."

"Here's fifteen bucks, keep the change." Cassidy says, knowing she's stiffed him, but the ride sucked and he was rude—screw him, she thinks.

Once out of the cab, she lets herself into the front doors of the grey office building, then past the security desk without signing in and down the corridor to the bank of elevators. Hitting the button, she checks herself out in the polished brass doors. She has her hair back, a Brooks Brothers blouse untucked and draped over a skirt—not a mini, but short and tight around her athletic thighs. She has no panty hose and is wearing a pair of high-heeled Ferragamo sandals. Not bad, for a Sunday, she thinks—not bad at all. She wants to look good for Carlos, but she doesn't want it to look like she put a lot of effort into her look.

Hitting the button again, because everyone knows that the more you hit the button, the quicker the elevator appears—right? The bell rings and the doors open to an empty elevator. Cassidy gets in, hits 27 and is on her way. Once on her floor, she quickly takes a left, unlocks and opens the regal double doors to her offices. She disarms the security system and turns on some lights. The florescent overheads make a little hum before illuminating the space. She immediately heads to her office where she does some quick housekeeping. After all, if Carlos wants to talk business, her office should appear impeccable.

She checks the route to her office from the front doors and makes sure that it is lit and clean. Once inside the corner office, she turns on the two Asian lamps that sit on opposite ends of her oversized teak desk. She turns on her computer and checks her messages. Looking up, she realizes its 3:45 p.m. and she has to get back down to the street level to let Carlos in. She gives her office another once over, checks her mini-fridge—it's got a couple of cokes, two bottles of champagne— always have to have some bubbly on hand, so you can celebrate those big deals. Today might be one of those times. Satisfied with her office, she gives the main hallway and reception area another inspection and then leaves the office to get downstairs to wait for her client.

Once inside the elevator that has a mirrored wall, Cassidy gives herself another inspection, pushes her boobs up a little, tucks some hair up, so that it doesn't fall and finally, checks her ass out. She doesn't quite know what to expect this afternoon, but she wants to look good, regardless.

Once on lobby level, she still has a few minutes before Carlos is due to arrive, so she gets out her bathroom key and uses the facilities. She's still got some butterflies, but that is normal she tells herself—completely normal. Walking out of the ladies room, she heads to the main entrance and right on time, she sees a black Mercedes SL500 sedan pull up and a driver gets out and opens the door for Carlos—who looks around before he moves toward the door. He says something to the driver that Cassidy can't hear, his driver, a non-descript black guy in a black suit nods as if to say, I understand. Cassidy is at the door as Carlos walks up; she opens the door and reaches her hand out to shake, and Carlos taking that hand, pulls himself close and kisses her on first her right cheek, and then the left.

"That's the custom in my country, Cassidy. I hope you don't mind?"

"Not at all, I apologize for being so formal. I find customs from other parts of the world interesting and some charming—like this one." She says.

Carlos smiles and quickly positions himself, so he can hold the door for Cassidy.

"Thank you, Carlos. You certainly are a gentleman."

"Don't hold that against me." Carlos says, with a sly smile that Cassidy cannot mistake as a come on.

"No comment. Let's get to my offices," she says, leading Carlos to the elevators.

Pushing the button, Cassidy says, "I appreciate you seeing me today. I'm eager to hear about the business proposal we discussed last night. You have really piqued my curiosity."

"Well, I was happy to get your phone call and am ready to talk business." Carlos replies as he inspects Cassidy from head to toe and letting her see him do it. This makes Cassidy a little uncomfortable, because she is really alone with this guy—no record of her in the building and no one else in the office—just the two of them.

"I hope you are ready to work hard, Cassidy. The opportunity I am about to tell you about, will require a large amount of your time and attention."

"I'm no stranger to hard work; I built this business—all by myself—with sweat, dedication, and knowing I had no one to lean on, but me. All that work created one of the more successful firms in this city, but you knew that. That's why you called me after all." Cassidy says looking forward as the elevator gets to the 27th floor and the doors open. They walk to her office and through the door, she left open. Carlos looks around, noticing they are alone, as he had hoped. He follows the tall blonde to her office, enjoying the view from behind. He smiles to himself, imagining what she'd look like with her ankles behind her head…..he recognizes his primal need for dominance and dismisses it.

"Can I get you anything? I'm afraid I don't have much to offer—some diet Cokes and some bottled water. Or, perhaps you'd like some champagne. I have a bottle in the fridge." She says, wishing she could take that back.

"Ahh—some champagne, sounds great—can I help you with it?" he asks.

"Sure, you can open the bottle; it's in that fridge over there. I'll scare up some clean glasses." Cassidy says, as she points to the fridge and excuses herself to get the glasses from the kitchen.

Alone in the kitchen, she really begins to get nervous. She loved the attention last night and the flirting was fun, but now she is alone with him and not so sure she really was wise in calling him today. She finds some champagne flutes in the dishwasher; she rinses them again, and heads back to her office to find Carlos sitting in her Herman Miller Aeron chair, with his feet on her desk.

"Nice digs, Cassidy. I like your office. When you are done with my project, you will have an office twice this size and a view like no other in Manhattan." Carlos says while smiling. "That's why we're here, so let's get crackin'." Cassidy says, workmanlike.

"First, let's enjoy a drink; I hate to work with a dry mouth, don't you?" Carlos asks, as he pours the amber liquid into the glasses.

"Well now that you mention it Carlos, a drink couldn't hurt." She says, taking the flute as he hands it across the desk. Cassidy feeling a little awkward, because she is on the client side of her desk—a side she is never on. She quickly raises the glass to her lips, when Carlos stops her and says, "A toast—we must toast!"

"Okay Carlos, you do the honors."

"Very well then, may we live long, love hard, and prosper." He says, raising his glass and drinking hungrily.

Cassidy a little taken aback by the "love hard" part says, "Salute," and sips her champagne.

Carlos gets up from behind Cassidy's desk and sits in the chair next to her and crosses his legs.

"I have to tell you, Cassidy, that what I'm about to tell you, must stay in this office. I count on your confidence, discretion, and loyalty," he says.

"You know you have that, Carlos. From the minute you walk into my office as my client, you get that."

"What I need from you, Cassidy, is more than what you give your other clients; I need your connections, your flexibility, and your complete devotion."

"That's quite a lot you're asking for. It's my turn to ask you what's in it for me, Carlos."

"More money than you have ever imagined; more cash than you've ever seen and more freedom than you could have ever thought possible." Carlos says, standing up.

"I'm about to offer you a once in a hundred lifetimes offer."

Cassidy clearly interested, is doing some active listening. She can't help, but think that this is too good to be true and there is a catch. There always is, and he's going to tell me what it is, before I commit to anything.

"So Carlos, why me? There are bigger firms out there; why my shop?"

"Because I have observed you, Cassidy—the way you conduct business; the way you carry yourself—the way you interact with your husband. You're hungry, but it's the type of hunger that can be trusted. It's not the type of blind ambition that clouds judgment. You are what this job calls for—it's that simple, need I say more?"

"If you say so, but until I hear what it is you are proposing, I can't say much now can I?"

"I know, you are at a distinct disadvantage here and I know a woman like you doesn't like that, so it's time for me to unveil my offer." Carlos says, sitting back down and refilling their glasses.

"I am involved in a business that has put me in a position of amazing liquidity and I need to make some investments so that my assets don't become liabilities." He says, looking out the window behind Cassidy's desk.

"How can I help you, Carlos? I'm a little confused here." She asks.

"It's really simple, but you will have to sign some papers, before I can tell you anything more."

"I don't know, Carlos, I don't like to sign anything before having shown it to my attorneys. This is really a problem for me." Cassidy says, getting out of her chair and getting her purse to get a cigarette.

"You don't mind, do you?" She asks as she lights it.

"No, I don't, but what I do mind, is your doubt, your lack of trust. This is for your benefit, as much as it is mine. I have a situation that I want you to help me with, but I must have a written agreement to engage any further. Is this a problem?" Carlos says with intensity.

"A problem? No. I just like to take precautions, because I don't like to be exposed or vulnerable, when I don't have to be." Cassidy says, then sits and sips her champagne, waiting for Carlos's response.

Carlos, now risen and pacing the office, begins to explain: "Once I have a personal services contract signed by you, I will then have the comfort I need to bring you more into the know."

"It almost sounds like you are buying my soul, Carlos, can I at least get 24 hours to review it myself?" Cassidy asks.

"That will be fine. The contract won't mean a thing, if you do exactly what is needed in this venture. It's for my protection, not yours."

"Okay then. When can I see this agreement, so we can start— or should I say, when I can start?" Cassidy asks, while taking a drag on her smoke.

"Oh, my. You are more ferocious than I thought—and I like that." Carlos says, sitting down again while he puts his hand on Cassidy's leg.

"Carlos, I am expensive, but I assure you, I am worth every penny, so let's quit the dance and get down to brass tacks. Show me the agreement and I'll think about letting that hand of yours stay on my leg—got it?" Cassidy now feels in control and looks at Carlos leaning forward putting her hand on top of his and helps him tighten the grip on her leg.

"Cassidy, come to my apartment Wednesday evening for dinner and we'll get started. Is it a date?" The handsome Latin asks.

"Yes, Carlos, it's a date. Send your car to pick me up here at 6:00 p.m. and we can get the ball rolling. Cassidy extends her hand to seal the deal; Carlos stands and gently extends his hand, so Cassidy must rise from her chair. When she does, he pulls her towards him.

"I must go now, Cassidy. Thank you for the time." He says, staring into her eyes.

"Wait, Carlos. One more thing…." Cassidy says, leaning closer towards him, "I expect the same discretion from you. If we are going to have any fun while making all this money, she gently grabs his crotch; I need your cooperation too."

Stepping back a little, and then back in for more, Carlos finds his lips and hips all over the woman holding his cock and future in her hands.

33

I step back, licking my lips tasting Milagro and realizing that I am at a real crossroads here. The woman I've fantasized about is now about to be mine. Well, not yet—I still haven't crossed the line of infidelity. I am standing right on it, but haven't crossed over—if you will. I have never cheated on Cassidy, since we have been married. Although, I have cheated on her in my mind, many times, but I'm not Jimmy Carter, and lusting in my head is not a crime or punishable offense.

Suddenly, Cassidy's image flashes into my head. I see her at her most vulnerable, needing me. I remember when we had no money and all we had was each other. I remember all day "bed-ins." I realize I have a conscience and it pisses me off, because now, I have the dreaded G-word—guilt. Guilt works on me in many ways, and right now, it's taking the fun out of this moment.

However, as I reflect for a millisecond on the guilt and step back from Milagro even further, now wiping my mouth, I hear myself say, "I'll help you, but I can't go any further with this experimenting. I hope you understand?"

"Martin, you surprise me. I thought you'd sleep with me first, and then tell me that, but I now know that you are most suited for the task I am asking of you." The Latin beauty says, as she readjusts herself.

"Milagro, I guess I'm old-fashioned. I love my wife—made a vow in front of people I love, and quite frankly, can't deal with the guilt. I know it sounds silly, but as God is my judge, Milagro, I want you, but if I can't enjoy you "guilt-free," I can't and won't go through with it."

"Martin, I admire you. You have integrity and that is why I want you to help me with my money. Do we have a pact?"

"Yes, Milagro, we have an understanding. Now tell me more."

"Well, I wanted to get your buy-in and now I have it. Let's finish the task at hand here, fluffing and drying the money that is and then later this week, I will explain everything you need to know about my storage and transportation needs. Now refresh my drink, and let's see how the cash in the dryer looks, okay?" She says, handing her drink to Marty.

"Sure Milagro, we can do that." I say, heading towards the dryer.

Both Milagro and I stand in front of the dryer and as I begin to open the door. Milagro says; "You know, Marty, I am going to make you very wealthy. It's too bad you won't be able to tell your wife about your windfall. Have you thought about that?"

"Well, no, but that's a type of guilt I can live with. I know that probably makes no sense to you."

"No, Marty, I do get it. You can provide for your family with this money and that's as good a rationale, as there can be. No one is getting hurt and it's really a victimless crime, so I see your reasoning. Am I right?"

"Yes, I guess you do know me better than I thought." I answer and as I am finishing my reply, I open the dryer door and what seems like a waterfall of twenty dollar bills, spill out.

Milagro reaches down and examines one of the bills. "It's perfect, Marty—worn, but not too worn. It looks like it's been in circulation and it will make the surprise for Carlos feel even more spectacular." She says and kisses me on the cheek.

"Thank you, Marty, you won't regret this arrangement. I promise."

"Great, I'm glad you're happy, because I didn't have a clue how this drying process would work, but I did get some Tyvek bags to hold the bills. The Tyvek won't rip and is lightweight. We use them for hangar storage, so I know it'll work for our purpose today." I say feeling good about my advance thinking.

"Good deal, Marty. Now, let's get this moving. We have four more packs of ten thousand to get done." Milagro, now speaking with the tone of a task-oriented woman, hands me the next pack for the dryer, and she begins stuffing the completed load in the bag. I load the machine— program it for 15 minutes, and get Milagro the drink she asked for.

Alone in my office, I take a deep breath. I feel a little bad about the grab and kiss, but I push that out of my mind, because I know I did the right thing. I just can't get my mind around what Milagro is really asking me to do, but I know I will find out when she's ready and right now, there isn't a law against drying cash. So, I pour the drink and check out my face in the mirror looking for lipstick residue, I'd hate to get caught with lipstick on my face when I walked away from the making "the beast with one back," that would really suck. As I'm walking back, I noticed Milagro is on her cell phone and quickly, as I walk in, she hangs up.

I dismiss it and hand her the drink saying, "You can use the phone in my office, if you want privacy."

"No, Marty, I was just checking messages. No privacy required— besides, we're partners now and I shouldn't keep secrets, should I?" She asks, taking the drink and turning to the dryer. "Why don't we use the other dryer now, Martin, now that we know that this works—we can finish quicker, okay?"

"You bet, I was thinking the same. Let me have another pack and I'll get another ankle weight to help fade and wrinkle." I say as I begin walking back to the office.

About an hour later, Milagro and I are loading the bags of cash into her hired car. She asks me to come with her to her place, to help unload.

"Okay, but can I have your car drop me close to home when we're done?" I ask.

"Of course, now, let's get going. I hate being out here with the cash. I feel exposed." She says, getting in the car.

It's a short ride to Milagro's apartment. The address I knew, because I had written it so many times on her dry cleaning tickets. Once at the building, her driver opens the door and welcomes us home. Milagro tells the driver to pop the trunk; both the driver and I head around the back of the car to unload. I let the driver know I'll handle this load and ask him to wait here as I will be right down.

I realize now I am going to get to see the inside of my dream woman's apartment, but somehow now, after the last couple of hours, it's just that—an apartment—not the scene of a bad mistake. I grab the five bags of cash and follow Milagro into the building and into the elevator.

On the 15th floor, we exit the elevator, Milagro grabs her keys, unlocks the beautiful mahogany door, and says, "Thank you, Marty.

Please leave the bags in the foyer and I'll call you to set up our next meeting this week. Be a dear and sign for me with the driver and tip him 20%, when he drops you off, okay? Have a good night." She says, as she closes the door.

Wow, that felt like the "bums rush," I think but, whatever. I get in the waiting elevator, then into the car and tell the driver to take me to The Mixer.

"I need a drink," I say.

"Very good sir, we'll be there presently. Will you need the car after that?"

"No, my good man," I answer, as I look at the buildings go by.

"I was instructed to sign the paperwork and give you a 20% tip. Can you handle that?"

"Of course sir," the driver replies.

"Good. I want to do that in the car, before I get out, okay?"

"But of course, sir. I'll see to that."

"Thanks," I say and return to my daydream, as the city goes by—wondering just what I have gotten himself into.

34

Snuffy can't stand the smell of garbage. It's not the usual kind of disdain for the smell that an everyday person would have. You see, Snuffy, while he was on the inside, he worked in the cafeteria. He started out at the bottom; washing dishes, garbage detail, cleaning out grease traps, and shit like that. It was those memories—the smell evoked in him.

As he roots through Carlos's garbage, his head is somewhere else, which isn't a good thing, especially when you are supposed to be looking for something and you don't know what you're looking for. Based on the garbage, Snuffy can tell that this guy is a bit of a neat freak. All the garbage bags are neatly tied and not overfilled.

There was a time when Snuffy was married and one of the things he remembered about wife, number one, was her unique talent for piling garbage on top of an already full bag of garbage and balance the shit till he would be reminded about taking out the garbage. For the love of Christ, she could have put it outside the door, just as easy, but no—she would balance that garbage so precariously, that when he would go to close the sack, it would fall all over—coffee grinds, food, and cigarette butts—all over. God, how he hated that!

Back to the task at hand, he picks out some cards from friends and receipts from neighborhood stores. He then takes out food menus and some dry cleaning tickets. Nothing unusual, run of the mill garbage, but if it's got a phone number on it, pull it and bag it for further inspection later has always been his motto.

After 20 minutes or so of garbage picking, Snuffy decides that's enough for today. You don't want to push your luck and have some citizen or your target come out or walk by and start asking questions, so he shoves his take into a plastic Ziploc bag and he's gone.

Garrett knew that getting the warrants to go through Carlos's phone records and set-up surveillance wouldn't be easy, but to make matters worse for him, it seems like Mr. Ferrar has some friends in judge's chambers that are pushing back and asking for more information— before they'll even look at the warrants and subpoena requests. This does not bode well for Agent Tedia. He kind of showed his ass a little bit with Carlos, assuming that he'd have the legal paperwork he needed in 48 hours, but it's been four days since their meeting and no warrant in sight. He can only think that this is giving Carlos a chance to cover his tracks and erase any kind of a paper trail he might have left out there.

Garrett was pissed and the more frustrated he got, the more he felt like throwing chairs and computers out the window. He felt like a car in park and someone was stepping on the gas with no where to go—then the phone rang.

"Tedia here," he answered, "how can I help you?"

"Tedia, it's me, Snuff. I have a present for you. When can we meet?"

Garrett snapped back, "Right now, meet me at The Alpine Tavern on 56th and 7th. You know the place?"

"I sure do. Used to cash my paychecks there a lifetime ago; I can be there in a half an hour." "Great!" Garrett said, "make it 20 and I'll see you there."

Carlos is signing the personal services contract he had his lawyer draw up for him to give Cassidy—this was no different than most contracts used for securing personal services, except that instead of a "morals clause," Carlos inserted a "subordination clause." This stated that at any time, the party involved—Cassidy, if she refused to do what was asked of her by Carlos, he could sever the arrangement and seek damages of no less than $500 million dollars. Pretty steep price for saying no to Carlos, but for what he would be asking of Cassidy, this was essential.

Tonight he would execute this contract and make Cassidy a wealthy woman—too bad she's married. He hates to make a widow of a woman, but he was certain once he initiates the work with Cassidy, the decision will be hers, not Carlos's. He's seen that scenario before and the outcome is never pretty.

Carlos calls his driver to remind him to pick Cassidy up tonight at her office at 6: 00 p.m. He'll have the home court advantage and he always prefers that. He felt powerful in his lair; no woman could refuse him here. He was going to prove that again tonight.

35

I am propped up at the bar in The Mixer, just looking at the Yankee game. There could have been a woman with her top off pitching to Derek Jeter, and my expression wouldn't have changed. I couldn't get my mind around what had just happened today. Focus was hard to come by; I could see the Yankee uniforms on TV, then my mind would wander to Milagro, then back to the Yankees, then to Milagro and then BAM—Walt slams a glass down in front of me and says, "Earth to Marty. Is anybody home? Hey man, snap out of it. What's going on with you? I haven't seen you this distracted in a long time."

I look up at Walt and simply say, "Choices, Walt, it's all about choices, isn't it?"

"Well, Marty, that's quite a profound statement coming from you. I don't mean any disrespect, but I recall a time when you thought everything was already planned and our actions were merely window dressing for pre-determined outcomes."

"Walt," I say tilting my head like a puppy trying to comprehend its owner's orders.

"I'm sure it's the choices we make that determine our fates. I'm sure."

"Okay, Marty; it's me, Walt. What the hell is going on with you?"

"Walt, I'm not sure, but I do know this, that I just made a choice that will change my life, and that's all I can tell you, that's all I will tell you."

"Well in that case, Marty, then I'd have to say in answer to your question, yes. We make certain choices in life that stay with us and if we make those choices with a firm conviction, that usually is an example of our character at work. So you see Marty, you have some character—you're not just a character."

"Yeah, yeah, yeah; another vodka and tonic for the character please," I say and light a smoke.

"What's up with you these days, Walt? I say trying to change subjects.

"Is there anything exciting happening in your life? What's going on with that truck full of money we talked about? Did it come just as you thought?"

Walt looks around the bar as if he was looking for a snoop and says, "Yeah man, it came just like the other one, except it showed up an hour later."

"So what does that mean now?" I ask feigning interest.

"Well, it means that there is something going on over there, but just what it is, I don't know." "Why, may I ask, Walt, are you spinning your wheels on this?"

"Marty, you of all people should know that I'm way over my head in debt, to the bank and to Keith, to my wife, and to five different credit card companies and that is just what I owe. Then factor in what my overhead to live is and I'm ready for bankruptcy. It eats at me every day and it's threatening my sobriety. That's why, Marty, I have to hang on to my hunch that there might be a big score here that could change everything for me. I still dream of giving back—to help others—the treatment center in the mountains. That's my destiny and this may be the path.

"Well, now that you know the schedule, what is your next step?" again feigning interest.

"Honestly, Marty, I don't have a clue. I think I'm just going to stake out these deliveries for a while longer to check out the whole operation. I have a bunch of questions that need to be answered, before I can even think about a way to get on the inside."

"Till then, Walt, keep me posted. I mean a score for you is a score for me." Marty says with a smirk.

"You bet, Marty. I can't share this with my AA sponsor, so you by default become my sounding board on this one—like it or not."

"Cool." I say and return to the game with my smoke and my drink. As soon as Walt answers the phone and walks away, I am back to thinking about Milagro.

Just then, my cell-phone rings and it's Cassidy, my caller ID tells me. I hold the phone away from my ear and give it a funny look—like I got busted for thinking about another woman, but I remind myself I can't get in trouble for thinking. It's my actions that will get me in trouble.

"Hey babe, what's up?" I say, "Sure, I'm on my way home now."

That's right, I think, with all that went down this afternoon, I forgot she was going in to the office today. She always says I don't listen—maybe she's right

Milagro is dialing Carlos's phone number, while she stares at the sacks of money in her living room.

"Hello, Carlos. Yes, I know." She pauses while he rambles, "I know. I'm still working on it. Then why don't *you* try to find a place then, to "rough up" fifty grand? Maybe I should take it to a Laundromat." She says into the receiver sarcastically.

"Thank you, Carlos. I appreciate your confidence in me." Milagro is now regretting this call.

The intent of her call was to make him think she *hadn't* taken care of the fifty grand yet,

"Yes, I promise. By weeks end—if I find a solution. Can I begin to take a regular amount out, when I've treated the cash and start circulating it here and there?"

Obviously, Carlos is distracted, because she has asked him this question before and each time he's flatly refused.

This time he says, "We'll see."

"Really?" Milagro responds.

"Yes, really. Now I have to go." This is the last thing he says and then click—he's gone.

That went better than she thought it would. He seemed to buy her story. Carlos *might* let her make a move or two on her own. This decidedly was a good call—a very good call.

I settle my bill for the drinks with Walt, who shakes my hand saying, "I'll keep you in the loop, my friend, be well."

"Thanks, Walt, you too," I say and head out the door into that color blue— dusk the color it gets, just before the night comes on. Looking both ways before I cross the street, I head home thinking that I can't tell Cassidy about this afternoon. She won't understand and she'll want to get involved. I can't let that happen—at least not yet.

Putting the key in the door, I turn the lock and I'm in. All of the stuff for supper is out, the stereo is still on, and going upstairs, I see that the TV in the bedroom was left on. Walking downstairs, I see a note on the fridge that says, *had to run into the office—should be home by 8:00 p.m. Love you-- C.*

I begin to realize I'm being paranoid because of what happened to me today and that it's all okay right now. I shouldn't read anything into Cassidy going to the office on a Sunday—nothing.

So I begin doing some of the prep work for supper. I guess I feel guilty and need to do something that will help me feel better about today's clandestine meeting, so I stay busy in the kitchen.

About 20 minutes later, Cassidy comes bouncing into the kitchen, grabs Marty's ass and kisses the nape of his neck.

"Wow, you're in a great mood, what gives?" I ask, as I lean into her kiss.

"Nothing. Isn't it okay if I want to kiss my husband on the neck?" She says pouty-faced.

"Well of course, Mrs. Tyroni. It's perfectly natural to kiss your husband. How about some more love for your man?"

"Don't push it, sailor." Cassidy says and dips some bread into the gravy that I have simmering on the stove.

"So, what did you need at the office that got you in there on a Sunday?" I ask almost ashamed of myself for asking, but I can't help it.

"Nothing, really—just a contract that needed to be reviewed and made ready for a Monday morning meeting. Now that it's done, I don't have to go in tomorrow, if I don't feel like it"

"Oh, you couldn't send someone, *you* had to get it?" I say with some attitude.

Now I knew I had done it—why would I accuse, when it's me who has misbehaved? I could see the look—I had now ventured into "look land"—that dreaded place where a husband goes when his wife just can't believe what she is hearing him say and what he's insinuating.

"What's that supposed to mean, Marty?" Cassidy says now hands on her hips. That loving wife that was once in the kitchen is gone and I know my mouth is what made her go away. My wife is like a sports car; she can go from happy to pissed-off in seconds flat!

"I didn't mean anything. It's just that you never go in on a Sunday. I figured it would have to have been something special, to get you there—that's all." I say, almost backing away and focusing on the sausage now sizzling in the frying pan.

"Well, I'll have you know *every* contract I execute is something special, so there it is, Marty. A contract—satisfied!" Cassidy says and storms out of the kitchen.

"You sure are a buzz kill, Marty, now I don't feel like eating." Next thing I hear is the bedroom door slam.

"Shit!—I think to myself—why couldn't I keep my big mouth shut? It's not like I'm squeaky clean here. I should have just left things as they were. She was happy. I was confused and we were going to eat ravioli—at least until I opened my mouth. What an idiot.

36

Garrett walks into the Alpine Tavern and almost immediately, the smell of stale beer and cigarettes hits his nostrils. He looks around and sees no sign of Snuffy, but then again, he's early. He lucked out and hailed a cab that seemingly caught all the lights heading uptown. In New York City, it's a funny thing. You can look up any avenue running south to north and see the sequencing of the stop lights. It's like a string of Christmas lights; they just turn green, one after another and if you are with a cabbie that sees this; his speed, will be dictated by the turning of the lights. It's really a cool thing that usually happens in the wee hours of the morning when your lit and it makes you feel like the King of New York—all the lights are turning green in your honor.

He finds a booth with a view of the front door, so he can see Snuffy, when he walks in. But just as he gets settled in, a waitress with a pile of hair almost a foot high, a short skirt and some serious cans says, " I'm Wendy, what'll it be?" She says this while chewing a piece of gum like a gangster from those black and white movies that Garrett used to watch on Saturday mornings.

"How about getting me a club soda, Wendy?" Garrett says.

"That's it? A club soda?" Wendy replies.

"Yes, just a club soda. I'm waiting on somebody." Garrett answers.

"Oh, I see, you'll order more then?"

"Look Wendy, if this is going to be a problem, I can move into another section." Garrett looks into Wendy's eyes and says.

"Hey, that's your call. For all I care, you can get your *club soda* from the bar yourself." Wendy says with some serious attitude.

"You know what, Wendy? That sounds great. Why don't I do that?" Garrett visibly pissed says, as he gets up and goes to the bar to get his club soda and a Coke for his soon-to–be-here associate.

Wendy looks at him and says, "Cheap jerk. Go fuck yourself!"

Well, it's good to see that none of the charm is gone out of the Alpine Tavern and its staff. Garrett thinks to himself.

Finally, after 10 minutes that seemed like an hour, Snuffy comes walking through the door. "Where you been? Garrett says as he points at his watch. "Have a soda on me."

"Thanks, Agent Tedia. Good to see you too." Snuffy says and lights a smoke.

"What have you got for me?" Garrett asks.

"Some receipts from around the neighborhood, take out menus, dry cleaning tickets, and stuff like that. They all have a phone number; I figured you could make some calls."

"You don't need to do any figuring; just gather information for me and I'll do all the figuring, okay?"

"Jesus, Garrett, who pissed in your cereal today?" Snuffy says as he hands the Ziploc baggie to the agent.

"Don't you worry about me; I'm just under a little pressure. Nothing I can't handle. Maybe the contents of this bag will help," Garrett says.

"What else have you got for me, Snuffy?" Garrett asks "Photos, license plate numbers—anything like that?"

"No, man, not yet I just got this stuff today, so cool your jets, I don't want to get pinched, do ya' dig?" Snuffy says draining his Coke as he stubs out his smoke.

"I hear ya', but I need info on this guy. Can you step up your efforts?" Garrett asks. "I'll make it worth your while."

"How are you gonna' do that, Tedia?"

How do you know what my while is worth?" Snuffy adds lowering his head between his shoulders like a vulture does when sitting and waiting on its next road kill.

"Trust me, Snuffy. I can come up with more funds if you come up with some real evidence for me, do we have a deal?"

"Sure, Tedia, We have a deal. How about you wet my beak for now?"

"Here's a hundred bucks," Garrett says as he peels away five twenties, "Now go find me something on this guy and be quick about it." Snuffy just grabs the cash, sticks out his hand, and after Garrett shakes it, he's gone. Garrett's eyes follow him out and he sees Snuffy chat with Wendy on his way out.

Garrett finishes his soda and tucks the Ziploc in his coat and heads out the door. It's then that Wendy says as he walks by her, "Even your friend thinks you're an asshole."

"Great," is all Tedia can think, I'm out trying to catch the bad guys and I have to take this shit from a piece of dirt like Wendy. Smiling at the gum chewing, bad hair, slutty-looking waitress, Garrett makes a mental note. No more meetings here, even for New York, this place is rude.

Back in his office, Garrett has all the contents of the baggie displayed out on his desk, and all he can see is garbage. Snuffy was right. Nothing here that can help, but he still has to do his due diligence, and he starts by calling the number for Meltzy's Dry Cleaning and One Hour Martinizing®.

"Hello, this is Agent Garrett Tedia with the FBI and I'd like to speak with your manager." "Well, I'm the manager," she says; "this is Bertha. How can I help you, Agent Tedia—was it?"

"Yes, that's right; I'm just doing some routine follow-up, maam. Can you tell me if you have a customer named, Carlos Ferrar? The name doesn't click in Bertha's head right away, but after a minute or so, she remembers that was the name of that guy who dropped off clothes using Milagros' phone number and then came in asking about the dry cleaning business.

Bertha is a simple woman with very little demands out of life and the next words out of her mouth, even Bertha, couldn't believe. "No, Agent, I don't think so. I know all of our customers. You must have the wrong dry cleaner." She says with a completely deadpan face and voice.

"Well in that case, I'm sorry I bothered you, Bertha." Garrett answers.

"No problem. Glad to help." Bertha says.

"If you do remember, you will call me, won't you?"

"Sure Agent, just leave me your number and I'll check with the other workers here." "Bertha," Garrett asks, "do you have a database or list of customers I could look at."

"Agent Tedia, we don't keep track of names—it's phone numbers we use. We use the last four digits of a clients number as an identifier. We don't keep any records like you are looking for." Bertha replies.

"Very well then," Garrett answers, "Can I call you back, if I have any other questions?" "Sure, but I hate to waste your time." Bertha now piling it on says.

"Well, I appreciate that, I really do." Garrett says and then hangs up.

Garrett looks at the two dry cleaning tickets Snuffy retrieved and scratches his head.

37

I am carefully measuring my thoughts; when I can focus, I have some amazing powers of observation. Right now, however, my head is filled with two things—money and Milagro. How can this be happening? The woman who is a main character in many of my sex fantasies is offering untold wealth? How can this be true? I need to get some proof that what she is saying, is for real.

Jerry Garcia put it aptly, "*when life looks like easy street, there is danger at your door;*" those lyrics have rung true many times for me. I have learned that when things seem to be going my way, I need to be on "extra alert," because when good fortune comes knocking, I have a tendency to let my guard down. It's then, when I am prone to mistakes. Mistakes that could cost me that good fortune I was pre-maturely rewarding myself for. This, I know to be true from first-hand experience.

Today, certainly will go down as a day I will never forget, but it's not over yet. Cassidy comes downstairs looking somewhat remorseful for her momentary rage. This means, or at least using my amazing powers of observation, that I might get lucky tonight. I still feel a little "randy" after my encounter with Milagro today. Sometimes Cass and

I aren't on the same wavelength sexually, when I want it. She doesn't or maybe I'm tired and she is all over me like "white on rice." Then I'll have to "phone-in" the sex energy, but that is what marriage is all about—putting your needs and wants behind those of your spouse and if your spouse does that, then it works. It's when one of the partners doesn't see the need to acquiesce to the other; that is when conflicts kick in.

That's never been a problem for me, since I'm a little codependent. Cassidy is pretty good about it too. I can recognize when Cass is giving in to me. After all our time together, I pretty much know what she likes to do and doesn't, so when she is saying, "yes" to something I want to do, that I know she doesn't like, that's when I smile on the inside. I know there is no greater act of love than that.

I love my life and don't want some silly scheme to screw things up. Both Cassidy and I work hard at this relationship and when something is working, why monkey with it? That's the "human condition," again, even when I know how good I've got it, I still tinker and tweak—always thinking I can make it better. Can I be mistaking happiness with boredom?

38

Carlos knows he is dangerously close to realizing his dream; he has his "money-making" operation in full swing with his nephew at the helm of the operation. He thinks he can carry on the operation for at least one more year. Right now, they are printing close to a pallet of twenties a day. That's roughly three million dollars every three days. His goal was a billion, but that's greedy. He'd have to stay in full tilt mode for three years and now with the FBI sniffing around, he doesn't think he has the team or the luck to run that long.

Right now besides him, Milagro and Jamie, the operation team consists of four Peruvian immigrants handling the actual printing. They have been threatened by the death of their loved ones back home, if they violate the work agreement Carlos contracted for them. So far, they have been good, hard workers; fear does a good job of motivating people.

Sliver had a tractor trailer customized, so it could accommodate the printers, the copier, and the count machines, along with a good supply of the raw materials needed to make the legal tender. This way, the operation was always mobile, a real stroke of genius. Too bad Sliver got sloppy, he had come in handy, planning and executing this enterprise, but business is business. The warehouse in Red Hook was Carlos's own private Fort Knox. The money was beginning to move into the local and international economy with no problems. The plates, the ink, and paper were all the real deal, so the only variable was the manufacturing process. That part they had down pat; it was the transporting of the finished product to the warehouse, then getting the cash into circulation that kept Carlos awake at nights.

The truck with the cash made the delivery into Red Hook every two weeks—early in the morning at different times, so not to attract attention. The delivery truck picked up its load from a different location every time. This way, no pattern could be determined by any pain-in-the-ass "lookey-looks." The Peruvians who drove the truck and loaded it, operated out of fear, so they performed exactly as told. For intimidation purposes, Carlos had to cut the tongue out of one of them, because the Peruvian asked Carlos a question he didn't want to answer. Carlos made quite a show as he removed the tongue slowly in front of the others. There was no doubt in their minds, he meant business and so they followed orders—no more questions—their families were safe and Carlos sent money home, as long as they did as they were told.

Getting large amounts of cash into circulation is where Cassidy comes in. Carlos plans on buying real estate and other assets, so he can in turn, sell them for a hefty profit. Turn his millions into billions, in a relatively short time, with Cassidy's contacts and instincts—he'll be able to pick up commercial real estate under the radar. She'll also be able to find him investment partners from her extensive clientele; some old and new money folks who would rather make money, than talk about it. That's who he was looking for—a tight-lipped, well-heeled partner, who can maybe lend some legitimacy to his fortune—Conserve-Reserve was a start, but he'd need more money-laundering vehicles and Cassidy was the key to a big one.

The next morning, all that Cassidy can think about, is that Monday mornings suck. She thought that once she owned her own business, Mondays would take on a different feel, but no. Mondays still suck. Probably because most everything else on the planet gets back to work on Mondays.

Cassidy knew that she'd have a busy day so her little white lie to Marty about taking the day off might be what is what is making "throwing the covers off and spinning to put her feet on the floor," so difficult today. She has a 10:00 a.m. staff meeting, then a lunch with Liz, and in the afternoon, she thought she'd do a little investigating on Carlos and Milagro. She hated to feel vulnerable and right now that's how she feels. At least until she meets again with Carlos. So she needs to stay busy, so her insecurity won't get the best of her. She also had to come up with a story for Marty before she announces she'll be at a business dinner later this week, knowing how jealous Marty is and especially after his little outburst yesterday, she thought it would be best to not tell him that it's with Carlos.

With all that on her mind, she spills out of the bed to see that Marty is already up. She smells the coffee as she throws on her robe, brushes her teeth, and takes her meds. She takes a little blood pressure medication as of late. With a family history of hypertension, an ounce of prevention is worth a pound of cure, is her motto. After that little routine, she makes her way downstairs.

Looking up from my paper I say, "Hey baby, did you sleep well?"

"You bet I did, lover. I always sleep the sleep of the dead, after we do the "wild-thing," you know that." She replies kissing me on the head and sitting next to me in the teak Adirondack chair we bought while on vacation in the Pocono's.

"Well, I thought you slept well, but I never can tell. Besides, I know you never really sleep well on Sunday nights."

"Aren't you the thoughtful man, but no matter how hard I try, Mondays just seem to feel the same—icky, but necessary," Cassidy answers, sipping the hot coffee with both hands on the mug, as if warming them.

"Speaking of Monday's, I say I'm going into the store around 10:00 a.m. today. We'll be busy taking in the weekend's dirty clothes. Bertha needs me as Cheech can't make it in today."

"How come at 10:00 a.m. and not sooner?" Cassidy asks.

"I am the owner; I must keep up appearances you know."

"You are so full of it; I have never met someone who thought they were as special as you, Martin Tyroni."

"Well, like I say, I may not be much, but I'm all I think about!" I shoot back returning my attention to the paper, looking at the sports section.

"Yes, Marty. You are indeed not much. I couldn't be more in love with you." Cassidy says, as she makes her way inside, "I'm gonna start getting ready; I'll come out and see you before I leave." Cassidy says, closing the door.

"Uh-huh." I grunt to no one there.

39

Walt rolls out of bed and hits the alarm clock. He knows it's 7:15 a.m. and he has an 8:00 a.m. AA meeting today. As usual, he contemplates not going, but as usual, he remembers how he felt before he got sober. That's all the motivation he needs. Alcohol and drugs kicked his ass and he tried everything he knew to do, to kick on his own, and nothing worked. Finally, he asked for help. Asking for help is hard for a man like Walt. He grew up in a family where when the going got tough, you sucked it up and worked it out or worked through it, but he was out of schemes then. The life had finally caught up with him. He called the only person he knew who would be sympathetic— Marty. Marty carted him to rehab in upstate Elmira and came every other weekend to check on his friend, bringing him cigarettes, books, and news from home. It was that experience in the treatment center that gave him the inspiration for wanting to run his own center, a place where healing happened every day—a place where a person could change their ways—a place where second- and third-chances began.

Walt reaches for his watch, slides into a pair of jeans, pulls a T-shirt over his head, and heads into the kitchen of the one-bedroom apartment he is close to being evicted from.

There, he pours a cup of coffee out of his dirty coffee pot; he knows he needs to clean it, but he keeps saying tomorrow. Besides, he thinks it tastes, okay. It's not like he's hosting breakfast every morning. As a matter of fact, it's been quite a while since he had a date or even sex, so the coffee pot is just fine, thank you very much.

Walt has had the delivery schedule to that warehouse in Red Hook on his mind all weekend. This Friday, if his schedule was right, there is another delivery. Walt has seen three deliveries now and the truck enters the warehouse at times ranging from 1:00 a.m. to 4:00 a.m. He thinks this Friday he'll make his move, but he'll need help.

The only person he could trust and who might help was his boy, Marty. They had done some crazy stuff back in the day, but holding up a truck, early in the morning in Red Hook, would be the craziest one; but he might go for it—he just might.

40

Bertha gets the store open at 7:00 a.m., so that the folks, who start work at 8:00 or 9:00 a.m., can get their clothes in for same day service on the way to the subway or to hailing a cab.

Have your dirty laundry in by 8:00 a.m. and we'll have it back to you by 5:00 p.m.—that's their promise.

This Monday, she knew would be different than the ordinary Mondays, because her first drop off was from none other than, Carlos Ferrar.

"Good morning, Bertha, it's Bertha, right?" He says.

"Yes, and you are Carlos Ferrar, right?" Bertha answers.

"Yes it is. I need this back today. Is that possible?" Bertha points to the sign-In by 8:00 a.m., back to you by 5:00 p.m.

"Great," Carlos says, "I also want to thank you for your time the other day. But I have another question for you."

"Ask away." Bertha says.

"Who did you get your dryers from? I think we could use one of those in the workout facility we are opening at our office," Carlos asks.

"Sure. We got these two from Temple Equipment in Queens; let me get you their number—hold on." Bertha says and heads to the office where she jots the number down and returns to the counter.

"Here you go. Ask for Keith when you call, and tell him we know one another. He'll give you his best price the first time, no haggling."

"Thanks so much. I appreciate your help. If I can return the favor, let me know." He says as he tucks the number into his breast pocket and leaves the store.

Carlos figures if Milagro can't get that money "roughed and ready" he'll show her how it's done with his own dryer. He could ask the Peruvians to do it before they band the twenties; besides, it's one more precautionary tactic. Milagro can sometimes be careless and with victory so close, Carlos doesn't want to let anyone or anything spoil his plan.

Carlos didn't sleep well last night. Perhaps, it was because he got teased by Cassidy and didn't get to close the deal. But he knows their next meeting will be here soon enough and until then, maybe tonight he'll order in. Did he feel like a blonde or a brunette? He'll have to give Madame Clara a call and see what's in her stable tonight. Carlos gets what he wants and tonight he needs to scratch his itch!

Agent Tedia has been getting in his office before 8:00 a.m. every day, since he started working this Federal Reserve case. He needed to show the brass that he was capable of running a major operation and being visible was key. Even if he was just shuffling papers around, he needed them to see that he was working.

He was looking at his "Wall of Truth" and the only dot he had connected was Sliver to Carlos. He knew that if he could connect the security firm murder to Carlos or to Sliver, that would bring him another step closer, but he had nothing. As a matter of fact, he had less than nothing. Only a hunch, and last time he checked a hunch, he got nothing—just frustrated.

He feels pretty good about his theory that Sliver stole the money trees. He also knew that Carlos and Sliver understood banking and money. He knew Carlos had a lot of money lately. He knew Sliver was murdered. He didn't know how they stole the plates; he didn't know where the money was printed, and he didn't know where the money was kept or how it was being moved around. Basically, he knew very little.

Snuff's garbage picking duty was getting Garrett just that—garbage. This Ferrar guy was very careful but Tedia knew like all criminal minds, they had a tendency to over think things and when they over think, they make a mistake. He was waiting for the mistake, but it didn't seem to be in sight. Garrett needed a break... he was running out of time. If he didn't have a solid lead in a few weeks, he'd be taken off as the lead agent on the case—standard operating procedure. If you didn't come up with anything in 180 days, another set of eyes were called in, and you went to the back of the line after you download what you don't have to the next agent in charge. Garrett had been at the back of the line for a while, and he didn't like it there, so he had to find something. He just had to. Maybe, it was time to play hardball with Carlos. Maybe Garrett could find a chink in his armor. He had one idea left, but he needed to get those phone records in order to carry out this last gasp effort. Dialing the phone, he jots some names on a pad. "Yes, Carlos Ferrar, please. Thank you." In a matter of seconds he hears, "Mr. Ferrar's office, this is Lindsey. How can I help you?"

"Lindsey, this is Agent Garrett Tedia, with the FBI. I was in your offices last week."

"Yes, I remember, Mr. Tedia. How can I help you?" Lindsey said very cold and businesslike. "I need to see Mr. Ferrar this Thursday. Does he have the time?"

"Well, let me see. I need to put you on hold for a moment, okay?"

"Yes, Lindsey, that'll be fine. I need you to tell Mr. Ferrar that I should have a warrant by then, and won't need an appointment, but because I'm such a nice guy, I am making an appointment."

"Very well, sir, just a moment." Lindsey said and before he knew, it Garrett was subjected to an infomercial on hold.

In two minutes, which seemed like eternity to Garrett, he hears Lindsey's voice, "Is 3:00 p.m. okay, Agent Tedia? Carlos can see you then."

"Yes, Lindsey, 3:00 p.m., Thursday will be perfect." Garrett answers.

"Then it's set. We'll see you at 3:00 p.m. this Thursday."

"See you then, Lindsey." Garrett says and hangs up. Game on, he thinks, but he has a lot to do before Thursday. Time waits for no one and he starts dialing again. This time, he is calling a friend, a friend who owes him a favor.

"Records, this is Monty, how can I help you?" "Monty, it's Garrett Tedia—I need a favor. I need some phone records, but I don't have a warrant. Can you help a brother out, my friend?"

"Can we talk it out over lunch?" He asks, "I'm in the middle of something right now, can you meet me at the Blarney Stone at 1:00 p.m.?"

"Sure, Monty, I'll see you there." Garrett says and hangs up.

A year ago, Garrett was working an identity theft ring in the Bronx, when he found out that one of the perps was Monty's kid. Garrett gave Monty the information because the kid had no priors and he was able to help Monty get his kid out of trouble. Monty won't hesitate when Garrett calls in the marker. Garrett knew that would be the case, so he had to choose the favor carefully—and this was the one.

The only problem Garrett had was that any information he would get from Monty, could not be used in court or to obtain a warrant as the information was gathered without the use of proper channels. But Garrett had to take the chance; he had no choice. Sometimes getting caught in the gears of the machine was necessary and Garrett was grinding right now. He had till Thursday to get what he needed to ask for a warrant and he hoped the phone records would be the thing. If he could find some calls to Sliver or anything that might link him to the Reserve Heist or Sliver's murder from those records, he might have the break he needed. Then again, he could come away with nothing and then what? He couldn't think about that now, he had to get busy.

The next challenge for Garrett was to get either the home phone number of Carlos or better yet, his cell phone. So far, the only thing Snuffy was able to dig out was a couple of dry cleaning bills and that's when it hit him. There were four digits on those bills and didn't the dry cleaner say they used the last four digits of the customers' phone numbers as an identifier. All Garrett had to do was figure what the first three numbers of that phone number are and he'd have something for Monty to look up.

He first checked and made sure that the four numbers didn't correspond with Conserve-Reserve, which was a good sign. He knew where the guy lived. If this was a home phone, he'd ask his friend at New York Telephone, what three-digit exchanges might be within that address area. Then, it would be good ole' fashioned detective work he'd have to do and by process of elimination, he might find the number that he was looking for.

An hour later, he had an Excel spreadsheet with 125 possible exchanges for that address. This was going to be a long morning; he got more coffee and shut his door and began dialing.

"Carlos, please." Garrett said, "Oh, I'm sorry. I must have the wrong number. Excuse me, please." He dialed the next number and asked the same question; got the same answer and moved through the list scratching off the phone number as he hung up.

41

I sensed that today was going to be busy in the store, so I poured a third cup of coffee. Whether this was to get some more caffeine in me or maybe I just wanted to prolong the time before going into work, in any event, I settled in with my third cup and lit a smoke.

I keep thinking about the meeting with Milagro. I wonder just how much money she's talking about. Will it be enough to start living like the "idle rich?" I have always loved that term; I wanted to be one of the "idle rich." Maybe this was my chance.

I have always felt destined for greatness, but deep down, I really wasn't willing to work for it. I wanted all that went with it, except the actual work. I knew this was a character flaw and that no one gets that kind of life handed to him unless they happen to be a member of the lucky sperm club, but for some reason I still had a feeling that this might be the ship I'd been waiting for to come in. How could I find out how much money she was really talking about? I'd need proof—fifty thousand was nice, and it had been a long time since I'd seen that much cash, but I needed more than that. I guess I have to ask Milagro for a round figure. Man, did she have a figure, I thought, but never mind that, she was only testing me. I have to move past that, this was business I thought to myself, just like Sonny Corleone said to his brother Michael in The Godfather.

The next thought I had was how would I keep this from Cassidy? If it were a real score, why couldn't I tell her? She was good about keeping secrets. Would she be mad because I didn't tell her up-front, sure, but once she saw the money and started to spend some of it, that would pass. I hoped that would be the case, but I wasn't sure.

The paper had been read and I'd finished my coffee. Now, I had no more distractions to keep me from getting down to the store. But first I had to take a shower and dress. I could hear Cassidy on the phone confirming her Monday morning staff meeting with her assistant, and letting her know she'd be there in about 30 minutes, I could also hear some *Grateful Dead* coming from the bedroom. I remember that Cassidy had never even laid ears on the *Dead*, until she met me and when I took her to her first show, she went absolutely berserk and fell in love with the scene and the music. When the show was over, she looked at me and asked where the next show was. She was hooked. Now, she was as devout as any Deadhead.

I could hear the tune *Sugar Magnolia* playing as I walked in; she was singing along with Bob Weir and applying eyeliner. I'm always amazed at the things women can do at the same time like drive and talk on the phone while putting on make up and smoking, and of course, mess with their hair. For some reason, I thought that was a god-given talent. I have trouble changing the station on the radio and driving, but then again, I was always a little less, shall we say—dexterous than most. I blamed it on my short, fat fingers. I have smallish hands and hate it. Whenever someone would refer to the age-old myth about dick size, and its relationship to how big your hands were, I always tried to say that they were wrong—it was feet (mine are a size 12) or hide my hands. My manhood was average, and I always wondered whether it was big enough. I guess I watched too many porn movies where the guys have those ridiculously monster "wangs," and thought mine should be that big. In any event, I smiled, watching my wife do her makeup to the sounds of Bobby singing and Jerry picking. Life was okay. I shouldn't want more than this, but it's that "human-condition" and my desire for "more" creeping in.

"Hey, babe, you look great this morning." I say.

"Thanks. Aren't you sweet," Cass coos back. "I have a day full of meetings," she adds, "and I need to be sharp today. I have to remember to not schedule such a heavy Monday. You know how I despise Mondays."

"Yes, I do, but just think you are one day closer to Friday."

"It'll be busy at the store too," I add.

Just as I step up to my side of the vanity to start the ritual of brushing, flossing, shaving, Cassidy asks, "Are you really happy, babe?"

"What do you mean, happy, you have to elaborate, honey?" I ask.

"I guess I mean do you have any regrets?"

"Well, a few little ones but who doesn't, but the big decisions I made like marrying you, living here, that kind of stuff—not at all; why?" I ask.

"No reason just curious, I mean. Wouldn't you rather be on some island in the Caribbean selling sandals and just watching sunsets and tourists covered in oil?"

"Well, I don't know about the tourist part or selling sandals, but the islands always have a primal pull for me. But I know our work here is the means to that end some day. Sure, we could sell everything, cash in and move to one of those little islands that our government doesn't pay attention to and live tax-free, but is now the time?" I ask.

"You are right, honey," Cassidy responds, "I guess I'm just in a Monday mood.

"I tell you what sweetie, I say, I'll pick up the latest Robb Report and we can look at those dream homes in dream locales and figure out our getaway tonight. How does that sound?"

"Can we over a bottle of wine? You can get two copies so that we can go back and forth." She says, doing her final primp.

"You got it, babe that sounds like a plan." I say, applying shaving cream.

"Good. I'll see you tonight around 7:00 p.m. What do you want to do about dinner?" she asks.

"I'll surprise you, okay?" I say.

"Cool. I can't wait," she says giving me an "air kiss" as she walks out.

I quickly think to myself that was a funny exchange; it's usually me who is dreaming longingly of retirement on some island, not Cass. Maybe telling her about this Milagro money, won't be as much of an issue as I'm making it out to be. This might just work out. Of course, I'd have to find the right time. It's been my experience that whenever delivering any serious news—good or bad—you need the right setting. For example, bad news, I usually delivered in a public place. This way, a violent reaction could be prevented. Cass did have some restraint. Very good news on the other hand, I liked to deliver in front of others too, it pumped my ego up, and I got "props" from everyone. But this type of news I'd have to deliver alone with her, because she'd have questions and I'd have some serious explaining to do.

But before I did any sharing, I needed to know just how much money Milagro was talking about?

Once I got to the store, all I could see is pile after pile of clothes. This morning was a big take; sorting and bagging will take till after lunch. Bertha had already got the same day stuff out and now, I would help tackle the rest. I ask Bertha if there were any calls for me and she said just one—from your Latin girlfriend. That was quick, I thought, but maybe I could use this opportunity to find out what my next step was. Just how much money was she talking about—I had to know.

Shutting the door to my office, I dial the number. I also commit the number to my desk blotter which is my unofficial calendar, rolodex, and PDA. I like to think I am "high-touch, not high-tech." I despise those handheld devices. People look so dependant on them and I have a skill for losing expensive things like sunglasses, cell-phones, and gadgets. Investing in a slick PDA, just didn't compute.

Milagro answers, "Milagro Perdido. How can I help you?"

"Milagro, it's me, Marty. You called?"

"Martin, so good to hear back from you, I have to change our plans. We need to accelerate things, so I need to see you today after lunch. Can we meet in front of Bloomingdale's at 2:00 p.m.?"

"Sure, Milagro, I can be there, but I have a question," he gets out.

"Yes, Martin, ask away." Milagro says.

"Well, we never discussed just how much this largesse was. Can you give me a ball-park amount?"

"Martin, I'd rather we discuss that in person. Two p.m., in front of Bloomies, okay?"

"Okay, but will you tell me then?" I ask.

"Yes, Marty. I will show and tell you, how's that?"

"That'll be fine, you know I was just asking, so I…"

Cutting me off, she says, "Two p.m. See you then." She hangs up.

Looking at the receiver I wonder—am I getting myself into something I will regret? Probably, but I am already past "go" and as they say, *in for a penny in for a pound*. Hell, I have waited this long for my ship to come in, so a few more hours would have to be okay.

Thinking just that I look at the clock and it say its 10:24 a.m., this was going to be a long morning. Now back in the work area, I begin sorting—men's shirts, women's blouses, and so on, stay busy and it'll be 2:00 p.m. soon.

Cassidy gets into her office, listens to her voicemail, sorts through the mail, and jots some notes down for staff meeting. She will have to mention to the team that she needs a list of every agent's listings and sales prospects. If she is going to commit time to work with Carlos exclusively, she needed to know what was going on with the rest of her operation. So in case this Carlos thing was a bust, she'd know what she had to fall back on. That's why finding out how much money Carlos was talking about, is critical.

The staff meeting was uneventful; everyone had a full plate and that made Cassidy feel good. She needed to keep the rest of the team busy, as they always were looking to her to see what her next big deal would be and right now, she didn't know what that was. She told them this morning she was prospecting, which meant she had nothing.

Even though she knew that Carlos wanted to see her at 6:00 p.m. on Wednesday, she needed answers now. She looked in her PDA and retrieved his number from her directory. She loved this particular PDA she had had some duds in the past, as long as her assistant would download the information she needed, it was great. If Cassidy had to do that, it would never get used. In any event, she dials the number.

"Conserve-Reserve, may I help you?" the perky receptionist says.

"Yes, Carlos Ferrar, please." Cassidy answers.

"Thank you, I'll connect you to his office." She says and the ringing begins.

"Carlos Ferrar's office, this is Lindsey how can I help you?"

"Is Carlos available?" Cassidy asks.

"He's not in right now; who may I say is calling?"

"It's Cassidy Tyroni. Can you have him call me? It's urgent."

"I'll let him know, Ms. Tyroni."

"Do you think it'll be within the next hour?" Cassidy asks.

"I would think so, but I can't guarantee it, Ms. Tyroni."

"Okay thank you Lindsey." Cassidy says, hanging up.

Twenty minutes later, the phone in Cassidy's office rings.

"Cassidy Tyroni, how can I help you?"

"You rang." The caller says.

Cassidy recognizes Carlos's voice. "Yes, I did. I have a big question, Carlos. I was thinking about this contract signing and I need to know, really need to know, just how much money are you talking about? Also, I'll need some proof of the amount. I have been hung out to dry before, based on promises or should I say, delusions of grandeur and this girl is too old to learn that lesson again."

"Oh my, Cassidy, you are the shark. You must be the type who needs to see it, touch it, and play with it. Are you?" He says, knowing full well that there is a double intandre there. "Look, Carlos, I don't have time for games. How much and can you give me proof?"

"Very well then," he says, "Meet me tomorrow for breakfast, 9:00 a.m. at the Clocktower Restaurant in the Marriott Marquis. I'll show you what you need to see, okay?"

"That'll be fine. Thank you for indulging me, but I just needed….."

"See you then, Cassidy." He says cutting her off and hanging up.

She looks at the phone as she hangs up. She spins, looking uptown, thinking, "How can I tell Marty about this?"

She also realizes that she is leading this Latin developer on and she really doesn't want to go through with everything that he is surely thinking. She wonders will this contract of his have a sex clause. Will she have to sleep with him to get what he says is this great prize? After all, she did grab his crotch and give him that idea. Maybe that was a mistake, but she knows that was what he wanted. She'd rather be in the driver's seat, than be pursued. Heck, one kiss and one squeeze, a commitment doesn't make, but she was sure he was thinking otherwise. Perhaps if the money was really all that big, maybe a courtesy fuck was in order. She hated to put a price on herself like that, but everyone has one.

She pushes back from the desk and leans forward as if she was listening intently to the noise that the city street was pumping out; but all she could think of was how hurt, how mad, and how crazy Marty would be if he ever found out. He certainly wouldn't understand that she HAD to sleep with Carlos to get the money they needed to realize their dreams. That just wouldn't fly. She loved Marty down to the very fibers in his soul and she didn't want to hurt him. He was a lazy man, but a good husband, who put up with a lot. He was a kind and compassionate dreamer that she knew she was lucky to have. Most of their friends were divorced and she didn't want to be among that number. Maybe she shouldn't do this at all. However, she was too smart and perhaps greedy to make that decision before hearing how much money was at stake, and what it would take to get it? She could wait one more day; she'd have to. There was no other choice. With that, her phone rang, she was certain it was Liz confirming lunch as she could recognize her number on the caller ID read out. Cassidy certainly couldn't say anything to Liz about this, so she had to cancel on Liz. She would be too tempted to tell her what she was up to. So she made her assistant cancel Liz; Cassidy was called into a meeting and would have to reschedule, is what the assistant told Cassidy's friend. Cassidy knew this was the right thing; the fewer who knew, the better. Heck, if she and Marty were going to slide off into the Caribbean sunset, they'd have to be extremely discreet, that she knew for sure.

42

Walt is opening up the bar for the day. He opens at 11:00 a.m. He knows he could do business earlier, but he didn't want to enable any alcoholics. They are usually the only folks who "need" a drink in the morning and he certainly could feel their pain, but he didn't need to look at their pain. Shit, he had enough issues and enabling others, didn't need to be added to the list.

He was hoping Marty would come by since he usually does on a Monday afternoon. Walt knows Monday is busy at Marty's store and that Marty liked a couple pops before heading home to the Mrs.

Today, he decided was the day he would tell Marty about his plan. Walt has a customer who sells equipment and the like, to dentists. This customer had always boasted of having access to chloroform and how he would one day use it on his wife, to shut her up.

Walt figured that he and Marty could sneak up on the truck driver and then hit him with a shot of chloroform. That would incapacitate him. The two would then drive the truck to this remote area he knew was safe; he had been to a couple of AA retreats there. It was just outside Huntington, on the island. Once there, they would unload the trucks contents into Marty's van. They would then leave the truck and drive away as a couple of rich guys.

Walt had done his homework. He'd seen no one trailing the truck. He knew the driver had a cell-phone, because they always made a call and then gained entrance to the warehouse. They'd have to move quickly, because whoever was on the receiving end of that call would be looking for the truck. Walt and Marty would have to be done in minutes. It could work; he played it out over and over again in his mind, trying to account for everything—every possible scenario. He thought he was prepared. Now he'd just need to get Marty on board. If Marty wasn't willing, he'd have to go it alone—drive the truck and download the money himself.

I was clockwatching when the phone rang. It rang three times before I realized no one else was picking up. "Hello, Meltzy's, Marty speaking."

"Hello. May I speak with the owner, please?"

"This is he, who's calling?"

"This is Agent Garrett Tedia, with the FBI. I had called earlier and spoke with Bertha and wanted to double check something. To whom am I speaking?"

"This is Martin Tyroni. Agent Tedia, was it?" I ask.

"Yes, Mr. Tyroni. I called checking to see if you have a customer named, Carlos Ferrar. I was told by Bertha that you couldn't share that information, because you didn't keep those kinds of records."

"Well, why do you want to know?" I asked.

"I can't tell you that, sir, but it is important and I'd rather not have to get a warrant to go through your records. We might just find something that the IRS would want to know," Tedia said sharply.

"Are you threatening me, Agent?" I asked.

"Not at all, Mr. Tyroni, but time is of the essence and if I had your cooperation, this could be over quickly." Garrett answered.

"Well, how do I know you are an agent and not someone looking for something else?" I said with some attitude.

"Good question, sir. How about I stop by this afternoon and we can discuss your customer privacy policy?" Garrett suggests.

"I'll be here at 4:00 p.m. today. Come by the store and ask for Marty, okay?"

"Okay, Mr. Tyroni. We'll see you at 4:00 p.m." Garrett says, hanging up.

Now I am feeling weird. I know Milagro said she and Carlos had a successful thing that had afforded them amazing liquidity. Could it be an illegal operation and was the FBI on to them? I also wondered if I could be implicated if I didn't cooperate. I thought about calling my lawyer, but I thought that would make me appear guilty—if I had a lawyer there while the FBI was asking for what seemed like harmless information. I just had to wait; this was another question I had for Milagro.

Garrett had made about 50 inquiries with no luck. He decided to ask the dry cleaner once more if they knew Carlos and his phone number. He knew using phone numbers was a common practice in these smaller shops, because people always lost their tickets but seldom forgot their phone number. Lots of small businesses use this as an easy identification practice.

"Hello, is Carlos there? So sorry, I must have the wrong number." Another crossed off exchange; this was getting old. He hoped this Tyroni guy would cooperate, because he had no way in hell of getting the warrant he threatened him with. Hopefully, his badge and some tough talk would get it done.

43

Milagro fished around in the ornate lock box for the photo she needed to settle Marty's mind and prove she was talking about serious money, rather than whatever amount his small mind might think of.

There it was. She looked at it and smiled. Carlos took this photo last month to make a point and she kept the photo. It was a Polaroid of Carlos holding up a newspaper with the date visible while behind him in plain view, were pallet after pallet of cash, stacked on top of one another. Each pallet she knew had three million in twenties on it, and from the looks of the photo, there were more than 300 million dollars visible. This should assuage Marty and actually, this photo made Milagro feel good too.

What didn't make her feel good was the way Carlos had been treating her lately. She felt of less and less use to him; she knew his pattern. When Carlos was through with you—you tend to disappear. This operation was coming to a close and Milagro had been instrumental in getting the security codes for the Federal Reserve. She was a good PR person for his business, but getting her share of the take from Carlos each month was becoming increasingly difficult. She had to now ask, when before, the money was wired into her accounts on and off shore without fail. This was troubling. She could read the writing on the wall and she wasn't going to be another statistic of Carlos's greed. She'd seen what happened to Sliver and knew that she was probably next. That would leave only Carlos, his nephew, and all that money. Milagro was going to get her share. But she needed Marty; she needed his help, his van, and his discretion. She knew he could be bought. Marty was perfect—aloof, trusting, greedy, and a little slow on the uptake. He would help for a few hundred thousand initially and the promise of more to come and then Milagro would slide under the radar far away with enough to live out her days comfortably. Carlos would look for her, but she knew how to stay gone. He wouldn't miss the money for a while, he'd miss her first. Then he'd conduct a count and put the two together, but she'd be long gone. She smiled, knowing this will work. It was drawing close to 2 p.m.; she put the photo in an envelope and placed it in her black Prada handbag, then readied for her meeting.

Sometimes it's not what you are thinking or what your intentions are, but it's your actions that define you. Nobody has ever been judged by their intentions. Too bad, because right now my intentions are really good, but unfortunately the reality is, that the actions required to achieve said goodness, aren't so good. It was Gordon Gecko who said greed is good, but that was easy for him to say—his greed paid off. I, on the other hand, knew my greed wasn't good and that I would be taking the risk of a lifetime to satisfy that greed, but I couldn't stop thinking about the money.

A few hundred grand would do me nicely to start; it would allow me to feel more in control. I said earlier that I never begrudged Cassidy for all of her success and money that went with it. I certainly got my share and then some. But if by chance, I could deliver a tidy sum to the family coffers—well it might give me a little more shall we say, "swagger." Or maybe I would keep it to myself; I could always say that business was really good. I could use a new car, just the other day my friend, Vinnie, had said he could get me an amazing deal on a used Bentley and while I was at it, I might even buy some jewelry for Cassidy. My friend, Herb, always had some "hot rocks"—or perhaps take her on a trip. It's been a while since we went away. Perhaps, buy her some beachfront land from Ruben—another buddy of his who sold a successful car wash and became a land baron in Belize. Who knows, I might invest the money in the market. God knows, I have plenty of contacts on Wall Street who could use some money to work with and watch it grow. By now with all this wishful thinking, I could feel the beginnings of a headache and I needed to settle down. It was 1 o'clock, so I decided to stop by The Mixer for a pop on my way to the Bloomingdale's meeting with Milagro; that would hopefully slow down my mind and put me in the right frame of thinking for the meeting.

There are times when a day seems like a journey— this was one of those days and I knew it. I walked through the door and into the darkness of The Mixer in the afternoon. I didn't bother to look around to survey the lay of the land. I just strolled up to the bar. Walt saw me the whole way and just as I arrived at the well worn bar. Walt pushed a tall, sweating drink at me and without a thought, as I had done a thousand times before, picked it up, took a swig, and looked at Walt saying; "My brotha' from a different motha', how are you?"

"Martin, I am so good that it should be illegal," Walt shoots back.

"Outstanding my friend, outstanding, because I sure need some good karma right now and this is the place I hope to find it. What's got you so happy, Walt? Somebody offer to buy the bar?"

"No Marty, not today, but if you know of anyone who'd be interested, I can always be bought, but you know that," Walt said smiling.

"Yes, Walt we all have a price—we all can be bought—it's all about circumstances—the way we react to them, and of course how much cash is involved," I say looking into my drink, almost trying to melt the ice with my stare.

"Marty, I have a plan—a plan that can make us a boatload of "fuck-you money," but before I tell you about it, finish your drink and I'll make you another and you can hear me out, okay?"

"Okay, Walt, I say, what you've got, can't be any weirder than anything I've got going on right now," I mumbled, so Walt couldn't quite hear me.

"What's that, Marty?" Walt asks.

"Nothing, I'm all ears and a little thirsty, so pour that drink and let's talk." I say while rearranging myself on the stool.

Walt pivots around and slides me the promised drink, then grabs a glass from the clean glass rack and shoots some Coke into it from the gun.

"Marty, pay attention to me. Remember I told you about the Korean kid from the candy store who came in that night?"

"Yes, the one who was talking about truckloads of cash—that kid?" I ask knowing the answer—since I have only heard Walt talk about this kid a couple dozen times already.

"Good, well as you know, I have been staking out the place in Red Hook and he was right; he was right about the truck coming in every other week in the early morning. I couldn't tell what they were hauling, but he was right about the schedule, so I am assuming he's right about the contents too."

"Walt, are you telling me you have been going down to Red Hook and sitting in your car waiting for trucks at 2 a.m.? Are you fuckin' drinking again?"

"No. Fuck you Marty! I haven't started drinking and yes, I have been sitting there waiting and my waiting paid off, just listen would ya'?" I could tell he was serious. I could see the look; I knew that Walt didn't want to be taken lightly.

"Alright buddy, let me hear what you're thinking." I said and settled in for some open-minded listening.

"Good, the way I see it, the next truck will come in this Friday night or Saturday morning, however you want to look at it."

"Okay Walt, I'm with you, keep going." I say.

"Well, I think we can intercept the truck a couple of blocks away from its destination, put the driver out of commission, since I've seen a driver without any passengers each time, then hijack the truck to a remote location and I've picked out a spot. Then, offload the cash into your waiting van and BAM! We're gone with a shitload of cash and no one the wiser, except you and me." Walt finishes this in one breath and stares at me as he catches his breath for what seems like an eternity.

"Well Marty, say something," Walt leans in looking for what he wants to hear.

I deliberately take a long pull of my drink and hold Walt's stare as I do it.

"Walt, have you lost every bit of your mind? Did you hear yourself? You said words like—put the driver out of commission—hijack the truck. I'm not sure you are a well man, Walt. That is absolutely the craziest thing I have heard in a long time and I have heard some smack, my friend" I say this and sit back straightening my spine and slumping my shoulders, my body language is screaming—no "fucking" way am I getting involved in this. Next, I put my elbow on the bar, grab my drink and ask, "Just how were you planning that we put the driver out of commission, Walt?"

"I thought we'd use chloroform. I have some. A customer of mine is a sales guy who sells the stuff and he did a trade out with me—drinks for chloroform. Don't ask me how it came about, you had to be there and I'm not getting into it—just know I have some."

"Well OK Walt, what happens if the driver has a radio or a cell phone and calls his buddies? What then, Closeau? Start shooting up the place? I mean really, Walt, you didn't expect me to go…Uhhh okay, I'm in or did you?"

"Well Marty, I didn't really know how you'd react, but it sounds like you don't want in. Is that right?" Walt now almost defensive, but a little hurt, turns to look at the lone customer at the bar who is focused on the *Wheel of Fortune* on the TV and then looks back at me; "Well, whether or not you're in, I'm going through with it. Too many things have passed me by Marty, I'm not going to have one more thing gnaw at me for the rest of my life. I'm going to do this whether you join me or not, and that's that."

"Walt, can we go into your office for a second; what I need to say to you, I don't want to do here, okay?" I say getting off the stool and start heading for the back of the bar.

"Marty wait! We don't need to go there, just say what you have to say here. I don't need to go into my office to listen to you tell me I'm nuts and that this is dangerous and stupid. I know that, but I think we, I mean *I*, can do this but it would be a hell of a lot easier if I had your help. You're the only one I can trust."

"Walt, I am so NOT helping you. I value my life and if self-preservation is an instinct you possess, you will forget the whole thing and go on with your life."

"Marty, I don't need a lecture; I need a partner. Are you going to help me or not?"

"Walt, my answer is no. NO FUCKING WAY—not in this lifetime am I going to help you get killed, or ruin your life. We're not kids anymore and we don't do that shit anymore. I have a wife, a home, and a business. I have some responsibilities and so do you. Are you prepared to throw all this away, because I'm not and I don't think you should? I can't stop you, I can only protest, which I do. I beg of you to change your mind—come to your senses and come to dinner with Cass and me Friday."

"Sorry Marty, I have plans." Walt says to me and turns to the bar and starts washing glasses, avoiding any eye contact with me.

I can take a hint, so look at my watch and sees it's time to go, but before I walk out, I get in front of Walt, grabs his face with one hand under his chin and squeeze his jowls tight together, then turning his head so he can't help but stare back at me and say; "I love you, Walt, this is not right and you know it—do the right thing here and leave it alone." Letting go of him, I see Walt look away and continue washing the same glass.

Walt looks up and says with no emotion or expression, "Thanks Marty, see you later."

I just shake my head, not believing what I have just heard here and walk out of the bar into the Monday afternoon sun. This day is definitely shaping up to be a journey—a journey into madness. That encounter with Walt was almost surreal…and where am I headed now? I think to myself. To meet some woman to talk about some large amount of cash; I sense there is some symmetry here, but I decide to just let it go. I can't begin to think this was all meant to be—like serendipity—not this.

44

At 2 p.m., a courier arrives at Cassidy's office and drops off a delivery for her. The receptionist calls Cassidy's assistant and the package is on Cass's desk, minutes after it arrived.

Cassidy sees the envelope on her desk as soon as she strides into her office after a late lunch at Katz's deli that she had with some people from the office, even though she canceled on Liz, a girls got to eat. She knows what's inside. It's the personal services contract from Carlos. He left her a message at 11:00 a.m., saying it was on its way and that she could review it, sign it, and they could get started after breakfast tomorrow, if she was so anxious.

She sits down and looks at the envelope for a minute before using her pearl handled letter opener from Tiffany's that Marty gave her when she set up shop. The contract was about 12 pages long. The first ten pages were pretty standard stuff—boiler plate content, but it was the last two pages that had the caveats is what she was looking for.

"If for any reason, the executor of this contract wishes to cease activity with the agent, the executor has right to any profits, whether they are real estate or monetary, that the agent may have gained in the course of the life of this agreement. Additionally, the agent in the instance of dissolution is required to remove herself from all communication to the executor and must yield to all requests made upon her, by the executor."

Well there it is, Cassidy thinks. The clause that the devil writes to those he engages business with. Basically, if Cassidy is asked to or decides to quit this arrangement, Carlos gets all her profits and her silence. Hell, he can even ask her to move out of New York City and disappear. Either there is really a lot of money at stake here, or this is one paranoid dude. Cassidy hopes it's the money. She decides not to show this to her lawyer and deep down, she never intended to. He'd never advise her to sign this. As a matter of fact, he'd advise her to run the fuck away from anyone who would offer such a one-sided deal to her. But for some reason, and Cassidy knows what that reason is, it's greed—she will sign this. She stuffs the contract back into the envelope and puts it into her Dunhill attaché case. Breakfast tomorrow will be a defining moment in her life she thinks, but after all, isn't life is a series of defining moments that dictate the rest of the moments of your life? You just had to recognize them and act. Cassidy was ready. Man, was she ready.

45

I am crossing Lexington Avenue, when I spot Milagro stepping out of a cab. All I can think of is how much I'd like to see her on all fours begging for more—more of me that is. I think I made the right decision; I'm here for the money, nothing more and nothing less. Because of the money, I have to stay focused, because if I don't, I might have to make a decision based on lust, rather than logic.

Of course, didn't I just turn down a friend who I've known virtually all my life and now I am on my way to entering into a scheme with a stranger? Man was this getting weird, but just like Hunter Thompson wrote, when the going gets weird, the weird turn pro. I was about to turn pro.

Milagro finishes paying the driver and when she looks up, she sees Marty, right on time. Good, she thinks; he is anxious. First he wants to see proof that what she's told him is for real. If he wasn't serious, he wouldn't want any proof.

"Hello Marty," Milagro purrs.

"How are you, Milagro?" I ask.

"I'm fine, thank you. Why don't we get a cup of coffee in the diner over there and I can show you what you asked to see." she says and puts out her arm for me to take. A fine couple we make, I think. I wonder if I could have gotten tail like this all along and I settled down too soon. But before I can follow that thought, I get a case of the guilts and remember to focus on the money—the money, Marty, I say to myself—stay on point.

The diner is pretty crowded for a Monday at 2:00 p.m., but I spot a booth along the wall and we make our way to it. Milagro slides in with her back to the door and I get the view I like in every restaurant. It's an Italian thing; never sit in a restaurant with your back to the door because someone may come in looking for trouble—at least you'll see it coming, as I'm thinking all this, it's then I realize, I watch too many movies. The movies make being a gangster so glamorous that you almost think that the gangsters' life looks good. In any event, I focus on Milagro and see she is looking around the restaurant trying to get a waitresses attention. When she does, the waitress makes her way to the booth, coffee pot in hand.

"You two gonna' order food?" She asks.

"Well, we'd like some coffee first, then look at your menu and decide, is that okay?" As I'm saying that, the waitress turns over Milagro's coffee cup and pours her some. She reaches over and does the same for me.

"Suit yourself, I'll be back in a sec, hon." I just look at her walking away, then turn to Milagro and say, "nice place huh?"

"Whatever, Martin, I don't want to be here long; the less we are together between now and Monday, the better."

I say, "Okay but what's happening Monday, Milagro?"

Milagro reaches into her bag and pulls out a pack of Dunhill menthols and extracts a cigarette from the green box. As she raises the smoke to her lips, I am right there with a light. She touches my hand to steady the cigarette and light her smoke. As she exhales the blue smoke, she pulls out a Polaroid and slides it across the table to me. I look into her eyes momentarily and then focus on the subject in the picture.

I recognize Carlos. I also take note of the date on the newspaper he's holding seeing that it was not long ago and then realize what I'm really looking at. Behind Carlos, all I can see is pallet after pallet, stacked with what appears to be cash—neatly stacked vacuum sealed bags. I can't tell how much money is on each pallet, but it's a lot of money. That much I can tell.

Before I can say anything, Milagro very matter of factly says, "Each pallet you see has three million in cash on it; you do the math, Marty, it's there. Do you believe me now?" I am still staring at the Polaroid, when I hear her say three million.

"Yes, I do, what's next?" is all I can muster, still looking at the picture.

"Good, I was hoping that would be your response. Now listen to me closely, Marty, because I don't want to have to say this too many times."

"I'm listening, Milagro, go ahead. Let me hear what you have to say." I say this and realize that this conversation is remarkably similar in many respects to the one I just had with Walt. This is one strange day, is all I can think—which is becoming a recurring theme.

"Marty, next Monday, you will pick me up in your van. I will blindfold you and then drive your van to the warehouse that you see in the picture. Then I will take off the blindfold. Once we are inside and you will help me load your van with cash, if we use the forklift, it should take us less than 30 minutes to load two pallets of cash into your van. Once we've loaded your van, I will blindfold you again and we'll drive north. Once we're outside Westchester County, I'll remove the blindfold and you'll drive to a location where we'll offload the money into another vehicle and then you'll drive your van home and wait for your next set of instructions. I will pay you $300 grand for this, do you understand?" She says and sips her coffee and takes a drag on her cigarette.

"I understand, but will Carlos know about this?" I ask, still looking at the picture.

"Let me worry about Carlos, Marty," Milagro sharply answers

"But what if we're followed?" I ask.

"Martin, I have taken every possible outcome into consideration—remember I'm a planner. I know when to make our move. We'll never be noticed, I have my methods. You are just along for the ride; this will be the easiest money ever made, as far as your part is concerned—no worries." Milagro finishes her coffee and butts out her cigarette.

"Are we together on this, Martin?" She asks.

"Yes," is all I can say. "What time Monday?" I ask.

"I'll call you and tell you where and when to pick me up. Just make sure you have a full tank of gas and that the van is in shape; I mean, I don't want to get on the road and have a tail light out. We don't need any curious cops to notice either, do you understand, Martin?"

"Yes, I guess I do. It sounds awfully simple, the way you describe it," I say.

"It is. Just do as I say, and on Monday, you'll walk away a lot richer." And with that, she pulls out a twenty dollar bill for the table and gets up.

"That's it?"

"Yes, Martin, that's it; I'll call you—till we meet again, be well." She turns and walks out.

The waitress returns and noticing the other side of the booth is empty; she looks at me and then the twenty dollar bill and says, "I guess you two won't be eating."

"You guessed right, what do I owe you?" I ask.

"Five bucks," she says as she grabs the twenty.

I respond saying, "Just give me back thirteen."

"Thanks," she says, giving my change and stuffs the rest into a pocket in her uniform, and walks away.

"What is happening to me today? Is everyone nuts, or am I the target of some cosmic joke?" I think to myself as I lift myself out of the booth, drain my coffee cup, and walk out of the diner into the bustle of Lexington Avenue and just stand there looking skyward.

I'd always felt like I was destined for something great; I'd felt that way since I was a kid; I thought that I was special—terminally unique. Could this be that greatness—the $300 grand—for sitting in a van, blindfolded, and keeping my mouth shut? Or, is it Walt's plan I am supposed to help with? Man, this is one freaky day. What else can happen?

I'm stunned—almost dazed, and then I am overcome with a feeling of confidence. Maybe my ship is coming in. Hell, why not me? Yeah, why not me?

That's it, Milagro thought. She'd played her hand. Marty knew what she was planning. Was she crazy? Why did she like this Marty fellow? What was it about him that suddenly made her want to spare him from Carlos' wrath...?

Sometimes when someone plays a part in our daily lives, like your mailman, or the kid behind the counter at the video store or coffee place, maybe even your dry cleaner—they become a trusted and familiar face. Somehow reassuring you that you are doing what you're supposed to be doing—doing what you planned to do—in control. These people become a part of your validation system. You interact with ease, once you get beyond the transactional nature of your relationship. You see these people more than those you love sometimes. So, if you were choosing sides and you had a choice of them or a distant relative, because they, the dry cleaner, are a known entity to you, you trust them and you trust in your knowledge of how they'll react to certain things. This is because they are more familiar, simply put; when you see someone over and over, it creates a feeling of security. You're so secure; you'll trust them with most anything.

Milagro ran that through her mind and she knew that Marty was her best option for this operation and time wasn't on her side. Carlos would never live up to his end of the deal he made with her. He'd have her deleted and live his miserable, filthy rich life guilt-free.

She'd planned this score for some time now and all that was left were two phone calls and flawless execution. Then she'd be free from Carlos, free from his influence. She would dissolve into the world and live a beautiful life—filled with sunrises, sunsets, and all the beauty this life affords us. She could breathe deep, look the world in the eye—no longer having to put on the armor she'd grown over the years—armor she needed to wear in order to survive. It suited her well, but it has grown too heavy these last months and it was her time. It was her turn to take off the armor and exhale.

Her next call was to the car rental folks in upstate New York, a town called Horseheads. There she would rent a van and park it in a remote location, a day or two before; then she would have Marty drive her up there. They would off load the cash, and she would drive away into the sunset—south—far south. Getting across the border in Mexico, won't be hard. She will be able to disappear.

She'd use a bogus identity to rent the car and use a fake passport to get into Mexico. She'd have to use a credit card to rent the car, but once used, she'll throw it away. So, her steps will end there, just in case anyone begins to look for her. She would also have the car destroyed in Mexico, so no trace of her or the car could be tracked.

She wondered if anyone besides Carlos cared. Her clients would give up on her after a few weeks and realize she wouldn't be back. Legally, no one had any claims—her rent was paid, the furniture and contents were paid and someone will eventually begin to put together that she was gone. No trace, there'd be no crying families, no press conferences—just one less person out in the world....

She would be invisible—literally, off the radar.

Her plan was coming together quickly; she must stay in the moment. Getting too far ahead would make her lose her focus and make a mistake—a mistake that would cost her her life. She was too close now to let this get away from her. She was too close.

46

Walt was trying to figure out what to do next; could he really do this by himself? He could certainly handle the stake out and identify the place in Red Hook where he'd intercept and he was always going to be the one who was going to incapacitate the driver. From there, he'd have to commandeer the truck by himself or maybe he'd rent a van and use that to stake the warehouse out in—and the van could be his get-away car, but off loading that cash into the van, would take time if he was alone. He'd have to settle for less of a score, only because he couldn't physically handle the load alone.

Then it hit him—just take the truck itself—like in the movie *Goodfellas*, when Pesche and Liotta hijacked that truckload of furs from Idlewild Airport.

He'd take a cab to Red Hook and wait in the shadows. Then, he'd take out the driver with chloroform, throw him out on the street, and then drive the truck, full of money, out to Long Island by himself. He would then off load in the privacy of a storage rental facility he'd kept for years that currently held what he got out of his first marriage and figure out what to do next with the money later. Why hadn't he thought of this at first? This was the best way—involve no one else. You hold your destiny in your own hands. His mind was now made up.

His next step was to visit the storage facility in Massapequa and make room for the loot. He'd also need to do a couple of "dry runs" from Red Hook to the storage locker, making sure he could take a commercial vehicle on all the surface streets between here and there. He'd also have to measure the gas tank situation. He didn't want to have to stop and get gas once he stole the truck. The drive to Long Island at that hour, shouldn't take more than an hour, but that meant at least 50 miles, so he'd need to have gas available, in case of a low tank. These were minor details, but Walt was proud of himself for thinking of them. He was energized again. Marty had deflated his sails for sure, but now he was back to full steam ahead. He knew now that he was going to succeed; he knew his life would change in five days. He thought now would be a good time to pause and thank his higher power for putting this opportunity in front of him. Okay, he wasn't sure if God had stealing the money in mind, but he knew that God wanted him to be happy and by changing his life's situation so that he could help others with the treatment center he would open using ill gotten gains was going to make him happy, then it must be God's will.

It's amazing the things we can rationalize away; what would a day be without a few juicy rationalizations. Walt was no stranger to this. Before he got sober, he lived several lives at once. There was his life at home with his family, and there was his drinking life, filled with mistresses, lies, and behavior he'd wish he could forget. At one point, he was so deep in his alcoholism and the life, that he told the same lies over and over so much, he began to believe them himself. He was so far out of touch with reality that he had created an alter ego and thought that was his reality. So believing that this whole scam and score was God's will was easy for Walt—he may be sober, but he still could rationalize and lie to himself.

He felt somehow secure and righteous that this was his destiny and he was its master; Walt was now ready; he began cleaning the bar with a new vigor. He even poured a free drink for the guy watching *Wheel of Fortune* and he started thinking about what he'd feel like on Saturday after this was over. Would he be different? Would he tell anyone and what would he do with the money first?—Questions that he relished pondering.

47

Snuffy was really beginning to get frustrated. This guy, Carlos, was good. He was careful with his garbage and he was careful with his comings and goings. He behaved as if he knew he was being watched. He also felt like Carlos was hiding something, but he couldn't tell what. He just acted a certain way. Snuffy was good at reading people; he sensed this guy was a snake, but he couldn't put his finger on what his scam was.

He knew he had to get creative, but what could he do? He sat in his one-room apartment and stared out the window. He stared at nothing, because his mind was going a hundred miles a minute and he couldn't focus and then it hit him—his friend Chip, from when he was on the inside—who talked about being able to tap into phone lines using the lines on the pole and a cell phone signal. Of course, Garrett wouldn't approve, because anything Snuffy discovered this way couldn't be used in court, but Snuffy needed something. He needed another angle and another way to get into this guy's life.

Snuffy had accumulated a little black book of thieves, sneaks, strong-arm men, con artists, and the like, when his time was ending in prison, knowing some day that he might need some of these men and their talents.

The last time Snuffy spoke with Chip he was working at a Radio Shack in a small town in New Jersey. It had been at least a year since they'd talked, so it was a long shot that Chip would still be at the last phone number that he had, but what the hell. He was desperate and maybe, just maybe, he would get lucky. Turning away from the window, he goes into his pine chest of drawers to get his book of names out of the sock drawer.

Why do we hide things in sock drawers? he thinks; Do we think that we can out smart cat-burglars by hiding things there? Snuffy was told by his burglar friends that they look first in the drawers, knowing just how silly people are and where they store valuables. In any event, Snuffy finds the book and calls the number next to Chip's name.

"Thank you for calling Radio Shack, how may I help you?" The voice answers.

"Hi, I was looking for Chip, is he in today?" Snuffy asks. The next few seconds seem endless when the kid on the other line answers, "Hold on, he's in back. Let me get him for you. Who may I say is calling?"

"Tell him it's his old friend, Snuffy."

"Okay, just a minute, sir." The kid says.

"Thanks"

After a minute, Chip picks up the phone, "Snuffy, is this you?"

"Chip, it's me—the one and only. I was hoping you were still there. How are you?" Snuff asks.

"Snuffy, I'm great. I'm the manager of this store now and I have a house here in Netcong and lead the life of a citizen, amazing, huh?"

"Amazing yes, but certainly better for your health and for your parole officer, I'm sure." Snuffy replies.

"You got that right. I even pay taxes—imagine that," Chip says with a smile.

"Well, I'm glad it's going well for you. I need to ask you a favor, but I can't do it on the phone. Can I come see you today?"

"Sure, Snuff. You remember where the store is?"

"Yes, just off Route 46, right?" Snuff asks.

"Yep, that's it—in the same strip mall. There is a Starbucks next door, can you be there at 4 p.m.? I get out today at 3:30 p.m. and that would be perfect for me." Chip says looking at a customer playing with the Zip Zaps.

"Four it is, Chip. I'll see you there, thanks man; I'm looking forward to seeing you."

"Me too, Snuff. It's been a long time. See you then,"—and with that, Chip hangs up.

Snuffy thinks to himself, as he hangs up the phone. "This might just be the break I needed. Perhaps, I can listen in to Carlos' phone calls for a day and hear something that'll give me the lead I need to help Garrett out with this guy."

Still frustrated with the task, but persistent, Snuffy decides to take a trip back over to Carlos's house for his daily garbage check; he knew he'd find the same shredded papers he'd been looking at for weeks now, but in his current line of work, you never know when someone is going to make a mistake that can help you, so grabbing a few pairs of surgical gloves from below the sink, he goes out the door.

48

I'm beginning to think that I might be going nuts. First, this Milagro business and then, Walt wants to hijack a truck filled with money. I can hardly keep up with all of the scheming? I'd have been a lousy spy for sure.

I had a little trouble holding all this to myself. I wanted to share it with Cassidy, but she'd freak out knowing that I was meeting with Milagro without telling her and she'd also get in Walt's face and read him the riot act, if I told her about what he was planning on doing. I certainly couldn't tell Bertha; I was all alone with this and it made me feel anxious to say the least.

Here I am, quite possibly on the brink of the biggest score of my life and I have so many unanswered questions. Of course, it was illegal as hell, and I don't even want to ask Milagro where that money came from. I don't want to know how she and Carlos hooked up, and I certainly don't want to know where Walt's money truck was coming from. I have no where to go with this guilt, fear, and confusion, so I head back to the store. I did after all, have a 4 p.m. meeting with the FBI to discuss Carlos. Now, I actually had something to tell them, but if I shared what I think I know about Carlos, I could screw up my own score. I might betray Milagro and for all I know, I could be considered an accomplice, because of what I know. Man, this was getting absolutely crazy and somehow I had to hold it together. I wanted to help Milagro and I want the $300 large. I want to stay out of jail and I also want someone to tell the truth to and unload this burden of information, but I just couldn't. You can't have your cake and eat it too, I thought—and then I thought what a silly analogy.....cake?

I decided on the way back to the store that I would stonewall the agent. Yes, Carlos was an occasional customer I would share and that would be it. I wouldn't bring up Cassidy's relationship with Carlos, unless asked let him get that information on his own. After all, she had plenty of clients I didn't know about. I would have to stay calm, be composed, and answer the questions convincingly.

I just knew it had to have something to do with all that money I saw in the Polaroid, but I knew nothing about that. Heck, as far as the FBI knew, I don't even know it exists. Hopefully, they didn't either.

I fancy myself a good liar, but Cassidy told me otherwise. She says I twitch my nose and hold my chin up when I'm lying, but I don't believe her. In any event, I hope I won't be asked any questions that would cause me to have to lie, but I needed to be prepared anyway.

I switched my train of thought to another track; this track was a lot more pleasant. I was beginning to think about what I'd do with

300 grand in cash. How I would spend it? How would I store it? What would I tell Cassidy, and would I tell Cassidy?

This was all very complicated I reminded myself, if I do the right thing here, then I thought—there is no right thing here—the money is stolen. God knows how it got there—into the warehouse that is, and now I am part of an elaborate scheme—where I'd be willingly blindfolded. There'd be clandestine drop offs and ultimately a measure of danger to myself and with the amount of money involved, I figured I was risking my life.

With the kind of cash Milagro showed me and talked about, I could sell the shop to Bertha, who I knew would buy it if offered and then I could talk Cass into using her real estate connections to find that secluded island in the Caribbean. The dream place where they could spend the rest of their days, lolling in the sun, becoming part of the landscape, blending in, sleeping in, staying up late, going to bed early, and watching sunrises and sunsets. Maybe they could even open a little business that would keep her occupied. Cassidy would like that. She needs to be doing—always doing. So the thought of her sitting around doing very little was probably a bit of a stretch, but I know she'd survey the island and figure out what was needed and throw herself into it—that was my Cassidy—perpetual motion.

Now yours truly, has no trouble doing nothing. Well, maybe I'd buy a boat. I might also take up deep sea fishing—yeah that's the ticket—fishing. Fishing was one of those activities where you could say you were doing something, when you really aren't doing a thing. That sounded good to me; I'd just have to sell it to Cassidy.

As I got a block or so away from the shop, I glanced at my watch and it read 3:30 p.m., just a half hour away from my meeting with the FBI agent. Feeling the way I do, I'd normally stop into The Mixer, but I thought it best if I avoided Walt for a while. I thought I'd give him some time to rethink his plan and come to his senses. So instead, I stop into Carvel for a milk shake, maybe the sugar will help. As a matter of fact, a Carvel cup on my desk would be a good prop when the agent comes by—I thought. He might think I'm just a big kid who still likes ice cream. How could I be involved in anything unlawful? I am thinking way too much—relax and be Marty. Just keep out of your own way, I remind myself.

Bertha was tidying up the front of the store, when she saw Marty heading towards the store. It was soon going to be the afternoon rush. How nice of him to help today, she thought. Today she could use the help. She wasn't feeling very good—her hips were giving her a hard time today. She had degenerative arthritis in her hips, one of those lovely conditions that she inherited from her bum of an old man. This job aggravated her hips every so often. With the bending, lifting, and wheeling the racks, there were days that when she sat down for longer than 15 minutes, it felt like it would take a crane to get her out of the chair. The hips would lock up and she'd feel the bone rub on bone when she'd try to move. She wished sometimes she had a portable morphine drip, so she could handle the pain.

Better yet, she'd love to have her own shop and then she could have someone do the work for her. Her mind wandered off until she realized she was dreaming. Her doctor had been nagging her to get her hips replaced, but she didn't have enough time or money to be out of work for six weeks, so she put up with the pain and chewed *Celebrex and Aleve* like *Chicklets*, but they didn't really help. She needed a cup of Oxy Contin tea to help this pain.

"Bertha," I said walking in, "I'm going to be in back, so just holler if you get busy and FYI, I'm expecting someone at 4 p.m... Will you let me know when he gets here, okay?"

He disappeared behind the counter and out of her sight.

Hmmmm, she thought, that was an unusual entrance for him. He's usually filled with questions about the day's business. He was definitely pre-occupied—this she could tell. If she knew anything, she knew her boss, that's for sure. It's probably one of his moods, or who knows, maybe his high-maintenance wife was pushing his buttons again.

Bertha was a big Cassidy fan. She admired her business savvy, the way she always seemed to be in control and put together, but she also knew she could be cold, calculating, and vindictive. Aren't all the business sharks that way? Bertha just figured that came with the territory. Marty made Cassidy seem more humane, Bertha thought. You just could see the way Cassidy loved him, the way she would talk about him when he wasn't around. She adored her husband. Bertha remembered something Cassidy said and it always stuck in Bertha's head. Cassidy said marriage to Marty, was like having a sleepover with her best friend every night. For some reason, that hit Bertha right in the heart; she may be a shark, but she was also a romantic—and a vulnerable girl too.

For reasons unknown to Bertha, she knew Marty's feng shui was out of sorts, but it was her experience that these moods always passed—usually pretty quickly. So she dismissed it and got back to straightening out the store, making coffee, and filling the chiller with sodas and waters. The customers didn't mind a little bit of a wait when you offered them something to drink. Those who would normally get edgy after waiting three minutes, if you gave them a beverage when that happened, they would be patient for at least another five minutes. So, the free drinks paid for themselves in many ways—goodwill always does.

I looked at my watch and it now read 3:53 p.m. I assumed the agent would be punctual, so I got up to go to the bathroom. When the phone rang, it was Cassidy. I could see her number on the Caller ID screen and all of a sudden, a wave of the guilt's hit me. So I hesitated, took a deep breath and gathered my thoughts, "Hey doll, what's up, where you at?"

"Just getting ready to call it a day, she said and I was thinking we'd meet at The Mixer for a couple of drinks. What dya' say?" she asks.

Instinctively, I almost say—okay. Then I remember I wanted to avoid that nutjob Walt for a little while, and I thought we'd discussed tonight, earlier in the morning, so I say, "You know, didn't we say we'd hang at home tonight? It's nice outside. We could open a bottle of nice wine and drink it in the courtyard. The plants look like they could use some music and our company. Plus, we'll look at those homes and islands in the Robb Report. Remember, does that still sound good?"

"You're right. I can get out of these panty hose, throw on my snuggies, and chill. Yes, that sounds great. I'll be home in an hour. When will you be there?" she asks me, as she is logging off her computer.

"I'll be home right around 6, give or take, twenty minutes. Okay?" I answer.

"Super-duper, I'll see you then. I think we have some food in the house. We can figure out supper later—love ya," Cassidy says.

"Love you too," I say, without thinking, because I do love her and will for a very long time. After hanging up, I look around and go into the bathroom to take a whiz.

It's 4 p.m. on the dot and in walks Garrett. He does a quick survey of the dry cleaning store. Garrett's training had become instinct—get the lay of the land and know where you are and where you're closest exit is—stuff like that. It takes all of five seconds before Bertha now behind the counter says, "How can I help you?"

Garrett sizes up Bertha then asks, "Are you, Bertha?"

"I am," she responds, "Who's asking?"

"I'm Agent Garrett Tedia." He says and he doesn't flash his badge in the traditional sense. He just puts his hands on his hips, so she can see the badge riding on his belt. "We spoke on the phone, remember?"

"I do, you were asking about a customer." She says feeling a flush of warmth rise on her face.

"Yes, I was," he says, "I'm here to see Mr. Tyroni, is he in?"

"I'll get him. He's in back," she says, looking into his eyes, "would you like some coffee, soda, or water?"

"No, just get me to Mr. Tyroni, thank you." Garrett says coldly.

"Okay, suit yourself," she says while turning to go get Marty calmly, but inside she is nervous as a whore in Sunday school.

She turns the corner and looks at Marty's office and doesn't see him. Then hearing the toilet flush, she knows where he is. Looking up while zipping up, he sees Bertha.

"Can I help you *B*?" I say.

"Your 4 p.m. FBI agent is here." She says.

"He is and how did you know he is an agent?" I ask.

"He told me, that's how I know," Bertha says sharply.

"Of course, he would; okay, let's go," I say walking towards the front with Bertha following behind.

Once I turn the corner, Garrett reaches out his hand with a business card in it.

"I'm Agent Garrett Tedia, you must be Mr. Tyroni?"The agent asks me.

"I am and please call me, Marty. I get nervous when people call me Mr. Tyroni, especially FBI agents. Nice to meet you, Agent Tedia." I say looking at Garrett and then the card he gave me.

"Why don't you come with me to my office?" I ask.

"Great." Garrett says and looks hard at Bertha as he follows Marty to his office.

Once in the office, I extend my arm towards the old, aged armchair in front of my desk. Garrett nods and sits, as I take my chair behind the desk.

"So, how can I help you, Agent?" I ask then take a pull on my milkshake.

"Well, this won't take long. I have a couple of questions and then I'll be on my way." Garrett says, as he pulls out a little wire bound book and pen and opens to about the tenth page while throwing the other nine over the wire coil binding the pages.

"Do you have a customer whose name is Carlos Ferrar, Marty?" Garrett now looking into my eyes and waits for the answer.

"Well, after thinking about what you said on the phone earlier, I guess I have to say—"yes, I do."

"Good," Garrett says, "then can you tell me, Marty, why your girl up there, Bertha would tell me you don't, Marty?"

"I didn't know you'd asked her." Marty said

"Are you hiding something about Mr. Ferrar, Marty?" Garrett asks, getting more serious and leaning into his questions.

"No, Agent, I'm not. I don't even know Mr. Ferrar, other than his dry cleaning habits." Marty answers.

"You're sure, Marty, because if I find out you're covering up something, that makes you accessory and that isn't good, Marty," Garrett now sensing he might be onto something, pushes harder.

"I mean if you have anything at all, you feel you need to tell me about Carlos, Marty, now would be the best time."

"Honestly, Agent, I don't. He has his shirts done here every week or so—suits and coats too—nothing extraordinary. He dresses very nice and wears expensive clothes, that I can tell you, because that's all I know." I'm starting to feel more comfortable and convincing, so I sit back and take the milkshake with me as I recline a little.

"As a matter of fact, Agent, he always pays in cash, so I don't even have a credit card number to give you." I add, feeling more in control now and not on the defensive. This is going well, I think.

"He uses cash only, you say? When was he in last, Marty?" Garrett asks hungrily.

"I don't know, I'd guess last week, why?" Marty answers quickly.

"I have my reasons. Is there anything of his waiting to be picked up?" Garrett asks.

"I don't think so, but let me ask Bertha. She'd know better than me." I say and call out to her. "Hey *B.*, come back here would you?"

"I gotta' go." Bertha says, hanging up.

Just then, Garrett looks at a light go out on the phone on Marty's desk; he'd noticed a line light up when he sat down.

"Marty, what do you need?" Bertha says walking in.

"Is there any of Mr. Ferrar's clothes waiting here for pick up?" I ask.

"I don't think so, but let me check." She answers.

"Okay, let me know—we'll wait." I say looking at Garrett who is watching Bertha closely.

"Just take a sec, I'll be right back." Bertha says, leaving the room.

"How long has Bertha worked for you, Marty?" Garrett asks.

"Forever it seems like," I say. "She is my right hand here. She really runs the place; I help her, if anything." I say with a big smile.

"I'm still troubled by her hiding Carlos from me." Garrett says, shaking his head.

Walking into Marty's office, she says, "Yes, he has an order ready to be picked up."

"Really?" Garrett asks; "when do you think he'll pick it up?"

"Could be today, just can't say." Bertha answers, looking at Marty now.

"Hmmm, how late are you open today?" Garrett asks.

"Six." Bertha answers.

"That's less than two hours," Garrett says, thinking aloud.

"Okay then." Garrett says, "I guess I'll just hang around then. You don't mind, do you Marty?" Garrett asks, as if he's telling me I shouldn't mind.

"Well, where will you hang around, Agent? We do have work to do around here?" I say readjusting myself in the chair; I don't want this cop hanging around for two hours.

"I thought I'd wait right here. I promise to stay out of your way, besides I still have a couple of questions I'd like to ask," Garrett says with a smile.

"Well, I guess I don't really have a choice then, now do I?" I say, almost expecting to hear him say, "yes, you do."

When Garrett says, "Well, the law says you don't have to let me stay without a warrant, but you don't want me to do that, I mean go get a warrant do you? That could get messy for you." Garrett says, knowing he doesn't have enough to get a warrant.

Now, I am totally unsure of what to do, so I look at Bertha, who is clearly uncomfortable. I then look back at Garrett, who seems smug enough, then I say, "You know Agent, why don't you come back with a warrant. I haven't done anything wrong and I've answered all your questions, so I guess I feel uncomfortable with you staking out my customers without a warrant to do so. So, *yes*, please go get a warrant. I guess I'll take my chances." I say not knowing where that came from, but I think I noticed Garrett shrink just a little, enough for me to know I'd done the right thing. I also noticed Bertha's spine stiffen a little, so I really felt okay with my answer.

"Marty, I was hoping it wouldn't come to that, but if you insist." Garrett says, standing up and looking down at me.

"Agent, I do insist. I appreciate your stopping by, but I have work to do, as does Bertha, so if you won't think us rude, please excuse us." I say standing myself.

"Okay, Mr. Tyroni. I will be back with that warrant. Don't think I won't and I'm going to turn this place upside down and inside out when I do," Garrett says, putting his little book back into his coat breast pocket while clicking his pen and putting it in his shirt pocket.

"I look forward to it, Agent." I answer, but I'm a little scared too.

With that, Garrett looks at the two of them and says, "No need to show me out. I know my way."

Once they hear the door close, they both look at one another and just exhale.

49

Snuffy gets to the Starbucks where Chip had asked to meet him
a little early; he wanted to make sure he got to this meeting on time so
he left the city earlier than he probably had to. He didn't want to get
stuck in the Lincoln Tunnel traffic—he hated traffic. He'd had to wait
in line all his life. Whether it was at the dining room table as a kid,
or for a shower while in prison or in the food line while he was in the
Navy he never got to the front of the line.

He was at the front of this line right now. He orders his Grande
Frappachino and realizes that Starbucks has made us all learn new sizes
to order your drink. He then grabs a seat outside the store, so he could
smoke. The weather was pleasant and he knew he'd get some good
people watching in, before his old friend arrived.

All he could think about as he lit a smoke was how was he
going to ask Chip if he would do him a solid by helping him tap in to
Carlos's phone? Chip sounded pretty reformed so this might be a long
shot, but what the heck, if he wouldn't help, he'd just have to keep
digging in garbage and putting up with Garrett's haranguing.

Chip recognized him immediately—of course he did. Snuffy hadn't changed; same leathered look, same cold stare—the type of stare that can only be cultivated on the inside.

Snuffy rose to greet his old friend; he offered to buy Chip a coffee, but he declined. Chip suspected that Snuffy needed a favor of the illegal kind; he didn't have any allusions that he was going to ask him about a surround sound system.

"Okay, Snuffy." Chip says; "What gives. It's been too long for you to call up out of the blue just to catch up. Who is it and how much "tap time" do you need?"

"That's what I like about you, Chip." Snuffy says; "No small talk, just business. You don't waste time."

"Well, I hate to wait, so what's the deal?" Chip says and pulls a smoke out of Snuffy's pack on the table and leans in for a light. As he lights his smoke, Snuffy says, "I need about 24 hours of "listen in" time; it's a guy in the city. I don't need to give you the details, but it's in a nice neighborhood. The pole is down the block from his house. I can't offer you much, but I think I can get you about three grand."

"Snuffy, no way, not for less than five thousand, I've got more to lose these days." Chip says and blows the blue smoke up in the air.

"C'mon Chip; I'm maxed out right now, three thousand is all I can get. My client doesn't like this kind of work, so it's coming out of my pocket." Snuffy says, sitting back in his chair. "Snuffy, for three thousand, I'll get you 12 hours of "listen in," that's it, take it or leave it." "Deal?" Snuff says and extends his hand.

"Okay, Snuff, where are we talking about?" Chip says as he pulls out a pocket notebook. "Give me that, and I'll write it down for you," Snuffy says reaching for the pad.

"I'll need the last four digits of the guy's phone number too." Chip says, stubbing out his cigarette.

"Perfect. I'll put it all on the same sheet—name address and numbers," Snuffy says, handing back the notebook to Chip.

"Here's the deal, Snuffy; I'll need the money Wednesday, bring it to me right here, same time, OK and I don't take checks, so cash is it." Chip says looking around, as if he was being tailed—it's a reflex.

"I can do that, Chip." Snuffy says; "When will I get my listen?"

"Thursday night," Chip says; "we'll do it in the early morning, this way you get the morning and afternoon. How does that sound?"

"The best would be around four or five a.m. Can we do it then?" Snuff asks.

"Sure, no sweat, when we meet on Wednesday, I'll give you some things that you'll need to get to help me out." Chip says, as he stands saying, "it was nice NOT seeing you again, Snuff. If you know what I mean."

"I do. See you Wednesday." Snuffy replies and watches Chip walk away.

Snuffy is all smiles on the inside. Garrett might not like his methods, but hopefully the results will get him something he can use to further his efforts. He drains his drink and heads for his car—a successful trip he thinks. Then he wonders if he'll hit any tunnel traffic at this time of day.

50

Sitting back down behind my desk, I notice Bertha turn to leave the room, when I say, "Whoa, where do you think you're going? We need to talk and we need to do it now." "Marty," Bertha says, turning to face me; "I don't know anything about this guy, other than that he came in here a while back and asked some questions about dryers. He said he was thinking of upgrading the workout facility where he works, then I get a call from the FBI asking if he was a customer. I told them I couldn't give them that information. I don't know why I did it, but I did. Maybe it's because I felt some kind of a connection with Carlos and wanted to protect him."

"Bertha, this guy, Carlos, is trouble. I just feel it in my bones. He's too smooth—he just gives me a bad vibe."

"Marty, I might as well tell you that while you were talking with *Officer Friendly*, I tried calling Carlos to let him know some flatfoot was in here asking questions about him." Bertha says as she grabs a smoke out of the pack on Mart's desk and lights up.

"What were you thinking? We have no idea what this guy is into and you're warning him to stay away? You could be implicated— obstructing something—hell, I don't know, but it ain't good!" Now I grab a smoke, light it and exhale deeply; "Bertha, you are to have NO contact with this guy, from here on out. Any dealings with Carlos, I'll handle. Do you understand me? Am I clear, here?"

"Marty," Bertha says; "I didn't mean any harm, I just was…I don't know—just doing what I thought was right."

"Well, stop acting on your instincts. Think Bertha, think, for all we know, this guy could be a serial killer and now, you may be on his list. I don't know, but shit! Just keep your mouth shut and if any more cops come asking questions, you don't know shit."

"Okay, Marty. I get it." Bertha butts out her smoke and gets up to go tend to the counter.

Now I feel a little bad for being so matter-of-fact with Bertha, but I felt I had to. This could blow the lid off my little score and jeopardize Milagro, who incidentally, I feel the same about as Bertha does about Carlos. So I might be a little conflicted, but like the saying goes, "I may not be much, but I'm all I think about." So I sit back, finish my smoke and start moving some papers around on my desk, but within seconds, my mind is a million miles away from paying the bills.

All I can think about right now is the effect this guy, Carlos, is having on the women in my life—Cassidy, Milagro and now Bertha. I feel a resentment creeping in.

Just then, the phone rings. Bertha picks it up on the first ring up front.

"Meltzy's, Bertha speaking. How may I help you?"

"Bertha, it's Carlos Ferrar. I got your message. What were you talking about?"

"Well, I had it all wrong. I panicked. I thought this FBI agent was in here asking about you, but he was a friend of Marty's goofing on him, you know how guys are. I'd never met this friend, so I thought he was the real deal." She was getting in deeper by the word, but she was proud of herself with this quick-thinking lie.

"Are you sure, Bertha?" Carlos asks a little more intense.

"Yes, Mr. Ferrar, I'm sure. Besides, why would the FBI be looking at you?" She asks, regretting the question.

"Bertha, let me assure you, I am a high-profile businessman in this town, with many enemies. Any one of them would have motive for throwing me under a number of buses. I'm sure you understand."

Whether she did or didn't, she just wants to get off this call.

"Yes, I do, but he was just busting Marty's stones." She answered.

"Bertha, I am sure you understand how much a message like the one you left, might upset someone, so I hope you're telling me the truth. I really do." He says this in a tone that instantly lets Bertha know that this guy doesn't need her protection.

"I am, Mr. Ferrar, I am." Bertha says, like a child who has been scolded.

"Very well then, by the way, I'll be sending my assistant to pick up my clothes. Oh, and Bertha, don't worry, you won't see me in your store again." He hangs up.

Bertha puts the receiver back in her cradle and goes in back to tell Marty about her exchange.

"Well, I guess that's okay Bertha. Perhaps, it will make this whole thing go away. Maybe, when his assistant comes to pick up his stuff, you call Agent Tedia and let him know. This way, we are being cooperative. It's been my experience that cops like it when you cooperate, ka-pisce?" I say.

"Yes, boss. I get it." She says, turning away.

"Good, Bertha. I appreciate it. I really do." I say, returning to the paper shuffling.

My thoughts begin to wander again and then return; maybe what Bertha did, is the best thing. I hope so, is all I can think. This weirdness and anxiety is beginning to make me real antsy.

It's almost time to head home and I have piled all the bills—paid none—just piled them in some kind of order that only I can figure out. Just then I remember that Cassidy and I were going to chill out at home, so I need to pick up some supplies—some wine, some bread, and some cheese. I thought we'd get the night started with a hunk of bread, hunk of cheese, and some chilled white wine. I also need to get a couple of copies of the *Robb Report Homes Magazine*, so we could do the—"wouldn't it be a nice thing." I love doing that, especially when Cass is into it too.

Walking into the house, I can tell I'm the first one home. I was hoping I would be. I love to set things up for Cass. I would get the wine opened, put it in a floor chill bucket, cut the cheese, put the bread on the cutting board with a knife sticking in it like King Arthur's sword in that stone, and lay the magazines out on the table. Sometimes after I'd do something like this, I would just sit back sometimes and look over the scene I created; it gave me a very "Town and Country" living feel, and I liked that.

I know exactly what I'm doing here. I am creating the perfect environment to tell my bride that I'm about to make a big score with Milagro and maybe tell her about Carlos and the FBI and Bertha, depending on her initial reaction. I'm not sure how she'll take it, but I can't deal with the guilt. I thought I could handle it, but I was wrong.

I remember when Walt was getting sober, he explained the Twelve Steps of AA to me. How he had to "clean his side of the street," so that he could look the world in the eye again. That hit home with me because right now I am feeing like I need to "sweep my street" and clearing my chest of this burden is the only way I think I'll be able to draw a deep breath filled with peace. That's all I want sometimes, is a deep cleansing breath.

I am only a week away from the biggest score of my life and I am excited with the thought of all that cash. I think if I explain it right, Cassidy will feel the same. I just have to explain my intentions, the why of it. If I can spin it right, she'll be "all in." I am always an optimist. I truly believe that if you change the way you look at things, the things you look at change.

Just as I am walking back into the kitchen to pull down the wine glasses, I hear Cassidy walk in.

"Honey, I'm home," She yells.

"In here," I yell back.

Walking in, Cassidy can see the scene Marty has set up in the courtyard and just looks at him saying; "I love you, Martin Tyroni, have I told you that today?"

"No, but you can tell me now." I say, looking into the crystal for water spots. Seeing none, I walk towards my wife and hug her tight.

"I love you bigger." I say.

"No, you don't." She says; "I love you biggest!" It's one of those hugs that seem to go on forever. I feel safe hugging Cassidy and I feel complete. As I kiss her on the lips, pressing hard thinking—God, I love this woman! Thank you.

Finally apart, she says; "Pour me a drink while I run upstairs and get out of these clothes and get into my "snuggies," Okay?"

"Sure, babe, I'll be out back, waiting for you. I'll turn on some tunes, so we can have some background. Anything you want to hear?" I ask, making my way to the den where the sound system resides. She's upstairs by now and doesn't hear me. I wait, but no answer. She didn't hear me, so I start searching for the title I feel like hearing. Finding it, I play some *Little Feat-Time Loves a Hero*—some of their best work, me thinks, and perfect for tonight.

Cassidy glides down the stairs and makes her way to the outdoor courtyard. She's greeted by her man who hands her the glass of wine, she'd been looking forward to for the last couple of hours.

"Wow, this is great!" She says; "This is all I could think about. God, I love you."

"Well, you seemed a little down this morning, so I thought I could help." I say while cutting her some cheese and ripping a hunk of a crusty French baguette.

"Here, eat something, I don't want this wine going straight to your head."

"I love how you take care of me."' She says, reaching for the glossy magazine on the table. "How was your day, Marty?" she asks looking at the cover of the magazine.

"Not bad. A little busy with a few too many moving parts, but okay." I say, grabbing some cheese and thinking if she only knew what some of those parts were.

"That's nice, how was the store? Did you have a good take today?" She says sipping her wine.

"Pretty good, probably $2,500 to $3,000, a good start for the week—steady." I say, pulling a pack of smokes out of the pocket of my slacks.

"How about you, how's the real estate game?" I ask as I pull out a smoke and light it.

"Actually, it's a little slow right now. Nobody seems to be looking or in any hurry to part with their money, so the team has been doing a lot of fishing." She says, reaching for my smokes.

"Well, I'm sure it will pick up." I say; "You guys are the best at what you do, so it'll happen." Leaning back, crossing my legs and exhaling a cloud of blue smoke as Lowell George belts out; *well they say, time loves a hero, but only time can tell if he's real, he's a legend from heaven, if he ain't he was sent here from hell.* Man, I love this tune, I think. It's perfect.

"Cassidy, I have something to tell you." I say still sitting back. "I can't wait any longer." She can tell by my tone that I have something serious to say and she immediately throws down the magazine and sits erect.

"Yes, Marty, what is it?" She says putting her wine down too.

"Well, I don't know how to put it, so I'm just going to go for it," I say, grabbing my wine and taking a deep drink.

"It's like this babe: you know Milagro, the woman who works for that guy, Carlos?"

"Yes Marty, of course I do, what about her?" she says weakly.

"It's nothing like you are thinking; I'm not having an affair or anything." I say, waiting for her to respond, but she just stares at the ground.

"Anyway, she approached me at that fund-raiser telling me that she had an opportunity that would change my life." I say putting down the wine.

"Oh, she did, did she?" Now Cassidy sounds a little defensive, but suddenly recognizes the scenario as it's similar to what Carlos said to her.

"Yes, and I met with her to find out what she meant, but before you say anything…." I say sitting forward; "I was only interested, because I wanted to explore it for us—for us, babe."

"I'm listening, Marty," Cassidy answers now taking a long pull on her cigarette.

"Well, we met at the store and she had me, get this—launder, or at least run though our dryers $50 thousand in new crisp twenty dollar bills." I say, waiting for her to speak.

"Go ahead, keep talking, I'm listening and believe me you have my attention." Cassidy now visibly concerned says.

"So, I help her with this money that is, and she tells me that there is way more money where this came from. So I met her again today, and all I'd have to do is simply give her a ride in my van to an undisclosed location and then help load the van with cash and deliver her to another place and off load the cash. I get $300 grand for this, sounds good, right?" I say, gulping my wine and refilling the glass in anticipation of the *freak-out.*

"Marty," she says putting out her smoke; "I think that is the craziest thing I ever heard, and you must be the most gullible guy to ever walk the earth. I am sure this hot-looking woman needs you, please, Marty, don't piss on my leg and tell me it's raining. I'm not that stupid! How long have you been seeing her and do you love her?" she says with tears in her eyes.

"Baby, it's not like that at all. As a matter of fact, she only trusts me because I DIDN'T come on to her when we were alone. I'm the only one she can trust and that's the truth. I love you and would never jeopardize us—you have to believe that." I say, moving closer to my wife.

"So, let me get this right. She picks you out of all the men in all of New York City to help her transport some cash and you get $300 grand for being a chauffeur? It just doesn't add up, Marty, we have a problem. You have a problem—I don't like this nor do I like the spot you've put me in."

Now she's pissed. She lights another cigarette and drains her wine and grabs the bottle and pours another.

She's doing just a little acting here because she knows she isn't "lily white" here either, but Marty doesn't know that.

"Cass, I have never even touched this woman. I have no feelings for her. I'm doing this for the money—$300 grand is a lot of money. We could get a head start on retirement with that. "We could get closer to one of these…" I say, pointing at one of the magazine's "drop-dead-gorgeous homes." Besides, it would be *my* contribution for a change."

"Marty, you'll never see a dime. She is playing you—sometimes you are so stupid." She says, knowing that will cut into me.

I've always felt like I wasn't smart enough. We've been together for so long and I've told her my deepest fears and secrets and now with that statement she was not fighting fair.

"Well, I know the money is there, Cass, I saw it." I say, almost pleading.

"She showed me a Polaroid of Carlos standing in front of pallets of cash, each pallet had $3 million dollars in cash on it. I saw it. Carlos was holding a paper that had last weeks date on it. She wasn't lying to me. I asked her to prove it to me, that's why she showed me the photo. Plus, she is afraid of Carlos. You need to be careful too." I say.

"You might be walking into a trap. I know he is a client—have you seen him since the Ball?" I ask, pushing the issue.

"This is NOT about me." she said taking a drag on her smoke, exhaling she continues; "No, I have not," now she was lying.

"I'm telling you the truth, Cass. I didn't have to tell you this, but because I keep nothing from you, I needed you to know."

Now I was relieved, cleansed—I told her. She'd reacted and it was all out on the table now.

"Well, I forbid you to help her and if you do, I will leave you, Marty. I don't want you to see her again. Do you hear me?" Cassidy standing now and begins pacing.

"But, I already gave her my word and said I would. I can't go back and tell her my wife said I couldn't help her. I won't do that." I say as I stand up too.

"Marty, I don't know what to say here, but I am really disappointed in you. I thought the days of "easy-money schemes" were behind you, and now this? What did you expect me to say? "Great, honey. Let's have a party! You're going risk your life over $300 grand. I'm proud of you—have you lost your fucking mind!" She exclaims while sitting down. "When is this $300 grand-ride supposed to happen, if I may?"

"Next Monday. She'll call me and tell me where to pick her up and then we'll go to the place where the pallets of money are. We'll load the van and then I deliver her to somewhere upstate and then wait for the next set of instructions for the next delivery."

It feels like I might be making a dent in my wife's armor, so I stay on the offensive.

"We could take this cash, plus what else I can make off of her which will be substantial and add our money and assets and get the hell out of New York. We could live in the sun; we could spend each day; however, WE want to. We'll owe nothin' to nobody. We'll live as we please—wherever we want. Think about it; it's what we've talked about. We just were handed the key to freedom. You've got to support me on this. You have to give me your blessing," I say really sincerely.

Cassidy is still in shock. This was not the evening she had planned on. All this was way too much for her to process, but one thing registered, she believed what her husband was telling her to be the truth. She can tell when he was lying, and he wasn't. She knew this.

But, why would Milagro approach Marty? What was Carlos's role in this?

Cassidy also had a secret she was keeping from Marty, but there was no way she was going to tell him about her dealings with Carlos. There was a lot more on the line there.

"Marty, if you feel you have to do this, then go ahead. I'm not going to stop you. You've already decided without me, so asking me for forgiveness rather than permission is a moot point. If what you say is going to happen, happens, then we'll have another discussion, but right now, I want you out of my sight. I'm sure you understand."

"Well as long as you're really upset I might as well tell you that the FBI was in the store today asking questions about Carlos, so again I warn you, be wary of this man, be very wary," I add with a smirk.

Cassidy gets up and gives me a look that I know and hate; she grabs the wine bottle out of the chiller, takes it with her and walks inside and heads upstairs. I count to five and hear the slam of the bedroom door and I breathe deep. I did the right thing. She'll appreciate my honesty when I show her the money. Cassidy will come around, I am counting on it.

In the bedroom, Cassidy is sitting on the bed with wine in hand and wondering if Carlos was behind this, she wouldn't put it past him. She couldn't ask Carlos, because if Marty was right, she would be putting her husband and the Latin Lolita in danger. She had to be careful and not let Carlos know that she knew any of this.

Maybe, she could leverage this information somehow. She didn't know, but she knew she didn't want to show her hand to Carlos—not yet at least—not just yet.

51

Carlos is early. He walks into the Marriott Marquis at 8:30 a.m., knowing he has 30 minutes to kill, before meeting the lovely Cassidy Tyroni. He takes the elevator up to the eighth floor, where the Clocktower Restaurant is. He looks around and sees the bustling lobby is jammed with people—all going somewhere. Some are heading to the meeting rooms, others waiting in line to check out, while others are just waiting to meet people. Carlos walks into the gift shop, looking for a little something to break the ice at this mornings meeting. Perhaps, one of those lighters that say; *I Love New York*, will get her to smile. He's seen her smoke, so he knows she'd use it and besides, he was going to make her a wealthy woman, so a cheap lighter should get her to smile.

Walking out of the gift shop, he greets the hostess who looks to be about 55 with glasses around her neck suspended by a beaded chain that looks like her granddaughter might have made and asks for a booth for two in the smoking section. The hostess, who looks like she'd rather be somewhere else, unceremoniously shows him to a booth. She robotically asks him if he'd like some coffee and when he says, "yes," she walks away, only to return with a glass pot of coffee and cream and sugar. Pouring him some coffee she says; "Karen will be your server, she'll be with you soon."

"Thank you." Carlos replies and adds cream to his coffee.

He takes out the lighter he bought, and places it in the plate that sits across from him. He checks his platinum Philippe Patek, seeing that its 8:50 a.m.—ten minutes till Cassidy gets there. He hopes she has the signed contract, so he doesn't have to waste time going over it with her and they can begin to get working. Maybe, he thinks, he might need to reserve a suite, so they can consummate the deal, but he isn't sure that's the right play, so he stays put and drinks his coffee.

His cell phone vibrates and although he despises the use of cell phones in restaurants, he looks at the number and takes the call.

"Jamie, why are you calling me on this phone? I thought we said never on cell phones." Carlos says with some attitude.

"Carlos," Jamie says; "I just wanted to see when I could call you to talk about a change in plans this Friday."

"Call me at home on the land line, Thursday evening. Don't forget, Jamie, Thursday after 5 p.m., okay? Got it?" Carlos asks.

"Thursday, after 5 p.m. is good," Jamie answers, "talk to you then." Jamie hangs up without saying anything else. Carlos looks around and snaps his phone shut, just as Cassidy walks up to the table.

"Something important on that call, Carlos, you look surprised." she says, pulling out her own chair, before Carlos can get up to help.

"No, not really. Just unusual timing for my associate to be calling, that's all." Carlos answers, placing the phone back into the breast pocket of his navy blue pinstripe Hugo Boss suit. Carlos likes expensive clothing. He likes the way it feels against his skin and he likes the treatment the salespeople give him in the shops on 57th Street.

"Well, I'm glad to hear that," she says; "because, I want you to be completely engaged at this meeting."

"Don't you worry; I am all yours this morning. Nothing could distract me, except your beauty." Carlos says salaciously.

"Cut the Don Juan-shit, Carlos. I'll drive that car, and right now, your car is no where near my garage, so put my little "grab" the other day, out of your mind. I just wanted to see how big your balls are." she says, leaning forward and touching his hand.

"What's this?" she says, holding up the lighter.

"I just wanted you to have something that would remind you of me, whenever you used it," he says, sipping his coffee.

"Would you like some?" He says, placing his cup in its saucer.

"Yes, please," she says, turning her cup over to receive the black liquid.

"Cream?" Carlos asks, as puts down the pot of coffee.

"No, I take mine black, but, thank you," she says, sipping the hot brew.

Just then, Karen, their server appears and hands them menus.

"I see you have coffee. Can I get either of you some fresh fruit juice?"

"No, thank you, Karen, Just give us a couple of minutes to look over your menu. Thank you." Carlos says, giving the waitress a big smile.

"Very good, sir, I'll be right back," she says, walking away.

"Are you a breakfast eater, Cassidy?" Carlos asks.

"No and I don't make my bed," Cassidy says.

"A hot breakfast for me is coffee and a cigarette. Do you mind if I smoke?" She asks.

"Not at all, hence, the lighter," Carlos smiles, grabbing for the lighter to light her cigarette. Cassidy leans in, allowing him to light her up.

"Thanks," she says; "you certainly are a gentleman. You're mother taught you well."

"Breeding is everything. Don't you agree?" he says sheepishly.

"Well, I guess so, but they say your environment has a lot to do with it too," Cassidy remarks. "I didn't ask to see you to discuss human behavior. I'm here to give you this," she says, pulling the contract out of her Prada portfolio briefcase. She plunks it on the table.

"I've signed it, so I'm ready to get down to business."

Carlos sits back and gives Cassidy a 500 watt smile and picking up the contract says;

"Well now, that's great news. I'm ready to work too, so let's get started."

Karen returns asking; "are you ready to order yet?"

"I am. Are you Cassidy?" Carlos says.

"Sure," she says. "I'll have the fresh fruit cup and brioche, please."

"Thank you." The blonde server says; "For you, sir?"

"I'll have the corned beef hash with poached eggs, wheat toast, and a side of your breakfast sausage." Carlos the wolf says almost licking his chops.

"Thank you. I'll put these orders in and be right back, more coffee?" She asks.

"Yes, please." Cassidy answers.

"I'm on it," the waitress says and quickly returns with fresh coffee; "your breakfast will be right up."

"Thank you," Carlos says, dismissing the server.

"Well, where were we?" Carlos asks.

"You were going to tell me how we begin making this vast amount of money you've been talking about. I've done my part—signed your contract. Now talk to me." Cassidy says, taking a drag on her cigarette and placing it in the ashtray.

"First things, first," Carlos says; "I need to know if you understood all the clauses on the contract?" He says, sipping his coffee.

"Of course, I did. I wouldn't have signed it, if I didn't." Cassidy says, recrossing her legs under the table.

"Okay. Have you got something to write on?" Carlos says, taking out a piece of paper and unfolding it.

"Sure do." Cassidy says, reaching into her briefcase pulling out a yellow legal pad and a Mont Blanc pen—ready to write.

"Good." Carlos says; "I like my women prepared, and you certainly are that."

"Carlos, enough with the compliments, I know that I'm good, so get on with it."

"Write this down," he says realizing that this meeting was going to be all business and no play and he reads off two addresses in Red Hook to her.

"I want you to inquire about buying these two properties for me, to start. I already own the warehouse between these two buildings, but I want the whole block."

"Okay. Do you know what they're asking price is?" She says, ready to write.

"Cassidy, they aren't for sale. You'll have to find out who owns them and make them an offer, they can't refuse. If you know what I mean." Carlos satisfied with himself says. "Right," Cassidy says, putting her pen down; "You want me to buy you two buildings in Red Hook that aren't for sale, and when do you want this done?"

"As soon as you can," he says; "if you'd like, we can go look at them tomorrow, after you have some information for me."

"In that case, Carlos, our meeting is over. I'd love to stay, but I have some work to do. Thanks for the coffee," she says, stuffing her pad back into her briefcase.

"Oh, and Carlos, don't call me. I'll call you. I don't want anyone in my firm to know that we are working together, Okay?"

"Sure, Cassidy, I know you're protecting yourself. I'll keep my distance. Remember, my mother taught me well," he says, looking up at the standing beauty before him.

"Good, I'd appreciate your discretion. I'll be talking to you soon," she extends her right hand and instead of shaking it, Carlos gives the top of her hand a kiss.

"Till then, Cassidy, till then," he says with that Cheshire cat smile.

Cassidy wheels on her Ferragamo heels and all that's left of her is the lipstick mark on the cigarette still smoldering in the ashtray.

That went very well, Carlos thinks to himself, very well. He reviews the contract, sees her signature, and waits on Karen with his breakfast. He's worked up an appetite. This woman intrigues him, and he can't wait to see her again, bedding her will be a challenge, but Carlos is up to it.

52

Marty wakes up on the couch in the den. Cassidy locked the bedroom door and he did some pleading to get in, but he gave up. He knows his wife and knows when she's dug in, so he settled for the couch instead of the guest room.

It wasn't so bad, he's slept on worse.

Shaking off the night, he goes to the bathroom, takes a leak, and wanders into the kitchen. He sees right away that Cassidy has already been up because the coffee maker is still on and her cup is in the sink. He probably shouldn't have opened that second bottle, but he did and slept through her leaving this morning.

He then spies a note on the black granite counter in the pass though into the breakfast nook. The note reads; *Marty, sorry I blew up last night. Let's talk today. I'll call you from the office—Love, Me.*

Marty knows he's in the clear now. He'll wait for her to call. She must have thought it over and realized, "what the hell." It seems like easy money, so why not us? Marty crumples the note, throws it into the garbage, and heads upstairs to get cleaned up for his day.

53

Snuffy calls Garrett and sets up a lunch meeting. He's got to tell Garrett that he needs some cash and why. Garrett will either tell him to go away, or give him the cash that he needs for Chip. But in any event, if he's going to meet Chip tonight with the money he's asking for, he'll need Garrett's help.

They decided to meet downtown, near Garrett's office—at a little Italian restaurant called, Stella's. It's a quiet, family place, with checkered tablecloths and Italian music playing. They have a great lunch buffet and Snuffy knows this place is too nice for him to get Garrett in any trouble by being seen with him. Garret agreed immediately, when Snuffy suggested the spot.

Snuffy arrived first, finding a table in the back, with a view of everyone entering the restaurant. He feels good about this meeting. He thinks Garrett might be pleased with the plan. He'd soon find out, because in walks Garrett, who spots Snuffy. Garrett walks to his table, sitting down without a handshake or a greeting.

"Talk Snuffy. Why are we here?" Garrett asks almost rudely.

"It's about our target, I still haven't been able to come up with anything, but I have a plan that is guaranteed to get us some info," he says smiling; "I have a friend who can tap into his phone line, without having to enter this building. He can do it, via, the telephone pole down the block," Snuffy says, looking for the waiter.

"Keep talking, I'm listening," Garrett replies, buttering a roll from the basket on the table. "My guy needs $3 thousand to do the job—I need some money," Snuffy says, finally getting the waiters attention.

The waiter walks up and says; "Gentlemen, welcome to *Stella's*. Will you be going to the buffet today?"

"Yes, we will." Says Garrett; "and we'll have two cokes. Thank you."

"Very good, sir, just help yourself to the buffet and I'll be right back with your sodas."

"Let's get some food and figure this out Snuffy. I hate to decide to break the law that I am paid to uphold on an empty stomach." Garrett says, getting up and heading to the buffet. "Okay, I hear ya'," Snuffy says, placing his napkin on his chair as he follows his employer.

Both men load their plates with some bowtie pasta, sausage, meatballs, and some spinach arabiatta, and cups of Italian wedding soup. They get themselves situated and begin eating. "So, tell me this again, for three grand, I get what exactly?" Garrett says slurping his soup.

"We'll get twelve hours of untraceable "listen time," and we'll get it Thursday afternoon till Friday mid-day," Snuffy says, breaking off a hunk of bread for dipping.

"Is your friend certain he can do this?" Garrett answers back.

"Definitely—he is a whiz; he should work for you guys—he's so good," Snuffy says proudly. "Well, if he's so good, why is he your friend?" Garrett says with a smile.

"Hey, that's not cool. I'm on your side." Snuffy says, wiping his plate with some bread. "Well, normally I'd tell you no way can I authorize this, but I've got nothing and the clocks ticking, so you caught me with no choice here. When do you need the money?" Garrett asks.

"Now," Snuff says; "I need to deliver it to him this afternoon. Is that a problem?"

"Yes, but no," Garrett says; "after we finish, we'll go to the bank and I'll withdraw the cash. I can't believe that I'm doing this, but I'm behind a rock here and need something."

"Great," says Snuffy; "You won't be sorry and I'll buy lunch."

54

It's almost 5:30 p.m., when Cassidy's assistant finally hands her the information that she was waiting for. Both buildings Carlos wants, are owned by the Banco Popular—the bank that caters to the Hispanic population of the Tri-State area. Cassidy sits back and smiles; she has done business with them before and has a good friend in the property division.

Getting Carlos what he wants, won't be a problem she thinks.

She goes through her PDA and retrieves the number, dialing it; she gets the automated attendant, waits, and enters the extension. Expecting a recorded message, she's surprised when she hears; "Properties, this is Michael."

"Michael, its Cassidy Tyroni. How are you?"

Cassidy and Michael met while doing a deal in Tribeca a few years back. The bank had foreclosed on some warehouses there and when Robert De Niro opened his diner there and some other developments started and as the neighborhood got chic, Cassidy took the eyesore structures off their hands and flipped them for a handsome profit that Michael benefited from on the back end, thanks to Cassidy.

"Cassidy, it's been a long time. I'm fine and you?"

"Michael, I'm great. I'm even better, because I am talking to you," she says smiling. "Why's that? How can I help you?" He asks.

"Well, it's easy. Your bank owns a couple of properties in Red Hook and I have a buyer for them." She says.

"You've got to be kidding me. What are the addresses?" The young man asks.

Cassidy reads him the addresses and asks; "How much do you guys want?"

"Wait a minute. Let me pull them up and we'll see what the story is; hang on," he says.

Cass can hear him typing away.

"Okay, I've got them. We got them in a foreclosure, a couple of years back. They appraised for $5 million each. I'll take $5.5 for each. We are not in the warehouse business and we don't need them, so if I can turn a million in profit for the bank, I'm a hero," the young bank official says.

"So for $11 million, I get them both free and clear." She says.

"Free and clear," he says; "you want me to write the paper on them?"

"Yes, I do. When do you need some money, Michael?" She asks, hoping for some time. "Well, because they weren't listed, I won't have anything pushing me, so we can say, Thursday, by 5:00 p.m. Can you get me $220 thousand, to hold them?" He asks.

"You bet I can. Should I use the same routing number as last time, Michael?" Cass asks, checking her file.

"No, we'll open another account for this. Call me after 10 a.m. tomorrow and I'll have it for you, okay?" Michael says.

"Done, Michael, I love doing business with you. I wish you held more property; we could both make a lot of money," she says, jotting down the information.

"Me too, my wife is decorating our house and it feels like I have a separate bedroom for the people at Roche Bubois. Everytime I come home, there's another piece of furniture."

"I hear ya', man. Who knows, maybe there will be more; my client is in a hungry mood," she says then thanks Michael and adds, "have a good night."

"Good night, Cassidy, I'll talk to you tomorrow. You made my day." He says and hangs up.

Cassidy is pressing some keys on her calculator and smiles. She just made $1.1 million dollars with one phone call. Carlos is already paying off. She quickly dials the phone; "Hi, Bertha, is Marty there?"

"Sure, Cassidy, I'll get him, hang on, okay?"

Marty answers asking; "Hey babe, what's up?" I answer, unsure of what I'll hear from her.

"How would you like to go to dinner at Palio tonight? I just made a big score."

"Sounds good. I'll need an hour or so to clean up and change. I can meet you there at seven-ish."

"Great," she says, "see you there."

"Babe, about last night…" I start to say and before I can finish.

"Water under the bridge," she says, "if you think you should do that run with that Latin woman then do it, I'll support your decision. I trust you, Marty."

I am speechless all I can muster is; "okay, see you there."

Hanging up, I just stare at the phone and think; "this must have been one hell-of-a- good day for her, or she's up to something." I never thought it was both.

Before Cassidy even looks up, she dials another number.

"Carlos, its Cassidy, the buildings are yours."

"Yep, that's right, both of them," listening to his next question; "eleven million. They need $220 thousand by tomorrow, at 5 p.m., is that okay?"

"Good, I thought so," she says; "I'd like to see them. Can we go there tomorrow around 11 a.m.?" she asks.

"Great, pick me up at my office at 11 a.m," she says, writing down some notes.

"You're welcome," she says, hanging the phone up; "you're very welcome," she repeats to herself out loud.

Palio is an incredibly beautiful, elegant restaurant, located in Midtown on the 4th floor of a nondescript office building. When you get off the elevator, it's like entering a world of polished cypress, mahogany, and teakwood. The tables are spaced further apart than in most Manhattan eateries, and that's why Cassidy selected it. She needed to tell Marty about this deal and the future of her business. It was important for her to share the truth with Marty. She flirted with the idea of keeping him out of the loop, but when she realized that Carlos was talking millions; well, it's hard to keep that much a secret. Besides, Marty shared his little clandestine operation with Milagro, which at first, made her feel betrayed and jealous, but when she looked at herself, she remembered something her father had said. He told her that "sometimes we fail to see our role in things, because we get so caught up in how it affects us. We get too close to the fire and forget that when we point a finger at another, there are four fingers pointing right back at us."

It's funny; she thought that as she got older, her dad got smarter.

She needed to come clean with her husband. There were many occasions when he made her furious. She also knew that she'd rather be miserable with Marty, than be without him. Too many of her girlfriends and their husbands took the easy way out, divorce, but Cassidy knew that relationships, long-term relationships, took work. It takes courage to be happy.

Again, her dad's voice rang in her ears. "You've heard the saying that the grass looks greener on the other side? Well, do you know why that is, Cassidy?" he'd say to her. He'd tell her matter-of- fact, "because the other guy is working on their grass. Your grass isn't attractive to you, because you don't care for it—you take it for granted. Most people don't have a lawn, take care of your grass, and another's won't make you envious. Want what you have my dear.

Cassidy missed her father. He passed away eight years ago, of a heart attack. He went just like that. No warnings, no signs, just one day, in his backyard while watering his tomato plants, he fell over and that was it. Marty was so comforting and every word he said soothed her. It was then, that she realized how special he was. No one knew her like Marty did. He had a way of making you feel special. The way he focused on your words and how you said things—she always felt he settled for her. He was one of the smartest men she knew, but he was bad at business—just didn't have the killer instinct. He liked people too much. She felt a warm sensation—she loved that man and she had to tell him everything tonight.

I am absolutely baffled when I hang up from Cassidy's call. Last night, she was leaving me. Today, she supports me and wants to put last night behind her. I know my wife and that is not the way she behaves. She usually would hang on to the resentment and beat me over the head with it, until I succumbed and gave in and did things her way. This was usually the underlying message in all of her lectures; "Why can't you be more like me, Marty!" God, how I would cringe on the inside, when it got to that, I thought her incredibly egotistical and selfish when she was like that and I really don't like her very much that way.

I have this theory that just about all arguments are based on the opposing parties saying or thinking, "Why can't you be more like me; can't you see how much better I am than you and that what I am doing is better for you?" Countries, religions, cultures—it didn't matter— most disagreements came down to that premise, "be more like us."

We all have defects of character and Cassidy's really only came out when we were in disagreement. So all things considered, it wasn't the worst of marriages. As a matter of fact, I think what we have is what most people wanted. I am way more than reasonably happy and I think Cassidy is too.

However, I know something isn't right in Denmark, and perhaps at Palio tonight, after a few glasses of fine wine, I'd find out. But right now, I needed to get out of the shop and get home and dress for dinner. Palio warranted a jacket and slacks, so I cleared my desk of any pressing paperwork, checked on a couple of things, and said *good night* to Bertha, who still was acting weird, but I had to get out of there without digging any deeper, so paying little attention to Bertha, I walked out and into the sun and the bustle of a city street.

55

"Hey Chip, Snuff here. I have the package, so I'll see you tonight at the same place, okay?"

"Yep," Chip answers; "I'll also need the target's name, and you'll need to get a cell phone that we can throw away, when it's done."

"A cell phone?"

Chip quickly answers; "Yes, and don't ask questions. Just do what I tell ya' and you'll get what you need, okay?"

"Well," Snuff says; "I have no choice here, do I?"

"No, you don't Snuff—Chip fires back; so don't forget. Got it?"

"Yes, I'll see you in a few hours." Chip hangs up, leaving Snuffy staring at his phone.

Well, I guess it's off to Duane Reed to buy a calling card and then a cheap cell phone, Snuffy thinks to himself. Hopefully, he can get it activated today. This was turning into a pain-in-the-ass. He needed to remember that he was repaying a favor to Garrett. He hated being in debt to people who made him repay them by having to do things he disliked…note to self—make amends quickly.

At home, I am staring into my closet. I want to look sophisticated, so I select a pair of Armani slacks and a Versace blazer that Cassidy bought, a matching Tommy Bahama silk shirt and a crocodile belt and some Cole Haan loafers.

Looking at myself in the full-length, I'm pleased, and think to myself—how nice this would look walking into some restaurant on an island surrounded by too blue water—some day—I reflected—someday.

Back downstairs, I pour a glass of Grey Goose on the rocks and turn on some Dylan—his lyrics make me stop and think… *Like a rolling stone, if you knew what a drag it was to see you, you'd know.* Damn, that Jew from Minnesota had a magic way with words—arranging them, delivering them, just so. It transports me back to another time. Music could do that; transport you to another time, change your physiology, make you feel the way you did when you first heard the lyrics, the melody—God I love that.

I walk around our home, looking at things that, with Dylan in the background, made me think of all the years and experiences Cassidy and I shared. It's the shared experiences, the way you think you know how another feels, and when it's validated, just how comforting it is to be with that person—a peaceful easy feeling. That's all I want—that easy feeling. The chance to take a deep breath and know it's all alright. That's all I want—is for it to be all alright, right now.

Draining my glass, I turn off Dylan, turn off the lights, and hit the street looking for a cab. Again, my thoughts shift.

"Man, wouldn't it be nice to walk out of my house and see the ocean, hear the surf, feel the sand beneath my feet and follow the calypso or reggae music to wherever it led me?" Just then, the sound of a horn honking, police sirens, and the airbrakes hissing on a city bus, startle me right off the island in my mind and back to the task at hand-hailing a cab.

Cassidy jots down the address of the warehouses she just bought for Carlos and puts it in her briefcase, turns off the banker's lamp on her desk, and says her good nights to the staff. On her way out, she sees the waiting car that she called to take her to the restaurant. Cassidy doesn't like hailing cabs, so she hires a car service and pays them through the business. Some day, she thought, she'll have a car and a proper driver, after she does a few more deals for Carlos—that won't be a pipedream, but a reality. Just like the queen of Manhattan real estate and hotels –Leona Helmsley used to do, until a disgruntled bean-counter in her organization turned her into the IRS.

But today, it's a black Lincoln that smells of stale cigarette smoke and aftershave and a driver who just says; "where to?"

After she gives him the address, she stares out the window watching the city go by. She begins to wonder what life outside of the city would be like—a simpler life—no crowds, no clock-watching, no emergencies—a softer and easier way. Maybe her husband was right; a little business on an island in the Caribbean was what they should really be working towards, instead of a Manhattan Penthouse or an estate in Larchmont.

Cassidy was conflicted for sure. What was the right dream?

I get to the restaurant ahead of Cassidy and let the hostess know that the Tyroni party is here and that I'm waiting for my wife. I ask the woman manning the desk who looks like a Mediterranean goddess dressed in a slinky black dress if she could direct my wife to the bar when she arrives. The hostess nods politely then shows me to the bar. But before she leaves I say; "You'll know it's my wife; she'll be the striking blonde that you can't take your eyes off of ."

The younger Sophia Loren-look-alike says; "she is a lucky woman to have an adoring husband like you, Mr. Tyroni."

Satisfied with myself at her reaction, I sit at a table for two in the bar and wait for the server to take my drink order.

No more than ten minutes after I'm seated, I see the hostess walking in with Cassidy. The two of them are smiling at one another, as if they are sharing a secret. The hostess arrives.

"Mr. Tyroni, you weren't lying; the striking blonde is here."

I get up and hug Cassidy and wink at the hostess, behind her back. I am the man.

Cassidy sits, just as the waiter brings my drink—a Grey Goose dirty martini.

Cassidy looks up and says; "That looks good. I'll have one of those please."

"With pleasure," the server says and vanishes to retrieve her libation and in a matter of minutes, there are two martinis on their table.

Grabbing my glass and holding it out to toast; "Here's to every man's dream—a woman with looks, who cooks, and has a big checkbook."

"Marty, you certainly are a romantic," she says laughing and sips her drink.

"Cass, right now, you are my world and whatever this life has in store for us, I want you to be by my side to share it."

"Sweetie, that's my wish too. We make a good team; we just fit and we were lucky to find each other. I'm a happy girl."

"So, happy girl," I ask; "why the celebration? Tell me about your score."

"Well, I'm glad you asked. As you know, I have taken on Carlos Ferrar as a client," she says, sipping the martini and putting it down.

"He is extremely liquid and wants to buy up some commercial real estate so he can diversify his holdings."

"Liquid isn't the right word." I say; "He is a goddamn tidal wave."

Thinking to myself, I don't like the way this is sounding, but I bite my tongue till I hear more—an open mind is what I need to cultivate here.

Cassidy leans in; "Sssh... let's talk at the table. You never know who could be listening."

I nod. I can tell when my wife is getting paranoid and I figure after another martini and some wine, that will pass.

So, we chit-chat about this and that, finish a couple of more martinis, and get seated. I asked the hostess to seat us at a banquette in the back, so we could really have some privacy. Once seated, another server hands me the wine list. Without even looking, I say, "We will have the Stag's Leap."

"Very good choice, sir," the waiter says and leaves us.

"I feel like some veal tonight." I say, as I look over the exquisite menu.

"What have you got a taste for tonight, babe?" I ask.

"I don't know, something light. I had a big breakfast and lunch today." She says.

The sommelier delivers the bottle, shows me the label, engages us in some conversation about the winery, and pours out the wine; I decline a tasting, because I hate that bullshit pretentious tasting ritual, since I have seen too many people act so pompous that it makes me gag. After we order our meal, I start in.

"Okay, back to your cash-rich client. Let me tell you more about the picture that I told you about last night that showed Carlos in front of hundreds of millions of dollars, Cassidy, I don't know where he got it. I didn't ask Milagro, but it was a shitload of cash. You need to be careful; I get a funny vibe from this guy."

"Honey, I entered into this arrangement with my eyes wide-open and made sure that I am not too exposed and liable." Cassidy said, sipping her wine.

"Good, because Milagro doesn't trust him and I believe she is afraid of him. I think he is into some shady deals."

"Well, I don't know about that. He simply explained to me that he has some cash he needs to move and real estate was the way he wanted to do so," she replied, readjusting her napkin. "Which is why I wanted to celebrate tonight. He just purchased two warehouses in Red Hook today with my help and my commission is a million plus!" She said, extending her glass for a toast.

"Well, that is something to celebrate." I say, reaching out to touch her glass.

"After I turn in the firm's part, I clear almost $600 grand. Not bad for a day's work, huh?" beaming she says.

"Yes, my dear that is some serious escarole!" I say taking a hard swallow of wine.

As I place his glass down, it hits me.... "Did you say, Red Hook?"

"Yes, why?" she asks.

"Well, I'm sure it's a coincidence, but have I got a story to tell you honey. It seems Walt is under the impression, based on some information he got from what I consider an unreliable source, that in Red Hook there is a warehouse full of cash, and every other Friday he said a truck makes a delivery of more cash. To make this story even crazier is that Walt is seriously considering hijacking –yes hijacking the truck and making off with the cash."

Looking across the table I see Cassidy shaking her head with her mouth open.

"I can't believe that I'm thinking this," I say, "but that photo I saw, looked like it was taken in a warehouse, but I couldn't tell you where it was. Wouldn't it be something, if the two warehouses were the same? You don't have the address with you, do you?" I ask.

"I do, but it's in my briefcase, which I checked at the coat check." Cass says.

"Give me the claim check. I'll call Walt. He'll know if the two addresses are close."

"You must be crazy, honey. Carlos wouldn't be stockpiling cash in Red Hook, and besides, I didn't want to say it to you, but I bet what Milagro showed you, was computer enhanced and it was a bullshit picture to get your appetite whet."

"Just give me the ticket and we'll see," I say, "besides, it was a Polaroid, so it couldn't have been enhanced."

"Okay, Columbo, here's the ticket," she says, fishing in her bag.

So I take the ticket and return with her briefcase, handing it to Cassidy because I can never find anything in any of her bags, but she can in seconds. Cassidy takes out the address she wrote down and hands it to me. I then take her briefcase and walk off to return it to the coat check and call Walt.

Cassidy now alone, looks around the restaurant at the beautiful people and drains her wine glass. Her mood has now gone from ecstatic to nervous. She hopes her husband is wrong, but for some reason her gut tells her differently.

56

I hand the briefcase back to the girl behind the counter, drop five dollars into her tip basket, and step into the foyer and dial up Walt.

"The Mixer, this is Walt," the big bartender answers.

"Walt, it's Marty, I've got a question."

"Well, I didn't expect to hear from you. What's up?"

"Well, I need to know if the address I'm about to give you is remotely close to that warehouse you have been talking about? The one in Red Hook," I ask and then read him the address.

"Marty, that is right next door. Where did you get that?"

"Well, I'd rather not say, but let's just say we need to talk tomorrow, okay?" I say hanging up.

Walt, not hearing the click keeps talking; "Marty, what's going on?" Realizing he is no longer connected, he places his phone down and looks out the picture window of the bar.

Returning to the table, I look at Cassidy and say; "Houston, we have a problem."

It's just then, that the server delivers our food, distracting us. We wait until he's gone and then Cassidy asks; "What's wrong? Did Walt know the address Marty?"

"Not only did he know the address, he says its right next door to the warehouse that has been getting the deliveries. Cassidy, I say, Carlos is into something and maybe we are the only ones who can connect the dots."

"Marty, before you go jumping to conclusions, let's think about this. How and why would Carlos be getting truckloads of cash delivered to a warehouse in Red Hook?" Cassidy asks, as she cuts into her grouper.

"I don't know, but I got a feeling that it isn't on the up and up. I told you an FBI agent came around the other day asking questions about Carlos." I say reminding her.

"I didn't know anything so I kind of stonewalled the cop," I add. "I was trying to protect my score with Milagro."

"Jesus, Marty," Cassidy said; "this is some serious stuff. I need to ask Carlos about this." "The Hell you do! If you tip him off, then we become a part of this. Right now, we are innocent bystanders. The minute we begin to act like we know something, we become accompli to whatever it is he's doing and I don't think that's a good idea."

"Well," Cassidy says; "what do you suggest, Sherlock?"

"I don't know, but our food is getting cold. Let's eat and let me think on this one. I don't know what to do, but I think we can make this work to our advantage, if what I think is happening, is true."

"What's that Marty?" Cassidy asks.

"I'd rather wait, and then decide," he says; "by the way, when will your commission come through?"

"Well, we have to give the bank the earnest money tomorrow by 5 p.m., so I should see my commission in about a week, after we close. It's an expedited deal." She says, as she lifts a forkful of fish to her mouth.

"So, you could see your money as soon as next Monday or Tuesday?" I say, cutting my veal.

"Well, probably Monday, because I told the bank we'd like to have the paperwork done by this Friday and do the deal Monday morning," she says.

"Good," I say; "very good."

"I don't like the way that sounds, Marty." Cassidy says.

"Don't you worry a pretty hair on your head, I wouldn't think of doing anything stupid. Let's eat and continue our celebration. I won't know anything till tomorrow. Anyway, so why worry, right?" as I raise my hand getting our server's attention and point to the empty bottle of wine and order another.

"Tonight it's your night babe!"

439

Cassidy smiles and says; "If you say so Marty, but I can see those wheels turning in your little head and it makes me nervous, that's all."

"Don't worry, please, I'm sure we are wrong, besides, I'm a little drunk," I say, "and I'm sure Walt was wrong too."

I may be saying this, but that's not what I'm thinking, as I bite into my veal chop. That is not what I am thinking at all.

After supper, Cassidy calls the car service and the two of us share a cigarette on the street while waiting for our ride. We finished the second bottle of wine and we're feeling no pain. Our car arrives and I help Cassidy into the passenger side, I go around the street-side and tell the driver our address.

On the way home, all I can think about is calling Walt in the morning and taking a ride to Red Hook, in the light of day.

All Cassidy can think about, is getting home and in the bed. It's been a long prosperous day and she is drunk, tired, and full.

Walt closes the bar at 2 a.m. tonight. It was unusually busy for a Tuesday night, but all he can think about was Marty's call and that he needs to talk to him first thing later on today. Something very strange is happening and Walt wants to know how Marty got that address, but he has to wait—he hates to wait.

57

Snuffy managed the trip and the money drop off to Chip in New Jersey, without a problem. He was able to get a cheapie cell phone and then have it activated. He provided Chip with 24 hours worth of time. Chip thought this would be enough. Now, all that was left to do on this "listen in" mission was to meet Chip Thursday afternoon at Port Authority, when he comes in by bus and take him to the location.

Now Snuffy needs to fill Garrett in today and let him know what was required of him. That was a tricky thing, because already Garrett has coughed up the cash and now he's needed to provide protection for the operation, while they do the deed. Simply put, he'd have to be there with his badge and credentials in case any do-good cop came by and started asking questions, while they were listening in.

Garrett shouldn't have a problem with this, unless he has plans for Thursday night, but knowing Garret wasn't in high demand, Snuffy suspected he'd be available.

"Garrett, whatcha' doin', it's Snuffy."

"Oh goodie, it's the most expensive favor-returning snitch I know." Garrett answers sarcastically.

"Don't be like that man, you're gonna' be thanking me when my man comes through and blows things wide open for ya'." Snuffy says, lighting a smoke and exhaling into the receiver.

"So what's the deal? I have no time for small talk today." Garrett says.

"My, are we on the rag today agent?" asks Snuffy, tauntingly.

"Cut the shit Snuff, did you do the deal?" he asks.

"Yes, I did the deal. Here's how it's gonna' go down. Are you listening?" Snuffy asks, realizing Garrett isn't in the mood.

"I'll pick up my friend at four tomorrow, and we'll meet you at Ray's Pizza on 75th and 8th, at 4:30 p.m., okay?" Snuffy asks.

"Okay, then what?" The agent asks.

"Well, from there, we'll go to Carlos's neighborhood. I'll have a van and we'll get to work—I mean Chip will get to work."

"Chip, is that your friend's name?" Garrett asks.

"Brilliant, no wonder you are a cop. You don't miss a beat." Snuffy says.

"Listen, you little pain-in-the-ass, if I wasn't at my wits end, I'd kick your ass."

"Hey, big fella, I'm just playing with you. Take it easy; this will be an easy deal. We just get ourselves in place. Chip does some magic and we are listening in to your suspect all night. Isn't that what you want?" Snuffy asks.

"Yes, I apologize for being so short, but I'm wasting time on evidence that I can't use, so we had better come up with something that will lead me to something I can use or else I'm off this case and sent to the back of the line and I can't take that." Garrett says.

"Don't you worry, my friend, I have a good feeling about this, so you just try to relax. Keep looking and following up on your stuff, and I'll take care of things on my end. Lighten up—you are pushing yourself too hard." Snuffy says with some concern.

"Don't worry about me; just be at the pizza place on time. I don't like waiting. Got it?" Garrett says with some attitude.

"Got it, boss, we'll be there." Snuffy says sighing.

"Good." Garrett says and hangs up.

Looking into the receiver, Snuffy thinks that he needs to help his friend out and hopefully this "listen," will get him the lead he needs and he'll stop breaking Snuffy's balls, at least he hopes so.

With the day to himself, Snuffy thinks he'll treat himself to a manicure and a shoe shine. So with business taken care of till tomorrow, it's off to the Vietnamese ladies on 68th street and then a stroll down to Bryant Park for an outdoor shine. A nice plan for the day thinks Snuffy, as he laces his shoes and then heads out.

58

It's Wednesday morning and Carlos is sitting in his den, reading the morning *New York Times,* when he remembers that he needs to wire some money into the escrow account set up by Cassidy's company. He also remembers that he needs to tell her that *she* will be buying the building. He doesn't want his name on any of the paperwork. He feels over-exposed, as it is.

He begins to wonder whether or not it was smart to bring Cassidy in this quickly. He's not sure if he can really trust her, so he decides that he'll conduct a little test today, when they go to see the building in Red Hook.

This will let him know, if he can count on her discretion, honesty and loyalty.

It's a simple test; he'll wire in more than she needs and see what happens. Will she "come clean" and tell him that there is more money than she needed or will she just carry on and not say a word. Money and greed are powerful things. He has seen greed cost people their lives. He has seen what money can do to people. It can change their loyalties. It can change their hearts and it can make them do things that they'd never dream of ever doing. Money is a controlled substance; it is addicting, and the saying that money isn't everything, was clearly written by someone without any.

Carlos smiles to himself—deep down he hopes she passes this test, but if she doesn't, then he'll have to take required measures. Once Carlos has been betrayed or made to feel like he isn't feared, then he needs to make sure he is feared and respected—just ask Sliver.

Carlos calls his banker in the Caymans and orders the transfer of $300 thousand U.S. dollars into the numbered account that Cassidy provided him with.

Cayman has proven a great haven for some of Carlos's money. His operation works this way—he takes the cash they print to his Red Hook storage facility, he then contacts his bank in Cayman. The bank sends up three men, via private jet, into Teterboro Airport in Jersey. They take his cash and stash it in hidden panels in the jets fuselage. Carlos bought the jet for the Caymanian bank and had the modifications done—all at his expense. The bank of course, has no problem with these transfers, as they take a healthy 25% service charge.

The plane comes into the U.S. empty, except for the passengers and some bogus files, so that when asked, they say they are here on bank business.

Leaving the country, all is the same—passengers and the bogus files. The cash is hidden and no one is the wiser, especially, the IRS and the pain-in-the-ass FAA and NTSB.

Needless to say since 9/11, much has changed in air travel security measures, but if you have the bread for a private jet, the security is a lot easier to work around. Besides, the flight is made every two months, so it's really just a routine visit. Each flight can usually move about $50 million. Carlos props up his offshore accounts with those funds. Now with Cassidy's help, he'll put the cash in circulation, via real estate purchases. His business, Conserve-Reserve, also pumps his cash into the main stream economy, via the bogus clients who his unsuspecting traders execute buys and sells for. Actually, it's a really slick operation; the real estate angle will help, because the amounts are so high that he won't have to warehouse as much cash. He always thought that storing the cash would be his weak link.

As a matter of fact, the next Cayman transfer was scheduled for next Tuesday, which means after Friday's delivery from the "print truck," the existing warehouse will be full. If he intends on stepping up production, he needs those buildings next door.

After getting confirmation of the successful wire transfer, he calls Cassidy to let her know the money is there for her to make the deal. He confirms their 11 a.m. meeting and the trip to the buildings in Red Hook that they are buying.

Carlos realizes Cassidy is pretty shrewd by wanting to see the buildings. She knows that if it's a valuable property, she can then make a pile of dough when he goes to sell it. But she doesn't know that he has no intention of selling that building. He'll have to act as if he might, just to keep her hungry. Acting and misrepresenting come easy to Carlos. He has no conscience; he bows to the altar of money, cold hard cash and with his operation in full swing as it is today, he will never have to worry about money again.

59

I am up early. After I connected the dots with the Red Hook building, I slowed down my drinking last night, realizing that I need to be sharp today. I knew I'd have to wait till at least 9 a.m., before I could call Walt. I knew Walt attended an 8 a.m. AA meeting, so I had to kill some time. I didn't sleep very well, but I managed a few hours.

Cassidy, who was pleased with herself and her big commission, finished the wine and had no problem sleeping. As a matter of fact, her snoring let me know she was deep sleeping.

But by 8:30 a.m., she was up, showered, dressed, and on her way out—when she remembered that there was a connection with Carlos, Red Hook, Walt, and Milagro. When she asked me about the connection, I simply told her that I wasn't sure, but I'd talk with Walt this morning and maybe I was right, but probably not so. No need for her to worry. I just wanted her to carry on as if she knew nothing.

All things considered, she stood to make a pile of money and if she needed to play along for a while, then she would do so. She couldn't fake worrying about her husband. She knew Carlos was a tough businessman and Marty was anything but. She also worried about the FBI. Marty might be walking into some rising water, but for now, she had no choice. She was Carlos's partner in real estate and Marty was her partner for life.

Rationalization is a tremendous human tool. Cassidy was able to rationalize away most of her worry today by believing that based on her husband's track record that he was probably way off and that Milagro was playing him for a fool. In any event, the way she saw it, she or Marty would not be going to jail anytime soon.

She did, however, replace her worry about Marty with the thought of the $600 grand that she'd be making on this one deal. Pretty easy thing to help you change the way you feel—money is.

I called Bertha at the shop, to let her know that I wouldn't be coming in till after lunch and to ask her if Carlos had picked up his order yet. He hadn't yet, she told me, but that he did call and she shared the talk Carlos and she had...

Now I was reduced to watching the clock. I had the *Today Show* on in the background, but Meredith and Matt weren't enough of a distraction for me. Every five minutes, I'd look at the clock again to see if it was past 9 a.m. yet.

Finally, at 9:15 a.m., I call Walt.

"Dude, it's me," I say; "What are you doing this morning?"

"Well, Marty, now that you've piqued my interest after your call last night, I guess I was waiting for you," Walt answers.

"Well, my friend, wait no more. You and I are going to Red Hook. I want to see these buildings and see if I can make anything out of a hunch I have," I say excitedly.

"Well, I suppose I could open the bar late today," Walt says; "but, we need to be back by lunch, okay?"

"Sure, I'm on my way over. I'll bring the van. I need to fill the tank anyway."

"Great," Walt says; "I'll see you in about 20 minutes then, okay?"

"Yes sir, 20 minutes," I say and hang up.

Now I am clearly in the middle of a situation and I don't know what I'm looking for. The picture I saw was the interior of a warehouse and I don't remember any signs or anything that would let me know that I'm looking at the warehouse. I saw in the picture that Milagro showed me, but I had a hunch. I think it's too much of a coincidence for Walt's money-warehouse to be right next door to the warehouse Carlos was buying. I had to be right and if I was, what would I do then?

I didn't have to answer that now, but by this afternoon, if I still felt like I was on to something, I needed to have a plan. Since I still had the Milagro excursion Monday, and today was Wednesday, that didn't leave me with much time, but it had to be enough time to come up with something—there was no other choice.

60

Carlos is going through his closet, looking for a suit for today, when he realizes that the shirt he wants was at the cleaners. He had forgotten to have them picked up the other day, and now he was in need. He calls his assistant and asks her to grab his shirts. He needs them home by 9:30 a.m.

After I pick up Walt in my white dry cleaning van, the two of us head over to Brooklyn Heights to gas it up. I don't use it for delivery, but merely as a means to run errands. I actually enjoy driving the van, since I don't do much driving. When you live in Manhattan, you merely store your vehicle for weekends and airport runs.

After we take care of the van, Walt begins giving me directions to the warehouse he's been staking out. I also have with me the address of the buildings that Cassidy just bought for Carlos.

Walt begins to start reminiscing about back in the day and the after hours club we used to frequent in Red Hook. It actually brings me back to a simpler time in my life—fewer complications and less responsibility. I smile and nod as Walt talks. Besides, there is nothing more exhilarating to hear, than an alcoholic talk about his drinking days. Walt speaks with passion about those days; he remembers things in full color and with such detail. You can almost see the "glass sweating" as he describes a drink.

The block that the warehouse sits on, is pretty bleak. No life to speak of and nothing but other warehouses all around it. Back in Red Hook's heyday, this was a bustling place with sailors, shipping types, and shops all around selling things that came into port. The streets used to teem with activity, cart traffic, trucks taking on cargo, and ships off loading. The longshoremen's union and organized crime lords were kings down here. You couldn't do anything, without paying "tribute" to someone and if you didn't, you weren't in business too long. But today, the streets were quiet with the occasional car or truck but generally desolate. This change came about because of 9/11; this port was so wide open that Homeland Security couldn't place enough agents and resources here, so they simply put quarantine on what was delivered here. It didn't take long for the traffic that came here to find another port, hence the saying, *any port in a storm.*

I then realize that this would be a perfect place to store anything that you didn't want to bring attention to. I begin to think about the photo and the pallets of cash. Somewhere I thought behind one of these warehouse doors sits a fortune. Just within reach, but unattainable.

Walt tells me to stop the van.

"There it is," Walt says pointing, "this is the one. I usually sit over there and wait."

I pull the address out of my pocket and ask; "Where is this?"

"Around this corner, go to the right and we'll find it," Walt says.

I follow Walt's instructions and sure enough, these warehouses all share an alley—back to back.

"Okay," Walt says, what's the deal? Why are you asking about THIS warehouse?"

Now I know it's time to tell Walt. I had thought about how I'd do this and what he'd say.

It was now "Go Time."

"Well, my friend, I've known you a long time and we have been through everything, so what I'm about to tell you, must stay here, cone of silence, okay?"

Walt nods and turns to look me in the eyes and says; "Marty, you are my oldest and dearest friend. Tell me what's going on." Taking a sip of my coffee I begin.

"Cassidy has a new client, Carlos Ferrar—a big-time money man. Carlos has a company called, Conserve-Reserve, which for all intents and purposes, according to Cass, is an ATM. Carlos is the one who gave her the address of this warehouse and the orders for her to buy it."

"Okay, I'm following you so far," Walt says.

"Well, there's more, so stay with me and listen. You have heard me talk about that hot Latin lady who comes into the store. Her name is Milagro and she is in business with this Carlos. She approached me at a fund raiser that Cassidy dragged me to and told me she would and could change my life."

Walt just stays fixed on my words and without even looking over at it grabs his coffee and takes a long swallow.

"So, I listened to what she had to say to me and what I'm about to tell you, is the truth. She asked me to 'dry' 50 large bills in my dryers for an event she was planning for Carlos. She's an event planner, or at least, that's what she tells people. When I "dry" this money, I think, well, she's doing this for charity. Carlos has a lot of money, so I think it's strange, but not the weirdest thing I've seen or heard of, you still with me, Walt?"

"Yes, I think so." Walt says, shaking his head.

"Good, because *now*, it gets weird. Milagro, the hot Latin chick, then tells me her plan, which involves me picking her up in my van and her taking me to an undisclosed location, where there are millions upon millions of dollars in cash. She and I will load up the van and take her to a location where she and the money get out. She says she'll give me a couple hundred grand for my trouble and discretion, and then to wait till I get instructions for our next little road trip."

I take a deep breath and look at the warehouse and then look back at Walt, who is staring out the window and asks; "When were you supposed to be doing this?"

"Monday, I answer; five days from now."

"So," Walt asks; "why are you telling me this?"

"Here's the deal; when I asked her to prove to me that this money existed, because I wouldn't go along, unless she could prove to me that this wasn't some bullshit prank, she showed me a picture of Carlos in front of pallets of cash. This cash was in what looked like a warehouse. Walt, I think the warehouse you have been staking out, is the warehouse where that cash is. Why else would Carlos want to buy the adjacent buildings?"

"Let me get this straight. This broad showed you a photo of Cassidy's client standing in front of *pallets of cash*? How do you know it wasn't a doctored photo?"

"Because it was a Polaroid, Walt," I answer; "and you can't doctor those."

"Holy shit, Marty, I think you might be right. If everything you told me is true, then you just might be on to something."

"You think?" I ask hoping for validation.

"I do." Walt answers, "the next question is; what do we do?"

"I have an idea," I say, "let's get out of here."

61

Cassidy gets to her office after a trouble-free commute downtown. Yesterday, she sent Carlos the routing number for her account, so he could wire in the $220 thousand that she needed to close this warehouse deal. She hopes that the money is in the account by now, so she checks and after typing in her access code, up pops the balance and the activity in the account for the last 15 days. There it was; a transfer of $300 thousand.

"Hmmmm," She wonders. She specifically told him $220 thousand. Why the extra eighty? Maybe it was a tip, maybe an oversight, or maybe a key stroking error. She thinks about taking that eighty grand and transferring it into her personal account. She begins to type in the account and execution order numbers, when something stops her. It's her conscience and her ethics; since she's in this for the long term it doesn't make sense to scam now, so for some strange ethical reason, she doesn't do it. She knows she should tell Carlos that she received the extra funds.

What did he want her to do with it, she thought. Telling him was probably the smart and the right thing to do. No reason to upset the goose that is laying golden eggs. So, she dials up the goose.

She gets his voicemail at work, so she tries his cell and after three rings, he answers; "Hello Cassidy. How are you on this beautiful morning?" Clearly he has caller ID, she thinks.

"I'm fine, thanks, Carlos, and you?"

"I'm good; looking forward to seeing you soon," he says; "what can I do for you?"

"Well, I received the wire transfer and there was eighty thousand too much. What's up with that?"

"There was, he says, smiling as he crosses the street, how much more did you say?"

"Well, exactly eighty grand. Was that a tip for me?" She asks coyly.

"A tip, he asks, isn't your commission on this deal, enough?"

"Well yes, but I didn't know how you operated, so I thought I should ask." Cassidy said, "I have another client who handles gratuities that way, so it's not the strangest question to ask."

Carlos stops walking and looks upward, as if he is thanking God for his good fortune. Cassidy had passed his test.

"Well, Cassidy, why don't you go ahead and take that eighty thousand and think of it as an advance on the next deal, he says. Take your husband out for dinner and have a big night on me."

"Carlos, that's incredibly generous of you. I hope you don't think that I can be bought or anything like that?"

"No, Cassidy. As a matter of fact, because you told me that there was an overage, tells me you have integrity and some business savvy. So the last thing I think now is that you can be bought or sold," he says.

"Good, because I'm all business and our relationship is purely professional." Cassidy says, looking out her window.

"That's too bad, he says; a woman like you with my power and money behind her, could really own this town, but I understand—at least for now."

"Thank you, Carlos, she says, spinning back around in her chair. So, I'll see you at 11 a.m., right?"

"That's right. Be downstairs at 11 a.m. and my car will be there," he says, walking again. "See you then," she says and hangs up. Just then, she hears a knock on her door.

"Come in," she yells, looking up she sees it's her assistant, with a cup of coffee.

"I saw you come in, so I fixed you a cup," she says, placing the cup on the coaster on Cassidy's desk.

"Thanks, babe; you read my mind," Cassidy remarks, as she takes a sip. "You look nice today, she adds"

"Thanks, Cass. You do too." She replies; "you really look happy, did a big deal go down?"

"Oh, you could say that," Cassidy answers; "you could say that."

"Good for you. You deserve it. You work hard and good things should come to you," her assistant says.

"That's sweet," Cassidy says; "you deserve it too. So I'm giving you a bonus. How would you like a five thousand dollar bonus this month?"

"Cassidy, I love you," she says, "thank you, thank you. You are the best." The perky assistant says, beaming, "I'll go now, I have a desk full of work, thank you, again."

Cassidy smiles, as she watches her assistant walk out of her office. What the hell, she thinks; I just got eighty grand and that girl keeps me on target, so five grand was a bargain. It's the least she could do; besides, loyalty is going to be important moving forward.

Garrett, looking out of his office window downtown, realizes how close he is to solving this *Reserve* heist and in the same moment, knows he has nothing. Carlos can't be linked to the actual crime; he has an iron-clad alibi. Garrett also knows his business is legit; he unofficially had a friend of his in the IRS check it out and it's squeaky clean. He also can't get Carlos to admit his relationship with the dead fat man. Every road he walks turns into a dead end. His "garbage picking" turned up nothing. Hell, he couldn't even get the dry cleaner to tell him anything. It's about then, when his phone rings; "Tedia here, start talking."

"Agent Tedia, this is Bertha from Meltzy's cleaners. You asked me to call you when Mr. Ferrar picked up his shirts. Well, they were just picked up."

"Great. Did he pay with the usual cash?" He asks.

"Well, not exactly. His assistant picked them up and she paid with cash. Does that help?" She asks.

"What type of bill did she pay with?" He asks.

"I don't understand, Agent." She says.

"What type of bill? Was it a twenty, by chance?" Garrett asks with some hope in his voice.

"No sir, she gave me a ten and a five." Bertha answers.

"Damn, Garrett says; are you sure?"

"Yes, I'm sure. I'm calling you, so you know that we're cooperative. My boss told me to say that," Bertha said.

"Well, thanks for that," he says; "if he comes back in, will you please call me?"

"Sure thing, Agent Tedia, sure thing," Bertha says.

"Good, and Bertha…"

"Yes, Agent?" Bertha says about to hang up.

"I'm watching you guys. Don't think I'm not," he says.

"I'll remember that, sir," she says and hangs up.

Now Garrett is really fucked. No currency to check; all he has to look forward to is the phone tap tomorrow night. Maybe Carlos will say something that he can follow up on. If he doesn't, Garrett will be back to square-one and with the suits upstairs breathing down his neck, he'd surely be taken off the case and have to go to the end of the bench and wait till his turn came back up, which if he figured right—wouldn't be anytime soon.

He had to catch a break—he had to.

62

Eleven a.m. sharp, and Cassidy is waiting in front of her building for Carlos. She doesn't like to wait for anyone; she thinks it's rude when she's left to wait and takes it very personally. But just as she's about to think of how she'd make this man's morning miserable for making her wait, a silver Bentley pulls up and out steps Carlos.

"Sorry I'm late," he says. "The garage was backed up and it took them 20 minutes to bring the car around. Can you forgive me?"

"Well, as long as you promise never to keep me waiting again for anything," she says, taking his hand as he helps her into the car.

"Never again," he says while raising his fingers and flashing a peace sign; "I promise." Getting into the car he turns to Cassidy saying; "I'm glad you wanted to see this building; it shows me you are a sharp forward-thinking, business person who takes her client's interest seriously."

"I do, Carlos," Cassidy says; "if this building is a piece of shit or you can't show me why you want this, I'll have to as your agent, recommend that you don't pursue the purchase. I can always get your deposit and earnest money back."

"Don't you worry; I think you'll see why I want this building. Just sit back enjoy the ride and we'll be there in no time. Can I offer you a drink?" Carlos asks.

"It's eleven in the morning, Carlos; I don't drink in the morning or for that matter, during business hours."

"Okay, don't get hostile. I was trying to be polite." He answers.

"Would you like some orange juice?" He says, turning to the window.

"No, thank you. I'm fine," Cassidy says, coldly.

"Well then," he says; "how are you and how is your husband— it's Marty, right? Did you tell him about our arrangement?"

"Of course not, I told him we were still working together— but I didn't go into any details," Cassidy answers.

"Good" he says, raising an eyebrow.

"I told him what he needs to know. Are you satisfied?" Cassidy says as if she's bursting his bubble.

"Quite," Carlos says; "I'm glad to hear that."

"We'll be at the site soon. I'm excited to show you the space and tell you my plans."

"Me too," she says; "I have a busy afternoon and need to back to my office, right after this that is if we are going to close this deal this week. Okay?" Cassidy says as if uninterested in his plans.

"Roger that," Carlos says, as if he's talking to his mother.

Not long after crossing the East River, they stop in front of a brown, dirty, building that looks as if it hasn't been given any attention, for at least twenty years.

"Here it is," Carlos says; "what do you think?"

"I think you are crazy; why would you have ANY interest in this dump of a building?" "Well, I'm glad you asked," Carlos answers; "Charley, can you drive us around the block please?"

"Sure, boss," answers his driver.

In a minute, they pull up in front of another warehouse that doesn't look much better than the other one.

"This is mine; I own this warehouse and I want the other one, so I can expand my storage space and make sure I have control over the next tenant."

"Carlos, this is friggin' Red Hook. Why would you own this building in the first place? You are a financier—not a storage baron."

"Well, you are correct, Cassidy." He says; "But until you see the inside of this warehouse, you won't understand, so let's check it out, okay?" He says visibly excited.

"Sure, anything you say; you're the client," she says, as he opens the door and gets out extending his hand to help her out.

Carlos has thought about this "move" all night and all morning. She passed the test. She showed some loyalty and he thought it important to show her his true holdings. He thought she needed to know what his buying power was. He wouldn't tell her where it came from, but she'd be impressed. Hell, it impressed him and he'd been around the block, maybe this would help her consider letting him have his way with her.

"Wait here for a minute, please," he says as he steps out of the silver Bentley.

Cassidy nods and watches him move to the door on the left of the truck entrance. She sees him unlock some kind of a box and then enter a code and stand there then she sees a green light flash. He then presses his thumb onto a pad next to the green light.

Carlos turns to her and waves her to join him. Once she is by his side, he opens the door and they step into an empty foyer. He then turns to his right and pushes what looks like an intercom, except after he pushes the button, a door slides open and he presses his thumb on another pad and then she can hear the door in front of them unlock.

Carlos turns toward Cassidy and says, "Close your eyes and take my hand please."

"Carlos, this is very weird and I am not in the mood for surprises or games, so cut the shit. OK?"

But Carlos insists and she gives in, so closing her eyes and extending her hand she follows his lead. She feels a dip in the temperature as she walks into a room that feels expansive. She then hears him flip several switches. Then she heard the humming sound electricity makes when it's powering up fluorescent lights. Behind her closed eyes, she could see that lights had been turned on.

"Okay, you can open your eyes." Carlos says; "but don't move; just open your beautiful eyes and see why I want that other warehouse," he says letting go of her hand.

Cassidy opens her eyes and looks at what seems to be a warehouse that is the size of two football fields. The warehouse is filled with what looks like boxes. She couldn't see for sure, because the boxes, which look about five-feet tall and five-feet wide, are covered with painters drop sheets. The boxes are in rows, lined up as far as she could see—the warehouse was filled with them.

"Okay, Carlos, you have a very big warehouse here; filled very neatly with big boxes, but what's in the boxes?" She asks.

"I was hoping you'd ask, come with me and I'll show you," he says.

"You see, Cassidy, I'm not a trusting person. You also need to know that you are the first person who I have showed this to—who doesn't work directly for me. But since you have signed that contract, technically, I own you—so to speak," Carlos says with a look that could scare a ghost.

"Yes, I'm aware of that, I'm also aware that it's cold in here and you need to know that I have no intention of sharing your secrets with anyone—not even my husband. You are protected by client privilege," Cassidy says.

"Good. As long as we understand one another, then what I'm about to show you, is for your eyes only. I'd hate to have to think about what a broken confidence would cause," Carlos says, as he leads Cassidy to the nearest box.

"Carlos, don't threaten me. You can trust me. Let's get on with this—I hate drama," Cassidy says visibly annoyed.

"Very well, go ahead," he said, handing her the corner of a sheet covering the box; "pull it off."

Cassidy turns back toward the covered box and slowly pulls off the drop cloth and sees a five-foot high, five-foot wide stack of twenty dollar bills neatly bundled. Carlos, to her right, pulls off another drop cloth to unveil another stack of money. He moves again to his right and yanks off another cover—again a five-foot high, by five-foot wide stack of cash.

Cassidy is speechless. She'd never in her life seen this much cash. She never dreamed she ever would. She'd held big checks, but not cash. She looked out over the warehouse and says; "My God, Carlos. Are all of these covered boxes, the same as these?"

"Yes, they are. Isn't it beautiful?" He answers.

"How much is here?" Cassidy says, moving closer to the pallet that she uncovered.

"How does three quarter of a billion dollars make you feel?" He says laughing.

"Jesus Christ, Carlos. Where did you get this?"

"Is Conserve-Reserve that profitable?"

"Well, it's one of the sources of this cash, but there are others that you don't need to know about, at this moment—pretty impressive— huh?" He smiles, knowing her answer.

"Carlos, this is amazing; are you telling me you need the other warehouse to fill with more cash?" Cassidy asks.

"Well, yes and no. You see, I'm also paranoid and this warehouse shares a back alley with the buildings we're buying and I need to know that I own that back alley too," he says putting the sheets back over the stacks of money.

"Well, I can certainly understand your paranoia, and as your agent, broker, and associate—I support this purchase," Cassidy says.

"Well, I knew that once you saw this, Carlos says; that you would understand."

"Oh, I understand, alright. I understand." is all Cassidy can say.

It was at that moment that Cassidy could feel the physiological change that greed and obsession produce in her. The greed swelled in her like a balloon filling with air; it was at this moment that she realized she wanted some— no she wanted a lot of this money. All that was standing between her and this fortune, was Carlos. Being the alpha female that she was, she immediately knew what she needed to do.

"Carlos, tell me about security here? I saw you entering codes, using thumb scans and God knows what else," she asks.

"Well, my dear, if I shared all these security measures and precautions that I've taken, then I wouldn't feel secure. Remember, I'm paranoid and this warehouse is my dream come true. I've worked all my life to be standing here and looking at this vast fortune. As much as I trust you and I do—or else you wouldn't be here. I can't share that with you, but just know that this building without me is impenetrable." He said, smiling the smile of the devil.

"Has anyone else seen this or been here?" She asked.

"Yes, three others have seen the contents. You must know that one of those three is dead—at my hand, because he violated our trust. I tell you, this not to scare you, but to let you know, how much I value trust and loyalty. I can smell betrayal. I can sense when trust is being violated, so please, don't make me get those feelings from you," he asks.

"Carlos, this is safe with me. I signed on as your associate, because you promised great wealth and now I am convinced that you can make that come true. So know that my loyalty is well in tact," Cassidy says with conviction.

"Can you keep this from your husband?" Carlos asks.

"Carlos, I have secrets from my husband that I will take to the grave—one more won't matter. Besides, he'll benefit from my loyalty. So why spoil it, right?" Cassidy again says convincingly.

"Good, Carlos says; I feel good about this. Now, let's get out of here you have business to attend to. I want that building."

"Okay, Carlos," Cassidy says; "let's buy you a warehouse in Red Hook."

All the rest of that day and evening, Cassidy could not get the vision of all that money out of her head. It was emblazoned in her mind. She was still able to function at a high level—making all the arrangements to close on the building, and conduct her regular business, but whenever her mind was left to wander, it went right back to the image of the warehouse that was full of cash. The greed and obsession was working its way into Cassidy's hard-wiring.

63

Thursday began like any other day for yours truly—shit, shower, and shave. Some morning small talk with the wife who had been a little distant last night, but I had seen her like that before. It was her way of concentrating on work and I am okay with it. It meant that she wasn't breaking my balls any way.

Perhaps, I had been pre-occupied as well; I had my own firestorm going on in my head. Walt and I spent yesterday afternoon discussing various ways of getting inside that warehouse in Red Hook. Walt thought his original plan would still work; I didn't.

We entertained different scenarios and quite honestly, none of them seemed remotely executable, but it had been less than 24 hours since Walt and I had discovered that perhaps, this was our destiny. But how could "breaking and entering" be justified? We rationalized that stealing from bad people and sharing with good people was something we could live with. After all, it worked for Robin Hood—and everyone loved him, except the Sheriff of Nottingham, who was himself, a bad man. Carlos now took on the role of our Sheriff of Nottingham.

I mentioned none of this to Cassidy, as a matter of fact, at dinner I deflected her questions. But I assured her the building they thought was near the building that Carlos wanted, was not what they thought. Cassidy who was distant, pretty much said; "That's nice, honey. It seemed too good to be true, anyway." She also went on to say that sometimes we want to connect the dots so badly, that we try to make things work, that never will. Like forcing a square peg into a round hole—it just won't work.

Quite honestly, I was surprised at how quickly she dismissed it, but I didn't dwell on it. I was in my own little scheming world. I almost felt that what was happening was surreal; I had some difficulty getting my mind around the juxtaposition that was happening here.

There I was last night, eating a normal supper with my wife and yet, my mind had me sneaking into a desolate warehouse with my alcoholic friend and stealing cash and living the high life on some island selling sandals, with my adoring wife, who is sipping tropical drinks—carefree.

This was the stuff of movies, I thought. Maybe, when it was all over, I'd write about it—that seemed like a worthwhile thing to do. But maybe, it was just better to keep it all to myself—the money, the dreams, and the plan.

What I now felt I knew was pride and greed; it crept up on me like a snake—subtle and cunning. I had always wanted more out of life, but this was now becoming an obsession. If I could only be absolutely sure that the money was in that warehouse, I feared going through with some plan and then walking into a warehouse full of Tupperware or some shit like that.

Thursday was always a busy day at the shop; customers getting their cleaning in, before the weekend—wanting to have it back that night, so the mornings were stressful. Today was no different. Both Bertha and I are working the counter and taking in load after load.

At 9 a.m., we stopped promising that the clothes would be back that afternoon. I organized the load for the pick up and then planned on taking the rest of the day off. This was OK with Bertha; she enjoyed the freedom of being the boss for the rest of the day.

When I was done and the clothes had been picked up, Bertha told me that she'd called the FBI agent to inform him that Carlos's assistant had picked up his shirts and that she paid with cash. I was glad she'd done so. I was even happier on the inside that Carlos didn't pick it up himself; hence, my little plan was still a go. The agent got what he wanted—cooperation from us and yet, he didn't get what he really wanted which was evidence, so everything was alright in my mind's eye for the time being.

I promised Walt I'd stop by the bar this afternoon, after the lunch crowd, so we could further plan our next steps. We really didn't have any first steps, but we still thought a meeting was a good idea.

64

Milagro was going through her things; she had acquired so many nice things—clothes, jewelry, etc.… She felt bad about knowing that one day she'd have to leave them behind, but she also knew that when that day came she'd have to travel light, she would need to be able to be nimble and blend into the world—relatively unnoticed, but with the freedom that the cash would afford her. She decided that she could take two suitcases with her on this trip. She had purchased cheap luggage in order to not draw attention to herself when traveling. She wouldn't need gowns, business suits, or smart ensembles—just casual, everyday clothing that she despised, but it would serve her purpose.

Her dream destination was the Mexican Riviera—the Mayan peninsula. She loved the ocean, the beach, and the smell of suntan oil. She knew she could blend in down there, either as a permanent tourist, or just a woman from Mexico City, who got fed up with the crowds and aggravation of city-living. It was a good plan; she would have to live modestly and not draw attention to herself. She was confident that she could and would live happily ever after—maybe even meet someone, but she really didn't care. She had lived alone for so long and was set in her ways. The thought of sharing her life and her money, didn't hold a tremendous amount of allure for her—deep down she was greedy.

She had finally, after weeks of sorting, shopping, and packing, put together what she would need to begin the rest of her life. It all fit neatly into the two pieces of luggage. Somewhat depressing for some, but for her, it was exhilarating. This was the beginning for her—she wouldn't have to live in fear of Carlos. She knew that once she was gone, he'd look for her. But he was so paranoid and obsessive of his money, that he wouldn't be able to tell anyone why he was looking for her or what was so important that he'd need to track her down. He'd take his loss with some disdain, but she knew he'd get over it. Carlos would know she wouldn't go to the cops, because it would make her guilty too, so she had that to fall back on too. She knew he would be furious to say the least.

She knew that he only visited the warehouse on Saturday mornings, after the Friday drops, so that he could count his horde—he was like the dragons she read about as a girl. They were greedy, selfish, winged creatures, that slept on their treasures and would not move, except for food or when threatened.

That's why she would make her move on a Monday. That meant he wouldn't be back to the warehouse for almost two weeks, because drops were scheduled for Fridays, so she was confident she'd be long gone before he even realized money was missing. She'd be safe and he'd never find her.

65

Garrett looks at his watch and sees that it's 4:15 p.m. He hoped
Snuffy and his friend would be here in fifteen minutes; he'd done his
part. He couldn't believe how low he was sinking—tapping a phone
line, without authorization could get him fired. He'd lose his pension,
his good name or at least what was left of it, and then what was left
for him? But he was blinded by the desire to make this bust go down.
Tonight he needed to hear something that would turn this case into
something.

As scheduled, Snuffy and Chip arrive in a van that has some
writing on the driver's side door; an address of a shipping business in
Flushing, as unmarked vehicles go, this would do.

Garrett gets in and the three men exchange greetings and off
they head to Carlos's neighborhood. In the back of the van Garrett, sits
on a milk crate. There is no seating, just boxes of electrical equipment
and some tool boxes too. "What's all this?" asks Garrett. "These are
the tools of my former trade," says Chip.

"Are you telling me, we'll need all of this shit to listen in?"
Garrett asks.

"No, just what's in the tool box, to your left and that listening dish." Chip answers.

"Hey, Snuffy, where did you get this van—by the way—we're not going to be pulled over, because the tags are outdated or anything like that are we?" Garrett says, sounding like a cop. "No, Garrett, this van belongs to my sister-in-law's ex-husband. It's clean—trust me." Snuff answers back.

"Good, I can't afford to be pulled over and neither can you two, so drive carefully while you're at it, okay?" Garrett reminds them.

Once they get in position and the listening device is set up, the three men settle in for a long night. The device is set up, so that when the phone rings in Carlos's house, a red light appears on Chip's oscilloscope and then he pushes another button and the conversation can be heard through the headphones that Garrett and Chip have on. When that light appears, that cues Snuffy to hit the record button on the tape machine. This way, if they don't understand language, they can play the tape and have it translated. That was Garrett's idea, suspecting Carlos, might pull that old trick.

At eleven o'clock, the phone finally rings. The red light comes on and Snuffy hits the record button. Chip and Garrett stare at one another hoping that this works. After four rings, the phone gets answered.

"Ola, Carlos, how is you?" asks the caller.

"Fine, what's up?" Carlos asks.

"Listen, we have to change plans. We can't make a drop tomorrow night." The caller says. "Why not," an agitated Carlos answers.

"We had a problem with the paper and then had to make some more ink, so we got behind and I'd rather make a full deposit in Red Hook on Monday; is that okay?" the caller asks. "How behind are you?" an aggravated Carlos asks.

Garrett's eyes are as big as saucers—paper, ink, deposit—all he can think of, is what he suspected all along—a counterfeiting operation. He is hearing details on the drops and the production. This is what he had been hoping for.

"We are 10 million light," the caller responds.

"Listen to me, you stupid mother fucker, I don't know how you got that far behind, but if that drop is any less than 100 million on Monday, I will have your tongue! Do you understand me?" Carlos in a hushed rage explains.

"And another thing," Carlos says; "I want you to call me back on 555-3467 in 20 minutes. I have some new coordinates and a time change that I don't want to say over this line. As a matter of fact, we've said too much already," the call then ends.

Garrett is speechless. He knows that he has hit pay dirt, but he has no location, no details—just that, he believes, based on what he's heard Carlos was behind the Federal Reserve heist and that he is printing counterfeit money, and a lot of it.

"Hey, Chip. Can you tap into that number Carlos gave that caller?" an excited Garrett asks.

"If it's a land-line, no, because I am only set up to listen to the number you guys gave me, but if it's a cellular then, no problem." The specialist replies.

"How can you tell?" Garrett snaps.

"Easy, I'll call the number from this disposable cell I have here and I'll be able to see if the signals match. If they do, it's all good. If they don't, we are out of luck." Chip says, with a cocked smile.

"But if you call, won't he have our number?" Garrett asks.

"Not necessarily, unless he has that phone right next to him and picks up the very second it rings, then yes, he would. But if he lets it ring for a second—one second—I can see the signal and hang up quick enough, so that he won't even know it rang." Chip answers.

"I don't understand?" Garrett answers.

"Neither do I," says Snuffy; "if it rings, it rings, he'll hear it, won't he?"

"No," Chip says; "you see, as the caller, you hear it ringing, but the speed of sound is quicker than the speed of electronic transference. So once I hear the beginning of the ring and hang up, the transfer won't occur; hence, no ring on his end," Chip says, proud of himself.

"In that case, Mr. Electronics, let's give it a shot, dial it now," Garrett orders.

"Here goes," says Chip.

Garrett hears Chip dialing in his headphones. He hears the beginning of the ring and then silence, Chip hangs up.

"Well?" Asks Garrett; "what's the deal?"

"You, my friend, are in luck. Your friend, Mr. Carlos, has asked the guy to call him on a cell. He's clever, but not clever enough for the Chipster here!" the ex-con says with pride.

"Okay, then. Garrett says, notably excited; what's next?"

"Give me ten minutes and we'll be in full listen mode," Chip says, already making adjustments to his scope and his transponder.

"Hurry the fuck up, the guy is calling back in twenty and we've screwed around here for 10 already we can't miss this call." Garrett says.

Chip gives Garrett and Snuffy the "fish eye" and gets back to his equipment.

"Don't worry; I'll get this done in seven minutes." Chip says.

"Well, quit talking and work!" Garrett snaps.

66

Friday morning beckons and Cassidy has to be downtown at 10 a.m. to close the deal on the warehouse for Carlos. She needs to stop by his office and get some papers signed—then to the closing attorney's office to wrap this up.

She sees that I am already downstairs in the courtyard reading the paper and having a smoke with my coffee.

"Good morning, babe, sleep well?" I ask.

"I did, as a matter of fact," Cass answers.

"I'll be home late tonight, she says, I have a late meeting with Carlos, to review and execute the closing and then celebrate his acquisition."

"Really," I say, "should I be concerned that you're dining and drinking with another man, let alone a wealthy, handsome, Latin?"

"Not a chance silly. You're welcome to join us if you like. I know you don't like those things, so I didn't bother asking. Wanna' go?"

"As a matter of fact," I say, "I would. You've been spending a lot of time with this guy and I think it's high time I marked my territory."

"You and that macho bullshit, will you never learn that when I said, *I do,* I meant I won't." Cassidy answers.

"Never the less, when and where should I join this celebration tonight?" I ask.

"Well, that's a good question. I'm not sure. Carlos hasn't told me yet, so when I find out, I'll call you, is that okay, green eyes?" She says, lovingly.

"Sure, call me at the store and if I'm not there, leave me a message. Walt asked me to help him at the bar today; he's installing a new dishwasher and needs my back."

"You, helping him," Cassidy laughs, "talk about a cluster fuck, what is he filming this for—the *Comedy Channel.*"

"Very funny," I say, "I'll have you know that when it comes to being a go-fer, I'm pretty good!"

"In that case," she says, "don't hurt yourself."

"Oh, I won't and you play nice with the other kids too," I say getting up and giving her a kiss; "have a good day and I'll talk to you later."

Cassidy smiles and walks into the kitchen and then is gone out the door. So I return to my paper and coffee, when the phone rings.

"Marty, it's Bertha. That agent is here again and wants to talk to you. He says it's serious. You'd better get here now."

"I'm on my way," I say, "tell him to have a cup of coffee and give me twenty minutes, okay?"

"Okay," she says, "see you then," she hangs up.

Now, I begin to wonder what's up. Perhaps, the FBI has something new; I can't imagine how it would involve me, but I'll find out soon enough.

67

Carlos is excited; the warehouse officially is his today and he can start installing the security systems he designed. By Saturday afternoon, the adjacent warehouse will be ready for Monday's shipment. Actually, his nephew's little fuck-up is working out okay for Carlos. It's allowing him the time to prepare for the delivery; he can start fresh there. He won't have to actually transfer from one warehouse to the other; he'll just start off loading in the new one.

He is already dressed and ready to be driven to the Conserve-Reserve offices to meet with Cassidy to sign the closing papers and get the keys to the warehouse. He calls his driver and has him come around to pick him up.

Once at his office, Carlos goes through the monthly financials, only to see that once again, Conserve-Reserve is more profitable than ever. His brokers are happy. They're getting bigger bonuses. It's good to be Carlos today, he thinks. The only thing missing for Carlos is total control. Milagro is still out there and lately, she has been bringing less value to the operation. She was instrumental in the beginning, getting the security codes at the Reserve and helping to get him set up in business, along with creating his public persona, but now, she was less useful. It was time for her to go away; he felt her loyalty shifting. He only felt her greed; her need for him to make deposits for her and for what—she wasn't even fucking him—it was time.

Carlos knew there was only one way to handle this—himself. Besides, he'd actually take some pleasure in this. It had been a while, since his blood lust kicked up and now at the thought of eliminating Milagro, he felt that old rush of adrenaline return, and after all, he was a stone-cold killer at heart. As he dials Milagro's number, he looks at his watch.

"Milagro, Carlos here, how are you today?"

"I'm fine, Carlos, what's up?" she asks.

"Well, I need a favor. I'm hosting a little dinner party tonight to celebrate an acquisition and I need a date. Can you join me tonight?" He asks.

"Well, I guess I can. I don't have anything planned. What time will you need me to be ready?" She asks.

"Good, he remarks and smiles be ready at 8 p.m. I'll have my driver pick you up. Wear something sexy tonight; it's been a while since I've seen your assets, okay?"

"Sure, Carlos, anything you like. After all, it's my job, right?" she says.

"I guess you could say that," he says, "just be ready at 8 p.m. looking hot."

Carlos hangs up and looks out the window of his office, looking down Park Avenue. He feels a rush of power course through his veins. Tonight will be glorious. Everything is coming together for him. He couldn't be more at peace with his greed, his addiction to money, and his plans. Again thinking—it's good to be me—it's good to be me.

Cassidy stops by her office to grab the closing documents and get them notarized by her assistant. As she is leaving, the phone rings, her assistant says, "Cass, it's the FBI and they want to talk to you."

"Huh?" Cassidy says, "did you say the FBI?"

"That's right, I'm putting them through now," the assistant says.

"Hello, this is Cassidy Tyroni, who is this and how can I help you?" she asks.

"Ms. Tyroni, this is Agent Garrett Tedia, of the FBI. Do you have a minute?"

"Do I have a choice?" she asks.

"No, I'm afraid you don't," the voice answers, this won't take long."

68

Walt is waiting for Marty, when he realizes that he won't be able to open the bar on Monday, because he'll be busy all day. He'll have to put out a sign saying something like: "Closed due to death in the family," or something like that. He's only done that once before, and that was when there was an actual death in his family. He's glad he didn't kill all the brain cells he had drinking and drugging or he might have overlooked that detail.

Marty is right on time and the two huddle at the bar with the map and a pad of paper. For once, Walt is glad his bar is empty. They can work on their plan in peace for a change.

I ask Walt for a drink to settle my nerves. Then I explain that I just had a chat with the FBI and they think Cassidy is in danger. This means our plans have to be flawless. As the two of us begin working, in walks Milagro.

"I'm glad you could make it Milagro," I say, "please sit down."

"Hi, I'm Walt," the big bar owner says, extending his hand.

"Can I get you anything?" he asks.

"Just some water, please." Milagro says, taking her place at the bar.

"Milagro," I start, "I hate that it's come to this, but based on what I learned today, we don't have much time, so we need to set this operation up quickly."

"I understand, Martin." the Latin beauty answers, "I hope I haven't put you and your friend here, in harm's way. Carlos is dangerous and we have to be precise or else it could mean our lives."

"We know that." Walt says, "so hear us out and let's get together on this or else no one wins. This is a sum-zero game and we need to be on the same page, so let's get started."

"Okay," both Milagro and I say and the three of us launch into it.

69

Cassidy calls Carlos, explaining that she will be an hour late with the papers and tells him not to worry. She reassures him that everything is still on target for him to take possession this afternoon. She also asks him where they'll be celebrating tonight and if it's okay to bring Marty. Carlos tells her it's quite okay, because he's invited Milagro as well. "It'll be a swell party," he says.

"I've reserved a room for us at The Columbus Club. You can tell your husband the party starts at 8:30 p.m."

Agent Tedia has been busy today; he has conducted interrogations with both Mr. and Mrs. Tyroni. Trusting them with valuable information and also letting them in on his plans only because he'll be using them as live bait. What he doesn't know, is that they have plans of their own.

The Columbus Club is a very private club that some of the most influential and powerful people in all of New York gather to party, do business, and enjoy the perks of being wealthy. Tonight is Carlos's night. He's reserved the Wine Cellar for dinner for four; he's selected a menu fit for royalty and he pulled some strings for some special after dinner entertainment.

Tonight will be a night they will all remember. Carlos will have a busy day. After taking possession of the warehouse, he will immediately begin working with his security specialists—setting up security at the new warehouse. He explained to the security people before that he is a collector of fine art and will be using these warehouses to store some of his collection after clearing customs, so that is why he is sets up such an elaborate security system. They set up his last system next door and will use the same technology here. They assured him it would be complete and activated by Saturday afternoon.

He also spoke with his nephew Jamie again, confirming the Monday drop at the new location. He asked him to make sure that he brought the workers with him, because there was some clean up and set-up work that he'll need them to do, at the new warehouse.

Carlos was feeling particularly pleased with himself today. He was in the home stretch of his plan. He was three shipments away from the target amount. That meant he could then get rid of all the production evidence—the tractor trailer, the copiers, the printers, the ink making system, and the paper manufacturing set up. Most importantly, he'd be able to destroy the printing plates—the link that could put him away. The only thing tying him to the heist—he thought.

He had a new timetable and knew that within 60 days, he was home free and could live wherever he wanted. Once he liquidated all of his New York assets and burned down the business, so to speak, he could be free of any responsibilities. His nephew and Milagro would be long gone, and it would just be him and all the money he'd ever dreamed of. Who said crime didn't pay? Carlos was close to the biggest payday of his life.

He was living a good life now, but nowhere like the one he would be living in South America. He wouldn't have to worry about anything down there. He'd live among the cocaine barons in Columbia; he'd have everything he needed—women, luxury, freedom, plus protection. The government could be bought; he'd never have to look over his shoulder. He would be a king and a master of the universe. He was getting all that he deserved—his planning was finally paying off—and it was like rapture.

Carlos and Milagro arrived first at the club tonight. Marty and Cassidy were fashionably late; they were ushered downstairs to the wine cellar. The cellar itself was over 150 years old as is the building above, but it had been rebuilt twice, but the cellar remained as it was back when it was built.

Carlos shared stories of past members of the club during pre-dinner cocktails that had been in this cellar—names like Vanderbilt, Morgan, La Guardia, and Roosevelt. "If these walls could talk," he

495

said, "the stories they could tell." It was rumored that in this cellar, Rockefeller negotiated the Standard Oil breakup with the President of the United States. This was a room of power and Carlos was the man with the power tonight.

They drank fine champagne and rare wines, feasted on food prepared by one of the finest chefs in the city, but the real highlight of the evening, was yet to come.

Carlos took them upstairs into the salon of the club. The club was now empty; it was only his party there, and he had a surprise in store for them.

All through the evening, Cassidy, Marty, and Milagro exchanged knowing glances to one another. Carlos, so self-involved with the event he had planned, missed the exchanges. He couldn't hear what the ladies discussed in the restroom and unbeknownst to him he was not the only one with a surprise in the room.

I was very pleased with the way Carlos addressed me. I wasn't sure how Carlos might treat me tonight. Would I be treated as merely Cassidy's husband and dry cleaner, or would he give me the respect I deserved? Wound-up was I—got the respect I wanted. I also got the attention from Milagro that not long ago, I thought I would never get. Tonight I moved with cool and with diplomacy, allowing my high-powered wife the limelight she deserved. I now knew that things were going to be fine. I felt it in my bones. For once, the planets were lining up for me.

Cassidy was having the time of her life. She saw her husband in a different light. She felt his energy and saw the light of one who knows emanate from him. She saw the beautiful Milagro look at her husband and wish she'd had a partner like that. She watched as he and Carlos spoke—men from different worlds, with different ideals sharing stories—each one more interesting then the last. She knew her husband had friends all over town but was surprised at how many Carlos and he had in common.

Carlos, ever the gracious host, began toasting, he even went behind the bar and pulled down the bottle of Louis XIV Cognac that was worth ten thousand dollars, pouring snifters for all of them. The night was building to a crescendo, as he had hoped.

Once they were all seated in the salon, several waiters wheeled in a baby grand piano. The four of them sat in silence watching the preparations for what was next. Now was the surprise he had been keeping from them. From around the corner, walked in Bobby Short. For years the voice of the famous Carlyle Room, Cassidy, Marty and Milagro just gasped. Bobby Short was here to sing to them, like the Kings of Versailles—they were treated to the velvet sounds of his voice and they sang along as if they were at a piano bar, except that the piano player, was Bobby Short—the king of café society. They sang until the early hours of the morning, laughing, drinking and shouting out requests of the legendary entertainer, until the sun began to rise and the dawn of a new day broke up the party.

Saturday was a lost day. The after effects of the previous night, kept Cassidy and I in the bed most of the day, only getting up to go to the bathroom and refill the water glasses on each side of the bed.

Carlos, having had too much to drink and feeling too good, dismissed the plans he had for Milagro that evening, and instead he made a move out of weakness that he would regret later.

Milagro being too sharp for even Carlos, began to execute phase one of the plan. She went home with Carlos, clenched her teeth, and slept with him. But like most men, once he had finished, he fell into the sleep of the dead. Milagro had made sure he wouldn't wake up too soon, so she placed a "roofie"in the drink she made for him—enough to knock him out for a few hours.

Milagro then took out of her bag some special clay that they use to fit people for expensive sandals and took an imprint of his thumb; she also knew where he kept his access codes. She then took out her Blackberry and sent them on.

After she finished with those tasks, she climbed in bed next to the snoring man and she slept until late afternoon, knowing that if she wasn't there when he awoke, that might raise suspicion.

Finally, late Saturday afternoon, Carlos finally came to. He looked next to him and he smiled when he saw that Milagro was still there. Hearing him rustle about, Milagro got up and began to dress for her trip home.

"Did you have a good time?" He asked.

"Carlos that was a magical night, you certainly know how to celebrate. Thank you for everything."

"Yes, my dear it was. Why don't you stay and have some brunch. I'll have some food delivered," he said.

"Thank you, but no, Carlos, my stomach is still full from the feast last night and not to mention from the drink. The last thing I need now is food. I'm sure you understand." She said slipping on her stiletto heels.

"Well, at least let my driver take you home," he said and called down for the car to be brought around.

"Thanks, Carlos, I'll remember last night forever." Milagro said piling it on and gently kissed him on the cheek, knowing that she was moments away from a clean get away.

"Wait a minute, darling, I have something for you," he said while walking into the back room where his safe was and where Milagro had been while Carlos slept. Milagro's mind and heart began racing. She hoped she had put everything back as he had left it, and hoped that maybe he was still a little fuzzy, so that if she hadn't, he wouldn't notice.

"Milagro, he said, come here."

Now her heart was leaping out of her chest; she didn't know what to do.

"Why Carlos, what is it?" She asked; "I'm ready to go."

"Wait one minute young lady," he said; walking out from the room, "I want you to have this."

Milagro saw a jewelry case in his hand; she felt her heart slow down.

"It was my mothers and you should have it now."

He handed her the case and she opened it. Inside was a beautiful broach of a black panther with emerald eyes.

"Carlos, it's beautiful. How can I accept this?"

"You have earned it; without your help, we wouldn't be here. I want you to have it." He said sweetly.

"If you insist," she said.

On her way down to the garage in the private elevator she looked down at the broach again. What was he up to she thought?

Or, was he really sincere? Milagro was genuinely baffled. Maybe she's misjudged him; maybe the exit plan wasn't a good idea.

The elevator door opened up on the Garage level and there stood a man with a black mask on and she heard the "pop" of the gun and that was the last sound Milagro heard.

On Sunday, Cassidy and I were up early, since we'd had plenty of sleep the day before recuperating. Cassidy checked her Blackberry and the e-mail from Milagro was still there—the codes were in tact.

Garrett Tedia was now in front of a room, full of agents. Behind him, was a map of Red Hook and on that map were two red stars, highlighting the location of Carlos's warehouses.

"I want to thank you all for being here on a Sunday. I know most of you have families and I know there are other places you'd rather be," he said, addressing the group.

Garrett hadn't felt the rush of adrenaline that he was now feeling—for a long time. No matter how long ago it was, he was in control of this operation and this was his moment. He knew what to say. How to direct and lead men was what he did best and here he was, back in the saddle.

After an hour of delivering the assignments to his men, he felt he was on the verge of changing his destiny. This wouldn't change the past, but it would certainly change the future.

If all his calculations were right, not only would he catch Carlos red-handed, he'd have solved the biggest counterfeiting scheme ever put together. He wished it was tomorrow and that this was all over, but he still had some work to do.

His meetings with the Tyroni's sealed the deal. He knew by watching her responses, that Cassidy Tyroni had not been a part of the counterfeiting operation. She was merely a pawn in Carlos's plan, but he had to due diligence. He also had to tell her when NOT to be with Carlos, so she wouldn't get caught in the crossfire or even have her name in the press. He promised her that.

Her husband Marty had been taken as a fool. Who would ever believe that a woman would give him a pile of cash for a simple ride upstate, but he also knew that greed blinded many and besides, from what he understood the woman who promised him was incredibly attractive, so maybe the guy thought he might get laid too.

In any event, he had grilled Martin like a whopper and the guy was clean. He also told Marty when to NOT be near Milagro or Carlos. The sting at the warehouse would be in broad daylight.

Carlos had planned a money drop for four in the afternoon on Monday; the location was his latest acquisition in Red Hook. The FBI staked out the spot all weekend. They watched the security firm install the system. They heard their radio transmissions as they exchanged directions and Garrett had his own elite group of security experts monitor the whole procedure—all unbeknownst to the civilians and of course, Carlos.

It was 2 p.m. on Sunday, when Walt knocked on our front door.

"Come in my friend," I said ushering him in, "I hope you had a productive morning?"

"Yes I did" Walt answered excitedly, "I can't wait to show you two what I've got."

"Well, come into the family room. Cassidy will be down in a minute. Sit yourself down and relax." I said.

"Hey Marty," Walt asked, "have you got any coffee?"

"Of course, I do. I knew you were coming, so we made a fresh pot—hang on. I'll fetch you some." I said as I headed into the kitchen.

Cassidy walked into the family room and seeing Walt said, "Honey, don't you look good today. Is Marty getting you something?"

"He is Cass. Thanks." Walt said, sitting back down.

"Good," she said, "how are you feeling about things?"

"Fine," he said, "that stands for fearful, insecure, nervous, and excited!"

"Good, that will keep you on your toes," she said always the shark.

I returned with a tray of three mugs filled with coffee. Handing them out, I said, "Okay, let's go over this one more time."

"Marty, I think we might be over prepared," Cassidy said, "so why don't we just sit for a minute."

"Where is Milagro? She was supposed to be here; it's not like her to be late. Why don't you call her?"

"Okay, I answered, you two just sit tight."

Just then, the phone rings so I answer it, "Hello, Carlos," I say, looking at Cassidy and Walt, with what can only be described as a confused look on my face.

"I'm fine. Finally recovered from Friday night, and you?"

"Yes, she's right here. Hang on. I'll get her. Thanks again for a great night. Here she is," I say handing the phone over to my wife.

"Well, I don't know, Carlos. We have company right now. Can this wait till tomorrow?" She asks.

"Great, I'll see you at 9 a.m. tomorrow," She says and hangs up.

"What was that, babe?" Marty asks.

"Not sure, but he needs to see me—that's for sure." Cassidy said, sitting back down.

"You don't think he....Walt says pointing to the TV—turn this up."

They focus on the TV to see Ernie Anastos, who is reporting from location. The location is the Heliport on the East side.

The reporter is saying, "As they pull the victim from the water, we can only report what the police have told us, the victim's name is Milagro Perdido, a New York event planner. No other information is available at this time."

"Well, now we know why she's late." Marty says.

"Okay, team time to re-group. We have to focus and get this done, for Milagros sake, we must execute and follow through," Cassidy says.

70

Garrett Tedia can only shake his head, maybe he should have moved in sooner. Perhaps she'd still be alive.

The initial reports he read say that Milagro Perdido was killed—execution style. The CSI on the case reports traces of semen in her vagina. No marks like she was assaulted, no clothes, no belongings—just a bullet hole in her forehead.

Garrett calls his task force leader into the office; "Jimmy, we need to change our plan. Instead of keeping people on the scene in Red Hook tonight, let's let the men go home and get back on site at 9 a.m. Carlos might suspect we'll be watching him, so he won't make his move till tomorrow. We'll tap his phones and monitor all incoming and outgoing calls, in case he does change things, but according to my information, he has no way to contact the delivery that's coming, so it should still be show time at 4:00 p.m. tomorrow, okay?"

"Agent, are you sure?" asks Jimmy, the team leader.

"It's no problem to keep them there Garrett."

"I know that, but I think a night of real sleep in a real bed will give our guys an edge that they'll need when this deal goes down. That's an order Jimmy," he says, sitting back down behind his desk.

"Understood," the cop says and leaves the office.

Sunday night at 3 a.m., Walt and I drive into Red Hook, directly to the warehouse. They know that it's now or never.

I ease the van in front of the warehouse and we get out. Looking around, I see that we are alone. I wave Walt over. We open the security box in front of the building. I begin entering the codes Milagro stole from Carlos. The green light flashes. Walt slips on the condom-looking thing over his thumb. Milagro, after making the impression of Carlos's thumb, discreetly called Walt to come to Carlos' apartment so she could give it to him, while Carlos slept.

The thumb recognition scan clicked and the door unlocked. I turn the knob and we are in a vestibule. Again, I open another security box, entering the stolen codes and one more time, Walt's rubber thumb clicks some tumblers in the lock and I turn the doorknob.

We both look at one another in the glow of the Maglight that Walt is holding and we feel the rush of cool air from the expansive warehouse. I am the first to enter the room. I point my flashlight in front of me to see the rows of boxes covered in drop cloth. Without missing a beat, Walt walks up and pulls a cloth off, revealing the neat stacks of cash. Walt and I look at each other and high five. This is exactly what I saw in the Polaroid that Milagro showed him.

"Okay, Walt. Before we start blowing each other, let's get going." I say, shining my light on the wall where the truck entrance door is. I slowly pull the chains opening the door and Walt runs out quietly, backing in the van. Milagro told us that each pallet had $3 million on it. We figured we could off load two pallets in 30 minutes. "Okay, let's do it," I say.

With that the two of us unload a rolling ramp from the van and begin filling the vehicle with cash.

In 30 minutes, we are looking at two empty pallets. Walt, without saying a word, gets in and drives the van out the door. I lower the door, step into the vestibule carefully shutting the door behind me then lower the security box door, and do the same on the front door and its security box. I hop in the passenger seat and we are gone.

Back at the Tyroni household, Cassidy packs. She e-mails directions to her assistant, calls her financial planner to leave directions for him, and finally, she goes on-line and prints two boarding passes. She confirms the limo for pick up and waits.

Walt and I get home on schedule; we moved quickly. I call Bertha, giving her instructions and then Walt gets on the phone to give her even more directions. She is now the proud owner of a bar and a dry cleaning shop, which she purchased for well below market value.

Cassidy hands the two of us our luggage and then without hesitating, she turns and locks the front door and we all get into the van.

Nine a.m., Monday morning, Carlos is waiting in his office. He's pacing the floor. He didn't expect the cops to find Milagro's body so soon. He knew she e-mailed Cassidy those codes, because on her person, he'd retrieved her Blackberry. But he knew that without his thumb, the codes were useless. He'd make this Tyroni broad pay—how dare she double cross him! Both her and her husband would pay for this betrayal.

Carlos calls Cassidy's office and gets her assistant, "I'm sorry, Mr. Ferrar, Ms. Tyroni has taken leave; we don't know when she'll be back. Can I help you?"

"No, you can't help me. Where the fuck is Cassidy? I need to know that now!"

"Sir, Cassidy's assistant says there is no reason to yell. I will tell her to contact you as soon as I hear from her, but I have no way of contacting her."

"What about her cell phone, her Blackberry, goddamn it! Get her now!" He says enraged. "Like I said, Mr. Ferrar, we can't communicate with her right now, I'm sorry. I'll be sure to give her the message," she says and hangs up.

Carlos bangs his receiver into its cradle over and over again, "Fuck, fuck, fuck!" He yells.

Now his survival and self preservation instincts kick in; he can't call his nephew to postpone the delivery. So he quickly calls his driver and asks him to get to the office now. He makes a call to his travel agent and books a flight to Bogata. He'll have to hire a mule deliver the money to him there. Carlos is coming unraveled now. He calls his banker in the Caymans and tells him to transfer funds to his Swiss account, but he learns his account has been frozen. Now he is panicked. Something is very wrong here; he'll have to sort all this out from South America.

On his way to Red Hook, he realizes that the FBI must have been tailing him and got to the Tyroni's. He also realized that had he not been so foolish with his trust, he might not be racing to his warehouse to take just a fraction of what he'd planned on keeping.

He reaches underneath his seat in the car and pulls out his nine millimeter glock. He's not going down without a fight.

Once Carlos reaches the warehouse, he jumps out quickly and begins entering the access codes, but nothing is working. This can't be happening to him; this is a nightmare! God, let me wake up he thinks.

As he turns around, he is faced by Agent Tedia.

"What's the matter Carlos, locked out?" the now cocksure agent asks.

"Fuck you!" Carlos says and raises his weapon. But before he can fire, a sniper drops Carlos where he stands.

71

A news reporter is speaking in a rushed, excited voice; "This is Jim Avila, reporting from Red Hook. Today the FBI brought down the mastermind behind the Federal Reserve heist. Carlos Ferrar was killed earlier today trying to get away from law enforcement officials in front of this warehouse. The warehouse that held, what officials say, is close to a billion dollars in cash—all counterfeit. They also have in custody several accomplices who were delivering another $100 million dollars in counterfeit money in a mobile money printing shop tractor trailer."

Behind the reporter, the camera panned into the open warehouse where FBI agents could be seen milling around in their blue windbreakers patting one another on the back in front of the stacks of bogus money.

"This could be the largest counterfeiting ring arrest in the history of the United States. The late Mr. Ferrar was also a respected businessman owner of Conserve-Reserve, a financial services company now under investigation by both the FBI and IRS," the reporter continued.

"It looks like the Agent in charge. I'm getting word—is about to begin to address the media. Let's go to City Hall where the press conference is underway."

"Good afternoon, I'm Agent Garrett Tedia of the FBI and earlier today; Carlos Ferrar was shot by sniper fire, while attempting to flee the scene of a crime. Mr. Ferrar is responsible for two known murders, as well as the robbery of the Federal Reserve here in New York. Mr. Ferrar is the criminal mastermind behind the fraudulent printing of almost 1 billion dollars in U.S. currency, along with setting up an elaborate money-laundering operation."

"Also seized at the crime scene was a modified tractor trailer that acted as a mobile counterfeit printing operation. Arrested were three Peruvian nationals and a relative of Mr. Ferrar. It is believed that the three Peruvians were held against their will and that the relative ran part of the operation aboard the trailer. He is being held without bail and is currently being questioned."

"I will now take your questions," Garrett said and without hesitation the reporters begin peppering him with questions.

Garrett smiles and says; "Okay first question."

72

Three months later

The sun is rising in the Rockies and Walt is heading to a morning meeting at the new Mixer Treatment Facility.

"Hey Walt, how you doin'?" asks the perky blonde counselor asks after catching up with him.

"I'm doing great, what's your story?" he asks.

"Well, we had one intake yesterday and I think we have one guy ending his treatment today," she remarks.

"Awesome, great work, Sharon. Opening this treatment center has saved my life and fulfilled a dream," Walt says.

"Walt, you've got that backwards; your center saves lives, without your financial backing, all of this wouldn't be here, we owe you our lives," she proclaims.

Who left these damn blinds open; I'm trying to nap in here, I think to myself.

Cassidy walking in to the room looks at me and says; "Martin Tyroni, for goodness sakes, you just woke up five hours ago, how can you be tired?"

"I came down to these islands to live in tranquility, and that's what I'm doing. Besides, what are you doing home? I thought you were at the store," I ask stretching my arms and yawning.

"Well, it's raining. If you haven't noticed and I didn't feel like it was worth opening the store," Cassidy adds. "Besides, it's not like we need the money—selling sandals was your idea. Besides, I need to tell you about a building that is for sale."

All I can think is here she goes again.

The End

Printed in the United States
207388BV00002B/183/P